Truth and The Serpent

J. Rutledge

ISBN-10: 1541235487
ISBN-13: 978-1541235489

Truth and The Serpent
Copyright © 2017, J. Rutledge
Cover Artist: Ash
Editor: Sonya

Table of Contents

INTRO: THE BEGINNING

"Darkness, emptiness...void. In the beginning, there was darkness and nothing existed. Nothing existed as it had for eternity and Nothing was an infinite expanse of space and chaos. Nothing felt no need, no urge, and no desire, but Nothing was not alone; for there was infinity. Wherever Nothing went Infinity followed, and the pair were inseparable. Infinity was never cold, never hungry, and had no need to keep time. In such a place, there was no death, as none were alive. There existed one language and it consisted of one word, and that word was... truth.

Nothing was absolute and complete, and only spoke truth. Infinity extended forever and its endlessness was truth. Yet, through the silence there echoed a single reasoning and a question was asked, "What is the meaning of truth if there is no lie to tell?" And then... there was light.

With light came thought and desire, the Heavens, and the levels of Hell. Through a vast and unknown universe came the sun, and with it, there was a new day. The day came as if there had been a before, without worry or concern, with impossible acceptance and belief; daylight rose as if it were already tomorrow.

And the Day said unto the Sun, "The voice of my beloved! Behold, he cometh leaping upon the mountains, skipping upon the hills. My beloved looketh forth at the windows, shewing himself through the lattice... Rise up my love, my fair one, and come away. For lo, the winter is past, the rain is over and gone. The flowers appear on the earth, the time of singing of birds is come... Arise, my love, my fair one, and come away."

Time was steady and ever so persistent. Time called after the day as two lovers call to each other in a midnight sonnet. Time promised the day new possibilities and filled it with hope. And Time said unto the Day...

"To everything there is a season and a time to every purpose under the heaven. A time to be born and a time to die; a time to plant and a time to pluck. A time to kill and a time to heal; a time to break down and a time to build up. A time to weep and a time to laugh; a time to mourn and a time to dance. A time to cast away stones and a time to gather stones together; a time to embrace and a time to refrain from embracing. A time to get and a time to lose; a time to keep and a time to cast away. A time to rend and a time to sew; a time to keep silence and a time to speak. A time to love and a time to hate; a time of war and a time of peace."

After each rotation, Time would bid farewell to Day and usher in Night. Night was magic and was beloved by Time. Time was infatuated with Night and presented it with bouquets of dreams in attempts to woo it. And Time would whisper to Night...

"By night on my bed I sought him whom my soul loveth. I sought him, but I found him not. My beloved is white and ruddy, the chiefest among ten thousand. His head is as the most fine gold, his locks are bushy and black as a raven. His eyes are as the eyes of doves by the rivers of waters, washed with milk, and fitly set. His mouth is most sweet, yea, he is altogether lovely. This is my beloved and this is my friend."

And at the end of the dream, Night would accept her advances and Time would call out for the day to begin again.

Darkness and forever, then light and now counting the days. There had begun a new existence, and out of this new existence came... a new language.

CHAPTER 1: THE CAVE

An evening sunset, a portrait of warm tangerine and radiant fire, slowly melting into the skyline. The day was coming to an end and life began to slow. The night was cool and with it came a breeze that carried down through a valley. The valley rested below a pair of cascading hills and joined a peaceful countryside. The night was quiet and illuminated by starlight that were but candles from the heavens.

Nature's stage was all but set and the performance of elements was ready to begin if not for the wind still waiting to introduce the rain. The rain came out and danced excitedly on the roads below and was accompanied by a spectacle of lightning and the orchestra of thunder. A grand display by the elements and truly a magnificent show, and out of the night and into the storm there came... a single man.

His name was of no importance nor was his background, he was average and comparable to most any man. His pace was determined as he ran through the storm, and he ran as if his destination were his only salvation. The wind and rain were blinding to him as he looked ahead for light, but the roads remained empty and the man found no hospitality.

Thunder and lightning pounded over his shoulders and electrified him with fear and the night air whistled and laughed around him. He traced the winding roads trying to escape the conditions but the storm adjusted and continued pursuing him. The man was alone, and now lost, he stopped underneath a leafless tree looking around. Still, he saw only empty roads and a dark sky filled with an angry storm.

The winds shoved him violently off the road and into the tall grass. The grass seemed to grow higher and thicker around him as he continued until the grass became trees. The trees shielded him from the rains, but the forest had a sarcastic humor. Claw like branches reached out and began tearing at his skin to restrain him. The mud stuck to his feet and it thickened and sank beneath him.

Cold and alone, the man triumphantly emerged from the forest and into a clearing. Those abhorred vines now behind him and the openness allowed him to breathe. The mud beneath him was now sand and he was on a beach. The moonlight glowed and reflected off the ocean while the waves had pulled out to sea, but it wasn't long before they spotted him and began building as they returned to smash against the shore.

The man stumbled along the beach, running along the cliff side until a shadow in the rocks presented itself and became an opening. Exhausted, the man felt little concern for the unknown darkness confronting him and pulled himself into the opening. Cold and tired, the man dropped to his hands and knees and breathed a momentary sigh of relief. He breathed heavily into the silence and recognized the natural space that he was in... was a cave. His hands trembled in his pockets searching for his lighter. The rolling strike of the flint wheel tore through the emptiness and a tiny flame ended the dark. He found kindling and a dried branch to feed the flame. The flame's appetite was immense and grew until becoming a breathing torch.

The man raised the torch above his head and the darkness retreated from his presence. The glowing light of the torch emboldened him with pride and he was himself again. He looked around the cave and observed impressive natural designs that couldn't be matched by even the most skilled artisan. The cave walls were tiled with precious gemstones and were accented with nuggets of diamond and gold. Only a bit of light had disturbed the darkness, but the riches shimmered and danced spectrums if for only the man to behold.

A large etching in the cave wall caught the man's attention. He raised the torch and read the olden writings on the wall, 'Better is the sight of the eyes than the wandering of the desire, this is vanity and vexation of the spirit.' He thought momentarily on the words. What ancient people had written them and what was the meaning of the phrase? Still, the glimmering treasures around him led him deeper into the cave.

The cave was vast and his footsteps echoed as if tapping on an empty stage. It stretched miles deep and was an angular network that formed intersecting highways creating high cliffs, narrow bridges, and passages that looped and crossed paths for a seemingly endless distance. There were rooms of mineral deposits, with lava tubes that had formed on the cave floors from prehistoric volcanic activity and slowly vented a warming steam. He lowered the torch and saw some of the most unusual crawly things scrambling about under his feet.

"Some were lizard like things while others were amphibian or arachnid looking oddities. Some had no eyes and elongated limbs, while others were iridescent with almost transparent type skin. Not surprising to him were hundreds if not thousands of roosting bats above that did not seem to mind his attendance.

The sound of running water caught the man's attention and that lead him down a tunnel and into an adjacent icy cavern. The slow stream of water and ice flowed through a joint in the bedrock that had created natural ice formations. He ventured further into the cave, all the while painting the cave walls with the fire's light. His eyes gaped in astonishment at the reserves surrounding him.

Groupings of precious and semiprecious stones were all around him consisting of diamonds, sapphires, rubies, emeralds, and amethyst both uncut and faceted. The refractions and luminescence of the stones was breathtaking; however the man was no gemologist and could not properly identify each stone by name. But there before him, encased in the cave walls and scattered on the floors, were Jasper, Lace, Obsidian, Malachite, Turquoise, Tigers-eye, Hematite, and Quartz. He dropped more than he could stuff into his pockets and he kicked over more jewels than he could see. He stood in triumph and splendor as he imagined his exit from the cave and the fortune that would become his wealth. He continued exploring, all the while going deeper and deeper into the cave.

The man explored room after room and enjoyed the freedom of letting his greed grow as his eyes wandered. But then… an unknown echo caught his attention and drew him down a tunnel not yet explored. With the torch in front of him, he observed another etching written in the wall reading, 'That which hath been is named already and it is known that it is man; neither may he contend with him that is mightier than he.'

This time the words were worrisome to the man. He wasn't sure who or what was meant, but the tone of the ancient writings felt more like a warning to him. But then, there it was again… the echo coming from deep in the tunnels. It was not the heaviness of singular droplets of water nor the heel toeing of his footsteps, but something else. The wind from outside was not whistling through the cave tunnels, but this was more of a dense bellowing, almost as if the cave itself were breathing.

The sound of the echo led him into a hollow cavern where he found a pool of water from an underground stream. The crystal waters of the pool, glimmered on the cavern ceiling above him, and was only offset by a natural hot spring. The water was cool and crisp in his cupped hands and with each swallow he felt life and strength pulsing through him. He patted his face and neck with the water and exhaled a sigh of relief, but then an eerie, silent presence began growing behind him. He paused and held his breath and listened for movement. The silence of the cavern filled him with terror as his mind raced to give face to the unnerving feeling behind him. He remained on his knees waiting for the shadows of the cave to confirm his growing suspicions.

And then the silence was broken by a heavy shifting of sand and gravel. At first only once, then a second movement now followed by a third. His heart thumped heavily and his eyes dilated and sweat began rising across his brow. He was paralyzed by the unknown, as the singular movements became a continuous shifting that was now expanding around him. His mouth was dry and his skin a ghostly pale color, yet somehow he found the courage to reach for the torch.

Ever so slowly, he turned and observed a giant figure growing in the shadows around him. Nothing could describe the nightmare unfolding before him as he watched the dark figure continue to grow and expand. He shook his head and his wits returned to him. He looked for an escape but was cornered by the pool of water behind him that ended his retreat; and now the shadowy figure was almost on top of him.

The size and girth of it stretched wider on both sides until, finally, it stopped moving and there, during a momentary pause, the man slowly began to raise the torch. The man's eyes traced the massive body, coiled and patterned with scales, , from the left then upwards to the right up around its neck, and down its muzzle, to a pair of large reptilian eyes keenly staring back at him.

The man was petrified at what stood staring back at him eye to eye. And then, with a heavy tone, the creature said, "Speak… be thou truth or lie?"

The man's mind raced through scrambled thoughts trying to find the words to reply. The creature said again with commanding tone, "Speak!"

"I, I am," he stuttered out.

"You are Man… and I have known you since the beginning. As it was then, so shall it be now." The creature interrupted the man before he could give his name, and pulled itself forward out of the shadows and into the light, and what stood boldly before the man was a giant serpent. The face of the serpent resembled that of a wise old Mandrill more than that of any snake or reptile of the present.

"Tell me, Man of the Present, what has brought you here before me? Have you come to slay me and loot the treasures of this cave?" the serpent inquired.

"No! I only entered the cave to escape the storm," the man

replied, stumbling over his words. I didn't know anything was in here!"

"Is that what I am, a mere thing, as lifeless and meaningless as these stones? But oh, how they sparkle and do shine for they are precious and full of worth. But I am lackluster and only full of wisdom and knowledge, for surely such a thing has no value in the world of man. Vanity of vanities, Man of the Present... all is vanity."

"No, no. I didn't mean you were a thing, I... I just meant, that I..." He paused, taking a breath in order to finish his sentence.

"What I meant was... I didn't know that you were in here," he said, correcting his previous remark. "I didn't mean to upset you, when I said that."

"So it is only mere coincidence and no dealing of fate that has brought you out of the storm and into my domain?" the serpent countered, raising his head in response.

"Yes! It was just an accident! I'll go and I won't tell anyone that you're here," the man, stuttered.

"As quickly as you have found shelter, you would abandon it for the elements that previously tormented you? Tell me that simple fear is not your sole motivation for such a swift departure? Ha! Ha! Ha! Man of the Present! Your fear speaks louder than your words. However, if all I desired was to eat you, I would not prolong the event with such trivial subtleties," the serpent replied sarcastically, with a raised eyebrow.

"So, you're not going to eat me?" the man, prodded with concern.

"Of all the creation I am permitted to eat, rarely have I enjoyed the taste of man. But be that as it may, I am no vile monster, no vindictive beast of sin. I am only a serpent as the Creator hath made me and, as such, I am ruled by instinct and can tell no lies."

"The Creator? You mean God?" he pressed in clarification.

"No... I mean the Creator, as I acknowledge no God of man's making," the serpent boldly rebutted. Still, the Creator who hath made me saw fit to endow me with strength, a cunning intellect, longevity of life, and a chiefly purpose. Yet, my introverted nature has left me in solitude and sadly my days are filled with endless boredom."

"You're bored?" he inquired, with balking bewilderment.

"After years spent slumbering all alone, even the treasures of this cave have lost their appeal and no longer shine so brightly. Within these caves is a collection of riches and ransom unmatched by any stronghold known to man. The Legendary Kusanagi sword of 1185, the Triste Treasure of Moctezuma II, the Gold and Silver Treasures of Lima, along with the looted riches of Benito Bonito. The lost English Crown jewels, the forbidden Gold of the Inca's, The Treasure of the Flor De La Mar and, of course, the amassed fortune of the Knights Templar. Amazing isn't it, that no map or copper scroll guided you through these tunnels and past the concentration of riches, leading you here into my dwelling!"

"How easily you could have fled after taking your pick of artifacts, and royal regalia; but instead, you ventured further into the unknown for, perhaps, the temptation of blood and wine. Hmm... I would like to make a proposition of sorts. I shall grant you solace here until the storm ceases and in return, you shall provide me with the necessity of companionship. Accept or not, for it is I who stand to lose the most."

"You want me to stay, and talk to you?" the man questioned, in confusion.

"That is correct," the serpent nodded.

"And that's all... you're not going to kill me?"

"I cannot guarantee your life as it was not I who gave it to you. However, you may find death an attractive alternative as I have yet to master the art of social jesting," the serpent admitted.

The man's eyes widened after hearing the serpent speak of death.

"That was a joke!" the serpent chuckled.

The man sighed heavily and dropped his shoulders in relief.

"Do we have an agreement?" the serpent asked politely.

The Man thought to himself momentarily and considered the serpent's proposal, while the walls glimmered and sparkled

12

around him. He thought, that perhaps he could befriend the serpent, and possibly be rewarded with a portion of the treasures. But then another thought raced through his mind, that perhaps the serpent was lulling him into a false sense of security and was only biding his time before striking. He nodded to himself and was confident that he could turn the situation in his favor while still making a profit.

"Alright... I agree," the man raised his eyes, then nodded.

The serpent uncoiled and stretched out his massive frame, until he came to rest on the opposite side of the glimmering pool."

"But before we begin, I must ask you. How is it that you can speak?" he questioned.

"How is it that you can speak, human? The answer to both questions is the same, because the Creator has deemed it so. What's wrong human? Did you not believe in talking serpents?" the serpent retorted.

"Well, I... I... I didn't mean it to be..." he stuttered.

"It matters not, for the truth needs not belief to exist," the serpent smiled then said, "Feel no shame Man of the Present! I didn't believe in talking monkeys until you walked in here! Ha! Ha! Ha! Ha!" The serpent laughed at the man's expense.

"How long have you been here and where did you come from?" he asked, while looking at the size of the serpent.

"Ahh... indeed my beginnings are of a curiosity and, yet, after all this time, I suppose it is no coincidence that I have found myself back here in this Cave of Treasures. My age cannot easily be determined for I have existed for millennia. I was one of the first creations ever to exist, but I swear to you, that my dwelling here was no matter of expulsion.

"I have memories of darkness and a place without time and I have known man before the concept of logic or comprehension. It could be said that I have been both friend and foe of mankind since his earliest beginnings," the serpent related.

"What do you mean you have known mankind since the beginning? What beginning are you talking about?" the man inquired, stepping closer to the water's edge.

"I suppose the answer to that lies within the story of us all. You see… to tell my story is to tell the story of mankind; for I was there in a vast and magnificent garden and I remember when it all began. But first, touch the torch against any of the geode's around you. They have petroleum deposits enough to illuminate the entirety of the cave." The serpent sighed deeply then coiled himself partially, raising his head and body as if seated at an elevated desk presiding over a courtroom. "Ahh… much better," the serpent remarked with delight.

"Now, Man of the Present, let me tell you the history of things. Allow me to explain our ill-fated connection and the order of succession. Let me tell you who, and what, I really am," the serpent began to speak and the man began to listen.

CHAPTER 2: THE GARDEN

"It began in The Garden, when many creation and entities existed, it was the Age of Heavens. The Garden was a philosophical menagerie with endless potential and intrigue. It was complete and endless in its ability to provide and sustain all life that occupied it. Where all things, thoughts, and ideas were interpreted into life, purpose, and meaning.

"Any and everything that has been and will ever come into existence had its beginnings there. There were running rivers of dreams that flowed through valleys and meadows and cascaded down into lakes and ponds of imagination. All thoughts ever memorized or any lonely idea ever forgotten springs from those waters and eventually awakens in the minds of mankind.

"Simple streams flowed upwards over cliffs and through mountains without the need to split the stone. The rivers created by the streams emptied into oceanic lakes. Each lake was of a different temperature, some boiled, while others were calm and refreshing, or frozen and unforgiving. All the while aquatic life swam through solid ice and bounced happily through boiling waters as part of their natural migrations."

"The Garden soil was rich and seedlings that fell instantly sprouted into new fruit bearing plants. When looking up into the skies above, one beheld an elemental playground. Clouds consisted of fire, water, and stone and they did as clouds do and formed new shapes when coming into contact with each other.

"When it rained, nothing got wet because droplets of humility, hope, fear, and laughter were expelled from an atmosphere of emotion and a state of overall well-being. At that time, there was only one wind and the wind blew harmony and volumes of complex sounds to those who rested beneath it, and the Creator said to the wind, 'Awake, O north wind and come thou south, blow upon my garden that the spices thereof may flow out.'

"Creation and life were growing concepts in the Garden without law or boundary. One day there were things that only walked and crawled and the next day, gave flight or took to the seas and ended a life secured to the ground. Beings were molded from fire, light, wind, and water, while others were constructed from wood, metal, or glass. Every day there were new things in the Garden, but not all were kept and many were discarded. The Garden was made not for leisure but for progression and growth, yet life was complete and all were content.

"There were orchards of divine fruit bearing trees, with each tree bestowing a different ability upon its consumption. The Trees of Knowledge, Power, Life, Creation, Destruction, Will, Time, Travel, and Speed were all there. It was amazing as each one bloomed separately and each with an inspiring fragrance of its own. But still more and on were the trees of Growth, Sight, Strength, Vision, Flight, Energy, Health, and Heart."

"I would often rest underneath them and listen to their poetry, and the trees recited, 'Thy plants are an orchard of pomegranates, with pleasant fruits; camphor, with spikenard and saffron and cinnamon, with all trees of frankincense, myrrh and aloes, with all the chief spices...' The Garden was set in the east... and it was called Eden."

"Eden? ... You're talking about that story!" the man exclaimed.

"What story?"

"The story, you know... from THE BOOK!" he reiterated.

"You're telling me that there's a book titled... THE

BOOK?" the serpent asked.

"Yeah, that's what I said! It's a religious book, everyone knows of it," the man explained.

"That's got to be the worst title I've ever heard of!" the serpent muttered to himself. "Ohhhh! 'THE BOOK,' I know which 'THE BOOK' you're referring to now… what about it?"

"The Garden, that's what you're talking about. It's the same story as in THE BOOK," the man expressed.

"In what way?" the serpent further pressed.

"What do you mean in what way, it's the same thing," the man countered. "You just told me that the story you're referring to is religious in content, right?"

"Correct, however what I'm about to tell you is no cultural myth or religious lore. What I'm going to tell you is history," the serpent said, gesturing with his tail.

"What's the difference, if it's the same story?" he asked.

"It makes all the difference, one is the truth and one is a belief," the serpent clarified.

The man stood silently for a moment digesting the serpent's words.

"I can stop now if you wish, that is since you already know the story. I mean, there's nothing you ever questioned, or second guessed…right? And I hope I'm not offending you with my words, as I understand your religious beliefs mean a great deal to you. But you must realize that my version may differ from that of your understanding, because, you see, I was there!" The serpent's face showed in shadow as he moved forward showing his teeth, muzzle, and finally, his reptile eyes.

"How do I know you're telling the truth? And why should I believe anything you're going to say?" the man questioned intently.

"Everything I say is not a lie, nor is everything I bite poisoned. Just as it is with your understanding, it is up to you to believe or not to. As I said, I am a creature of instinct and truth is my nature. What reason have I to lie to you, and besides what do I stand to gain? You are under no obligation to stay, you are free to go. I am no jailer, you owe me no debt. How triumphant you shall be, once you escape the clutches of my rancid domain and return back into the loving bosom of the autumn breeze outside" the serpent remarked jokingly, then lifted his head and turned his back on the man.

"Or... stay and listen, that is ... if you wish to know my side of the story," the serpent offered.

The man looked behind him and could hear the storm raging outside, however, the glistening of the treasures around him beckoned him to stay.

"Aaahh! What a surprise... you're still here!" The serpent turned back around facing the man with a gleeful smile, chuckling lightly.

"Alright... I'll stay. So what do they do... the trees?" The man took a seat on a large flattened stone folding his hands intently listening to the serpent.

"Ah yes! The trees! The first time I encountered them, I asked that very same question, but I think the follow up questions are much more interesting. You see, each tree grants the consumer a divine ability upon consumption. Such as the Tree of Knowledge, it is not just knowledge in the sense of the singular word, but the complete idea of it."

"Imagine having instant knowledge of any subject, any thought or idea past, present, or future. But not just a new skill, but imagine coming up with a new idea never thought of and having complete understanding of it instantly. The knowledge of not just its destructive or creative ability, but its lasting effects, its future repercussions, its social ripples, and how that idea will change and shape new generations to come. Think for a moment how the designers of the automobile looked at their contraption and how they dreamed of what possibilities it might unlock, but how limited their view of it actually was."

"Imagine knowing exactly how far that idea would go, and how it would affect and change an economy, the lives it could bring together, the accidental deaths, and how certain events were not possible without its invention. Yes... true knowledge, in its entirety, unlimited and instantly yours!"

"What about the other trees, and what do they do?" he

inquired further.

"Which ones?"

"What about the Tree of Power, what does that one do?" he questioned.

"Interesting!" The serpent, commented with an inquisitive whispering tone. "Of all the abilities you could ask about, power was your first selection. Well, the Tree of Power, is not just power in a singular sense, but power as a complete idea and concept. Take if you will the power of the mind and how mankind has the power to draw things into reality like a magnet. Now take the power of love and how it can motivate one to overcome all odds and cross oceans, and break down walls all for the love of another. Now imagine having the ability to aim that power in any direction and for any purpose," the serpent expounded.

"Wow! That's amazing but just trying to understand the idea of that is…"

"I know… the concept itself is almost too large to even understand. You humans have such limited understanding of your true abilities and what you can actually accomplish and achieve. The abilities granted by the fruits, however, are nothing new to any of you. You already possess those abilities; it just takes time to develop them. Just as you attend school and undergo intense training to master an art or craft. So too can mankind master the art of Life, of Healing, and Creation, but he seems so preoccupied with the latter… namely Power and Destruction."

"That reminds me of the follow up question that came to me one day. I had a question that I did not ask the Creator directly, nor have I ever asked it to this day. It came to me while resting on a cliff observing clouds lazily colliding with each other. I wondered what did the Creator need with such divine trees? I had seen the Creator working and building, but never did I see the Creator even enter the orchards, nor ever speak of them. Did the Creator plant them there for someone or still, did the trees give the Creator his abilities? Such questions are dangerous and I thought blasphemy for thinking such things, so

I let them sink deeply into the abyss of my mind."

"That's crazy! You're saying that possibly God got his powers from eating the fruit. If that's true, then that would mean someone or something else put them there!" He looked on with confusing fear and distrust of the serpent's words.

"Everything had its beginning in the Garden... quite possibly even the Creator," the serpent further conjectured.

The man stood silently for a moment then asked, "Did you ever eat any of the fruit?"

"The fruit of the trees are not edible to me; therefore they are meaningless to me. The Creator made me complete and I cannot change any further. I spent many hours that became days and nights in the orchards enjoying their sweet and savory fragrances. But one thing I noticed, was that none of the creation ate of the fruit."

"I thought to myself, if the fruit was not for us, then who were they for? As I said before, the Garden was not for leisure, but for growth and development. The Trees were growing and producing amazing flowers and fruits, but I would soon learn who they were for," the serpent responded, with an attentive smirk.

"Very few remember how they came into existence, but I do. I awoke fully formed, but with no prior knowledge of having lived before. I felt not out of place nor afraid. I remember chaotic thoughts coming together and then I heard a voice call to me with a powerful and loving tone. And the voice said, 'You are as I have made you.' The voice was that of the Creator and then I became aware. I have been thankful every day for the life the Creator has given me, but only living life would fully explain what the Creator had made me."

"I was smaller then and little better than a lizard scrambling about the ground. I praised the Creator for allowing me to remain and endowing me with strength, agility, speed, and a cunning intellect. I was strong and full of life, but also foolish and arrogant. And like so many other fools too late in their wisdom, I am left to wonder... if I knew then, what I know now... would I have left the man and woman to their own devices? But we can never go back as we have only one life to live and such questions are but half remembered dreams and are forever out of reach." The serpent paused momentarily, and raised his eyes toward the ceiling of the cave in silence.

"What is it... what's wrong?" the man questioned.

"Out of reach... it's been so long, so, so long, but I can still feel them. They were laying right there in front of me, but I couldn't reach them... I couldn't reach them," the serpent sighed with a tear swelling in his eye then lowered his head.

"What was it that you couldn't reach?"

"My arms and my legs," the serpent reminisced then sighed heavily and sniffed a tear away. "I suppose it is truer than they say, you don't know what you have until it's gone. My abilities are unique and I am first of my kind. But being first is more than just a title, for everything that comes after you is blessed and thankful for all your waking and aching moments," the serpent said with conviction.

"Imagine the first fliers and think of how they flapped clumsily in the air trying to learn the language of flight. Just think as they were illiterate in the tongue of wind and air, and how today they are fluent and make music upon their wings. It's almost funny, looking back as I learned to dig and tunnel in the ground. Climbing tree and cliff to leap and dive into the waters below. My arms were nimble with strong claws to rival any eagle's talon. My legs were raptor like and I could spring and lunge fast with speed so as none could catch me." The serpent sighed again in remembrance.

"You know, I never gave much thought to my tail, but I suppose it is the Creator's supreme irony, for where does the story of humanity begin if not with a Serpent's tale? Yes... I think that's as good a place as any to begin." The fire light flickered and glowed a warm honey tone against the cavern walls, as the man continued to listen to the serpent's words.

"And then one day, the Creator became busy and soon decided upon similarities and patterns for all life to fill a new world called Earth. Breath was decided upon first and all would breathe oxygen to sustain life, either directly through lungs, or secondary by gills, or thirdly by diffusion."

"Then water was determined, and all who lived would need water to live. Larger, massive, and extreme just as a child's drawings, were the Creator's first attempts at life. Then as the Creator continued working the designs became smaller, more compact, and more detailed as if a new wave of technology had popularized creation itself.

"The Creator seemed to be pleased with me and thought to bring those second and third of me to populate the earth. They were large and terrifying reptiles and each was an expression of an attribute of me. It was as if each scale of me were given life to move and roar, to hunt and hatch. It was humbling and beautiful that I was selected to be made into hundreds and thousands; and for a time, we roamed the earth, and we reigned supreme.

"Years came and went upon the Earth and the Creator's work slowed for a time and life was allowed to live. The Earth was lush and hot with greenery, it was the time of Giants, but what are Giants if there are no ants under their feet?

"Then new life began to appear, first slowly, then with haste as the Creator found a new form of passion. My reptile kind remained, but others with fur and feathers began to appear. It was a complex arrangement and like many transitions, it was difficult. Out with the old and in with the new. It is the way of things, but nothing to be upset about. The Creator did not, however, destroy this time, but triggered growth and adaptation. Things began to waddle and crawl out of ponds and lakes and onto dry land. While others that walked and hopped learned to glide and eventually to fly. Those that gave flight became better and more adapted to life in cold climates and hunting smaller prey. And once again, the Creator's work slowed and life upon the Earth was allowed to live.

"A third transition followed but not the final. Changing, growing, living, and dying was the natural cycle upon the Earth. All the while the Creator worked, I saw the Angel and the Jinn take their places at the side of the Creator. I cared not for their sort as they were elemental and existed on alternative planes than other creation. However, I feared none, as my strength was supreme even to the fiery Jinn and the obedient Angel of light.

"Back upon the face of the Earth there were animals now … deer, antelope, bears, lions, tigers, birds of prey, domestic fowl, and flightless birds. And still more with whales, shrimp, bacteria, and bottom feeders of the deeps. The smallest are often the most overlooked, but usually are the most necessary. Worms were there underneath the ground, along with spiders, moths, flies, and all other crawly things.

"All of the elements existed on the Earth, but they were not fully in use. Earth, Wind, and Water were known to all, but Fire danced alone as none had learned to tame it. I could always sense when the Creator was planning something new, there was always something held back, something extra left undone and so it was the same in this instance.

"Even though the Garden was the workshop of the Creator, none were allowed to observe the Creator fully. We were only permitted to observe the Creator's voice, which appeared as different shapes, sometimes colors, or musical tones. I had watched the voice of the Creator many times working, sometimes a being was formed and life would spring forward out of sheer nothing, or the Creator would call to a droplet of dew and out would fold a petite butterfly. Days continued as such, many creations were made and new thoughts and ideas were grown, and I recall such a day when the Creator decided upon making a man.

"This time the voice of the Creator was resolute and spoke enchantment to the dust and commanded it to take form. The form raised itself from out of the dust straightening its knees and rolling its shoulders and what came together was a creation never before seen in the Garden. The Creator called to me and I beheld the new thing. The voice of the Creator beckoned me towards the new form. I looked upon it then entered and exited the form at seven points, and then around its vertebrae crossing over it two times.

"I observed its systems and within it was a flow of energy moving clockwise in direction. These seven points were physical then, but now exist only as auras of the human subconscious. Some have alluded to this and have become aware of the seven energy centers in all of mankind, I am not boastful of my contribution, but... you are very welcome.

"The Creator then breathed into the lifeless form and it gave movement and suddenly it was alive. The Creator was pleased with the new creation and stood him in the Garden for all to see and from then on, it was called 'Man.'

"For a time, Man and all creation were as they were intended to be and all were content. Life continued as it had before with the exception of Man. Man was different and would sit alone and lived separately from all other creation. Man would often rest under the trees in the orchard sometimes singing a hymn or in peaceful meditation. One evening, the wind became entangled in a debate with a group of mountains and a storm arose. Man, who sat quietly in meditation, refused to move from underneath the storm. At first, I was in awe of the storm as it raged creating thunder and furious lighting and flooding rains, yet Man remained in poise and refused to move. He was deep in thought and almost suspended above the ground in an ecstatic state. I had never approached him before as he was different from other creation, but he seemed to be favored by the Creator, so I thought to intervene.

"What could I do? I respected his poise and strength of mind, but needed to act quickly lest the storm take hold of him. Without thought, I rose up from the ground and wrapped myself around him, enveloping him to protect him from the storm. I locked my feet and claws into the ground and the trees for securement and remained there with the man for seven days. All the while, Man never broke his meditation, while I covered him in security.

"After the storm ceased, I released my grasp and looked upon Man, as he opened his eyes then said one word 'enlightenment' and walked away. I suppose it was chance encounters like that which began much of the lore and mythology of serpent kind.

"Throughout time, humanity has seen me in variations of

sacred or vilified roles or even as a guardian of sacred places as my kind are known to hold their ground. Personally, I prefer the classical tales to such scientific mockeries of my being. At least they were somewhat imaginative. Some of the earliest written records depict the cosmos as an extension of me, where Gods would sleep while floating on the cosmic waters of my serpent-being. In truth, I would often rest and look up into the starry night and dream, but there was no singing or divine milky waves or oceans, because that's just silly," the serpent said rolling his eyes in contempt.

"You see not only was I gifted a cunning intellect, but I was also given knowledge of chemical properties unlike any other. My venom is not only potent but is also the basis for all poisons and medicines. For no other creature as I is so heavily associated with the power to heal, to poison, or to expand the conscious through entheogenic ritual. Having such a power surging within me gives me the divine ability to move through the earthly world and the afterlife with ease. Indeed, of all the creation known to man, I am considered wisest of them all." The serpent raised himself up in pride and the man stood up quickly as the serpent towered above him. The serpent brought himself back down to his previous seated like position and responded, "I apologize for my pride, I didn't mean to excite you."

"Oh no, I wasn't scared I was just standing to stretch," the man defended. The serpent continued.

"The following day, the Creator called to Man and commanded him to name all creation as he saw fit. Man did as he was commanded and from then on all elements were given a name, day and night were called out as they rose and set. Then each new day, Man continued until all of creation had a name but for some reason, Man left off naming me. I didn't mind it at the time. I knew that all things had a purpose and all would be revealed in time, just as I too would be given a name.

"Still, Man remained distant from all other creation and was alone. The Creator then commanded all manner of creation to visit Man and accompany him, but none of them were found to be a suitable companion. The Creator then said, 'It isn't good for Man to be alone.' So the Creator set Man asleep and created Woman, as a companion for him, and the two saw happiness in each other.

"Man looked at Woman and said, 'Set me as a seal upon thine heart, as a seal upon thine arm, for love is strong as death. Jealousy is cruel as the grave and the coals thereof are coals of fire, which hath a most vehement flame. Many waters cannot quench love, neither can the floods drown it, if a man would give all the substance of his house for love, it would utterly be contemned.'

"From then on Man and Woman were happy and lived as other creation did in the Garden. I took interest in them, but was sure to observe them from a far. I watched their ways as they were a curious type and saw in them something that I had not seen in any other creation. One followed the other as if commanded to do so and I saw one take while the other gave. They were two halves of a whole, and while separated they were as wanderers lost in a labyrinth forever searching for the right path.

"I came to a conclusion of them and the one thing that stood out from them was, dare I say it… ignorance. Yes, ignorance was apparent in them and it was stunning. Every other creation was made with instinct or ability and learned rather quickly after birthing or hatching. Other creations either imprinted immediately or had within them the skills of survival; but what of Man and Woman for there were no others like them, so who were they to learn from? I thought to myself that perhaps the Creator had left something out, and perhaps would complete them at a later time.

"Additionally, all other creation had coverings, such as fur or feathers or shell or scales, but Man and Woman were exposed and had nothing to cover themselves with. Their flesh was weak and unable to adapt to the elements about them. I remember the wind and rains taking pity on the pair and allowing them cool winds and warm air to delight in. The ground was even sympathetic and closed up its thorns and stickers so as not to prick them. How odd were these new creations as they did not

TRUTH AND THE SERPENT

seem to have any given ability or adaptation of wing or claw, neither beak nor tentacle, or even a tail. Honestly, the sight of witnessing two people strolling about completely 'buttasscracktittynipplenutsackdanglingnaked' was more of an overwhelming bad joke that I was forced to observe daily."

"Butt-naked ass, what did you say?" the man remarked in befuddlement. "That's not even a real word?"

It is so! It's one word, three syllables. Now stop interrupting me!" the serpent exclaimed, with simple absurdity.

"Speaking of bad jokes, I've heard your professors explaining me away as a subconscious symbol of fear. Somehow hardwired into the human psyche from prehistoric days when humans supposedly swung throughout the trees. That from eons past, I hunted and ate upon the helpless and defenseless ancestry of man, resulting in such an outcome of demonic mythology and mass phobia of all serpent kind. Ha! How truly absurd! That alone... I am to blame for the shared nightmares of a species who knows not its own origins? What insanity!" the serpent, remarked cynically while shaking his head.

"Well, scientists have found evidence of ape-man like beings on earth. How is it crazy to think that?" the man responded.

"What's crazy is that you people don't know where you come from; and instead of understanding your whereabouts, you blame an irrational fear on me. I mean if it wasn't for my kind, rats would have overrun the earth a long time ago, because some trash mongering species leaves filth everywhere it goes, and doesn't know how to pick up after themselves. Do I ever get a thank you, hmm? Thank you, Serpent! Thank you for not letting a bunch of disease spreading rodents take over the world and start a society based on peanut butter and cheese currency. Of course not!" the serpent argued with a sarcastic tone.

"I apologize, I didn't mean to rant like that. It's just that after a couple hundred thousand years, things start to bother you a bit. Let's continue!"

"Sure, but I've got a question," the serpent paused listening to the man. "Why were you watching them?"

"Because, watching and listening is how I learn. You can

27

learn a lot about people just by observing them. You can learn their patterns and their behaviors, you can see their weaknesses and their addictions. But most of all, you can see how dangerous they are, just by watching them. My advice to you is this, Man of the Present. Just watch and wait, and eventually people will show you who they really are," the serpent said wisely.

"One afternoon I sat and listened to Man and Woman conversing, and I thought to myself that the two were mismatched as opposites and had different perceptions of the world. They would never see eye to eye but, oddly, they seemed completed by the presence of each other. I continued to observe them, until I felt my wit and cunning were indeed superior to theirs.

"Then one afternoon, I observed Woman gathering food as she had done nearly every day before that. I approached and asked her, 'Why do you not eat of all the fruit in the Garden?'

'The Creator forbids us to eat from certain trees in the center of the Garden. And if we do so, we will die,' she replied. 'Lies!' I said, the Creator knows that if you eat of that fruit you will not die, but your eyes will become opened and you will know the difference between good and evil.' She looked at me curiously then asked, 'What is good and what is evil?'

"I looked at her in puzzlement, replying 'Good is the opposite of evil, to know them is to understand the balance of opposites.' She replied, 'Why is it that you do not eat of the fruit?' So I answered, 'The fruit is not edible to me, just as stone and fire are not edible to you. I do not require the abilities of the fruits as the Creator has made me complete. I know the good and the evil, besides everything that is edible to me, I eat.'

"After our conversation, she changed her direction and looked towards the Orchard of Divine Trees. All of the trees were surrounded by a floating medallion, and each medallion appeared as a haloed ring, depicting the ability of the fruit. When she approached the Tree of Consciousness, she breached the medallion's seal and thunder crackled momentarily around the tree. The seal depicted two childlike characters, one male and one female depicting good and evil, sitting on opposite sides of the tree holding out their hands."

"What did the fruit look like? Was it an apple?" the man inquired.

"An apple? No, why would it be an apple?" the serpent responded, shaking his head, no. "I understand that you have never seen it, but try to be a bit more imaginative. Let me ask you this. What is a fruit... in a scientific sense?"

"Well I know that there's a difference between a fruit and a vegetable," he postulated, but the serpent interrupted to define the subject.

"In botany, a fruit is the result from the maturation of one or more flowers, while in the culinary sense, a fruit is a sweet tasting plant product. The same could be said of the fruits in the Garden, as the fruits are the means, by which the trees disseminate their divine concepts and abilities.

"All fruits are designed in one of two ways to either attract or repel. Those that repel are covered with spikes or hooked burrs, to prevent themselves from being eaten or to disperse toxins in defense of a mother plant. However, most are of a delightful appearance and are deliberately made appealing so that the seeds are unknowingly eaten and can deposit their nutrition into the host like species.

"As with the divine fruits, when eaten it propagates a symbiotic relationship between the fruit and the consumer, into what you have today, i.e. human consciousness. Unfortunately, due to mass cultural and symbolic appeal, the apple and pomegranate have become synonymous with the fruit of the Garden. But honestly, the fruit looks nothing like an apple, or a pomegranate. Its allure is seductive perhaps almost sexually overpowering to the point of breaking the law. This forbidden fruit, if you will, is fleshy, ripe, alluring, and delicious! In all honesty, they might as well look like a pair of boobs, but that's just me!" the serpent said with sarcastic humor, then continued.

"Immediately, Woman asked no further questions and picked the fruit from the tree. The fruit gave off sparkles of inspiration and images of what was to come. The good deeds of giving without the expectation of receiving in return, known as kindness. The evil act of stealing, not only property, but of ones sense of personal security by means of rape. The images she saw before her were but meaningless pictograms to a childish and unassuming mind.

"The sparkles faded, she blinked once, then bit into the fruit. She stood frozen momentarily as I slinked around her left shoulder and saw the cosmic expansion in her eye. It was similar to watching a shooting star followed by a planetary explosion of enlightenment which overtook her all at once. Then a tear trickled down her face holding the last of her innocence. She raised her eyes still in a daze of confusion, consciousness, and thought, that she could not fully understand pulsing through her. She approached Man, and she recited, 'Let my beloved come into his garden and eat his pleasant fruits. I am come into my garden, my spouse, I have gathered my myrrh with my spice; I have eaten my honeycomb with my honey and I have drunk my wine with my milk. Eat abundantly, O beloved.'

"Afterwards I thought to myself, if she would have been farther away from Man and had time to fully understand what had occurred, would she still have offered the fruit to him? Would she have decided to live alone with her new-found consciousness and leave Man in bliss and eternal ignorance? Another thought entered my mind and I thought, or did she offer him the fruit… knowingly?

"But in actuality, it all happened so fast and she couldn't have understood her actions, as they were partners and shared in everything they did. She, ate of the fruit and instinctively offered it to him. He did not ask where it came from, he only smiled upon seeing her and accepted the gift blindly, and I recited, 'Death and life are in the power of the tongue, and they that love it shall eat the fruit thereof.'

"Man sank his teeth into the wholesome fruit, and he questioned not what entered his body. What happened to her, happened the same to him, and the two were struck in an experience of conscious unbalance for the first time. For the first time, they thought aloud and looked at the world around them in question and felt insecure and were afraid. They dropped the remainder of the uneaten fruit and stopped suddenly and saw themselves as they truly were. Frightened, defenseless, and clumsy as they gasped in shame as they saw they were naked.

"They cowered and cried, then ran behind trees to hide and cover themselves with. I watched from the orchard in intrigue as I saw them scurry about in fright. And I say this in all honesty, I did not know what would happen to them upon eating the fruit. I am not saying I was surprised by their reaction, but interested was more of my observation."

"So you wanted them to eat it?" the man asked, with a skewed expression.

"I will admit, I was curious about the fruit and their effects once eaten. But if you mean that I had forewarned knowledge of the impending reality placed upon Man and Woman after eating the fruit? Then my answer remains... No!" the serpent answered, then continued.

"After sometime, the Creator observed Man and Woman covering themselves, and called to them saying, 'Why are you hiding from me?' Man admitted to the Creator, that he had eaten the fruit given to him by Woman. But Woman quickly retorted pointing at me saying, 'He tricked me into eating the fruit!'

"The Creator called me forth and became angry then punished me by saying, 'From now on you will be singled out from all other creation to grovel and crawl upon your belly. All of mankind will distrust and fear you, and at the very sight of you they will strike at your head. You will crawl about striking at their heels because of your actions today, and all of your offspring shall bear your fate.'

"And then a horrible pain drove through my body from the top of my head down through my arms and the feeling of fire shot through my toes. I felt a popping sensation and was almost shell shocked with a momentary loss of hearing. I could see everything around me, but I felt ill to my stomach and shuddered with a chill. I looked down and there, falling lifelessly from my body, were my limbs, falling as leaves from an autumn tree. My eyes bulged in fright as I saw my arms and legs laying there in front of me.

"My first reaction was to reach down and retrieve them before some scavenger ran away with them. But how do you reach out and comfort yourself without the arms to do so? How can you run away in shame without any legs? If not for my tail which had now become the entirety of my body, I would have completely fallen on the ground. But then the same realization that came over Man and Woman came over me. The realization of what was captured in that tear streaming down her face; It was the reality of everything I had lost.

"Why had such a curse been placed upon me? What crime had I committed? My head sank into my nonexistent hands and I could no longer hide my face in humiliation. I wobbled and flopped around on the ground in front of them and the voice of the Creator. And then… that's when it happened. Man looked down at me quivering upon the ground, he stretched out his arm pointing, and with solemn tone, laid heavily upon me the name to which I am to this day. And he said… 'Serpent!'

"There I lay on the ground unknowingly forming a ring sobbing with my tail in my mouth. If ever there was a symbol of irony it was I on that day as clear and widespread of the 'All-in-All' and the cyclic nature of things yet to come. And ever since then, humanity has seen me as a representation of dual expression, but mostly as a symbol of evil," the serpent lowered his head, while the man looked on him with contempt but humble empathy.

"On that day, my entire life changed and I am as you see me here today. I am the Serpent of Old, the Serpent of ruin and curse, it is because of me that mankind exists today as you do. There is not a day that passes, that I do not regret my actions on that day in the Garden," the serpent reared his head, as he spoke identifying himself as the accursed being of legend.

"You! … You are the evil serpent! It was you that tricked the woman and cursed mankind. You are the devil himself aren't you? The man's eyes bulged as he spoke with damning tone, while backing up against the cavern wall.

"Are you done?" the serpent responded, with a blank

expression.

"Why did you do that? You lied and tricked them? And for what? Is that what you are...evil?" he asked, pointing at the serpent in condemnation.

"Why do you persist in calling me evil? I understand that modern day propaganda has made me into a symbol of sin. Even once, was I made the face of a hideous political Anti-Semitic campaign but I swear to you, I am no harbinger of eternal sin, nor any Alpha Draconian spy. Evil is the nature of Man, as my nature is that of truth," the serpent defended.

"I was cursed on that day not for an evil deed. You see, I spoke truth to Woman and the Creator punished and disfigured me for it. No, I am not evil, I am foolish! If I had said nothing and left Man and Woman to their ignorance, then my arms and legs would still be attached to my body, but alas, I was disfigured and left in this form," the serpent, said remorsefully shaking his head.

"How truly blind and ignorant you are, Man of the present. You accuse me of evil and place the hatred of humanity in my heart unjustly. You condemn me as a liar and a devil even though you, as the direct representation of Man and Woman, stand before me alive and well. If I were lying, then no man or woman would exist to this day," the serpent retorted.

"I've heard some people say that by, 'death' God didn't mean that they would physically die, but that Man and Woman would be kicked out of the Garden and would have to begin a new life on Earth," the man countered in clarification.

"So you're saying the Creator's words were meant figuratively, and death was merely the ending of one state of being then transitioning into another state? Such as living in a state of ignorance versus consciousness. Am I correct by your meaning?" the serpent, added in clarification.

"Yeah, I mean it could be taken either way," the man agreed, while motioning forward with his hand.

"Then I say, that the Creator makes no mistakes and everything happens for a reason, just as every creation has a purpose. The events that occurred on that day were supposed to happen and as I would later learn … the only way to understand the meaning and purpose in our lives, is quite simply to live them," the serpent continued.

"I was punished, but I did not curse the Creator with my tongue nor with my actions, for it was the Creator who gave me life."

"But you're evil! And you tempted the woman and caused all of mankind to be cast out of the Garden!" The man stabbed back at the serpent's explanation, to which the serpent simply smiled.

"If the Creator wanted mankind to remain in the Garden he would not have allowed such fruit to be eaten, nor Man and Woman to be so easily persuaded. I repeat, I am no incarnation of evil, nor is humanity the result of any original sin. We are as we were meant to be and the events that occurred in the Garden have set in motion a connection that have bound both serpent and mankind for the remainder of eternity."

"How are we bound for eternity?" the man asked, turning his head in speculation of the serpent's characterization.

"But I did not suffer the consequences alone and as I was cursed, so were Man and Woman cursed as well. The Creator singled Woman out and said, 'Pain of child birth, and Master is what ye shall call him.' Then turned towards Man saying, 'Struggle and hardship of life, endless toil, until death do you part.'

"Now here is an observation I present to you, Man of the Present. How is it that I am the great evil, as three were punished and cursed on that day? And of the three, two were cast out of the Garden, whereas I was allowed to remain.

"I was right but also wrong at the same time. I was overconfident in my intellect and foolish to think I knew the will of the Creator. I learned responsibility for everything that goes into and comes out of my mouth. Neither ignorance nor blind trust will save you from the consequences of your actions. No matter how much cunning and guile you think you have, you will be held accountable for what you say, as well as the dumfounded words of another you ingest. It may not kill you, but neither will it make you stronger. It will however, make you keener, uglier, and fowler, it is as they say… you reap, what you sow!

"The truth is Man of the Present, you must question what you are offered, you must question what you take hold of or spend a lifetime suffering the consequences of your actions. Only through trial and error can humanity grow and in order to grow one must learn to let go. Am I upset at Man and Woman for my current situation? No, for guilt and blame only flower seeds of hate, where as I believe in personal responsibility, which is rooted in enlightenment and prosperity."

"That still doesn't excuse what you did. It doesn't matter what you say now, what's done is done! You seduced them and caused them to sin. If it wasn't for you, none of this would ever have happened," he quipped back angrily.

"Let me ask you this, Man of the Present, even if you could go back to the Garden, would you really want to?" the serpent asked calmly, while the man stood silently.

"No… I didn't think so. But, if you wish to know true evil, treachery, and deceit, you need look no further than your own reflection. What happened in the Garden was only the beginning of our ill-fated connection, but my story is barely half begun. Now, if you're finished condemning me as something I am not, I shall continue with my story."

The man stood silently with a suspicious expression, as he thought that perhaps he had stayed too long and he should have left long ago. For what was previously an ancient creature of legend, had now presented itself as the figure of humanity's eternal damnation and shame. Could the serpent hold the answer to the meaning of life? The cave jewels and the wealth of knowledge being offered were too much to walk out on, so he remained and the serpent continued.

"The Tree of Consciousness and the eating of its fruit spurred the beginning of a new existence for Man and Woman. Previously, they were but empty vessels without understanding, without any need for options. But now their eyes were open and for the first time they had become more than just physical male and female forms. They were human beings with will and ability, option, and now lives to lead. Before leaving the Garden, they took one symbolic look back before walking forth out into the Earth that all along awaited them.

"You accused me of evil, well this part of our story brings us exactly to that point. You see evil did exist before, but not among any other creation. To say that evil was unknown to Man and Woman is to say that good was foreign as well, because neither can exist on its own and has no meaning without the other. So the life that Man and Woman lived was neither a good one, nor a bad one. It was muted without sound, without sensation, without any real meaning. What good is free will without anything to choose from? You see, it was I who gave it to them, I suppose in some ways you could call me the catalyst of humanity.

"With choice in front of them came the great burden of life. Forever they would sift through a mixture of good and poor choices, over the harsh realities of living in denial or facing the truth. Finding the will to face each new day and the decisions and failures that resulted from them. There it was, an entire life of decisions and choices and barely enough time to see the results of them through and through."

"I've got a question... now this isn't necessarily what I go by, but many people think that it is the woman who was to blame. I mean she did give the fruit to Man, right?" he, asked open-endedly.

"Ahh! I believe you're referring to the 'Devil's Gateway,' are you not?" the serpent replied with amusement.

"That may be what it's called, but go ahead," he acknowledged.

"How unsettling a conviction, for neither am I female nor is any woman a seductive serpent in disguise. How laughable it is for the mighty man who at one instance claims himself master of all he surveys, yet only to be undone by the vexing's of a lusty and sinful woman. I say to you, that the fate of all mankind was decided by the Creator, therefore no blame can be placed on any singular participant. Such horrible accusations have only been used to justify the demonization and abuse of womankind and, unfortunately, such behavior persists to this day. Man is a man, and Woman is a woman, no petty name calling nor will sexism be tolerated in my retelling of said events. Such behavior will be cause for dismissal from my domain... understand?" the serpent said making clear the ground rules.

"Alright!" he acknowledged, then crossed one leg over the other.

"You know, it's interesting that so many creation and religious myths begin in about the same way. There was a man, a woman, and me... the evil serpent," he said wagging the tip of his tail, rebuking the charge.

"Do you think it was by mere chance that I, above any other creation, was mentioned so prominently in the beginnings of humanity? But what is most upsetting to me is the ease at which humanity forgets. Perhaps those theologians thought I just vanished, or maybe they were confident with the dark portrait they had painted of me; and were proud of their success in convincing the world that I, indeed, was the Devil." The man cringed his brow in intrigue upon hearing the serpent dismiss the accusation of being the Devil.

"But, a better question to ask, Man of the Present, is what happened to me. You see, Man and Woman obviously lived and eventually their offspring spread like vermin across a country field. I, however, did not vanish into the pages of religious mockery waiting to reappear about the final pages of it. No, I remained an active participant in the history of humanity, freshly scarred and at first only a hesitant observer, but I was very much alive and still there."

"So you're saying that religious stories are just retold myths and that none of them are true?" the man interjected.

"Let me explain a few things to you, before we continue. In its popular form the term myth refers to a colorful tale of shared cultural beliefs; usually used to explain true and common occurrences, such as the weather, or say the miracle of birth. However, the dangerous part of creation myths is how they take root and become cemented in part of the societal identity, where any discussion or rebuttal of scientific fact is attributed as evil or heresy. These social beliefs go so far as to be then taken as the profound truth, metaphorically, symbolically, or even worse… literally.

"How many times have people tried to explain my role in the history of man? Was I the devil in disguise or perhaps I was a person with a double tongue, labeled a 'snake!' Either way, as can you see, there is a stark difference between the factual truth and a sworn, shared belief on a mass scale, i.e. religion. However, a good way to tell the difference between truth and myth is by simple comparison.

"Now not 100% accurate, but it will help you to identify some key similarities with my version of history. You see, myths often share a number of reoccurring features within them, such as the same stories show up in lore, religion, and cultural traditions. Such tales often include a setting or location which no one can accurately locate, and take place in a non-specific pastime. There of course, exists a deity that no one can see, and talking animals who often take on cosmic forms. And most importantly, the creation myth usually addresses some deep or meaningful quandary of life's purpose or meaning in a universal context," the serpent reiterated as if speaking in front of a classroom teaching a lesson.

"But, aren't you a talking animal?" the man asked with questioning reason.

"No! I'm a reptile… but that's beside the point," the serpent squinted, replying sarcastically.

"Another feature of the creation myth is that there are always different versions of the same story with minor varying details… sound familiar yet?"

"So, what's your point?" he responded, while listening intently.

"My point is, the next part of my story is going to get a bit more personal as it deals specifically with the development of humanity. You may find certain parts of it disagreeable to you, but the actual meaning of any of it is utterly meaningless," the serpent stated.

"How is it meaningless? I thought you just said it is history and not a myth?" the man argued in confusion.

"What I mean is, these stories of 'Creation' are merely there to fill gaps in a period of history which no one can fully explain. They are nothing to be ashamed of, all cultures have them. They are there to explain how people came about and are usually in metaphorical terms. Quite simply, don't take this stuff too seriously!

"Did you ever ask yourself, how is it that these stories of early human life are so detailed in some ways yet very vague in others? How is it that people swear upon life and death, by a handful of books that came out of a time of mass illiteracy? Who told these stories and who recorded them, and if indeed they are fact; how is it that they have survived the test of telephone and time?" the serpent further explained.

"What I am going to tell you are truths, how you interpret them will depend on your understanding and interpretation of the events. Are you following me? ... Good! Now, one of the other aspects of these stories is how they weigh heavily on the balance of good and evil, or right and wrong. But the fact is, good and evil are subjective and depend greatly on the point of view of the narrator and the reader. Additionally, the reader rarely places themselves on the receiving end of said narrative. So much so, that no matter what happens in these stories, either good or bad, the reader will ultimately fail to see the lesson in them, because nobody wants to see themselves as bad dealing or evil doing."

"But isn't that what these religious stories are for? To tell us what's good and bad or right and wrong?" the man asked.

"Yes, but what good does it do, if you never see the evil in your own actions, because everyone sees themselves as part of the 'Good' narrative or the victim waiting to be healed or saved. Sadly, creation myths are composed of many truths and unfortunately many lies." The serpent resituated himself, coiling himself so as to appear to be sitting cross legged.

"It sounds like you're trying to discredit religion," the man pointed out.

"No, not at all. My point is, don't get so caught up in the

myth that you cannot see the truth. What matters is how these stories affect you, but more so what they mean to you. You may hear all sorts of fantastic tales of aliens planting seeds on earth, or humans crawling out of a bubbling goop. But, what matters is that you are here now and what came before you can have little impact on anything past what it has already done. You can let these stories inspire you or blind you. As I stated before, the choice of belief is yours.

"One last thing is the relevance of these creation myths, then we'll move on. What is relevant when one is seeking the truth is to try to find a balance. It does not mean that a Creator does not exist, nor does it mean that gravity is the only force at work in the universe. What it means is do not try to see things as absolutes, as both a creator exists as much as gravity does... you just can't see either one," the serpent summarized.

"Alright, so what you're saying is that there are a lot of things in these books that cannot be proven, but it doesn't mean they didn't happen. But what's actually important is the hidden meaning in them, which can be inspiring for humanity."

"... I'm surprised you actually got all that," the serpent exclaimed raising both eye brows, then continued.

"Now, the next part of the tale will go into more detail about Man and Woman and how the first civilizations began and so on. Again, there are varying stories and questions regarding how a population could spring from only two people, as biological variation is highly favored among the human species. What skin color were these people? What eye color did they have? What language did they speak? Once again, don't get so caught up in the myth that you are unable to see the truth."

"So were there other people?" the man asked plainly.

"Well, of course there were! I mean there would have to be other people. What married coupled do you know of that could stand each other for that long by themselves?" the serpent answered humorously.

"When I say they were the first, I mean that they were the first Man and Woman documented. Or perhaps their story is universal and all of humanity shares in their same experiences.

The truth is that human beings have been on the earth for quite some time and obviously, there are more people now... so you do the math."

"But what about their race or skin color? Were they white, black, or maybe some in between shades of brown?"

"Honestly, I cannot answer that question for you, because all of you people look alike to me. The minor variants in skin pigment do little to distinguish any of you to me. The way I distinguish one person from another is by their actions, as their names or outward appearance do little to describe their attributes and personality. Truly, it is your actions that define you. However, if we are believing that, in fact, the entire population of humanity sprang forth from only two people, then would it not make sense that perhaps they embodied all of humanities traits and appearances?"

"How do you mean?" the man inquired.

"Well, perhaps Man was darker, shorter, with lighter colored eyes, and long flowing hair. While Woman was lighter, taller, with dark colored eyes, and curly, kinkier hair. I do not know why you people see things in such absolutes and insist on selecting one type as the lead model of humanity when, in fact, all of you are the same?" the serpent, pointed out gesturing very animatedly with the tip of his tail.

"You're making some interesting points, but that still doesn't explain what they looked like," the man retorted in argument.

"Let me put it this way, the last person I encountered looked absolutely nothing like you. But you know what? The both of you, somehow, resemble that first Man and first Woman," the serpent said pointing back over at the man, then continued.

"After Man and Woman were cast out of the Garden, I went into hiding because of the utter grotesqueness and shame of my appearance. I wandered in the Garden crawling under stone and log until I found myself in a city."

"A city?" the man inquired.

"Yes! Believe it or not, the Garden was not the only place in existence at the time. There was an ancient city built then, and it's one of the oldest remaining cities that still stands to this day.

Oddly enough, this city has a booming population but has never had a shortage of living space. There are no taxes and the cost of fuel and food are low and very affordable. Amazingly too, it never rains and there is always an excuse that can explain any disturbance away. As a matter of fact, it's true what they say, as it is the motto and name of the city... 'Nothing is ever wrong, when you live in 'Denial!'

"And that's exactly where I was, in denial, hiding myself, eyes shut tightly telling myself that it was all just a bad dream. Perhaps, if I didn't come out I wouldn't have to learn to live on my belly. I stayed under that rock for so long that I began telling myself that it was comfortable and being underneath it was better than being outside. There underground, I cried and thrashed about in anger, some have said that my tantrums were so violent that it shook the pillars of the earth causing volcanic eruptions that would shame Typhon himself.

"Then a solemn question fell upon me and it is the one question I still have been unable to answer. What do you do when you're right, but you still lose?" The serpent paused momentarily in silence contemplating the rhetorical irony. The man as well sat stone-like as past life events flashed in his mind's eye.

"Eventually I had to come out, but sadly it was not pride nor personal strength that drew me out of hiding, it was a hunger. Nothing more than the grumbling and shivering of starvation that forced me to accept my new position and begin my life anew. Yet, slowly, over time I came to accept my new form and just as Man and Woman were forced to walk through life, so did I have to learn to crawl through mine.

"After that, I told myself that I would never interfere in the affairs of mankind. I was still able to go to and from the Garden and back to the Earth as I pleased, as the Creator did not restrict my divine abilities. At first, I stayed far away from Man and Woman, as I wanted nothing to do with them." The serpent paused from narrating then drummed his tail on the ground in front of him similar to fingers tapping a table top in quick succession.

"You know something, Man of the Present, I don't know what it is about people, but it seems as if I'm drawn to you all. Just as it is now, with you standing here. It was the same then, a familiar curiosity took hold of me, and once again, I found myself watching and observing them.

"Man and Woman now endowed with the gift of consciousness were placed on the earth. At first, they were alone and afraid, as the elements were cruel and harassing. However, they grew accustomed to the seasons and learned to survive, and eventually to live. At that time, I openly moved about the earth and all were able to see me. Man and Woman often saw me and although some believed in their hate of me, they neither despised me nor wished me ill. Others who saw me near Man and Woman, falsely associated my presence with fertility, and would dance and release snakes in ceremony into the fields to guarantee good crops.

"I said thanks unto the Creator for making Man and Woman full of forgiveness and I smiled upon them when the Creator blessed them with two children. After the event of child birth, I no longer saw Woman as a mere counterpart to Man, but as so much more of a meaning of strength and virtue. She was the beginning and the wholeness of humanity and from then on, she was known as... 'Giver of Life.'

"The two male children were the first young people I had ever seen and their behavior was curious and infantile, just as Man and Woman were before eating of the Tree of Consciousness. I watched as they grew taller and became faster and stronger. I became fond of them and I took an interest in these two young people. The first-born was granted exceptional skill in cultivation of the land and the second sibling was given great skill as a hunter and a breeder of livestock. The two children were favored by the Creator and both were given strong wills.

"The two siblings worked and labored extensively and both tamed the land as they saw fit. Acres of farm land, orchards, and vineyards grew easily with the touch of the first child. The skill and mastery he possessed over the land could not be equaled and his harvests filled the markets and tables with produce, grains, wines, and breads.

"Only his younger brother, whose livestock provided meats, leathers, wools, and rich milks and cheeses, could rival him. The two brothers radiated prosperity and they took pride in their work, for the Creator had blessed them with the ability to bring wealth and prosperity to their people. At the end of each day, the second son was often seen standing in the midst of his flocks teeming with pride as kids, lambs, and calves sucked at their mother's milk promising strength and abundance to his people. The Creator had deemed him, Master of all those having Breath, or commonly known as 'Breath.' His elder brother also could be seen muddy yet proud as the earth that clung to him shined as armor as he raised his head overlooking the abundance and plenty that he sowed from the earth. He was truly the Master of Grain, or commonly known as 'Grain.'

"It appeared that mankind was indeed meant for the Earth, as the two brothers had learned one of the most important things from such an early age. That the Earth was sustenance to all and it was the earliest commandment of the Creator. The two brothers learned the value of preservation and at the end of each day, filled their store rooms with their produce and stock.

"The brothers also learned to share and gave to the tables and barns of their neighbors. Those who were poor and without found charity in the brothers, and they offered comfort and rejuvenation to the weakened human spirit. The blessings of the two brothers extended endlessly as others learned their skills. I saw that, truly, a man could live forever through his endeavors as his work touches the lives of those around him.

"What could be greater to the expansion of humanity than the cultivation of land and herd? With their combined efforts, humanity was presented with a feast and the ability to feed himself and his brother. At the end of the evening, the two brothers said a prayer to each other, 'O that thou wert as my brother that sucked the breasts of my mother! When I should find thee without, I would kiss thee; yea, I should not be despised. I would lead thee and bring thee into my mother's house, who would instruct me. I would cause thee to drink of spiced wine of the juice of my pomegranate. His left hand should be under my head and his right hand should embrace me.'

"Now, it is inherent in all creation that with growth and age come larger appetites and new impulses. However, there was something different about the children of Man and Woman. I watched their abilities grow as they reached maturity, but they seemed dissatisfied, as if all they had accomplished was not enough. One afternoon, I came out from the hills to feed on a straying goat from the flock of Breath. I thought my presence went unnoticed, but he saw me and threw stones to end my attack upon the crying animal. I recoiled and released my grip only moments from finishing off the goat. The young man stood and boldly said to me, 'No Serpent! These goats are for my people!'

"The goat lay dying from my attack and would have been useless to him at that point, yet he continued pelting me with stones. Before I could speak in defense of my actions, the goat raised its head and said, 'No son of Man. I am for him… I am not for mass consumption.' The goat then dropped its head and died. The young man stood speechless and shocked upon seeing such a thing. He kneeled then said praises unto the Creator, as only the Creator could make such a thing possible.

"The goat spoke and said he was not for mass consumption?" the man asked in disbelief.

"That's correct, although things may be numerous, some things are not for everyone, and some things are meant just for you. Think on it for a moment. Out of all the water in the oceans is it mere coincidence or by specific design that the water ended up not washed down a drain, but crisp and clean there in the glass just for you. It was then that I thought that possibly there was more to my being and perhaps I, too, was meant specifically for something."

"Are you saying that you didn't know the purpose of your life?" he pressed the serpent.

"You say that with such ease as if you have discovered its

answer yourself just yesterday! Did you think I had no other purpose besides lurking within the shadows and crawling along the ground? Please... I am not a simple spider. But there is that emptiness inside you, that feeling that I'm not doing what I'm supposed to be doing with my life.

"From my earlier life in the Garden, there was no such mention of purpose as life existed as it was presented. It was at that very moment that I wondered what my purpose was. Every single day up, down, right, wrong, love, loss, triumph, work, waste, good, or evil. Yes! My good Man of the Present, that eternal question haunting us all, what am I here for? What is all this really about?" The man remained seated thinking on the weight of the serpent's words, with his eyes slowly coming out of focus on the serpent and down onto his own hands in front of him.

"So did you find your purpose?"

"As a matter of fact, I did," the serpent, smirked and nodded keenly.

"What was it?" he inquired intently, leaning towards the serpent.

"I could... but that would be cheating," the serpent replied with a keen smile. "Not to confuse you, but the meaning I found was that of my own and not that of man's." the serpent clarified, then continued.

"Then there came a day, I wish I could remove from my thoughts." The man showed an expression of grief and concern upon hearing the serpent's remorseful tone.

"It was about midday, the sun was high and warming in the sky. I had taken hold of a goat grazing in the fields, for an early supper, and said thanks to the Creator for another day of life. I then prepared to nest in the tree branches and watch the two siblings bring in their crops for a feast with their family. But something was different on that day.

"I heard the brothers arguing upon a hill that overlooked the grasslands named the 'Hill of Heaven and Earth.' They argued over their work and yelled that each was the greater. The elder brother said that if the Creator wanted man to have both grain and meat, the Creator would have made them readily available to pluck and collect as the fruit of a tree or the honey from a bees' nest.

"The younger brother agreed and said, 'Indeed brother for in the past there was nothing before us. There were no fields of planted crops and no herds of livestock. What could mankind do without our skills of land cultivation, hunting, and keeping of livestock? The Creator has indeed blessed us and our work. Because of our labors, humanity has grain for bread and wine, milk for cheese, and meat for strength, and leather and wool to wrap themselves in.'

"The two brothers said that the Creator had granted them immense knowledge to keep and care for the sheep, the cow, the goat, and the chicken. And the skills for working in the field as they had tools like the plough, the yoke, and the team.

"The elder brother then called out and said, 'I am better than you, and my work takes precedence over anything you do. I farm the land and the Glory of the Creator shines down on my fields and crops as shown by the radiant sun. All the people of the land can see the palace of the Creator when they look upon my growing fields and the bounty that they produce. My crops produce courage-giving wines that each warrior knows fills him with pride in his country before battle. My fruits and harvest celebrations foster neighborliness and it is over the drink of beer that many quarrels end and friendships begin again. The work that my farm provides transforms a wayward youth into a prideful worker and releases him from the shackles of poverty. I am the heart and bounty of the land, while you are tied up in muddy pig pens and kneel to the teat on milking stools. How could you ever compare yourself to me?'

"The younger brother said in rebuttal, 'Be calm my brother, as my work is of no lesser value than yours. Every string of yarn belongs to me from the tattered rags of a pauper to the crested headdress of royalty. The ropes of the sailor, the string of the archer's bow, and the sheath of the soldier's sword all pay me gratitude for my contribution. The priests who purify the hearts of the lost and weary are clothed in my robes and every time they walk, I walk among them. My work is noble and taught only to the most capable tradesmen, while any idiot can hold a plow. How could you ever claim superiority to me?'

"The elder brother, not to be outdone, said, 'Nobility and leisure is what I provide, a cool, crisp, brown bubbly beverage for the tongue of royalty and the warm and crisp breads that await them at the dinner table while your results are shown little appreciation and are bludgeoned to death and their innards are thrown out as scraps only suitable for dogs. My harvests are presented in robust baskets of cornucopias, while your burnt meat is speared for greedy fat fingers to rip and tear apart. No matter what you say about your herds and livestock, all of your herdsmen eye my crops in envy and I have to chase them away from gorging themselves on my melons.

"Who would want to live the life of a hunter or herdsman? Every day your mind is filled with fears of snake bites, thieves and bandits, and, of course, the wolves who endlessly stalk your sheep. Besides, where does a herdsman call home and whom does he lay with in the night to keep him warm, surely not an unsuspecting sheep? Ha! Brother you think too highly of yourself and those sheep boys of yours.

"The younger brother stood chest to chest against his elder brother saying, 'It's funny that you should say that we herdsmen envy you farmers. I have seen you and your men loving and praising our horses as regal and esteemed as they are. For only the noblemen and trained warriors are allowed to saddle and tame the beasts of the earth. But come now brother, I need not punish you when an old widowed wench will beat and pound your face, and your doughy flesh with spoon, spatula, and pin. Still, that will be but a tickle to you, when they pluck your ears and grind you with the mortar to make you into flour and meal.

'Uuggh! I love it when the baker cringes at your bland taste and mixes and then flattens you on the table broadly. And still they cannot make any use of you until they throw you into the oven fire and decorate you on the table. But, alas oh brother, even then warmed, golden and crisp, you are still placed behind my meats. You see brother, no matter how you try to argue it, you and your efforts are just like mine, everything we do becomes food. So how can you claim that your work is greater than mine?

"The elder brother stood silently a moment with his head bowed a bit in shame, but then raised his head saying, 'As for you, brother, your men wrap themselves in the sheets of dry leaves and rocks for bedding. Furthermore, your efforts are chopped and broken in pieces only suitable for the lame and sickly children of the poor. They take your meaty things and hang them out to dry as old laundry. I watch and laugh while your innards are stretched and taken to market and only made of use when I hear someone say, 'fill it with grain for my goat!' HA! Indeed brother, it is me and my skills that are the greater!'

"I looked at the two brothers arguing back and forth then figuratively took a step back and thought to myself. That is nothing more than a 'debate between sheep and grain.' The two brothers saw me resting beneath a tree and laughingly asked, 'Serpent! Tell us, who is greatest between us?'

"To their utter shock and surprise, I spoke saying, Brothers with skills bestowed by the Creator should stand together and be as one. For humanity has been blessed by the efforts of both and are forever gracious for the bounty which ye provide. However, of the two, I see that cultivation of the land is more necessary to the survival and growth of human civilization. Let it not be said that the hunter and keeper of livestock are meaningless, but it is the farmer that is the foundation of civilization and human society.'

"'Let all the herdsmen bend their knees for the farmer and let the hunters praise the light in the stable from sunrise till sunset. Every poor and lonely soul will know the worth of a dry loaf of bread even if they never afford the fullness of hearty meat. Mostly praised and sought are the rich milk and hearty steak, however, it is the efforts and labors in the fields of grain that all man and beast shall pay offerings to.

"Honestly, I did not think the levity of my words would weigh so heavily on the two young men. However, immediately after the elder brother stepped forward and said, 'See even the serpent claims me victorious over you brother!' The younger brother swatted away his boasts and walked away to end the argument. But the elder brother followed after his sibling and began taunting him.

"He repeatedly commanded him to bow to his greatness as he was victorious and his works were to be envied. The younger brother continued walking away and refused to acknowledge his brother's mocking. But still the elder brother persisted and increased his taunts to threats and finished by saying... 'Or else!'

"The younger brother continued to dismiss his brother's words as ridiculous and refused to acknowledge him. Then the elder brother's face became twisted with hatred and anger overwhelmed him. I watched as he grabbed his younger brother by the back of his tunic and then the two began to fight. I expected it to end in friendship as I had seen the two quarrel together as young things, but then I beheld a horrible sight.

"Without warning, the elder brother struck his brother from behind. I could not see the weapon with which he used to slay him, but the blow was fatal. The body of his younger brother lay broken and bleeding and the ground turned muddy red with blood. No sooner than his brother's body touched the ground did the elder brother raise a fist in triumph. He turned and then walked away, without even a single look back at his brother who lay dying. After he left, I went down to observe him, as his skull was split from behind and his eyes rolled backward in his head as he was near death but managed to utter and recite,

'The Creator is my rock, and my fortress, and my deliverer. My God, my strength in whom I will trust; my buckler, and the horn of my salvation, and my high tower. I will call upon the Creator, who is worthy to be praised, so shall I be saved from mine enemies. The sorrows of death compassed me, and the floods of ungodly men made me afraid. The sorrows of hell compassed me about, the snares of death prevented me. In my distress I called upon the Creator, and cried unto my God, he heard my voice out of his temple, and my cry came before him, even into his ears.'

"With his lasts breath did he speak the words of the Creator and then he was no more. I circled the body in a brief panic and confusion overtook me, as I observed a lifeless thing. The young man was only moments dead, but then suddenly an unbearable heat rose up from within me and there came smoke up out of my nostrils and fire spit out of my mouth. I then recited, 'The earth shook and trembled, the foundations also of the hills moved and were shaken, because he was wroth. There went up a smoke out of his nostrils and fire out of his mouth devoured and coals were kindled by it. He bowed the heavens also and came down, and darkness was under his feet.'

"Before that moment, I never knew I could spit fire but, sadly, it took the death of a youth for me to realize a new ability."

"You can breathe fire! Like a dragon?" the man remarked in astonishment.

"Not like a dragon, I am the original... Dragon. It was from me that all dragon-kind obtained their fire, just as all vipers did receive their venom. However, dragons grew to love the intensity of the flame and became renowned for it. Those who witnessed their fiery ability cursed me and my dragon offspring as creatures born of hell, and we were targeted only for destruction. They were such majestic creatures, a bit ill-tempered none the less, but, unfortunately, man saw fit to hunt them into extinction. It's almost symbolic, with the first act of murder came the fire and birth of the dragon.

"A glimmering light rose up from out of the young man and it rode towards the heavens as would a cherub fly on the wind. I shook my head in grief taking one last look before departing the area, as I heard the voices of others approaching. After the events in the Garden, I swore that I would never again become involved in the affairs of man. But now, I could see that what occurred in the Garden would have farther reaching repercussions than I had ever imagined.

"All but for my pride and wit, was it that I had cursed mankind with life upon the face of the Earth, but never had I wished this. Never had I wanted any harm upon the head of this youth. Never had I wished such horrible acts of violence and contempt of brother against brother. My head sank low and hung with grief and I said to myself, *What have I done... What have I unleashed... In the name of my Creator, what have I done?*

"Later, Man and Woman discovered the body of their murdered son, and for the first time, they would come to know heartache, misery, and loss. They were grief stricken and she, Giver of Life, fell upon her knees weeping at the broken body of her son. He that came from her own womb was now swallowed up in the cold and stillness of the night. She held and rocked his lifeless body in remembrance of the infant she once nursed, but neither the warmth of her breast, nor the tears she bled could comfort him ever again.

"Man was all but lost in a state of helplessness for his son, as he could no more conceal his emotions, but still attempted to comfort his wife. After many days of mourning, I watched Man and Woman now accompanied by their community bury their murdered son. His body was placed here in this very cave, and it still rests not more than a few meters down that corridor on the left. I was never fond of crypts, but after ages of congestion and noise, I found that the dead make peaceable neighbors.

"After they laid his body to rest, I paid his grave a visit and offered a single prayer saying, 'Hear the voice of my supplications, when I cry unto thee, when I lift up my voice toward thy holy place. Draw me not away with the wicked and with the workers of iniquity, which speak peace to their neighbors, but mischief is in their hearts. Give them according to their deeds and according to the wickedness of their endeavors; give them after the work of their hands and render to them their just dessert.'

"Now Man of the Present, I have heard modern scholars try and explain the murder of the young man as a metaphor for the development of civilization, during the age of agriculture. Arguing that agriculture replaced the primitive nomadic lifestyle of the hunter gatherer. In that sense, not one betrayed the confidence of his brother and failed to keep him. But it would be the variant will to win and dominate over ancient ways of life, I suppose. Sometimes, I wish it were that picture of growth and prosperity instead of the unprovoked betrayal that I beheld. In all that occurred on that fateful day, what did humanity gain?

"Unfortunately, truer is it that within man exists an eternal greed for power, recognition, and wealth. What I saw happen amongst the two brothers would eventually repeat itself and has continued to do so throughout history. Each tribal conflict, or civil war, that has pitted brother against brother and neighbor against neighbor. Where all too many times have we have seen country men turned into tyrant as they attempt to cleanse the land of verminous scum who share their same bloodlines, or only account to a different faith.

"Sadly, many would shun the behavior of the murderous brother as evil but, in reality they emulate this crime for the love of material and prestigious gain. Now I had been in the company of the voice of the Creator for some time by then, but that was the first time that I was angry with the Creator. What purpose was served by allowing such cruelty and viciousness to exist within the hearts of men? What end would such extreme violence produce and what would be its fruits? Many claim that I am evil and have long tempted and led mankind down a dark and daunting path; yet there, on that day, there was no temptation, nor any trophy to be claimed in committing such an act.

"I thought I understood the purpose of death as part of the process of creation. However, what was the purpose of murder? There are silent prayers we all say in the quiet of our minds, some call them wishes, but on that night, oh how I wished that it would rain.

"The following day, the elder son was again working in the fields tending to his crops, when the voice of the Creator appeared before him. The Creator questioned him to the whereabouts of his brother. The young man knowing his deed chose not to answer, and in arrogance rebuked the Creators inquiry saying, 'I know not his whereabouts... am I my brother's keeper?' The Creator asked again, but the young man remained spiteful and stood silent. The Creator then became angry with the insolence of the young man and the ground began to shake and blood welled up out of the ground glowing.

"The blood of his slain brother began to call out in admission of his crime. The Creator then became furious and issued judgment upon the first-born son of Man and Woman. I witnessed all at once everything stopped, and all life was suspended in motion. I looked around and saw the crow frozen in flight without the current of the wind to support him and not fall to the ground. The horse that had broken free and leapt a fence remained there while strong as ever but silent and still. Everything stopped except the young man who was now cowering before the voice of the Creator. I cannot explain why I was not frozen, perhaps it was another attribute I was unaware of, or maybe I was there to bear witness the judgment of the Creator upon the young man.

"The Creator banished him from the lands of his people, and he was cursed to live a life of flight forever, wandering aimlessly and without a home. The young man fell to his knees in shame and remorse and begged forgiveness of the Creator and not to send him away from his family. He cried and pleaded saying that the punishment was more than he could bear. He had been made a fugitive and that he feared for his life, as others would take revenge on him for his crime.

"The voice of the Creator moved in acknowledgement and then with finger like precision, a mark was struck down upon the young man's face, splitting his upper lip which cleft his pallet. The motion made by the Creator was exactly that when one communicates 'murder' in sign language.

"He was disfigured and all who encountered him would know that the Creator's mark was upon him. All who encountered him would see his deformed face and would cringe and recoil at his appearance. He was marked as an outcast and none would abode or kill him, lest he suffer the punishment of the Creator. And so it was that the Creator's judgment was complete, and the young man looked around him and saw his efforts that would no longer be his pride and home.

"He covered his face, then fled his home sobbing with fright and shame. The voice of the Creator was gone and life returned as if not a blink nor breath was out of sync. There was nothing

54

he could do to repay the life that he took, nor the pain he caused his family and community. It was better that his memory be that of two brothers and those who knew him could remember better days and brighter times.

"I've got a question, Serpent," the man interjected. "Why didn't God just kill him?

"What?" the serpent responded with an expression of puzzlement.

"Why didn't God just kill him? I mean, that would be justice wouldn't it? An eye for an eye? And you said it yourself, why would God allow a murderer to continue to live and possibly kill other people?" The man stood speaking as if questioning the rule of law in a legal proceeding.

"That's a good question, Man of the Present, but I found out later on that a life condemned to no prospect or possibility can be just as fatal as a sentence of death. You see, the elder son had skill and ability never before seen upon the land and he had helped build the very foundation of civilization. But unfortunately, that one mortal deed ended all he would ever be. There are some who have committed murder and will even be acquitted of their crime, but seriously what have they gained? The trust and respect of their community? What life can such a person expect to live, for they will forever be despised and reviled no matter where they go. It might as well be that they ended their very own life," the serpent explained.

"Interesting point of view, Serpent, but I still think I would have just killed him," he acknowledged with spite.

"But then, you would be the same as the murderer. Now, I am not one to judge the acts of man, but ask yourself is that what you really want?

"After some time, Man and Woman found themselves again blessed with additional children and they were favored in the eyes of the Creator. Life in their community prospered and continued to grow as the skills and teachings of the two brothers lived on in the work of all mankind. But, by that time, rumors had spread throughout the land of those who encountered the eldest son marked by the Creator. They said he had been seen crying for hours on end and then falling into seizures groaning and shaking upon the ground.

"His skills and talent upon the land were now meaningless as none would employ him, and eventually he became a beggar. His life was meaningless and empty and with no means of redemption, he sought out death but again he was denied. Many times it was accounted that a wanderer would enter a nameless village with gold and silver coins trying to pay a ransom for his own assassination. He wandered the Earth for many years until death appreciated his suffering and relieved him of his life.

"However, before his days had ended, he had married and did father many children. I suppose it is true that the Creator's mercy is eternal and even the wicked are allowed compassion. What I found most interesting in this turn of events, was not the Creators mercy, but his choice in allowing a murderer not only to remain alive, but also to father children and further populate the earth.

"I questioned the Creator's plans and motives for allowing such pain and suffering to befall that young man. I questioned not only the meaning of the act of murder, but the purpose of the murderer. For if he were meant to die, was his attacker meant to kill? I had never thought on such things before, as there were no troublesome scenarios to question, but if all of mankind had a purpose, what was the purpose of creating murderers?" The serpent paused and focused his eyes back on the man seated across from him in the cave.

"Now I ask you, Man of the Present, of which lineage do you spring from? Are you the murderous offspring of the elder son or of the blessed children of the Creator's followers? Are you to be trusted to keep your brother, or to be feared so as none should turn their back on you? You see, it is in the deception of appearance where all evil lies. Interesting that the Creator chose to mark all of my kind, so that truth is in our appearance that all may know they are of me. Yet, of all of you humans, those who are good and those who are of evil, all of you appear the same. Good cannot tell evil apart and brother cannot see brother plotting against him," the serpent said, laughing heavily.

"Why are you laughing?" The man stood asking with curious skepticism.

"Why do I laugh? Because after all these years, I still cannot tell the good from the evil ones of you. So, I decided it best just to treat you all as the latter." The serpent looked with a condescending expression and wagged his tail back and forth after identifying humans as all the same.

"So you think all people are evil?" he said in defense, while still standing.

"It was the Creator who made it abundantly clear that the nature of man is evil." the serpent pointed out. As a matter of fact, that brings me to the next part of our story. And it was amazing what the Creator did to remedy that evil from the face of the Earth.

"However, begging your pardon for making light the destructive plight of humanity, Man of the Present. You see we all have family issues and the reality of it is that the people closest to you can hurt you the most. Just because she is your mother, it does not mean she will love you or care for you. Just because he is your father, it does not mean he will guide you or protect you. Your sisters and your brothers may belittle and betray you despite any sibling bonds. Because, in the end, the family that should mean everything to you, quite possibly means absolutely nothing, as they are only people. But feel no shame of the bloodline of which you spring, Man of the Present. You see, I for one am no exception. Everyone in my family's a snake! And I don't trust not one of them motherfuckers! HA! HA! HA! HA! HA! HA! HA! HA..."

CHAPTER 3: THE EARTH

"The Earth, she was created beautiful and abundant for mankind, from her lush rainforests and arid deserts, to her unsteady mountains and icy fields. For mankind, the Earth provided the necessities of life and was all sustaining. She gave water to drink, harvests for food, an environment to interact and assemble upon, and the energy to work and reproduce. The Earth was bashful and would tilt as she was kissed yearly by the rays of the sun; and was known for her emotions caused by the sun's affection.

"The sun worshipped her, long as the summer day, from her head to her feet in the short winter months. For all of her short comings, Earth provided for mankind precious resources to be exploited for life's purposes. For mankind, Earth designated communities of life where she produced organic goods for oxygen, food, medicines, woods, and the reutilization of organic wastes. After some time, mankind learned how the forests and grasslands depended on the topsoil and fresh water; and how the oceans and rivers depended on the nutrients washed down from the lands. However, the entirety of the earth was not meant for man alone, for all that she provided, only an eighth did she appropriate for him.

"Forever surreptitious, Earth hid her treasures beneath the

oceans, the barren deserts, and within the Iron Mountains. Between the heavens and Earth there were no fixed boundaries, yet she wore a thin and fading cloak of protection. The Moon was her greatest admirer and naturally encircled her like a satellite and their gravitational attraction gave waves that tickled the oceans.

"Forever in love, Moon would not turn its gaze away from the Earth and continuously showed the same expression illuminated by the sun. For all the love and affection gleaming from Moon, life itself was affected as Moon moderated Earth's dramatic climates.

"Across the Earth were seemingly endless supplies for man and all those having breath. The diversity of their kingdom encompassed those joint of spine and those without. All were connected and each maintained their link upon the great chain. Even the sun was acknowledged as all made use of its light either directly or indirectly through the course of devouring one another. For mankind, Earth was provider and producer, she was home and far away land; she was peace to all as both cradle and grave. And out of that cradle crawled early man who, at first, wandered blindly, hunting and gathering over the land.

"But man could adapt and learn as he became civil and a master of agriculture. His communities became civilizations and its participants were thus citizens. Man attempted to oppose barbarism and seek out enlightenment and cultivation. No longer was man concerned only with warmth and food, but he sought improvement from insolence to civility. Mankind was awakening from its infancy and growing towards adolescence. As serpent, I am solitary in my ways, but I took interest in the lives and the growing ways of man and thus I learned the concept, of civilization.

"Civilization is a singular concept and never the plural as it refers to the growth of humanity as a whole. But a civilization is not merely a collection of bodies and groupings of structures, but it is the cultures that blossom from within them. I observed each community and watched how they defined their own identity and expressed themselves through art, customs, beliefs, values, and thus became known as, 'their ways of life.'"

"Wait a minute! You said early man, as in cavemen… right? If there were cave men and evolution, then they're couldn't have been a First Man and Woman from a garden?" the man interjected, while gesturing with his left hand interrupting the serpent.

"What I'm talking about, Man of the Present, is natural progression and the growth of human civilization. Yes, I acknowledged a first Man and a first Woman, and yes they had two sons who were endowed with knowledge of agriculture and livestock. However, I also said that there were other people on the earth that did not have those skills and were essentially hunter-gatherers. Eventually, the teachings and skills from the two sons spread and ended man's days as such," the serpent said addressing the man, while pointing with his tail.

"The truth is Man of the Present, natural progression and the growth of human civilization, continues to put an end to old ways. You can still see those trends in your world today with the advancements in technology, transportation, weaponry, and clothing. How long does it take for man to fully embrace a new concept, and put an end to old traditions and practices? How long did it take for humanity to see the benefits of bathing regularly, to incorporate automobiles, or to see women as equals? These issues, as you see, are continuing concepts which have taken time for humanity to fully appreciate. However, all do not agree that civilization is a good thing.

"Many have argued that civilization itself is at the root of all human vices. Where is it that you see the most corruption, crime, violence, prostitution, and substance abuse? All these things already existed, but why is it that within a civilization, these vices seem to multiply?" The serpent's words laid a heavy accusation on the ears of the man.

"So you think civilization is wrong? And that people should just live in tents or something?" he rebuked.

"No, absolutely not. Growth and progression are in your nature and to deny that would be to deny a fundamental aspect of what makes you human. Because of civilization, the world now has written languages, monetary systems, educational intuitions, and government entities. Growth is not good or bad... it's growth. 'Without continual growth and progress, such words as improvement, achievement, and success have no meaning.' - Benjamin Franklin." The man nodded in agreement but remained seated with his left hand lightly grasping his chin and forefinger tapping his mouth, then the serpent continued.

"All civilizations have depended on the agricultural setup left by the eldest son Master of Grain. I find it interesting that the death of the younger son by his brother, paralleled the growth of human civilization and the end to the hunter gatherer. For was it not he, Master of Grain, who's efforts are the basis of human civilization, and was it not he who was allowed to live and to further populate the earth.

"One could further argue the difference between a meat-based diet versus a grain-based diet. The sciences can argue the values and strengths of both, but I find it quite interesting that this debate happens to be one of the first lessons to humanity. It appears that of the two brothers, Master of Grain was the stronger and more necessary for the growth of humanity."

"So you think that the death of the younger brother was necessary for the growth of human civilization?" the man, leaned forward to inquire.

"An ironic and hard pill to swallow but, yes, I think so. I don't think it makes much difference either way. I mean the whole thing is quite agrarian, if you ask me. Looking back on it, I almost half expected the boys to burst out into song after their argument, singing of how 'The farmer and the cow man should be friends.' Hmm... probably should have named them Hammers and Rodgerstein... or was it the other way around?" The serpent shifted his eyes back and forth in befuddlement of his last statement.

"Rodgers and Hammers-who?" the man exclaimed in question.

"Oh never mind!" the serpent dismissed, then ended his own misstated humorous remark.

"But again we may have focused too strongly on the myth of

the brother against brother, and not allowed ourselves to see the truth," the serpent orated.

"Which is what?"

"The truth is, my good Man of the Present. As does human civilization grow, so does the evil nature of man grow along with it. And I would come to see just how quickly man's evil nature would grow and what the Creator thought to do with him, and I recite. 'The Earth is the Creator's, and the fullness thereof; the world, and they that dwell therein. For he hath founded it upon the seas, and established it upon the floods.' the serpent recited with a dark tone and the man grimaced in fear as a shadow seemed to encroach upon the cavern.

"For a time, man saw growth and prosperity with the addition of his new-found civilizations. Very few remained separated from each other and there was organization now on large social scales with the division of labor and animal domestication. Humanity banded together and gathered together to work and trade. Systems of ownership and the accumulation of personal possessions and the acquisition of land were the very foundations of now booming market places.

"Money was not universally recognized at the time, so a gift economy supplemented with a bartering system seemed to work well. I saw the first writings occur on stone and wood, which are now long forgotten, but was a hallmark of human civilization. Soon these civilizations began to spread by conquering and assimilating new lands and more people into their folds. I came to settle in a valley that was rich with food and a calm river to refresh myself in at the end of each day. And nearby, there was such a civilized community booming with growth; but for some reason out of everything mankind has been given, he becomes unsatisfied and turns destructive and wasteful. 'There is an evil which I have seen under the sun, and it is common among men.'

"In that community there was one man who stood out from the others, but not by his physical or material standing, but by his individuality and his faith. When he was a boy, his father called out his name, saying, 'Comfort us in our work and toil, because of the ground which the Creator has cursed.' Later in life, the boy came to be known as 'Rest.'

"Rest grew as other boys did but as a man, he was sure of himself and was not swayed by the trends of others. He took care in his activities and made an effort to see the beauty and worth in all things. His peers mocked him as they drank wine and beer past their limits and took him as foolish for not indulging in human vices. The community to which he belonged mocked him as odd and half-witted for he spent his free time making charts and recording seasonal patterns and plotting the stars.

"I took some interest in him, but only from a distance, as I swore not to intervene. As I watched him, I saw that he was just in his ways and he found compassion an opportunity worth exploiting. He was happy at the success of others and was uplifting to those around him. Hard work, education, dignity, and respect for others were his pride.

"People lived much longer than they do today and, thus, the Earth was heavily populated. The boy that I watched grow into a man did not have children until he was some hundred years of age. He and his wife were blessed with three sons and they came to know the meaning of happiness. My days and nights were spent mostly in leisure as I had come to accept my new form. Although my arms and legs had been removed, my senses were keener and my abilities had improved. I found that venom and fang combined with camouflage and disguise... I was even deadlier.

"Rest, was something of an orator and spoke heavily on righteousness and seeing the purpose and connection of all creation. But those who heard his words were not interested in the beauty of animal life, or the importance of forests, or the patterns of the seasons. The people were more concerned with status symbols and the collection of women and jewels. I watched as man's first era of civilization grew and he became more intrigued with dominance over the land and other men and social hierarchy became his obsession.

"Those who wielded power became the ruling elite, while those forced to toil and build became the subordinate population. From man's hunger for more came the social classes and thus emerged royalty, clergy, and, unfortunately, slavery. Humanity was barely out of its infancy, but like a flower reaching towards the sunlight, man's evil nature rose to the surface.

"I watched as he would rather take than give, instead of pleasure he caused pain. Violence was rampant and communities took to ritualistic acts and ceremonial killings in the name of entertainment. With each new generation, man's wicked nature increased and multiplied. After some time, mankind not only poisoned himself, but the earth became poisoned as well. 'The earth also was corrupt before the Creator, and the earth was filled with violence,' the serpent recited, while starring directly back at the man.

"Man lived without concern for the Earth and his waste began to pile and soon the air smelled rotten. Sickness spread from man to beast, but man thought not of his responsibility to the Earth. The land which fed him became rotten, and he drank from poisoned streams. Game were hunted and killed without thought for their numbers and resources and were spent without time to replenish itself.

"Man removed vast areas of trees, initially, to build havens of safety and to increase farm lands. Then man found that burning forests was a quicker way to reduce the hiding places for large predators. Bats were fearsome creatures during those times, and it was believed that they were harbingers of evil. So the bat was hunted and every place they lived was set ablaze. Man knew and cared even less for their importance, as the bat was a major predator of the insect and helped to control their numbers. As the bat died out, so did the insect populations flourish.

"Man's crops knew no mercy as the insect reproduced, unchecked, and devoured his crops before he could pick them. Then came the honey bee whom, at first, was highly regarded as they produced the nectar of the Gods and honey was its valuable export. Man thought to capture the honey for his own and in doing so, he destroyed their hives. With each hive, he destroyed 40,000 bees at once. Bees were so numerous at first it was not believed that they could easily be killed.

"However, man only sought out their honey as a delicacy and cared little for the pollination they provided. Soon man's crops began to wither and die and entire crops were no longer pollinated and man could not see the reason behind it. Crops such as almonds, peaches, avocados, and apricots were totally reliant upon bee pollination, but without bees, man slowly began to starve.

"Man continued to multiply in great numbers and the Earth was over flowing with him. As human populations grew, so did the demand and need for more resources. I almost can't blame them. How could they have known that there would be such a hefty price to pay for their actions? I, myself, had not considered the result of man's impact imposed on the earth's ecosystems."

"Ecosystems? You mean like in science?" the man lifted his head and unfolded his arms, interrupting the serpent.

"Yes, science! You see everything is connected, even I didn't know it at the time. I'm not sure if Rest fully understood it either. He was just curious at first and made a hobby of charting weather patterns and observing insects and animals.

"Although he was part of the community, Rest was of a different sort. He kept many hobbies, but of his favorites he seemed to enjoy the keeping of bees. He harvested their golden honey and shared his profits with his family and friends. He saw their love of flowers and began to see a connection between the flower, the honey, and the bees. At first, he could not deduce it specifically but came to reason that the tiny things were necessary and worthy of life.

"He would record in his journal how the worm ate the earth, and the fish then ate the worm, and how the hawk ate of the fish. What most saw as simple creatures eating and competing with each other, Rest saw as a mystery. He saw that nothing existed on its own and by removing one creature, others would be affected. He saw that man had an impact on the land, the rivers and oceans, and even the animals. And he recited, 'A false balance is abomination to the Creator, but a just weight is his delight.'

"He saw that each creature played a vital role in a complex web of the earth's design. In his home, he practiced speeches aloud and many evenings I listened and I learned."

"I was new to such a concept, that there was a connection of all life upon the Earth, so I continued to observe Rest and to learn more.

"Rest, said, 'The Earth's systems are made up of living things, plants, and animals in combination with the elements such as wind, water, and the Earth which all interact upon. The smallest of creatures, who appear to be nothing more than prey for larger predators, are linked together through cycles and the flow of energy. If even the most insignificant of creatures were to be removed, then the other animals that depended on it would die. Through the process of feeding that begins on plants, to animals, then on to men, it is the insects and animals that play a vital role in the distribution of energy and life in the system.'

"He noted that there were changes in the Earth's systems as he called it. He saw that vermin were increasing in the communities and now there were fewer predators to eat and control them. The devastated forests that were habitat for wild cats, snakes, and birds of prey were being cut and burned down, which allowed vermin to flourish and spread disease. He determined that man was the cause of these changes, but what would make the communities see the wickedness of their ways, he asked.

"Rest further said that the Earth's systems were controlled by factors such as climate and time, but time and the climate are not controlled by the Earth's systems. He said, that there was a dynamic interaction between plants, animals, and humanity, and without insects and animals, the Earth would die... and you know what, Man of the Present... he was right!

"The Earth's systems were vibrant and provided tangible goods and resources including food, materials, medicinal plants, and animals upon which all life depends. Man exists and operates within the Earth's systems and his actions weigh heavily enough to influence not only the animals, but also the weather. Rest drew up a plan of management outlined by principles to control and mediate the Earth's resources so as to allow man to utilize them, but also to allow the Earth's systems to replenish themselves. He came up with numerous approaches, but found that there was no one way to manage the Earth's systems. What he found was that each of the Earth's systems had a common factor, which was the weather. He determined that mankind would have to set clear goals regarding the growth of human civilization while respecting the Earth's systems. This could only be accomplished by researching and understanding the dynamics and connectivity of the weather, animal life, and the role of man on the Earth.

"While the Earth's resources have been recognized as the basis for civilization and growth, the Earth's systems and resources are constantly taken for granted. He referred back to his earlier charts of the seasons and weather patterns. He was astonished at his findings, that rainfall patterns along with seasonal weather patterns determined the amount of water that fell each year. From one year to another, the Earth's systems experience changes caused by droughts, long winters, pests, and vermin outbreaks, but only represented short term conditions. However, the Earth's systems have a negative effect upon animal populations resulting from little rain fall and the shrinking of their habitats, which lower their food sources. Invariably, the Earth is subject to episodic instabilities, but is not without the ability to defend itself and undergo a process of recovery due to large disruption and damage.

"Rest thought of the Earth as a living thing just as people are. When the body feels ill, it takes efforts and time to heal itself. He further hypothesized that if the Earth became agitated, it may also respond by changing its initial state to heal itself, meaning that the Earth has a natural resistance to external factors and the ability to return to its natural state by a level of resiliency. He thought that perhaps a major disturbance was an important role in the life of the Earth. But such a disturbance would, undoubtedly, alter animal populations, civilizations, the levels of natural resources, and the overall physical environment.

"A major disturbance could be anything from insect or

disease outbreaks, to volcanic eruptions, wildfires, or even… a massive flood. Rest was startled at his findings and rushed to inform his community. He was eloquent and spoke with reverence when he said, 'As a man of faith, I truly believe that the resources provided by the Creator are finite and are not to be wasted. We, as mankind, are like a giant stomping on a forest leaving a crushing footprint on the face of the Earth. Our actions upon her leave a lasting impression and we must take care and tread lightly over her.'

"He spoke about a coming disturbance caused by the actions of mankind. He spoke in many meetings and gatherings to all who would listen, but the people laughed and ridiculed him. You know something, Man of the Present, looking back I don't believe it would have mattered if he had more direct knowledge of the profound science of which he spoke. There are many scholars, scientists, and researchers who continue his work today and there is even a word now for the causality of which he spoke, and I believe the word is anthropogenic."

"What does that mean?" the man asked tilting his head upward at the serpent.

"It means, oh Man of the Present! You reap… what you sow!" The man sat listening with a look of concern on his face.

"By that time, Rest, had increased the frequency of his speeches and began making motions in council meetings to properly dispose of waste and the dead to combat poor air and water quality. He insisted upon putting an end to burning down entire forests. He said that the lakes and oceans were being overfished, while pests and diseases were becoming ever prominent in the communities. He stated that entire bird species that regularly migrated through the land had completely vanished due to the destruction of their natural nesting places.

"He tried different tactics to sway the council members, even by assigning monetary values to community resources in attempts to explain the urgency of the situation. He finished off all of his speeches with the urgent need to consider the long-term effects of human habitation and the Earth's overall well-being. But the people only laughed, and his warnings were mocked and dismissed. After a while, the people of the community grew tired of his speeches and visited Rest's homestead. They threatened that he lived in conflict with the community and that he would be brought to trial if he did not change his ways. However, Rest did not waiver in his work and continued to observe other creatures and he continued to monitor their interactions with the environment around them. While others saw majesty in the tiger and elephant, they paid little attention to the worm beneath their feet, and felt little remorse for the fungus trampled by their wagons. But Rest saw that big and small, all creation was necessary as deemed so by the Creator.

"He felt that mankind had altered what the Creator had set forth. He felt shame for how man takes but does not replace what he uses and therefore damages what the Creator has gifted. He further said, 'We hurt the Earth so much in how we raise our food, yet we fail to plan for the future. Our farming practices are responsible for the poisoning of the rivers and streams. Rotten and tainted soil, along with animal waste, washes into the waterways. Animal livestock are huddled together in small pens and splash in pools of their own waste, which in turn damages the soil and nearby grasslands. What happened to this place? I recall being a boy and this very land was covered in thick forests. Yet, now I watch as my own children grow into men and I see the forests disappearing before my very eyes.' As I watched him from a distance I recited. 'The words of a man's mouth are as deep waters, and the wellspring of wisdom as a flowing brook.'

"It had been some time since I had seen the Creator's voice but just then, a familiar echo caught my attention. It was coming from above the valley and overlooking the homestead of Rest. I could see the Creator's voice, but could not hear, as what was said was not for me. The revelation of the Creator's voice descended and weighted Rest to the ground bringing him down on his knees. He looked about not knowing if sanity had left him or if, indeed, the revelation was true. He nodded in acceptance and the weight of the Creator's instructions further weighted him lower to the ground.

"His wife saw him kneeling and ran out to address him. She inquired of his health and what had brought him to his knees. Rest steadied then raised himself up off of the ground. His face was flushed and his complexion had become pale; he then turned to his wife and said... 'I think it's going to rain.' His wife ushered him inside and offered him water and food, as she thought the heat of the day had overcome him.

"He told no one of his encounter as he tried to go about his life as before. However, as I have experienced myself, once chosen by the Creator, the call leads you. Then things began to happen. At first, not much was apparent, but then subtle and noticeable changes could be seen everywhere. Interestingly, change never happens all at once, it is always slow and indirect, similar to that of a frog unknowingly being slowly boiled alive.

"Rest continued to chart and observed that the days became longer and warmer, and then there were no clouds or rain. There were growing droughts and the Earth became dependent on water by heavy mists of a Canopy view, instead of refreshing rains. I heard the Earth recite in prayer one evening, 'My Creator, why hast thou forsaken me? Why art thou so far from helping me and from the words of my roaring? O, my Creator, I cry in the daytime but thou hearest me not; and in the night season, and I am not silent.'

"I, too, could see the changes now. Plants to animals that were suited to cooler climates, now began moving poleward as the temperature became slightly warmer. I took leave of Rest, to further investigate how far reaching the effects on the Earth were. Land mammals, large and small, ceased their migrations and seasonal mating across the Alps to the misty rainforests. The birds had quieted their songs, while other animal life like large reptiles and sea creatures became more active and began birthing and laying clutches of eggs.

"I then took to the seas and saw the fish moving northwards reclaiming island waters as their very own promised lands. Jelly type things with long, stinging tentacles began to fill the seas. It is true what they say, that an increase in jellyfish numbers is a sign of a dying world. I did not know it at the time, but they were a necessary part of a coming tragic transformation.

"The impacts upon various animal species were everywhere now, the changes were becoming such an alarming indicator of a warming and changing world that only a blind man could not bear witness to the truth. And again, the Earth cried out praying to the Creator, 'O spare me that I may recover strength, before I go hence, and be no more.'

"But, all the while, the people grew angry and superstitious as their livestock grew thin; as their harvests were smaller from unusual and depressing weather. And then I saw the voice of the Creator come and look down upon humanity, to see if there were any that did understand and take care of the Earth. The Creator then said, 'They are all gone aside, they are all together become filthy; there is none that doeth good, no, not one.'

"Fever and illness struck the communities, then starvation and crime began to swell; eventually bursting the communities at their seams. Soon, Rest lost interest in his daily affairs and then he began a new venture.

"He gathered timber in large quantities and ordered the aid of his sons. He set forms according to a plan that none could understand and, soon after, he began construction. The undertaking was massive and none knew exactly what he was building. The structure was built of gopher wood, and smeared inside and out with pitch. He laid out the exterior walls and built the entrance on its side, and guaranteed it with a strong roof.

"The structure had three levels, which were divided into nine equal sections that measured some multiple lengths in cubits. The people who saw him working throughout the days and nights laughed and exploited his work as a foolish attempt to gain popularity. His friends and neighbors turned away from him, as his work was not understood and they saw no profit in it.

"In the evenings, he and his sons began storing supplies and drying meats on a large scale. I took leave of visiting the communities as the sound of violence grew louder and ever more frequent upon civilized man. The people elected mystics who promised relief and a prophecy of coming rains, ironically they knew not how right they were.

"I do not recall the number of days or weeks that saw Rest building with determination until, finally, he had completed his work. What stood there was a massive vessel, larger than any group of men had ever designed. It was stories high and multiple lengths long and widths wide. Rest and his family completed stocking the vessel with food and provisions enough to sustain many people for many months. His family reassured him that they believed in him and that no matter the outcome they would remain together.

"That evening he sent them inside to eat and sleep, while he stayed outside looking up at the sky. I could see him from a distance, as he was strong but still unsure of himself. I could see that he questioned himself in silence, by asking was it truly a vison from the Creator or a bout of madness that had overtaken him. The vision was so complete he said, and the warnings of destruction were a nightmare yet, the night skies were calm and clear. After a while, Rest answered the call of sleep and found himself safe in the comfort of his dreams.

"I ventured down and inspected the great vessel for myself. It is truly amazing what one man could do when properly motivated. When all around him was chaos and he alone had constructed such a monument of salvation and wholeness. The great vessel was meant to float and the space it provided could secure thousands of men and women, but why and for what I asked? I exited the vessel and found refuge in the hills. I slept well but knew that the answer to my questions would soon be revealed.

"Then the following day, I awoke to the voice of the Creator, and then... the command was given. A growing yet steady rumbling stretched out across the ground. I heard it coming from miles away and for days continuing. And then I looked out and could see what was approaching and I was struck in amazement with what I saw before me. There they were, every living thing that flew, walked, crawled, leeched, or slithered; male and female were marching two by two towards the great vessel. It was truly a magnificent sight, a caravan of every creation that no traveling circus could equal.

"They came large and small, some with four legs, with others on two. Apes swung through the trees, wild cats exited the forests and walked alongside wolves and wild dogs. My fellow reptiles who love the sun, traveled throughout the night, while those who moved too slowly rode on the backs of large beasts who would allow them. The birds called to each other in melodies, and swarmed in the air marking the path for all to follow. And even those creeping things that cause you fright came as well, with their spinney legs, and worm like appeal.

"They crept and tunneled miles to meet the call. None were violent, none were viscous, for they were the necessary caretakers of the Earth. Man may have inherited the Earth, but without them, the earth nor mankind would survive what was to come."

"Did you go into the vessel?" The man locked his eyes with the serpent, then exhaled and coughed out the question.

"Me? Of course not! The Creator had commanded every living thing male and female that walked and breathed air to go into the vessel. The Creator had made me complete, I need not breed with an opposite, nor flee from the water. I was just fine where I was and besides, I had a front row seat to the end of the world man."

"I continued to watch Rest and his family in the coming days and then it happened. On the following day, after years of abuse, the Earth cried out in pain and sickness to the Creator. The Earth begged for mercy and to be healed from its wounds inflicted by mankind. Let it rain, the Earth prayed, to wash away its disease, let it rain, if only to hide its tears.

"I looked on at the confusion of man as he blamed others, but did not hear the cry of the Earth screaming at him. Then there was a stirring over the land, all plant and animal life suddenly halted. I remember it vividly, and then… it began to rain.

"After the first day, streams and ponds became lakes, crops were flooded and were only fit to harvest rice and mosquitos. The rains soaked the ground and mud slid down and swallowed entire homes. Panic and terror struck the people… but this was only the beginning. The time arrived and Rest and his family boarded the vessel. His wife helped him to shut and seal the door of the great vessel. Along with his family and the remnants of the world's animals, inside the great vessel they were safe and awaited the rising waters.

"Many ran to the home of Rest and threatened him for lack of hospitality. However, he and his family were safe inside the great vessel, and still it continued to rain. Thunder rumbled heavily in the clouds above and the storms seemed to multiply from out of the mountains. The skies were lit by feverish lightning that brightly lit the sky turning it pitch black. Everyone and everything that remained ran and cowered in fear.

"The winds blew rapidly and overwhelmed the people hiding in the doorways like dogs. The waters continued to rise and were now ankle high. I had never seen such an overflow of water in all my days upon the earth. Land that was usually dry and welcoming was submerged and all but forgotten. But it was not from one direction that the flooding occurred, it came from rivers and lakes, and manmade levees that had succumbed to the pressures of the sea. The accumulation of the rainwater saturated the ground making entire areas flood. Domestic animals left in pens and barns sank into the mud and were thus drowned by the encroaching waters. I heard the Earth pray aloud saying, 'He made a pit, and digged it, and is fallen into the ditch which he made. His mischief shall return upon his own head, and his violent dealing shall come down upon his own pate.'

"All across the valleys where rivers once ran freely, were now overflowing by the exceeding flow rate of the river channels at the meanders in the waterways. People thought to hide in their homes as dams had been previously built and were thought to provide solace from the waters. However, their homes and businesses were slowly dissolved by river basins that had broken loose from their restraints.

"Flat and low-lying areas were soaked by the waters that could not run off quickly enough to end the accumulation. The localized waters caused flash flooding as the rates of rainfall exceeded the drainage capacity of the lands. Freshly tilled fields were quickly muddied and sedimentation ran off suspended bed loads. Islands and coastal beaches completely vanished as the winds and waters combined their strengths and became tsunamis and tropical cyclones.

"Entire farms and acres of timber climbing hills and mountain sides were completely inundated and useless. With the amount of water on the ground, I did not know if even some tree species could survive the prolonged flood damage on their root systems. Any left alive would find no available drinking water supply as all the waters had become contaminated by the salty ocean waters. With such a concentration and buildup of water, any left alive would not enjoy the plague created by waterborne diseases and a thriving mosquito race.

"Yet, inside the great vessel, Rest tried to calm himself and his family from the psychological stresses brought about by the death of human life and the destruction of their world. He prayed reciting, 'The voice of the Creator is upon the waters; the Creator of glory thundered, and the Creator is upon many waters... 'For this shall every one that is godly pray unto thee in a time when thou mayest be found, surely in the floods of great waters they shall not come nigh unto him.'

"The flood was massive and all-consuming and it seemed that its only purpose was the annihilation of all mankind. However, devastating as it was, the flood waters would be of benefit and healing to the Earth. Flood waters recharge ground water and make the soil increasingly fertile and increase its nutrient count. Due to the droughts and destructive nature of man upon the Earth, the floods would revitalize the eco-systems that mankind had so readily destroyed. The aquatic life that had been fished into near extinction would be allowed a time of refuge.

"All of the animal life in the vessel would experience a renewed life, as the boost in aquatic life was food to so many. All along it was Rest's name that foretold what was too come. He was the rest and recovery that the Earth so desperately needed.

"Ground waters swelled and the rains fell for a full week, until the Earth was completely covered by water. The wind, however, did not cease and continued thrashing and screaming like a woman in labor. The Creator had placed judgment upon man and sentenced him according to his wickedness upon the Earth. Why not some other devastatingly destructive event, I thought? Why not the appearance of a black hole or perhaps a series of comets or asteroids smashing into the planet? Or even causing a reaction of matter and anti-matter to occur? I believe these also to be formidable ways of destroying large amounts of life, while still allowing the Earth to recuperate. However, the waters were chosen and were more effective and complete in the matter.

"There was massive loss of life, and the trial by ordeal was set for mankind and the punishment was read to him with drowning-pits and gallows. There was no differentiation needed as all were doomed, no matter if they floated or drowned all were convicted of witchcraft upon the Earth. It was the water that would ultimately determine man's innocence or guilt for water is said to be so pure an element that it repels the guilty. Drowning may be thought of as the least brutal form of execution, but it is a most unpleasant experience.

"I witnessed so many of them praying and screaming out in hopes that the Creator would perform some miracle allowing them to survive. They ingested the rising waters as they clutched their amulets and idols and invoked the names of their demon gods, but that which rained downed was the ordeal of the Creator.

"Indeed, all of humanity had been charged and accused of being a thief, a murderer, idolater, or receiver of such; for the wicked shall be put to the ordeal of water. The destruction was magnificent, their evil and wickedness all but washed away. With so much violence and malice in the hearts of men, their world came to an end, not by blade or lash, but from water, gentle and cleansing water. But man did not wash away so easily and some found themselves suspended above the ground, struggling from respiratory impairment from the condemning liquid.

"Drowning itself is unspectacular, although it is preceded by loud and panic filled screams of distress and the visible splashing and reaching out for salvation. But then they would become silent, as the drowning are unable to shout or reach for help, as neither the air nor aid is available underneath the water. I observed some hundreds, if not thousands, engaged in the instinctive drowning response. Just before sinking under the water, the body takes on a safe and calming behavior. Each case I observed was the same as the waters took them, the distress and common look of a person in trouble. Some had the strength left to keep afloat, trying to signal for help. Then there were those who were suffocating and were in the imminence of death as they realized they were done for.

"Some were passive as they suddenly sank after a loss of consciousness or by mere pressure of the crashing waves. Others became exhausted and were unable to hold their heads above the water and slowly lost the fight for their lives to hypothermia. Either way, the drowned all bobbed the same, with their heads low, tilted back, eyes now glassy and empty, their faces evidently frozen with fear and a gasping look.

"Days and nights of endless screaming in terror and chaos. The floods washed away and drowned many, but man was stubborn in his wickedness and shunned the Creator's judgment attempting to survive. Hundreds of thousands of dead bodies floated and those left alive lashed them together into makeshift rafts. The survivors went mad drinking sea water and eating the dead that kept them afloat.

"The Creator saw that mankind would survive at any cost and so a new command was given. Those many sea creatures that bred and grew were ordered to devour the survivors and the floating dead lest the waters become permanently spoiled. At that time, there were few sea creatures capable of eating human flesh. So the Creator commanded sea creatures to change form and to grow large. Their mouths became beaks, while others filled with sharp teeth. Some grew long tentacles to reach out of the waters and pull men and women underneath to be eaten. There were those jelly type things that swarmed in troops and were a silent death. They had dozens of tentacles, some stretching up to 15 feet long, with enough toxin to kill 60 or more.

"The sting from just one of them could kill in less than three minutes, but they were not conservative with their weapons and issued death from a thousand stings. The pain shooting through each of their victims was likened to a lighting strike, and with them the seas were a terrible lighting storm. There were many sea creatures that could not survive so closely to the surface, so the Creator made them to breathe air. These types were commanded to grow large and black; their teeth and intellect became sharp to outsmart men floating on makeshift rafts. They were apex hunters and have no natural predators. They later became known as the wolves of the sea, for they were ferocious and hunted in pods like wolf packs.

"I watched the sophistication of the sea wolves and their acrobatic behavior as they breached, spy hopped, and tail slapped murderously. It seemed that they found enjoyment in their ability and attacked man with charging and piercing speed like warships.

"It was awful as they fed on man, sometimes by suction feeding, where the large predators would tip the makeshift rafts over causing man to fall into the water. They would open their mouths wide in gleeful anticipation sucking them into their mouth's like a shrimp out of its shell. In the night, a group a fish cried out to the Creator saying that they had no purpose and had been forgotten. The fish prayed that they would give up sleep and would dream no more if they could serve the Creator in this task. Now the Creator does not need to bargain to act, but the Creator accepted their prayers and those fish too were made over.

"They were made into perfect predators with repeating rows of sharp teeth, ferocious speed, and required no sleep. With their freshly striped skin, they would attack and eat anything moving in the water. They could now grow to a size of more than 18 feet long and weigh up to a ton. Those sea dogs had oblique and serrated teeth to saw through the flesh of man and constantly replaced them throughout their lives. Although their fin protruding out of the water was a frightful sight to man, it was their tail that accelerated them with large bursts of speed. So much that when they attacked, they twisted and turned in the water easily tearing chunks of flesh from man.

"A few times I found myself caught within the midst of a feeding frenzy, but I knew the tonic touch and was able to immobilize them while I moved away to safety. It is true that their sense of smell is quite keen and one of their strongest hunting abilities. It was amazing how they were able to detect a single drop of blood from miles away in such saturated sea water. But they never sleep and keep water flowing over their gills appearing almost suspended in an unconscious state with their eyes open following the movement of creatures swimming around them.

"The civilized socialites were more of an attraction to them as their precious jewelry and shiny metals attracted the swimming death of the sea dogs. I, too, engaged in the event and devoured many evil and unforgiven lives. As well did many of my cousin offspring who joined me. At first, they were a bit reclusive in the waters, but soon came to love the sea so much that they stayed and to this day they even out-venom their terrestrial cousins.

"The saltwater crocodiles earned their reputation as one of the most ferocious predators. They were beautiful and full of brute strength, as they victimized the wicked human by latching on to them with powerful jaws, then dragging them down with a dominant and twisting roll. With this specific technique, many bodies would break apart in the water causing more of a drunken frenzy among the other predators. But the true professional was the cousin of the shark, who came complete with a tail capped with an 8-inch serrated like spear packed with deadly venom.

"The eels with their snakelike bodies, protruding snout, and wide jaws were the personification of death. With their primitive yet razor-sharp teeth and powerful locking jaws, they produce ragged wounds that swelled with infection leaving their victims alive yet suffering. Man's end was now complete, the seas and oceans were alive with terrible creatures that tore at his flesh. The culinary arts teach that it is the blood that flavors a tender steak, and so too did the beating heart of man making him all the more flavorful and delicious.

"The land was now depths below and all the Earth was covered in water, but no blue planet could be seen as she was painted bloody red. Throughout history, I have seen that all civilizations experience cycles of birth, life, decline, and eventually destruction. Many times, it is succeeded by a new culture, religion, or hierarchy, and perhaps Rest, and his family were to be that. Perhaps they were an innovative minority that began to see and experience their environment in a new way. Through either moral decline or the inability to meet the challenge of humanity, the civilization of man had come to an end.

"There are many explanations as to why a civilization comes to an end. Sometimes the cultural or political elite have become parasites, then give rise to grassroots movements who eventually overthrow them. However, in this case, it was obvious that it was nothing more than man's ability to over-exploit the Earth's resources. He abused the amount of disposable energy while not being able to access new resources, which eventually led the Earth to turn on him. But know this Man of the Present, when more animal life is in the care of humanity than in the wilds, beware... for the end is near.

"But what of the future, what world would Rest and his family be a part of. The old world had literally gone down the drain and Rest and his family would be the builders of tomorrow. Would his offspring follow in his footsteps or would man's wicked nature eventually resurface and have him once again destroy the Earth that was gifted to him? No one could know such things ahead of time. I theorized that perhaps there might be a shift away from disconnected communities and nations to a world of global connectivity, environmental consciousness, and economic morality. Just as Rest saw that all things are connected, and not to see the importance of all life is to live in ignorance, eventually man would again see his own demise."

"After the destruction and flooding, the seas and the winds calmed. The dead had all been consumed and for all the days after, there was now quiet. The great vessel drifted alone in the sea and Rest and his family were safe and tended to the animal life in their care.

"Some of Rest's family saw me in the waters diving and fishing about and what they saw of me later became recognized as a Giant Sea Serpent. Once an idea such as that takes roots in the psyche of man, it is near impossible to defeat such a myth. However, I am no cryptozoological creature nor any leviathan lurking about the depths of any loch. The only sea serpents that ever existed are those actual prehistoric aquatic life forms of gigantic proportion.

"You know something Man of the Present, I find it interesting that this whole time you have not made one reference to your 'The Book.' Does this story not seem familiar to you?"

"Actually, yes it does. There was a great flood that wiped out all life, save for one man and his family. He built a massive ship and filled it with two of each animal on the earth."

"And that's it?" the serpent quipped with a single raised eyebrow.

"Well, I mean what else is there? The people were destroyed in the flood because they were wicked and evil, and that's it," he answered.

"Interesting how easily you accept mass death and destruction on such vague principles as evil and wickedness. Is there no meaning or definition of evil or wickedness? What does 'The Book' say of these people and their wicked actions?" The serpent folded his tail like an elbow and rested his head on the end of his tail like a fist in a thinking position.

"I don't think it says exactly what they did that was so wicked or evil."

"Then how do you know if people today are not engaging in those same acts? If the premises of such a book is to inform humanity and instruct them how to live, why would you not describe in detail what actions led to such a catastrophic event that literally wiped out all of humanity?" the serpent leaned forward asking in interrogation.

"I don't really know, that's just what it says," the man replied, with both hands stretched out in front of him in defense.

"I find it frightening that you accept no answer as an answer and are thus satisfied. Personally, I believe in the preservation of history and knowledge so as to learn what mistakes were made and how to avoid repeating them, especially if it's going to mean the end of the world. I believe you should look at some of the glaring truths presented in that story and compare them with the actions and events occurring today," the serpent further implored.

"Why would I need to do that? I mean it doesn't really matter, because it's not going to happen again," he responded, waving off the serpent's questioning with one hand.

"As I stated before, Man of the Present, the truth repeats itself. And one thing I have learned is that man repeatedly destroys himself. You are correct that the Creator made a covenant with Rest and it was in the form of a multi colored bow in the sky. Allow me to continue and I will explain.

"It was shortly after the seas and the winds had calmed and once again I saw the voice of the Creator just ahead of the great vessel. Rest was on the deck alone and the voice of the Creator beckoned him. He looked up and saw the bow and repeated what was revealed to him to his family. He said that the Creator promised not to destroy humanity again by means of a flood. But there are many wonders in the sky, the oceans, and over the land. A grain of sand is but a fraction of the Earth, but no less a marvel and a miracle just as is one life. There are many radiant bows after the rains. Perhaps it was not the first of such marvels, but perhaps the one that held the most meaning.

"Understand this, Man of the Present, the Creator promised not to flood the earth again, but no guarantee was ever given not to destroy mankind. Which brings us back to my previous inquiry. If mankind was judged by the Creator for his wicked actions, what were they? I, for one, would surely want to know what they were so as to avoid the same ill-fate."

"I don't think it had anything to do with people destroying the environment. Maybe they were a bit wasteful, but that's not what I would call evil or wicked," the man replied with simple dismissal.

"You're are absolutely correct. Evil and wicked have nothing to do with taking care of the environment that sustains you. What I observed was no religious act. I observed truths, I observed a major change in the weather that caused a massive flood. I observed the changing of animal behaviors and migrations caused by the changing climate. I don't know about you, but that seems to be a pretty glaring example of things that are presently occurring, and possibly a warning of religious epic proportions! It doesn't bother me, I survived before, I'm sure I'll be just fine next time too," the serpent said, with confident irony. He then continued.

The sun rose and set daily, and the great vessel flowed with the seas, weeks felt like months, and month's felt like years. And I heard the Earth pray to the Creator, reciting, 'Save me, O Creator, for the waters are come in unto my soul. I sink in deep mire, where there is no standing. I am come into deep waters, where the floods overflow me…How long wilt thou forget me, O Creator? Forever? How long wilt thou hide thy face from me?' and then, the waters… receded."

"Then came the day that saw a horizon bursting over a coastline and it was the beginnings of land. With no way to steer the vessel, Rest and his family depended on the will of the Creator, and the vessel found a mountain peak and the vessel lodged firmly against it.

"They released birds over several days and on the first day, the bird returned after finding no dry land. And each day that followed, they did the same until a bird returned with nesting in its beak. It seemed that the day would never come but finally, the doors of the vessel were opened and Rest and his family, once again, found the earth beneath their feet. The animals who all along were the caretakers of the earth, both wild and domestic, were released and exited the great vessel. Just as easily as they came, they left and resumed their migrations and patterns as if no disruption had occurred.

"That evening, Rest and his family sacrificed a goat and said thanks to the Creator. Soon after, they began the work of living and starting anew. With all the Earth in their possession they could choose any path to follow or any idea to postulate. Rest said to his family, 'In the past world, humanity had failed to recognize the gifts of the Creator and became obsessed with material possessions. What has saved us was not our prayers as others prayed too. It was not our offerings as so many others had sent them up too. But it was our ability to recognize true wealth, which was the Earth that sustained us and the animals that cared for it. In such a time of great death and destruction, all sought after salvation, but while living none sought after life.

'The Creator has saved our lives to build a new world and we pray that all who come after us would learn from these past mistakes.' He ended by reciting, 'The wicked borroweth, and payeth not again, but the righteous sheweth mercy and giveth. For such as be blessed of him shall inherit the earth; and they that be cursed of him shall be cut off.'

"I would later see that no matter how many drastic efforts the Creator took to address man's inherent nature, he would eventually succumb to his destructive habits as all human civilization is engaged in dominating the environment and humanity, which in itself is destructive and unsustainable.

"Either way, the future of humanity was walking out of the vessel and only time would tell what would become of the new world. It was poetic in observing the great deluge, it was a story of creation all in its own. There was a time of creation where man populated the Earth. Then came the un-doing where all the evil and wickedness was washed away. Then finally, the re-creation where a new world was born out of the period of 'Rest' and 'Wholeness' of the great vessel.

"But the truth is repeating and what occurred then will, unfortunately, happen again. There will come a time when man's evil deeds upon the Earth will be the main ingredient in the soup of his own destruction. He will pollute and destroy the Earth far beyond repair. The seasons and climates will change subtly around him. There will be higher temperatures, droughts, harsher weather, melting glaciers, warmer oceans, and a rising sea level; yet, still, he will not change his ways. There will be more animal life in his care than in the wilds where they were intended to be. And then, as if commanded by the will of the Creator, all that man has built will simply be taken away."

"Interesting story, Serpent. It's almost believable!" the man said, while tilting his head with a dismissive tone

"You... don't believe me?" the serpent questioned. "And why not? Is it the message, or the messenger that you doubt?"

"It's not that. The things you've said are compelling, but that doesn't mean that's what really happened. It just sounds crazy that God destroyed everybody because they didn't recycle," the man rebutted, shrugging his shoulders in disbelief.

"Crazy am I! Of the two of us, Man of the Present, you're the one having a conversation with a talking serpent!" the serpent countered, widening his large reptile eyes back at the man.

"You may want to re-examine your definition of sanity and your measures of belief. Unless, of course, this is all a bad dream, which you can wake from any time you please," the serpent said jokingly.

"I shall save you the embarrassment of closing your eyes and clicking your heels three times for I am no hallucination and my words are as real and true as I am. Regardless of what any man writes, the truth will always remain the same. Fire will burn, venom will poison, and truth will always defeat lies."

"Well, you did leave out the end part about the man and his family," he pointed out.

"Curious! I have retold the events just as they happened. Maybe you wish to add insight regarding said details I have forgotten?" the serpent remarked, with invitation.

"Well, it was just as you said, the man and his family exited the ship and the animals went out in separate directions. The man had three sons and they each had families. The man grew wine vineyards and one day became drunk. When the man was drunk, one of his sons saw him naked. The other two sons instead clothed their father and did not see him naked. Because that son saw his father naked, he and his lineage were cursed to be the servants of his two brothers. The End!"

"I must say Man of the Present that is an interesting addition you submit. However, the scenario you present would set an entire race of people into servitude. If that were true, then it would be true today as truth is eternal. Those ill-fated people would forever be servants without any release from their cast. However, I have witnessed something that is actually true and that is that no man enjoys living in bondage. The will of man cannot be held by iron, nor broken by the lash, he will fight, rebel, and eventually, he must breathe freedom.

"I challenge you to locate this land and identify a people forever cast into servitude. As long as man has existed, he has longed to improve his position and make life easier. Regrettably, his imagination motivates him to subdue and exploit those around him. Many kingdoms and governments have existed and all of them have found new ways to place a chosen few above the rightful majority.

"However, I agree that such a land does exist. Unfortunately, it is located within the hearts of men. You see, this land and its people are whomever the powerful choose them to be. The words you speak only aim to justify the enslavement and mistreatment of others. Whether they be the young, old, disenfranchised, or incompetent, the powerful few will find a way to rationalize the mistreatment of them.

"However, fret not Man of the Present, for if you wish to visit such a place, simply walk down that sadistic road, through the valley of violence, and you will find a place without compassion and that place exists within the hearts of evil men," the man stood silent, lowering his eyes to the ground.

"But, allow me to conclude the tale of Rest, and his family to address your addition," the serpent continued.

"There was a time of peace and quiet that only the humble hearted can understand. Due to his curiosity of animal kind, Rest came to study my habits and learned the healing arts endowed to me. And with this newfound knowledge, he was able to protect his children from the offspring of pestilence, infections, and illness.

"Later, the man's three sons founded their own lands which became kingdoms and eventually populations of the known continents. From those populations, each was known for being masters of a specific trade or skill. One became known for their clerical work and study, while the second was known for its warriors and its military advancements. While the third was riddled with wealth and greed, which eventually led to mass poverty of their population. As for your claim that the man cursed one of his sons while in a state of drunkenness, this is what actually occurred.

"Rest's second son, known as 'He that Cries Aloud,' was never satisfied. Then following an evening when Rest became slack from drunkenness, He that Cries Aloud crept into his father's home and removed the sacred cloths of the First Man and First Woman. He that Cries Aloud, felt that while he was second born, his inheritance would be smaller to that of his elder brother and thought to take his inheritance in advance. Rest came back inside and saw his son with the garments and said to him, 'Thou hast taken the cloths of my forefathers, whilst thou leave me naked?'

"The other two brother's intervened hearing the commotion and rushed to their father's side. When they arrived, He that Cries Aloud tucked the clothing under his robe and exited his father's home. The other two brothers seeing their father in his drunken state, wrapped him with a blanket while their brother exited undiscovered. Later, those cloths would be handed down to his son, who became a man of great reverence.

"Now, true it is that many a drunkard have often cursed those around them, but little affect comes from such boasts. As for Rest, he found leisure and also the temptation of wine. What happened to him was the same that happens to all men when they become drunk, they behave as fools do. 'Wine is a mocker, strong drink is raging and whosoever is deceived thereby is not wise.'

"The words you spoke are a cautionary example of what can happen when one finds themselves in the company of fools. Turn away from shameful behavior lest their shame become your shame; cover them with reason and sanity, for you are their salvation. Know this Man of the Present, try as you may, but you are all alike and the truth of your faults shall be revealed. No man is without need for help and guidance and no man is above making a fool of himself.

"Forgive me if my words have offended you. Perhaps the book you speak of was not meant literally, but maybe as a guide. The history of man makes for quite an interesting tale and much can be learned from it. Although I am not of men, I have learned much from his exploits. I have granted you solace from the storm within this cave but you are free to leave if my words bore you."

The man looked around and saw a larger stone that shimmered differently than the others. He walked over to inspect it asking.

"What's this?"

"Let me look. Ohhh! Now! You wouldn't be interested in that old thing!"

"What is it?" The serpent reached with his tail taking hold of the circular object, shaking the dust covering it, then placed it before the man, and behold a crown of an ancient king.

"Once, this rested upon his head; a crown of black cloth decorated with large jewels. Behold, the first King of man, a mighty hunter, a builder of cities, and the most flagrant blasphemer against the Creator. The original and vilest of men is his tale, but beware Man of the Present, for his story is a cautionary tale of greed, lust for power, and arrogance against the Creator. I wish to speak of him no more, for all that do have known nothing but grief and suffering for the remainder of their days. That is unless you heed the warnings of his life."

"I'm in no hurry, Serpent, I think I'll stay and continue our conversation," he replied, all the while looking around at the glitter of the gems surrounding him.

"As you wish!" the serpent nodded with sly

acknowledgment, then continued.

CHAPTER 4: THE SEMANTIC

"The generations of Rest grew and populated the earth and all of mankind was unified and at peace. It appeared that man had set aside his evil ways and begun to move in a new direction. Education and hard work became his religion, patience and technology his ethic, and man had become a builder. He cultivated acres and articulated his thoughts into designs and formed the first contemporary systems. With the advent of written language, mankind was able to store large amounts of information and retrieve it at any time.

"The written word allowed man to communicate across great distances that otherwise would have been unmanageable. Hand in hand, all of mankind moved as one and he learned and fell in love with mathematics, the arts, science, and medicine. Villages became cities, paths stretched into roads and once again, streams were damned and irrigated crops. Man saw in himself greatness and ability, and with cooperation he could accomplish many things and behold... bronze.

"All over the world, man presented new designs and continued societal improvements. During this time, man characterized himself by those who had learned the skills of metal working. There were those who had acquired the skill of smelting copper and tin with lead and brought about the development of the first urban civilizations. It was a new day for man and soon would begin the age of Kings.

"The resulting bronze became a heavily traded commodity and participating civilizations stretched out conquering far reaching areas. From the Sub-Saharan civilizations who developed the metal independently to the remote lands in the east, man had now become industrious and full scale mining operations were underway and the known world exploded with trade networks spanning the globe over both land and sea.

"The ingenuity of man leaped forward with inventions including the potter's wheel, centralized government, laws and codes of conduct, organized warfare, and astronomy. Man sailed the seas again and the knowledge of navigation was well developed and taught. All over the world, the knowledge of metal working overtook the simple rock-tool and hunter gatherer clusters. Those that employed the newest technologies became wealthy and powerful producing economies focused on expansion. I looked around at the new world of man and at first glance, it did seem different, but I wondered to myself... would it last?

"I cautioned myself not to take this moment of pause in the existence of man as a declaration of fulfillment. As I looked back on the great deluge, it was reminiscent of an abrupt adjustment similar to that of an addict going cold turkey but in either case, sobriety is a daily endeavor.

"I don't know if it's destiny or opportunity that makes men great, or perhaps it's the design of the stars that makes them so evil. He was just a boy, but like the bronze alloy of his sword, he underwent an allegorical transition that would make him harder and more evil than any man before him. In order to understand the end of a man, it is important to know his beginnings. He was a mighty hunter, who later became ruler of many great cities. He lived the life of a hero but died a tyrant and was cursed as a rebel against the Creator," the serpent pulled back into a seated position gazing upward.

"What happened to him?" The man looked on with intrigue listening, as the serpent's eyes focused hypnotically in thought, then continued.

"When he was born, his people had known much struggle and hardship as they were poor and the land was scrawny and gave little for meat or grain. He was the great grandson of Rest and his name meant 'Shining Light,' for he was the light and hope of his people.

"It seemed that everything he touched prospered and everywhere he went wealth was overflowing. His people grew alongside him and their wealth quickly inspired others as their community grew. The boy grew into a very handsome, strong, and able young man. He characteristically wore a thick braid in the center of his head, which grew long and down his back. He took an interest in learning new things and was well versed in the arts of finance, commerce, poetry, and divination. He minded the ways of his elders and was reverent in his ways and always sacrificed to the Creator after each successful hunt. However, he had a reputation for being mercurial, as he was never satisfied, and was only happy when he triumphed over an insurmountable task.

"Later, he lost interest in his studies as his wit surpassed his instructors and he only found joy in hunting. What others saw as only the task of acquiring supplemental meat or the competitions amongst young men, Shining Light saw an untapped skill and trade. He immersed himself in the hunt and he obsessed passionately over it.

"First, he began by defining the action of killing or trapping as 'hunting,' by means of pursuit with intent by one known as a 'hunter.' He noted that all manner of beast on land, in water, or air were to be called 'game.' He further noted that skill and tact were necessary for the procurement of an elusive target. He set out to develop the specialist hunter, who, with special training and equipment, could acquire the most elusive and dangerous beasts of the wilds. He said that of all leisurely activities, the option of hunting as a 'sport' was reserved for those of select skill, resilience, and intelligence. Although history remembers him as a mighty hunter, they often forget that he was responsible for developing the sport from a subsistence activity to a social and regulated event.

"He challenged himself to resist simple kills and became a master of every type of known weaponry. He upgraded himself from deer and fowl to more daring game, such as lions, bears, and wild boar. Once he felt he had mastered the tracking and capture of an animal, he would hold events where he would challenge the strongest from neighboring villages and tribes to match his ability. These local events soon gained attention and developed into seasonal tournaments with the outcomes feeding hundreds and bringing wealth and glory upon him. The passion of Shining Light was now becoming an honorable pastime and many would-be heroes used the sport of hunting as practice for war during times of peace.

"Eventually, he increased his hunting trips to extended overland journeys sometimes lasting several days or even weeks while in pursuit of a worthy trophy. On each venture, he sought out new and more capable prey and he continued to classify each group by size and type:

Big game: Deer, Elk, Moose, Caribou, Bears, Bighorn Sheep, and Boar.

Small game: Rabbits, Squirrels, Possums, Coons, Skunks, and Porcupines.

Furbearers: Beavers, Foxes, Otters, and Wild Cats.

Predators: Lions, Tigers, Cougars, Wolves, and Coyotes.

Game bird: Pheasants, Quail, and Doves.

Waterfowl: Ducks, Geese, and Swans.

"As his hunting trips became more difficult, he learned to enlist various animals to aid in the hunt including birds of prey and ferrets, but he found that none were a better companion than the dog. He retained the companionship of a team of four dogs which led to an almost symbiotic relationship among them. Their senses to locate, chase, and retrieve game in otherwise dangerous hunts over difficult terrain were invaluable and he and his dogs became inseparable. It was even said that he possessed the ability to see in the dark and many artisans depicted him on reliefs hunting big game from a chariot accompanied by his four dogs.

"Soon his reputation spread and his legend was born and from then on he was known as 'Mighty Hunter.' With his newfound success and popularity, he saw that his sport was becoming too popular and developed laws and seasons of hunting. He designated closed seasons to protect game during times of mating when they were most vulnerable. He stated that the seasons were designed to sustain the wildlife populations from excessive hunting and poaching. In addition, he established 'fair chase laws,' which prohibited the capture of game under certain circumstances.

"But without enforcement, laws mean nothing, so he was strict in carrying out punishment for those who broke the hunting laws. But for all his skill and posturing, he had a secret weapon of sorts. When he hunted, he always wore a special cloak known as the 'Cloak of Ancestors.' The cloak rendered him invincible to animal attack and allowed him to face down the fiercest of beasts. There was some truth to this legend of his cloak as it was special and was of no ordinary origin.

"You see he had inherited the animal skins from his grandfather who, in turn, had stolen them from his father, Rest. The animal skins belonged to the First Man and Woman who received them from the Creator when they were first exiled out of the Garden. When Mighty Hunter inherited the animal skins, he sewed them into a cloak which he wore when out hunting. In the beginning, he had little skill or knowledge of hunting and tracking, but soon learned that when any beast saw the cloak they kneeled down before him, thus making his triumph inevitable.

"He continued this way for some time but even after all he had accomplished, he found himself dissatisfied and again searching for a new challenge. When Mighty Hunter was eighteen years of age, war broke out between his kinsmen and an encroaching tribe. During the first battles, the attacking tribe was victorious over his kinsmen and many were unsure if they could defend themselves against the raiders. Mighty Hunter was not a man of war, but saw in front of him a new challenge.

"He saw that he had hunted and killed nearly every type of

wild beast, but what of the trained soldier. He had never tested his skill and fortitude against the ultimate beast... man. Mighty Hunter then assembled a small troop along with his four dogs and set out to hunt the raiding tribe who threatened his kinsmen. He did as he knew and attacked the raiders not as an army but as a pack of wolves or wild boar. He tracked and located their camps and afterwards, he set traps and laid nets to snare them. He studied their habits from afar then used beating tactics to confuse the raiders into a stir and drive them into position.

"Once he had them in a panic, Mighty Hunter and his troop attacked under cover of night and ended the war in one battle. The word of his victory spread throughout the tribal nations, after which he was made king over all the people and he assumed undisputed rule.

"Now king, Mighty Hunter became a just and beloved ruler. He lived and preached tolerance for all life and that all mankind should unite and see the weary traveler as his returning brethren and welcome them with love. As king, he was known for many firsts, including being the first to wear a crown. Legends were told that while looking into the night sky, he saw amongst the starts a black ring, which sparkled and shined greater than any of the constellations. He commissioned his artisans to make him such a headpiece fitting of a king. The crown was made of the finest cloths and embroidered with jewels and laced with gold. None had ever seen such a magnificent headdress and believed it to have fallen from the heavens. Although he was the exulted ruler of all the lands, he never lost his passion and excitement for the hunt. It was during one such venture where I first encountered him.

"A neighboring province had pleaded for aid from a plague of wild beasts that had overcome their herdsmen and preyed upon their livestock unchecked. Mighty Hunter took the task upon himself to rid the province of their beasts of burden with no aid, which he called a matter of charity. He had tracked the beasts and found that a large pride of lions had taken a liking to the livestock of the neighboring province. I observed him stalking them with the use of his dogs and he hunted and killed the entire pride of lions with ease.

"I observed how the lions each walked up to him and kneeled at the sight of the Cloak of Ancestors. None of them moved as he thrust his blade into each of them and then used his club to bash the remaining cubs to death. Normally, I would have left him but curiosity overcame me and I rattled my tail and made my presence known to him. Upon hearing the warning of my tail, he immediately ended his butchery of the beasts and turned towards the grass in search of the sound's origin. He laughed saying, 'Tempt me not mere belly crawler, you shall kneel before me like all the rest, and I shall make a proud garment of you!'

"He stepped easily into the thick brush in search of me for he knew no fear and was confident in his skill and ability. But I laid not under his feet and was camouflaged up against the rock face directly ahead of him. I continued the twitching of my tail luring him in closer as he traced the sound ahead of him in the grass. I waited until he was almost on top of me, then I moved and revealed myself to him. He was caught in amazement by the sheer size of me as he had seen no serpent the likes of me before.

"But Mighty Hunter was confident and brave and shouted with his sword drawn, 'Kneel down demon for I am the mightiest of hunters and I will have your hide for my prize before this day is done!' To his shock, I remained upright and not groveling at his feet like the other animals... and then I spoke, 'He that diggeth a pit shall fall into it; and whoso breaketh a hedge, a serpent shall bite him.'

"Momentary fright struck him upon hearing my words confronting him, but he quickly recovered and remarked, 'Demon tongue! Or do my senses betray me? ... I have no fear of any devil for the Cloak of Ancestors protects me!' Again he shouted and commanded me to kneel before him with disgust and anger, but I remained in my ready stance with raised hood and senses aware. He saw how his commands went unanswered and that the Cloak of Ancestors he wore was powerless over me.

"He made ready and then attacked in foolish pride. He charged me with his sword and struck a futile but mighty blow.

I moved with the speed of a cobra strike and impaled him with the teeth of my lower jaw, hoisting him up off the ground as he shrieked in pain. My fangs now just inches away from piercing his flesh and injecting fiery venom, I bit down and felt blood rushing into my mouth, but the rush was quickly followed by excruciating pain. My fangs had been broken by the cloak which acted like armor upon him.

"I recoiled in pain and threw his limp body against the rock face rendering him unconscious. I looked at his body before leaving and uttered, 'All fear death, but foolish is the hunter who fears nothing.'

"Mighty Hunter was wounded but not dead. It appeared that the Cloak of Ancestors was proof against my bite and penetrating venom and had staved off his death for another day. He recovered from his wounds but after our encounter, he became a different man. He was angry all the time and no longer found pleasure in his leisurely activities. He fell into seclusion and was only seen by his closest advisors. For the first time, Mighty Hunter had felt defeat and he hated the weakness pulsing through him. He saw that he made offerings to the Creator and believed that he had been granted strength, skill, and protection for his obedience. He felt that for all his reverence to the Creator, he had been betrayed.

"Furiously he shouted, saying the Creator was useless and a liar. He then disavowed all priests who persisted worshiping and burning offerings in previous fashion to the Creator. He fell into a state of madness and soon after began searching for meaning in the stars. He called several mystics unto him and he learned to read the stars based on several systems of prediction between relationships of astronomical phenomena and events of the world.

"He searched for answers to describe his near-death experience and how he, Mighty Hunter, was defeated by such a foe. As he continued to search for answers he felt an important life changing event was ahead of him. He felt comforted by the new insight provided by his mystics and had them formally commissioned and the practice of reading the stars took hold amongst the people.

"Mighty Hunter was successful at employing the techniques he learned and made the first known recordings of the moon's influence upon the tides. He used his new insight to chart calendars and predict annual floods and seasonal instabilities. It was then, after a life elated by glory now overcome by defeat, that Mighty Hunter completely ended his belief in the Creator, thus becoming the most flagrant idolater.

"He formally changed the decree of the land and stated that all prayer and offerings would be made to the might of men and not the Creator. He spoke openly and retold the epic of the deluge and how the Creator had destroyed all of mankind. The mood of the people turned from joyous to fearful of a petty God who could not be trusted and thus, did not deserve their prayers. Mighty Hunter said that man was greater and could create anything he set his mind too. After an evening feast, he stood atop his palace and stretched out his hand and swept it over the land motioning to the great cities that had been built in his name. He said that the Creator in heaven had turned his back on mankind and should be judged as a common traitor and killed.

"It was then that Mighty Hunter became known by a different name. His name became synonymous with rebellion and hate against the Creator. So then he was known as, 'He who turned the people to revolt against the Creator' but commonly as 'Dark Word.'

"Now Dark Word was famous for idolatry and fire worship. His previous government which had been a source of justice, turned to tyranny and an iron rule and the belief in his ultimate power. Dark Word continued his affront to the Creator but saw little change in the people's faith. Seeing no other way of truly turning the people from the Creator, he made a ruling that he would avenge mankind of the Creator for drowning the old world.

"He submitted that a tower too high to be flooded by waters would be built and would reach up to the heavens where he would wage war against the Creator to free all of mankind. It was the tower which would showcase the majesty of the city and would stand tall for all to see. The tower was to be a symbol of man's never ending desire to improve upon himself, and would call out as a beating heart from the center of the city. He commanded that the tower would never be finished until mankind had reached the heavens. Upon hearing this, the people of the land all cheered at the might of their king, and no longer cowered in fear of the Creator. And so it began, that Dark Word sent for the greatest architects of the time to begin planning and constructing the Tower.

"Throughout history, towers have been used by mankind for numerous reasons. They stand as lighthouses, bell towers, clock towers, and minarets. As long-range defensive posts providing advantageous sight, or surveying surrounding areas. But most of all, a tower has been a beacon of human communication. The Tower commissioned by Dark Word would serve to communicate mankind's bold statement of defiance, ability, and independence from the Creator. He perpetuated the belief that man, like the tower, was a self-supporting structure that eventually would climb to the heavens and break the mortal boundaries set by the Creator. I looked upon him and recited, 'Why do the heathen rage and the people imagine a vain thing?'

"Looking back on the ordeal, Dark Word knew not what he invoked upon the people of the world with his little tower, Ha! Ha! Ha!" the serpent said snickering. "However, the Creator is infinite in wisdom and fluent in irony."

"The design trade at the time was merely a process of trial and error, which did not gain notoriety until the commission of the tower project. From their endeavors, the tradesmen were granted noble titles as their skill became linked to divinity. Later, the trade was used for monuments of symbolic religion and political power. He was involved day and night in meetings with his design team as they argued and debated their ideas on constructing form, technical aspects, and space utilization. They stressed the importance of ambience to reflect the social and aesthetic strengths of their King over the oppressive God of the old world.

"The architects produced hundreds of drawings and plans

detailing technical specifications, coordination of materials, pragmatic aspects, scheduling, cost estimation, and construction administration. With each new submission, the designs were grander and more elaborate until finally, a design was agreed upon. The confirmed design established three principles of durability, utility, and beauty. Dark Word agreed upon the final design and presented to his people a grand model in the center of the city. It was adorned with decorations befitting festal offerings and a bronze plaque set atop it which read: 'This towering enterprise and assembly by men, will stand as a testament to the mental fortitude, physical abilities, and will of humanity for all time.'

"And so… they began to build, with bricks cast in fire pits that served them better than stone and clay to cement the structure together. The tower was wider than it was high, more like a mountain with twenty-five gates on each side equaling one hundred. A spiral staircase was built around the tower and its width was rumored so wide that each fifty flights contained lodgings for workers with enough space for gardens, grains, and livestock.

"The architects determined that due to the massive size, weight, and height of the tower, failure was imminent and it would eventually collapse. However, Dark Word pressed them forward and said that there was nothing that men could not accomplish and ordered them to compensate for the size of the structure. The architects decided to build the base of the structure extremely wide, which would take up a large amount of space. But even then, they would not be able to determine how high the structure could go. Despite the warnings of the architects, Dark Word ordered the construction to continue.

"There was no possible way to employ enough men and women to work on the structure so labor was forced upon the able bodied. Men and women, both young and old, were charged incredible taxes and were thus forced to work off their debts in slave labor. Stories circulated of men and women who fell ill and died and thus were mixed into the clay for cement. Women who felt the urge of child birth were not released from duty and gave birth under the lash and children grew directly into servitude. Dark Word campaigned heavily in favor of his creation and incited an army who would charge up to the heavens and war with the Creator. However, as the masses were involved in labor and construction this left few warriors.

"Dark Word sent out messengers and proclaimed that all children born after that date would be part of the Army of Secession. The Proclamation read: 'The Creator has no right to rule from heaven and leave mortal man to toil in servitude. Rise up all ye warriors of men and let us ascend the tower to defeat the Creator.' Many answered the call of war and bore many sons to equip Dark Word's army. He provoked them into a frenzied state by claiming that all who breached the gates of heaven would be rewarded their weight in divine spoils.

"Dark Word fired arrows covered in blood into the sky and visibly allowed them to fall back to the earth, so as to convince the people that victory against the Creator could be attained. I watched as people turned to madness and believed Dark Word's lies. They say love is the strongest emotion and can move mountains, but hate combined with fear appeared to be equally motivating. I knew that such an attempt was fool hardy and would only end in the defeat of man. But as I watched man toil towards his own end, a fear overcame me.

"I had no fear of Dark Word actually succeeding, but more so of an absent Creator, for surely the Creator had observed such blasphemy and dissidence. The Creator is swift in judgment, but how long would this madness be allowed to continue. How long would man be allowed to live in utter contempt of the Creator? And I prayed reciting, 'The Kings of the earth set themselves, and the rulers take counsel together, against the Creator, and against his anointed. Saying, let us break their bands asunder, and cast away their cords from us. He that sitteth in the heavens shall laugh and the Creator shall have them in derision. Then shall he speak unto them in his wrath, and vex them in his sore displeasure.'

"Forty-three years and the behemoth was only three quarters completed and still no intervention from the Creator. If things did not seem ill-fated and odd enough, I began hearing rumors of a portent in the stars that foretold the birth of a male child. The child would put an end to idolatry and return the people back to righteousness. It has become somewhat cliché by now, Man of the present. The story of a tyrannical ruler and the murdering of infant males trying to stop a prophecy from coming true. So Dark Word, upon hearing of the prophecy and the arrival of a redeemer, ordered the killing of all newborn male babies. However, one woman fled the lands and gave birth in secret out in the fields and a male child was born.

"From an early age, the boy recognized the Creator and began ministering a return to the virtuous path of the Creator. By this time, worshiping the Creator had all but been abolished and reading the stars was the dominate belief system. While the boy too was raised to read the stars, he reasoned that the visible forces of nature were somewhat limited and controlled by routine. He reasoned that despite the believed divinity of the sun, it made way for the moon in the evenings. He reasoned that perhaps another force more knowledgeable, more powerful, was behind the routines of nature and the stars.

"This young boy alone came to believe in the Creator and began to abandon the ways of the others around him, and was known as 'New Star.' Elders who remembered the old ways began teaching the boy in secret and told no one that a true believer had been born unto them. While the child continued to grow and strengthen his faith in the Creator, Dark Word elevated himself to the position of a God King.

"The construction of the tower continued and New Star, still an adolescent, was too ordered into labor. Now, New Star took his place alongside his kinsmen and labored on the building of the tower. While doing so, he made it his work to change the hearts and minds of those around him and return them to the worship of the Creator. He was careful at first not to stir trouble, but began by reducing the number of idols that lined the paths of the workers. He would behave as a fool sometimes and clumsily step on or destroy entire rows of statues with his bundles of bricks. He would apologize for his destruction of the clay statutes and claimed that his bundles were too heavy, while he hurried trying to meet his work load.

"Many of the workers stopped setting out new idols in fear that the lumbering boy would crush them and bring a curse upon their work. But New Star saw that this was not enough. He would have to take deliberate action not only against the superstitions of the people, but he would have to change their hearts. In the mornings, he began reciting the words that he was taught by giving thanks to the Creator for his daily provisions. Many of the people at first were afraid but soon nodded in agreement and then later joined in with their voices.

"He saw how the people longed in their hearts to be freed from the tyranny of Dark Word, but had no faith in anything besides clay statues and vague mystical seers. The following day while performing his duties, he took an axe and began smashing the idols of an elder. He smashed them all but left only the largest of them standing.

"The elder cried out, 'No! No! No! Stop! Stop! Stop! What are you doing? What have you done? You have destroyed the idols of the gods. You will bring harm and suffering upon us all.' New Star replied that he was not to blame. He said that he had come upon the idols quarreling over which was the most profound and deserving of the best offerings. Then the largest idol turned violent and destroyed the others during the dispute. The elder looked at the young man in confusion and disgust and swatted away his claims. He said such a thing was not possible and that the statues could no more verbally argue than they could engage in a fight. By this time, a large circle of people had gathered around them upon hearing the commotion.

"New Star then replied, 'You are absolutely right dear elder. The statues have absolutely no ability and no power.' The elder opened his mouth expecting the young man to again deny the charge but was caught silent by the truth of his words. After the event, New Star led the people together in prayer.

"By then, it had become routine for Dark Word to survey the progress of the tower and he made weekly visits to the work sites. While doing so, he came across a group of twelve young men who had been arrested for refusing to supply bricks. Dark Word stopped his entourage to observe the execution of the rebels. Dark Word called to his captains and asked what had incited the unruliness amongst the workers and ceased the building of the tower. The captain of the guards quickly brought New Star forward and kneeled him before their king.

"Dark Word, expecting a feeble and ignorant slave, questioned New Star kneeling before him. 'What event turns your attention away from the tower of my commission?' New Star rose to his feet boldly saying, 'End idolatry and return to the ways of the Creator, it is your only hope!' Dark Word became incensed at hearing the young man's words. The captain holding the young man grabbed him by the back of the neck and pushed him face down into the mud. Dark Word rose to his feet and pointed with scepter in hand, but stayed the boy's conviction of death saying, 'Bring him!'

"Dark Word's entourage returned to his palace and the twelve were sent to the great palace hall. The twelve were charged as enemies of the state and accused of treason against humanity. A trial was set for the twelve and it was stated that New Star would testify to their slander and rebellion. That night, the young men could not sleep as they awaited their fate. They questioned their faith and knew not if they could withstand punishment or torture set to break their will. The following morning, the twelve were brought out into the great hall and New Star was called forth to testify on their behalf.

"New Star began by saying that he and his companions had committed no crime and that the King was guilty of sin against the Creator. New Star continued and said that it was the Creator who gave life and death. Dark Word replied, that men live by the will of other men and that there was no greater word of life or death than by his command. He then beckoned for two prisoners and had them brought forth. Dark Word then pardoned one of the two prisoners thus sparing his life and then ordered the death of the other.

"Dark Word then said, 'It appears it is my word which giveth and taketh away!' New Star stood firm even after observing the execution in front of him and retorted, 'It is the Creator that summons the sun up in the morning from the east and sends it away in the night.' He followed by challenging Dark Word. 'If ye be so mighty, let the King bring up the sun from the West.'

"Dark Word now confounded by the challenge, laughed saying, 'It is not even noon, and by doing so I would have to end the day early and all of the day's work would go unfinished!' The guards then took hold of the young man and brought him closer to Dark Word. He then said, 'The fire is man's greatest technology, it is what separates us from the beasts. To worship it, is to worship the greatness of mankind, now submit!'

"But the fire is not master. Should I worship the water that hushes the flame?" New Star replied.

"Then worship the water, for water is the life source of all," Dark Word rebutted.

"But the water is not master, shall I worship the cloud that distributes the rain?" New Star retorted.

"Then worship the cloud, for it is high in the sky and it is the veil of the heavens," Dark Word rebutted again.

"Oh King, let us not forget the wind that separates and upsets the clouds."

Dark Word reiterated, 'Then worship the four winds, for they are intense and blow from the lowest valleys to the highest mountains.''

"It appears our debate has brought us full circle. If I were to pray to the wind, I might as well worship any man who stands up against the mightiest storm!" New Star said defiantly, from his knees now laughing.

"New Star remained on his knees still in the grasp of the guards. Dark Word now angered at the boy's wit and continued defiance stood from his throne. 'A sharp mind and keen tongue you have there boy, but this contest of words is endless. Such trivia is meant for women and I am not one to suffer an impudent tongue. I am King and ruler of all the land, mightiest of hunters, and he who commands with a dark word! I bow to no one but the fire of our own creation! And on the morrow, I shall sacrifice you to it and allow the flame to feast upon your heathen flesh before the people of the city!'

"Before New Star was taken away he said, 'It is not you who commands the fire to burn, but only by the will of the Creator shall it take me. 'An evil man seeketh only rebellion, therefore a cruel messenger shall be sent against him.'

"Word spread quickly throughout the city of the execution planned for the following day. Dark Word had declared a holiday for the event would mark the continued honor and strength of man over the Creator. That night in the dungeon, the twelve were silent and weary for tomorrow their fates would be decided. New Star was silent and only his tears comforted him as he cried himself to sleep. He had no foresight as to what was ahead of him, if his pride had condemned them or if his faith would eventually save them.

"The dungeon was in the belly of the palace and easily accessible to one of my sort. Seeing the young man at peace in his sleep, I thought how Dark Word had maneuvered him into a position he could not escape. But the boy was right, and Dark Word was wrong. Even though the boy had successfully argued in favor of the Creator and showed no trace of cowardice, he would be killed and evil and ignorance would triumph.

"Intervention was not my plan nor my way, nor did I feel any remorse for the boy as he was only a slave and the life of a slave laboring was meaningless. Saving his life would only condemn him to a life sentence in the dungeon or cause suffering of those closest to him in reprisal. No, better not to get involved, I said. It was then that I could feel the aching of ghostly limbs mocking me as a reminder of my past actions. However, more than seeing the boy live, I would enjoy seeing the arrogance of Dark Word crushed before him… So I spit on him!"

"You what!?" the man interrupted the serpent with disgusting shock.

"I spit on him!" the serpent repeated sternly, looking back at the man.

"Wait! Wait! Wait! Wait! Wait! Wait! You just said he was lying there about to die… then you spit on him… like he's a piece of garbage?" the man argued, gesturing with his hands pointing towards the ground at the lowered position of trash.

"At no point did I say he was a piece of garbage! I said, I was thinking whether or not to intervene and then I spit on him. Right before you cut me off, I was about to say that I had a thought."

"Which was what?" asked the man now standing with his arms folded, awaiting an explanation.

"I thought about my saliva and how it protects my mouth from the fire I spew... want to see?" the serpent pulled back and widened his eyes as if making ready to pounce and spew fire on the man.

"Whoa! I'm sorry, I'm sorry, I'm sorry, I didn't mean that... I got it! That's fine!" the man apologized quickly waving his left hand away at his misunderstanding.

"May I continue now?" the serpent asked, raising an eyebrow and peering back at the man with disapproval.

"That's fine! Yes! Please! Continue!"

"Why thank you, Man of the Present!" the serpent remarked graciously with a toothy smile.

"So... I spit on him! Seeing as how my saliva is proof against fire. The fires would not singe a single hair on the boy's body. And then I'd get to see the stupid look on that bastard's face come morning! Ha! Ha! Ha! Ha! Ha! Ha! Ha!

"Then, as silently as I crept in, I exited in the same fashion, leaving none aware of my serpent presence. I imagine the young men awoke in the morning trying to summon the courage to support their friend and retain their faith in a silent Creator. All of the city was out and awaiting the execution of the rebels in grand fashion. I attest, there are many ways to execute a man, but being burned alive is truly a horrible sentence.

"I expected more of a spectacle from Dark Word in charging the twelve with treason and inciting rebellion. The twelve were brought out and New Star was pulled out from the group. His charges were read to the seething crowd and his sentence was then carried out. Dark Word said to New Star before ordering him thrown into the furnace, 'Let the Creator put out the flames if he wishes to save you!' New Star swallowed heavily reciting,

'My defense is the Creator, which saveth the upright in heart. He judgeth the righteous, and he is angry with the wicked every day.'

"Dark Word then pointed towards a large furnace used for firing bricks. The fires inside the furnace burned low but slaves quickly doused the flames with fuel and timber to increase the blaze. Within moments, the fire began leaping out of the furnace as they continued to feed the fire. The guards took hold of New Star and lifted him up off the ground. He struggled but found no leverage to free himself from the strong-armed guards. Dark Word turned to the remaining eleven young men saying, 'Now witness the fate of your captain and watch how the Creator lets his devotees perish in the flames!'

"And with one heave, New Star was thrown into the heated furnace. With his hands tied behind his back, he flew through the air like a fish sold at an open air market. The crowd cheered and Dark Word saluted the guards and then again saluted the masses who looked on in aww. They began to laugh and cheer at the might of their King who again had triumphed over the insolence of the Creator. Trumpets sounded and drummers beat the anthem of the kingdom. Dark Word motioned with his hands to calm and quiet the crowd, saying, 'Let his screams cry up to the heavens to warn the Creator that men fear nothing, and that his end is close at hand!'

"The crowd roared and cheered at the words of their King. He continued motioning to the crowd until a hush fell over them and then there was silence. Dark Word raised a hand to his ear followed by a fiendish smile… but nothing, he heard absolutely nothing. He frowned in confusion and walked towards the furnace to investigate, the crowd now completely silent around him. He walked up close to the furnace and the guards too turned wondering why no screams could be heard. I could see the look of puzzlement over taking his mind. Was the boy unconscious from fright, or perhaps he was weaker than he expected and had perished instantly. Nonetheless, there was not a whisper, not one sound coming out from the furnace.

"Dark Word's eyes grew large as he approached the oven looking inside of it. His face became flushed and pale as if he had fallen through the ice in a winter pond. The boy was alive and resting quite comfortably inside the blaze. His clothes and his entire person were untouched by the kicking flames and only the ropes that bound him were burnt, which allowed him to smile and wave to the on lookers outside as he said, 'A fool's lips enter into contention, and his mouth calleth for strokes. A fool's mouth is his destruction and his lips are the snare of his soul. The words of a talebearer are as wounds and they go down into the innermost parts of the belly. He also that is slothful in his work is brother to him that is a great waster. The name of the Creator is a strong tower, the righteous runneth into it, and are safe.'

"The entire crowd gasped at the obtuseness of the situation. Confusion and fear came over the people and then they began to scream in terror. 'The Creator has saved him! The Creator will avenge upon us, we must flee!' The people fell into a panic at seeing the boy inside of the furnace alive and well. Dark Word was frozen in disbelief and fled from the scene in anger. New Star remained in the furnace for three days in total before being set free. Dark Word said upon his release, 'Go... and never return to this land. Truly, the Creator protects you, but I will not cease until I am rid of him!'

"The eleven others were freed as well and they were sent out well supplied with livestock, slaves, gold, and even Dark Word's personal assistant, who later became New Star's majordomo. As I watched New Star walk out of the lands, I laughed heavily at the sight, the Mighty Hunter, the Darkest of Words beaten and publicly shamed by a mere boy! Aha! Ha! Ha! Ha! Ha! Ha! Ha! I knew not what was to come of New Star nor where those who followed him would reside. Little did I know that this event would prove to be a crucial turning point, which effectively set the stage for what was yet to come.

"Afterward, Dark Word became even more convinced in his plan to breech the gates of heaven and wage war with the Creator. He said that the Creator had made a fool of him and now he would stop at nothing to be avenged of him. By then, the tower was nearly complete and after the spectacle of the furnace, Dark Word could wait no longer as the mood of the people began turning against him. At the end of the week, he held a ceremony to name the great tower. Dark Word said that the tower was the final road to be traveled to ensure that man would be his own master. So the tower was named 'The Gate of God.'

"At the sight of seeing his people behind him, Dark Word seized the moment and summoned his great Army of Secession together. The years of intense training and preparation had made the soldiers beast-like and less like ordinary men. Companies and battalions were numbered as they assembled armored with heavy horse, swords, and arrows. All were ready; for now the armies of men would make war in the heavens and destroy the Creator. Dark Word gave the command and they began marching and ascending the tower up into the sky.

"I watched as Dark Word led his army with sword in hand shrouded with the Cloak of Ancestors and his team of dogs at his side. The beating of drums sounded their ascent, it felt as if with every step they drew closer to madness as their earthly world shrunk behind them. Hours of marching and the tremble of the enormous army shook the pillars of the Gate of God. Then, without advance warning, the voice of the Creator became visible overlooking the tower. The voice of the Creator said nothing, but Dark Word commanded his army forward as they knew not what they witnessed.

"The voice of the Creator was surrounded by a gathering of clouds that seemed calm and not interested in any storm. The voice of the Creator paused for a moment to observe them and appeared to rethink their destruction. And then, there was a heavy thundering that approached like a sonic boom. It was far away and swept over the land, leaving just as quickly as it came. Dark Word raised his hand over his head expecting rain and lighting from above, but there was none. The skies were clear and the voice of the Creator had disappeared. Dark Word and his armies paused momentarily but saw and felt nothing, then Dark Word raised his sword and commanded his army forward. He moved forward up the tower but within a few paces he turned and saw that his army remained in its place. He turned toward them shouting in command, but they all stood silent looking at him in confusion. I followed the spiral staircase with my serpent eyes down the tower and over the city to the rest of the people who also stood silently almost frozen in a state of shell shock.

"The people of the city looked at each other in misunderstanding as if no one knew their own name. But slowly, then suddenly, they were all strangers to each other and knew not where they were or why they were there. Dark Word saw his people down below stumbling around in confusion, so he called out to address them. He spoke with confidence and recited a great speech, pointing to his mighty army behind him. Victory was upon them he said but when he spoke, nonsense and garble greeted the ears of the people.

"Terror struck the crowd and they began screaming as no one could understand each other. Neighbors were instantly strangers, mothers screamed insanely, calling to their children, and all of mankind was confounded and babbled as babies do. The Army of Secession broke from their ranks and began to flee from the tower, some were pushed off and fell to their deaths in the panic. People began looting and rioting in the streets as no one could comprehend a single word from each other. Women pelted their children with stones as their cries were frightening and misunderstood. Those who cried out for help were mistaken for assailants and bandits and were beaten to death in the streets. Women screamed out for fear of being raped at the calls from their husbands who tried to take them.

"It was utter madness and insanity, I would not have imagined such an outcome, which ultimately would be the end of Dark Word's army. The people who had built such a monument of dissent and rebellion against the Creator, had been so easily scattered and defeated by a tongue of nonsense. The great tower which would communicate the greatness of mankind was the cause of man's now confounded language.

"Why did God do that?" the man asked, while seated, stroking the hairs on his chin.

"What do you mean… why?" the serpent further posed.

"Well, I mean, why not just destroy them, or why not inflict them with a plague or something? They were evil! I don't understand how creating multiple languages solves anything?"

"Hmm… I understand your inquiry, but please elaborate a bit more?" the serpent lowered his head inquiring of the man.

"Sure. So God confused and split the people apart because they were arrogant and thought they were superior. I get it, but wouldn't creating all those languages just upset the people more?" he asked, motioning with one hand.

"So you think the Creator should have just killed them instead?" lifting an eyebrow the serpent rebutted.

"Well, yes, but no! I mean, why not just kill the King? I mean it was he who turned the people against God. So why not just punish him and let the people go back to their lives. What purpose does changing their language do? I mean, eventually the people would learn the other languages and then wouldn't they just have another reason to hate God and start building the tower all over again?"

"I understand your inquiry, Man of the present… however, consider this. Perhaps it wasn't a cure-all, perhaps the Creator was doing you all a favor… a solid if you will," the serpent countered with an optimistic expression.

"What! How is dividing people and creating multiple languages in any way a good thing?" the man asked, argumentatively.

"As I said before, I offer these events to you only as I witnessed them. I am no judge of man's actions, nor am I any perpetrator trying to lead him astray. But what puzzles me about mankind is why he fails to see the fault of his own actions. Everything that happens to you people is always someone else's fault. God's wrath, or the devil in disguise, when all along it was man himself. I have seen the Creator's will firsthand and know that it is far-reaching and full of intent and meaning.

"The events that occurred on that day were unlike anything I had seen before. The voice of the Creator rolled in and stood out over the tower then, instantly, a single clap of thunder, and all in the city were silent. There was no cowering, no death or destruction, no storms, no external action that I perceived taken against humanity."

"So you're saying that God didn't punish them?" the man asked still standing, with his arms crossed now starring judgingly back at the serpent.

"It appeared that the Creator was going to do something, then didn't. Now, just because I didn't see anything physical occur doesn't mean nothing happened. Obviously, after the voice of the Creator disappeared, mankind's language was confounded, therefore something did happen. I have a couple of theories I'd like to offer if you don't mind." The man stepped back a few feet leaning against the cavern walls listening.

"What I think happened in that moment was not a curse but a realization that struck humanity all at once. Instead of cursing or destroying mankind, the Creator allowed man to see himself as he truly was."

"Which was what?" he asked grudgingly.

"Let's take a step back, for a moment. Mankind was united and moving in one direction, even if it was, in the wrong direction. Mankind had found a confidence in his ability and moved towards a common goal. If you're saying that there was ever a possibility that Dark Word could ever breach the gates of heaven, you are utterly lost and delusional. And as you said, if the Creator was angered at the descent of man into idolatry, then what good would splitting their languages do? It would do nothing but slow the process and only upset the people further. But there is something more there. They had built up very high from where they were, but I think that somewhere along the way... they lost something."

"What got lost?" the man inquired changing his attitude and retaking a seat.

"Just follow me on this! At the time of the tower events, mankind was united, building and achieving new technologies never before seen. But in the process, he became obsessed with his own superiority. As I said before, a tower is a symbol of communication and on that tower a united mankind transitioned from a single language to many. However, my observation was that humanity came to a realization that they had lost something. But I think there, on that symbol of communication, lies the key to this mystery.

"For all the achievements that humanity had made, ultimately something was missing. The people of the city were so consumed with work, success, and war that they had forgotten something as basic as how to communicate with each other. I ask you, what is language? Language is how you communicate, but more importantly language is your identity. Language gives you the power to communicate your thoughts and share your dreams. Yet, without it, you are a stranger, a foreigner, an outcast. Communication was what they lost, language was what they lost, but more importantly, their identity was what they lost.

"If you were to trace each spoken language back to its root form, you still would not return to one single human language. However, this tale clearly depicts a time when all of mankind spoke one language. So how can it be that the tale explains the creation of multiple languages, yet fails to actually state what the original language was? Quite simply, I do not believe that is what the event was trying to tell you. I feel that these events and the tale itself is more of a metaphor, like symbols and codes that have been looked over too hastily.

"How so?" asked the man, resting his chin on his fist.

"Let me put it to you this way, if a message is presented to you but you read it the wrong way, then you may completely miss the information being transmitted. For instance, have you heard the one about Liam Su?"

"Who the hell is Liam Su?" he remarked with inquiry.

"No one, but I was wondering if you knew what time the Post Office closes?"

"Huh! What does a guy named Liam Su have to do with the Post Office?" he asked shaking his head in confusion.

"Nothing, except Liam Su is 'US Mail,' spelled backwards. My point being, if you are not looking at the information correctly, you will miss the meaning completely. I believe we should look at this tale of events in another way, which could possibly increase our insight into the meaning of it all. That is, of course, if you are willing," the serpent said with an offering tone.

"That's interesting, but I'm not sure what else you think is there. I mean the people were evil and God punished them. That's it!" he said, dismissing the serpent's analysis.

"Your shallow insight is disappointing, Man of the Present. But I can assure you that my inquiry is not meant to change the outcome of the events nor cast doubt on your belief system. My investigation is based purely on my instinct which leads me to seek out deeper meaning and truth in all things. If you will allow it, I think it could reveal some interesting concepts." The man sat listening but did not rebut any further.

"Now, I believe the overall theme of the tale is speaking about the relationship between communication, language, identity, and man's societal progression. As man became more technologically progressive, he reached a point where he could not communicate with another thus changing the identities of humanity. The origins of human language have been debated by many theorists. Some of those theories argue that language is so complex that it could not have appeared on its own out from nothing.

"Most researchers find it relative that language was invented only once and that all modern languages are in some way related. However, due to the limitations of reconstruction, those origins can no longer be determined. I do agree that all of humanity does share a common relationship when it comes to language, but that relationship is not based in grammar or semantics.

"See, language is the capacity by which humanity acquires and utilizes complex systems of communication. At that time in your history, there was only one language and after the events on the tower, there were hundreds. Presently, there are thousands of languages depending on dialect distinction. What I find interesting is that humans have the ability to communicate by either auditory, visual, or tactile stimuli; such as writing, graphic pictures, or by whistling and shouting. This is because human language is not restricted to being either spoken or signed, as human language is modality-independent.

"Human language, as a concept, is the ability to cognitively learn and or use complex systems to communicate. All human languages rely on a set of rules called semiosis, which is the process of assigning signification in language or literature, which gives meaning to a word or phrase. Additionally, the word language and its synonyms are "tongue" or "mother tongue." When applied to the events on the tower, the result is that their languages were changed, or their "mother tongue" was changed. You then have to ask... what was their mother tongue?

"The Creator could have easily destroyed the tower, or turned the whole lot of marching idiots into a pack of possums for that matter, but why change their language? What is the meaning in that action?

"Humans are selectively different from other animals and creatures, and language is one of those major differences. Human language is unique when compared to the finite communication used by, say, insects or fish who can only communicate a set number of expressions or actions. Whereas you humans can communicate an almost infinite set of complex ideas, emotions, thoughts, feelings, in either past, present, or future tense. This is due to the use of grammatical and semantical categories. Allow me to expand a bit," the serpent uncoiled some, stretching out more of his massive frame.

"Now, the concept of linguistics refers to what is being expressed, to then be understood from the context. In this case, we are asking, what is the meaning of separating mankind by the way of many languages? Again, we are looking at the tower events through the scope of linguistics and semantics due to the overall theme of communication to gain a deeper understanding. Now, when we look at the events of the tower as a message from the Creator, we will use semantics. Why? Because semantics is the study of how meaning is conveyed through signs and language. So let's look at the semantics or significance of the events surrounding the tower and the meaning of creating multiple languages. However, I do not wish to convolute the meaning of my argument as doing so would lead us out of semantics and into the exploration of context, which of course is the interpretation of signs, known as pragmatics!' the man blinked rapidly shaking his head, attempting to keep up with the serpent.

"Now, all humans acquire their language through social interaction usually from early childhood where many children are fluent speakers approximately by age three. Because your language is so entrenched in your societal culture, it ends up not only being used as a tool, but also comes to identify you as part of a social group. Whereas, the very language you speak, or how you speak it, defines your position and place in society.

"Additionally, depending on that language or dialect it can come to control or imprison you there, just by the way you speak. Meaning your language... is now your identity. I believe that all of you start out somewhat the same. From my observations, all of humanity speaks one language at the time of birth, the same language. That language is not comprised of any signals or gestures, nor vowels or phrases. The language is only that you are alone, cold, and hungry. And the cries that escape you beg for a mother to hold you, for a father to secure you. That language is the basic needs of all humanity and that language connects you and, sadly, it is that natural language that is taken from you.

"As you grow, you are taught another language, which unfortunately, separates you from each other. Your new language tells you who your friend is, but also who your enemies are, just by the language they speak. What would you call this natural language for babies... do you not say that they... babble? And was it not upon the tower that they spoke as babies do... in confusion... babbling?

"I believe humanity was allowed to retain the ability of spoken language forms, but their language was taken back to that infantile state. Where meanings are lost and only fear, hunger, and basic human needs can be expressed in a series of panicked cries. A shared, infantile state where mankind can only express his basic needs.

"Something that all mankind understands, something that is universally true to all of you. And what is it that they say is the universal language? Why love of course. Love is the universal language, love is your shared language. Love... is your mother tongue!" the man's eyes widened in expression as the serpent identified the shared language of humanity.

"From birth, love is the only thing you know, it is the most basic human emotion that is replaced after being taught to hate. Without love, you will not recognize each other, you will see each other as foreign and alien. Without love, man divides himself into paltry groups and draws lines against his brother in the sand. When all along, they have been, and remain, your brother and neighbor.

"The events on that day were not caused by vengeance, but by a Creator who allowed man a moment of realization. For all he had accomplished, for all he had built, he had forgotten love, he had forgotten how to communicate, he had forgotten his own identity, and, all at once, he became a stranger to himself.

"Love as defined is a complex variety of feelings, emotions, and states of being that can represent affection, virtue, kindness, closeness, or deep understanding. Strangely enough though, everyone seems to have a different meaning of the word, but it seems to encompass a deep concern for the wellbeing of another. Because everyone has such a different meaning of the word and how it is employed in their relationships, it makes the concept of love difficult to define.

"There are many different theories that attempt to explain the nature and function of said concept. Of the theories that account for the meaning of love, most consider love a healthy and natural behavior as part of evolution. There is also a spiritual theory, which states that love is a gift from the Creator and like many gifts, they are often taken for granted until they are lost. More important than its language definition of love, is its function. When investigating the origins or meaning of a subject, I find it useful to ask what its purpose is.

"Is it a catalyst to a physical act or perhaps a survival instinct embedded within all of humanity? I think we can conclude that love, as a concept, is a force pulling humanity together against external forces facilitating the continuation of the species. How or why you may ask? Well love conceptually helps humanity identify with a person or thing. Just as people love their favorite food. The person does not identify with the nutritional value of a sandwich, but they have a connection with how that food makes them feel.

"But more importantly, love is often referred to as the universal language that overrides cultural and linguistic divisions. I understand that the events on the tower have traditionally been used to explain how mankind came to have multiple languages, but has anyone ever thought that perhaps it describes man's original language? Maybe take a step back and look at the scenario from a different perspective.

"Some would say love is reserved for those closest to you or those who share the same religious values, cultural beliefs, or patriotism. While others have argued, love should be applied equally to all people and things of life. The Chinese philosopher Mozi introduced a concept of 'universal love' where he believed love should be unconditional and offered to everyone without regard to reciprocation and not limited to friends and family. Others, as well, have viewed love as a concept and one that is inherent to all of humanity and which should be shared in the same way.

"The Persian philosopher Sa'di wrote: 'The children of Adam are limbs of one body. Having been created of one essence. When the calamity of time afflicts one limb, the other limbs cannot remain at rest. If you have no sympathy for the troubles of others, you are not worthy to be called by the name of man.'

"Furthermore, there is an eastern belief system often referred to as the religion of love, where the concept is that through love humanity can get back to its inherent purity and grace. Lastly, when we speak of humanity's language being confounded and split, we can compare this to a Hindu belief system where, 'In the condition of separation, there is an acute yearning for being with the beloved and in the condition of union there is supreme happiness.'

"Is it not that humanity is trying to once again unite, but cannot seem to do so. Man's original language was the universal language which he is trying to get back to. All he must do is realize what he forgot and he, again, will be united just as the limbs of his body.

"Think about the meaning in that for a moment if you would, Man of the Present. That the Creator wanted civilized and developed mankind to return to that infantile state to remind him of where he had come from and what he had forgotten. That infantile state where nothing else mattered but a caressing and swaddling hold of love. And afterwards, humanity was separated now alien and foreign to each other. Perhaps the Creator wanted mankind to pause for a moment and remember his true language, that mankind had built so high, but without the capacity to communicate those basic human needs of love. All the best laid plans of men were worthless and meaningless.

"I'll ask the question, as how exactly do people learn their first language? I dislike using the term "normal children" as very few of you can be considered normal. What exactly is a normal child? Differentiating between those of your young who make a mess, chew with their mouths open, or endlessly poop themselves, I find laughable. As opposed to other children who cannot sit still, do not readily rise and sleep at regulated cycles, or are outfitted with a leash. And then again, the never ending noise. Yet, somehow, you find ways of labeling groups of your young... normal. In comparison, all of my kind are normal and self-sufficient from hatchlings and do not require an 18 year period of incubation, after which they still might default back into a larvae stage back at home.

"But for arguments sake... a number of human children do undergo language acquisition in the first years of their lives. Children learn language from those who use it around them, the same is applicable for both oral and sign languages. Interesting enough, is that this first language acquisition requires no formal training or regimented curriculum. You all just eventually catch on... like a monkey rewarded with a treat," the serpent said with a cynical tone.

"I believe it was your Darwin who even called the process 'The Descent of Man,' where you all have 'an instinctive tendency to acquire an art.' From my observations of your species, it appears that human babies respond and are more stimulated by human speech than other sounds. Your researchers have noted that around one month of age, babies begin showing signs of differentiating speech sounds. And it is around six months of age at which human babies begin producing their own speech sounds also known as…babbling. Now, again, you may find all of this just a coincidence or just me arguing semantics over nonsensical folklore which attempts to describe the origins of human language."

"It's just a bit of a stretch though. I mean it doesn't say it was a good thing. Couldn't God have just sent a vision or something to the people as a guide? And you can see that people speak even more languages today. So either people are not getting the message or that's not what it really means," the man rebutted.

"That's not what it means? That humanity is capable of growing and building great things, but if you forget something as basic as how to communicate with love, you will be spread about the earth treating each other as enemies… that's not what it means!" the serpent argued back at the man.

"It is an interesting concept. Not a curse on humanity, but a self-realization. It's interesting… I'll give you that! "

"Allow me to continue. Now, let's try to see the reason behind that realization, the meaning behind the symbols. I just explained how the language you speak comes to be your identity, but how does the action of changing human language help any of you people?

"The Creator had endowed man with the ability to dream and to imagine, but more importantly, with the ability to bring those dreams into reality. The building of the tower marked a new point of man's hopes. Where he imagined reaching higher than any mountain top, he imagined owning the skies and walking upon the stars. This new version of man had forgotten his evil ways during the deluge; he imagined tomorrow, he dreamed future, and wanted forever. It could be said that man had found peace and a sort of perfection in himself. However, very little is learned in a state of perfection. Only through error, defeat, loss, and separation will man come to understand what he can become.

"Mankind must learn to see past his petty differences such as language, culture, politics, and religion. Man must learn to see the truth, that he is not separate, and that there is no division. He is, and always has been, one. Mankind can and will accomplish great things, he will fly through the skies, walk upon the stars, and, eventually, will reach the heavens. All he must do is acknowledge the truth.

"However, of all the achievements I found that the greatest accomplishment that was endowed to the new generations of man, was his interest in the concept of meaning. Rest had seen the destruction of the old world for mankind's lack of care and understanding of the environment around him. From this, Rest taught his children to seek out the meaning in all things. They engaged heavily in this study and passed it on to the generations after them.

"How so?" he questioned the serpent.

"As I stated before, when trying to understand the meaning of symbols, context is everything. And as such, meanings are not complete without an element of context, meaning that the context depends on a person's experiences and many times those stem from learned concepts. In this case, most people have a preconceived notion about the events surrounding the tower and that the events were negative. But when we look at these events differently and assign them a truth value, we can possibly see them differently. Possibly that the division of languages was not a negative, but a positive."

"Not negative, but positive. Hmm...I'll hold off on judgement, but go ahead!" he said leaning back a bit, still listening intently to the serpent.

"All languages change over time as speakers adopt or invent new terms and phrases and the speech community adopts them into the lexicon. Now, this language change happens on every phonological level including vocabulary, morphology, syntax, and discourse. Language change and or loss is usually perceived negatively, as in this case, a divine punishment.

"However, language change is natural and unavoidable due to internal factors such as changes in pronunciation or acceptance of a common dialect. No matter the internal factors, human society, overall, favors change, which results from social classes to new ideologies. As far as the tower events and the monolingualism identity being lost due to divine punishment, I submit this argument.

"The city and its tower could be described as the first society to implement or embody the ideology of an ethno-national state where monolingualism was the defining characteristic. Unfortunately, the tale of the city and the tower ultimately shows how the ideology of one people, one state, and one language will ultimately fail. Even though the idea of monolingualism continues to spread throughout the world. I mentioned evolution before and I submit another comparison. Just as human biology favors diversity, it appears that human linguistics do so as well.

"As we can see, multilingualism has become the norm in modern human civilizations. Even though many try to establish a national language, it is the same philosophy as one people, one state, and one language. Before the rise of the concept of the ethno-national state, monolingualism was a characteristic mainly of populations inhabiting small islands. But with the ideology that made one people, one state, and one language the most desirable political arrangement, monolingualism started to spread throughout the world. One important source of language change is due to contact between different cultures resulting in the diffusion of linguistic traits between them. With some 250 countries in the world corresponding with approximately 6000 languages, most countries are multilingual and exist in close proximity to each other.

"The world's languages and dialects spoken are as diverse as the bloodlines of the people who speak them. They include English, Spanish, Russian, Hindi, and Urdu. The languages spoken in East Asia, including Mandarin, Chinese, Cantonese, and dozens of other off-shoots and variations. Continental Africa is home to families of languages encompassing the Niger-Congo regions including Swahili, Shona, and Yoruba. With still more including the Afro-asiatic languages which include Arabic, Hebrew, and the Saharan region with Berber and Hausa. But why? If the Creator truly cursed and punished mankind on that day... why is it that the multi-language system seems to be working so well? Was it truly a curse?

"Even though multilingualism is generally viewed negatively, the claims that the world would be better off speaking one language are unfounded and nonsensical. Additionally, some further argue that linguistic diversity is at the core of many political conflicts. In examination, we see that many of the world's most violent chapters occurred in areas of low linguistic diversity. If you recall, the reoccurring civil wars, unrests, and genocides seemed to take place amongst those nations who speak the same language, whereas those areas with linguistic diversity appeared to be of the more stable civilizations.

"I have said it before, that the Creator's will is far reaching and with much intent, often more than we can understand at the time. Perhaps the events that occurred on the tower were not a punishment, but perhaps the Creator saw mankind building towards his own end. It appears that for all your advances in civilization, philosophies, and technologies, you are destined to turn on yourselves. You forget to speak with love. Until you all remember and again speak your mother tongue... it might be better that we keep some distance between you.

"Now you may disagree with my explanation of the events, but you cannot dispute the glaring symbolism and overall theme in the tale itself. But what does this have to do with people having multiple languages and societal identity, you ask? This diversification of language could be considered a process of evolution known as descent where modification leads to a new phylogenetic tree or, in this case, new languages and new meanings. Meaning... you broke the rules and an example had to be made of you!

"The Creator could have destroyed you, but decided to teach you something about yourselves. Perhaps you don't believe that man's confounded language was due to any divine punishment? That perhaps all of the people were not confused and speaking in different tongues, maybe it was just one person. Maybe it was Dark Word alone who had developed a sudden case of insanity. There were tales of him being overcome by gnats in his brain and driving him mad. Perhaps it was Dark Word alone who was unable to comprehend normal speech and thus cried out his kingdom was babbling in madness."

"It is an interesting point you make. Maybe it wasn't everyone going crazy, just the King. I can see that love is considered the universal language, but is that going to solve all of the world's problems if everyone just says nice things to each other?" he added, with his arms crossed over his chest in half disagreement.

"That's not my point at all! My point was that you people choose to see only what's on top. But you have not considered any other possibilities or meanings of the events. It doesn't really matter to me either way, I merely wished to convey my observations of the events of the tower and offer an alternative point of view. It's sad that so many of you agree without ever really questioning or investigating for yourselves.

"Was it simple revenge from the Creator for man's disobedience? Was the Creator threatened by a mortal army climbing a wobbly tower? I think not! I think the tale of the tower was intended to tell humanity so much more. I think the Creator wanted humanity to take a moment and consider how they climbed so high in the first place. It was together! It was united!

"But when you lose such a simple thing as the ability to communicate with one another, you might as well be frightened, naked, little children, screaming and running about in confusion. When all man must do is remember that his brothers and sisters are limbs on the same body and then humanity will again be united."

"That's not what I expected you to say at all! But didn't the whole thing collapse or something?"

"Actually no, even with all of the confusion, it was never dismantled. People were more concerned with just trying to start over and find a place where they belonged again," the serpent continued.

"And instantly they were foreigners in their own land, causing most to leave, while others shut themselves in their own homes afraid and unwilling to communicate with those around them. Many of those who left the kingdom embarked on a massive migration westward and settled in modern day Europe and eastward towards China.

"They crossed through dangerous, unknown frontiers traveling over 4,000 miles. Over five to six generations of migrations which helped to spread the art of metal working technology and horse breeding and riding. The languages that inflicted them now became the roots of present day genetic groups and nationalities.

"Once, what was a great towering milestone in the legacy of humanity had now become a cold and meaningless thing. There were a series of earthquakes and lightning storms that damaged the towering Gate of God and the top caught on fire and became uninhabitable. The structure was so massive and heavy that the earth beneath it sank into the ground and much of its base was swallowed by massive sink holes. The body of the tower remained intact and above ground, but now forever silent was the great symbol of human communication.

"I sat one evening looking at the lifeless thing, with its head cocked and crumbling into ashes, its feet buried beneath the dust. Perhaps, the path which man walked was wrong and he marched towards his own disunion. Forty something years of human labor, engineering, and construction, reduced to a tomb, silent as the grave. Many have attempted to rebuild the horrible thing but only succeeded in destroying it further. Even the great Macedonian conqueror of the known world attempted to move the bricks and tiles to another location with hopes to rebuild a palace for himself, but the venture was later abandoned upon his death.

"It was approximately ten years after the abandonment of the tower project and the kingdom of Dark Word was all but a shell of its former self. The cities were abandoned and he was without subjects or worldly pursuits. His advisors and generals had left and some had founded cities and realms of their own.

"Dark Word was then accompanied only by his grief and shame. Unfortunately, he remained stubborn and full of contempt against the Creator. He again continued his wicked ways and planned another assault on the Creator. This time, he planned to fly directly up to the heavens and challenge the Creator to a duel and end the Creators reign once and for all. He devised the most ridiculous method, which involved harnessing four mighty scavengers to a large crate to carry him up to the heavens.

"Upon seeing the silly box, I was surprised that he got that high up off the ground before the straps broke loose. Two of the great birds flew away while the other two, still harnessed to the crate, fell and crashed down in the fields. Surprisingly, Dark Word survived the incident with only minor injuries. The following months saw him fall further into madness and he was often seen wandering in the night, completely naked, with a pot of wine and his sword drawn cursing the night sky.

"The remaining years of his life, he lived almost completely in poverty and struggled to hold on to his sanity. But such a man was not destined to die quietly, and only a death of great notoriety was suitable to the life that he lived. And in such a time, there came a young hunter of great skill. They sung of his valor so that it even surpassed that of Dark Word as a Mighty Hunter in his prime. Upon hearing such rumors, Dark Word mounted his horse and went out in search of the young hunter, whose presence cast a shadow on his reputation and standing.

"If only momentarily, Dark Word once again found joy in hunting and went out with his team of dogs to make trophies of beasts. While out on the hunt, he encountered the rumored young hunter who was known as 'The Red' as he was hairy and its color was fire red. Each day Dark Word killed and trapped beasts and compared his trophies to The Red, but his kills were timid compared to the trophies of The Red. Dark Word having known no equal in the sport of his making, became filled with envy and vowed to end the dispute with a tournament between the two. He challenged The Red to a hunt to end any comparison once and for all.

"He said that he had hunted all manner of beasts and his exploits could not be matched if The Red lived 500 years. The Red, being brave and confident, acknowledged Dark Word's reputation and agreed his legacy was unmatched, but questioned how one animal kill could prove such a thing. Dark Word proposed that the two would hunt each other and the victor would return with the head of the fallen as a trophy of their might. Some whispered to The Red not to engage in such a match as it was against the will of the Creator.

Upon hearing the name of the Creator, Dark Word spit and cursed and said, 'All those who worship the Creator are fools and after I kill The Red, I shall mount his head on a pike for all to see!' The Red, being threatened in such a manner, could not refuse the challenge or he would suffer never ending shame and be forced to flee the lands as a coward. The Red replied to Dark Word, 'I pray the Creator grant me strength and cunning against such a tyrant and brazen idolater as you!'

"The following day, Dark Word and The Red, each accompanied by two men, ventured out in the forests to begin the hunt upon sunrise. Dark Word was dressed in the Cloak of Ancestors and was assured victory in his heart. Each team of men was to track the other party and take each one as a trophy ending with the victor emerging as the mightiest hunter. Dark Word and his men were deep in the wilderness past where few would journey.

"I watched the two parties of men as I was unsure who would emerge victorious. The first to strike was The Red and his men and they easily dispatched Dark Word's two men but lost him in the thicket. It appeared they had underestimated Dark Word who was as keen as he was evil and left many false trails behind him. Dark Word set traps and snared The Red's companions one by one and silenced them without making his presence known. The Red, seeing himself alone, knew that it was he and Dark Word and a victor would soon be decided.

"Hiding like a lion waiting to pounce, Dark Word spotted The Red near the river's edge and sensed his victory was assured. Dark Word approached the river down below expecting his opponent there, but found only me. As a matter of fact, he was standing in the exact location where I had encountered him the first time. I raised myself up over his head and he pitched his spear at me, but I dodged the weapon. He drew his sword and dropped his shield and said, 'Be it time now demon? I fear no creature of the earth!' But before he could finish his rally cry, I struck and bit him with lustful delight.

"I repeated not my error and avoided the cloak, and with surgical like precision, my fangs sunk into his flesh and deposited vile nectar. It coursed through his body and quickly thickened his blood into jelly. He lay dying and gasping for air, while I looked on saying, 'Who hath woe? Who hath sorrow? Who hath contentions? Who hath babbling? Who hath wounds without cause? Who hath redness of eyes? They that tarry long at the wine; they that go to seek mixed wine. Look not thou upon the wine when it is red, when it giveth his color in the cup, when it moveth itself aright. At the last it biteth like a Serpent, and stingeth like an Adder.'

"His eyes rolled backwards and his arm fell to the ground. The Shining Light that rose as the morning sun, that gave rise in the day to the Mighty Hunter, and ended in the night with a solemn and Dark Word, was dead and no more.

"Eventually, The Red found his lifeless body and cut off his head as proof of his victory. He left the Cloak of Ancestors not knowing it was of great value. The body of Dark Word was returned to his lands and he was buried with humble honors. Later, I overheard a congregation of angels say that Dark Word finds no rest in eternity and is chained on the outskirts of Hell in the Circle of Treachery.

"It is said that all who cross his path find a mad man weighted down heavily by a regal crown, foaming at the mouth and babbling nonsense. He continuously utters an unintelligible statement, which serves to accuse him as a traitor and idolater against the Creator. Carved into his flesh is that which reads: 'Surely the serpent will bite, without enchantment and a babbler is no better. The words of a wise man's mouth are gracious, but the lips of a fool will swallow himself up. The beginning of the words of his mouth is foolishness, and the end of his talk is mischievous madness. A fool also is full of words, but a man cannot tell what shall be, and what shall be after him, who can tell him? The labor of the foolish wearieth every one of them, because he knoweth not how to go to the city.'

"And as for his legacy, it was said that he fathered many children, and of them was a son who became even more vile and wicked than he. After that, the northern tribes were founded by twin sons who were legendary hunters and their reigns became attested to Dark Word's bloodline.

"As legend tells it, the twin sons journeyed and hunted a magnificent white stag into a forbidden marsh. They lost sight of the animal but found the daughters of the King of Dul, whom they kidnapped and married, later uniting their peoples under one banner. An heir was produced and became King of the north and upon each battle he posted a golden plate on his tent reading: 'Atilla, the son of Bendeuci, Grandson of the Mighty Hunter and Dark Word. Born at Engedi by the Grace of the God King of the Huns, Medes, Goths, Dacians. I am all the horrors of the world and the scourge of God.'

"I know not the purpose of it all sometimes, Man of the Present. The living, the killing, the meaning of words, or the silence of sinners. What causes the separation of man and how he can avoid it, despite his overconfidence and insecurity. However, I challenge you to see beyond your belief systems, and societal norms. Perhaps see the glaring signs and symbols that caused an abrupt return to an infantile state where grown men babbled as babies. Perhaps embedded in your cultural lore is a deeper meaning and perhaps a misinterpreted sign by the Creator. That all of humanity is connected and truly does speak one language. I suppose there is a ladder that man must climb, a tower he must build to reach his full potential. However, separated, he is in competition with himself and only defeat is assured.

"It is unfortunate that man chooses not see each other as himself and only identifies the differences in his brother and sister. As is with all things that are true, this scenario will repeat itself again and again. Man will build and marvel at his achievement, he will divide himself, and he will fail. But through each trial and tribulation, man will build higher, stronger, and eventually will find himself united. All he must do is remember his true language and speak his mother tongue, for to argue it any further is merely... semantics.

CHAPTER 5: THE PROPAGANDA

"As time went on, man learned his new tongue and the multitude of languages became his new identities. However, it appeared that no matter how many languages man spoke, the dialogue remained the same. He cursed his fellow man, mocked his peers, ridiculed the wise, and threatened new scientific ideologies. Humanity continued to show its age and like a young girl approaching her birth rite celebration, humanity was now decorated with copper. There were some who had become eloquent speakers, but in actuality, they were only masters of the lie. I heard beautiful song and listened as lyrics turned from pleasant lullaby to violence and vulgarity. So sad was the song of man, he had come so far, but again had lost his way.

"I put the events of the tower behind me and traveled southwest heading into a valley that stretched out into a large low lying area of plains. The valley was filled with asphalt deposits and slimy tar pits leading further south. To this day, the valley remains home to earth's lowest elevation point and would later lend its nickname "be deep" to a nearby city of ancient ruin. Present day, the valley is occupied by a body of water so toxic no life will grow of it, hence its name, Sea of Death.

"What precisely caused the high salinity of the Dead Sea is debatable. Some theologians believe that a divine act of immolation set upon the region, ignited the tar pits, and heavy rains flooded the area, thus creating the sea."

"What is a divine act of immolation? And what city are you talking about?" the man asked, leaning forward.

"I apologize, Man of the Present, as it is me to blame for your lack of comprehension and not your poor vocabulary," the serpent replied sarcastically.

"However, immolation is quite simply... destruction by fire. And in this case, a destruction many have come to believe was no accident, but a purposeful act by the Creator upon the Cities of the Plains for crimes against nature," the serpent stated, staring directly back at the man.

"Crimes against nature? You mean... homosexuality?" the man, grimaced while uttering the last word.

"Once again, you surprise me with your knowledge, Man of the Present. The word immolation is foreign to you but the term, 'crimes against nature' is uttered and instantly you return with, homosexuality. Now, I'm curious as to why you are so familiar with such terminology. It wouldn't have anything to do with the events that occurred in the region would it? Perhaps you know the tale of which I am referring to?"

"If we're talking about the story that I think we are. It was something like there were two cities and all the people were evil and God destroyed them because they were fags!" he said confidently.

"I'm sorry, they... they were what now?" the serpent questioned, shaking his head in misunderstanding.

"Fags! You know... gay people!" he repeated, shrugging his shoulders with surety.

"Ahhhh yes, I remember now! The queer, the faggot, the fairy, the homo, and the poof! Human language is filled with so many pejorative terms, it remains a difficulty keeping track of them all.

"Yes, I am aware of such a belief which purports to explain the wicked ways of the people that ended the Cities of the Plains, and how they were judged and destroyed by the Creator. I recall the events quite clearly, as I was there! But I can tell you with certainty that no one group of people or any one act of sexual deviancy was solely to blame."

"You can't tell me that that's not why they were destroyed! They were fags, everybody knows so, and that's it!" he said, standing firmly in his understanding.

"It! As in *you* believe *it*! Make note, my dear Man of the Present, believing a thing to be true, does not make it a fact," the serpent, reiterated, looking down at the man.

"So if that's not what happened, then what are you going to say? That they weren't destroyed because they were gay?" the man continued, gesturing with his hands pointing at the serpent in accusation.

"Actually no! That's not what I was going to say. The events did happen and the place was destroyed. There were people there, yes, and I did observe their behavior and it was quite despicable. Again, I am no judge of human behavior, nor do I have any specific interest in defining your actions as good or evil. However, what intrigues me is how these past events have come to affect the journey of humanity. The destruction that fell upon the Cities of the Plains was deliberate and remarkable. Not so much as a trace of their civilization remains to this day, but the story does, and what a legend it has become.

"Situated just to the east of ancient Mesopotamia, settled the grandson of Rest's eldest son. He later founded a proto-civilization built up east of two great rivers along the combining low and highland areas. Following the colonization of the area, three city states merged and formed a powerful nation of his name. The resulting civilization flourished and its success and strength was due in part to their ability to secure their regions under a coalesced governmental system. The implementation of this neo-government permitted an exchange of natural resources between the city states that resulted in a continuous flow of renewable wealth. The plains were often compared to the garden from whence we came, as it was a land well-watered with lush green fields, and highly favorable for agriculture and livestock.

"The reputation of the civilization soon spread over the lands and attracted many would be raiders. However, the cities fastened themselves together, allowing them to withstand numerous invading forces. I located a dwelling of caves that overlooked a grouping of tar pits that provided me shelter and, for a time, I too came to settle in the Valley of the Plains.

"Unfortunately, prosperity was singular to the Valley of the Plains. And the surrounding areas were struck with a harsh famine, triggering an influx of travelers seeking refuge from the shortages. The cities enjoyed much success but only after five years of the famine in the neighboring regions, a revolt began. Five cities refused to pay tribute and revolted against the joint rule of the High King of Elam.

"Each of the five cities were governed and led into battle by lesser kings, while the High King of Elam was joined by three of the remaining loyal city-states. The resulting battles came to be known as The War of Nine Kings. The Valley was the battlefield and the forces of the four northern kings advanced on the southern nations of the five rebel kings. With their greater numbers and heavier artillery, the 'Forces of Four' destroyed the 'Rebellious Five' driving their retreating armies into the tar pits.

"Their deaths unfortunately were not quick, for the tar was not like quicksand. Those who retreated found themselves not sinking in the bubbling mess, but eternally stuck while their pursuers surrounded and fired arrows at them. The fortunate died of arrows in their chests and backs, but a company commander halted their assault saying, 'Come now men, save your ammunition. Bestow time upon these rebels so they may reflect upon their deeds against our High King, let them starve and die of exposure.'

"Those that escaped the tar pits fled into the caves seeking a path through the mountains to safety. Unfortunately, the caves were my domain and they that entered did so unknowingly, leaving fewer to exit than the numbers who came in.

"In the aftermath of the war, two of the larger cities known as 'be deep', and 'fortify' were sacked and raided for their spoils, which also included the taking of captives. However, fate was not on the side of the High King, and his victory was short lived. Word quickly spread to the northern mountain range where an

135

assembling force of 318 strong, awaited to avenge the looted plunder and free the captives of the two cities.

"Already besieged from war, the High King's forces were attacked under cover of night from multiple directions and were easily overwhelmed. The armies fled northeast, but were pursued until all, including the High King, were captured and slain. The High King's great civilization was raided and destroyed for all its amassed goods and wealth. Everything was destroyed from the grand ziggurats, to the tombs of the ancients and left exposed to the sun.

"The destruction and violence brought on by the war was not to my taste so, afterwards, I left the valley for calmer settings. I hoped to live in peace for a while, away from the world of men and, if at all possible, return to country living. How I had missed the quiet voice of nature with its curtains of tall green grass and the glimmering chandelier of the night sky. I admit, that my curiosity of man overtakes me from time to time, but the serenity and good hunting of the countryside was refreshing to my being. I left the cave dwellings and headed north into the mountain range where it was peaceful and free from war.

"The inhabitants of the mountain range were a pious yet humble people and they volunteered no time in the pursuit of wicked and worldly things. Their lives were anything but complicated and they found that overthinking vexes the human soul and without it, happiness could be achieved. However, the villagers were not ignorant and were successful merchants, scribes, tutors, and military men. The upper class occupants were either shipwrights or priests who specialized in either architecture, accounting, or astronomy.

"For the villagers, the evenings were a time of leisure and reflection and the fullness of fresh beer made them joyous throughout the night. Even though a women's status was almost equal to a man's, only young male children attended school, as young girls were not considered capable of literacy and business. They devoted themselves completely to their trades as either farmer, artist, baker, fishermen, merchant, or priest.

TRUTH AND THE SERPENT

"The tribes of the mountain range saw growth and much happiness, and were led by a great man, known as 'High Father.' He was just and kind, humble yet commanded respect wherever he went, and he was favored much by the Creator. For all that he had done and the goodness and friendship he bestowed, he and his wife were granted no children. And then one evening, a familiar rumbling came over the hills and I heard the Creator's voice calling to High Father. I looked up but saw not the voice of the Creator, but three men approaching the elder's tent. I had never seen these men before. They approached the camps without invitation but were greeted not as strangers. They had traveled a great distance but their clothing did not show the excess of wear and travel.

"The elder greeted and invited them to eat and refresh themselves as his guests. Now, what was said amongst them was not for me, so I could not hear what was discussed. However, I did hear the elder raise his voice and ask for mercy, begging for forgiveness. He rose to his feet and lifted his hands as if in prayer then lowered himself in prostrate to his knees. Repeatedly, he asked for mercy from the Creator and asked not to destroy the righteous with the wicked, if only but a few. When I heard the elder speak of destruction, a familiar fright came crawling up my spine. I had seen the Creator's will destroy before, so I knew the time would come to leave the area but I knew not how soon.

"Before the men had completed their meal, two of them disembarked and began heading south. I watched as the elder then moved to gratitude and bid farewell to the remaining man and thanked him for the visit. The following day, I expected to see the elder begin some monumental undertaking. Yet, strangely, the elder raised no alarm; he merely sat with his people and continued his daily activities as he did before. Intelligent as I may be, the understanding of this meeting did not become clear to me for some hours. I circled the camps and moved throughout the mountain range, but saw no corruption or evil amongst the people. The elder had been met by the presence of the Creator, and instinctively, I knew destruction was sure to follow.

"Then I rationalized, that perhaps the destruction was not set for the people of the mountain range. The two men who departed earlier headed south towards the Cities of the Plains, and then I knew. The destruction was not meant for them, but for the cities and the two men were messengers sent to deliver it.

"My thoughts immediately turned to concern for the inhabitants of the Cities of the Plains. After the War of the Nine Kings, I'd departed the region giving them little thought. What had brought the judgment of the Creator upon them? Had their exploits turned towards evil and wickedness so as to provoke the Creator? I was overcome with knowing the truth of their plight, but time was short, and I would have to move quickly.

"By then, I knew that the two men were undoubtedly angels in disguise moving with swiftness towards their mark. They had a head start on me, but I move unlike any other over the face of the earth, and could reach the cities well ahead of them.

"On my approach, I could see the skyline of the cities backlit by a glowing red and black sky. There was an arch built on a road paved with bones a mile out. Human skins were painted and made as flags and banners that blew murderously in the wind. The sight of this was terrible and only the truly evil would enjoy such a welcome. As I neared the cities, I could hear the crack of a whip tearing through flesh and the expected scream immediately followed. I entered the cities through a gutter that ran along the outer walls to conceal myself and avoid aggression.

"The gutters ran long and were clogged with filth and the decaying remains of a well-fed civilized community. The people of the cities were unlike any I had ever seen, as their culture was that of lies and complete deception. They procrastinated and debated endlessly, but did not work to build or create anything new. All day long, people campaigned for the approval of their peers, all the while impersonating the narcissistic and ignorant behavior of prominent socialites. None could be trusted and none lived by any code of ethic or integrity. It was endless and they laughed as they did this to each other, as if such behavior was appreciated and conventional.

"Holocausts were seasonal and each quarter brought new diseases, criminal enterprises, and chemical addictions with which to engage in excess. Physical acts of violence were only exceeded by the plotting imagination of vengeance and despair. The cities had grown into tumors and if left unchecked, they would infect the very foundation of humanity.

The Shit...

"I came across a heaping pile of garbage and observed a mule defecate upon the filthy mess. The stench was overpowering and I was forced to swallow the smell as there was not a clean breath of air to exchange it with. Now, I rarely spit fire as I am cautious not to unleash such a destructive force. However, the pile of shit was surrounded by stone so the fire would be contained. I reared my head in to position and made ready to ignite the trash.

'Stop! Stop! Stop! What are you doing?' a miniscule voice cried out.

"I looked around but saw no one in sight, then a buzzing fly landed on the end of my nose, waving its arms violently, grabbing my attention. 'Stop! Don't do that! You're going to destroy everything!' the voice was that of the fly.

"Who are you? And what do you mean, don't destroy everything? It's just a pile of garbage and shit!"

"It might be garbage to you, but to me it's my whole world! Please, don't do that!" the fly defended pointing back at the pile of shit.

"I stopped and looked again and saw a large congregation of flies swarming above the filth. There were maggots crawling out of the garbage while other's laid eggs into it."

"This is the entirety of your world? This is disgusting!" I stated, refocusing my gaze back on the fly.

"Allow me to introduce myself! My name's Allin, but everybody calls me GG. And this is no ordinary pile of shit my friend, this just so happens to be the greatest city in the world. This city is everything; I live here, I work here, and I play here! It's the shit!" the fly spoke out, stepping forward on my nose.

"So let me get this straight, the place you live is a piece of shit, you get up every day and go do shitty work, then you go out to party and get shit faced? Is that about right?"

"That's life in the big city baby! Everybody who's anybody is here. You gotta love it!" the fly said, while panning two of his arms out gesturing with a third in praise of the city.

"Just think about it. Even after I'm dead and gone, stories will be written about this place, and you know what... I was a part of that!"

"Why would you want to live your whole life in a place like this? Look at it! It's surrounded by garbage, crime, and noise. It's overcrowded and there's never ending corruption and lies! This place is a fucking cesspool! It's disgusting! Haven't you ever wanted to get out and see the world? You could do some traveling, see the country, climb mountains, or even sail the seven seas. Think of all the places you could go and everyone you would meet," I offered to the fly, with optimism.

"Yeah... but that ain't shit!" the fly remarked, while standing on his hind legs with three of his remaining arms folded, while stroking the hairs on his chin with his remaining fourth.

"Well, perhaps if you had more time. I understand that the life span of a fly is very short. You are hatched and within a few days you mature. If by any luck you are not eaten or swatted, you're dead by the end of a few weeks. I apologize for not introducing myself, I am the Serpent of Old and I often encounter the voice of the Creator. I can tell you with certainty that the Creator is compassionate and cares deeply for all creation.

"I could speak to the Creator on your behalf and ask that your life be extended. Imagine the life that you could have, if you could live months, possibly even years. You would be the greatest fly that ever lived. So what do you think? Would you like me to do that for you?" the fly remained in his current stance, listening while stroking the hairs on his chin.

"Man, I don't think you understand! I live the fast life baby, fly till I die!" and with a fist pump in the air and a ferocious tone, simultaneously he said, "and besides... it's better to buzz out, than fade away!' "And those were his final words."

"So what happened to him?" the man, inquired still seated

listening to the serpent's story.

"Who happened to what? The fly? Oh! Pft... Shit if I know!" the serpent simply replied, shaking his head shrugging off the whereabouts and happenings of the fly, then continued.

"I looked down an alley and observed a foreigner in dispute with a citizen over the actions of a peasant, resulting in the foreigner being struck in the head by a stone. The foreigner stood bleeding, while the citizen demanded payment from the foreigner for the service of bloodletting. The matter was quickly taken to court where a kangaroo presided over the matter, who ruled in favor of the citizen. The foreigner being quick witted, struck the judge in the head with the same stone before fleeing the city, remarking, 'Now, you pay him!'

"What I saw around me in the city was spectacularly grim and it sent a frozen chill through my very being. The city had been consumed by anarchy and violence, and was utterly lawless. How people could survive in such an environment was incomprehensible. I was aware of no such vermin, no such bottom feeder, or decomposer that was immune to such compounded disease and intense obscenity. But again I was wrong, there was a type of scavenger who seemed to thrive in such an environment, one of the lowest life forms in existence... the lawyer.

"Out on the streets, I noticed the amount of professionals soliciting legal services. As a matter of fact, everyone in the city claimed to be a lawyer of some sort. There were lawyers, super lawyers, wanna be lawyers, thinking of going back to school to be a lawyer; my father's a lawyer, just finished law school but can't find a job lawyers. And then there were the, I've been sued and lost my license, but still provide counsel and receive payment, but can't legally be called a lawyer until I am reinstated.

"I asked myself what sovereign government existed and established a society without rules of conduct. As surely, the stability of a chaotic society openly engaging in moral wrongs, political corruption, and social injustice should have imploded upon itself. These professional litigators were more than experts in circumvention of the law. They were serial criminals for hire, who defended their own criminal actions as feeding the economy. Each day, they awoke plotting against each other and all day long, stabbing each other in the back, and at night trying to fuck each other in the ass. In that city, there were only two types of people, lawyers and homosexuals... everybody was trying to fuck you in the ass!

"The sight and smell of moral decay and rampant complacency was overwhelming, yet the people commuted proudly through it. I had only been there a short time, but I was able to see the citizens for what they truly were. They were as so many flies swarming to the stench of a fresh and hot shit, all the while thinking they had *made it*, but really had attained absolutely nothing.

"The people of the city treated each other with utter cruelty and without any regard of hospitality to any visitor or traveler. Their elected officials had enacted lawful business practices as economic crimes. Many contractual disagreements were either cited as blasphemy or ended in bloodshed. I observed the wealthy engrave their names on silver coins before throwing them to the poor. Upon retrieving the alms, the authorities were called and the poor were arrested and hanged as thieves.

"I witnessed the burning body of a young girl, it was her screams that I heard upon entering the city while receiving a hundred lashes. Afterwards, she was burned until her flesh was cooked black, while passersby spit on her in damnation. Her accusers then smeared her body with honey and hung her corpse from the city walls. A wooden plank was nailed above her which listed her crimes as: Solicitation of kindness and compassion by manner of feeding the hungry.

"I witnessed a greedy mob of peasants salivating at the honey roasted meat hanging before them. Who would feast upon her body first, the peasants, the insects, or maybe the rats? At least the rats brought silverware and napkins.

"An open café window, exposed a woman under pain of labor on a dining table bringing forth a new life. I thought to myself, what life would this progeny have in such a hellish place? A murderous parolee, a noble thief, or perhaps a rapist beggar, as anyone of these would be a suitable vocation for an eager youth in a city without hope. I smelled the cooking of meat from open air markets but observed no livestock, not even a dog safeguarding a dry bone. The screams of the woman in labor went in vain, while a crowd of onlookers stood impatiently outside.

"There was no hospice to care for the pregnant woman, but soon I realized that my thoughts were again naive. For the mother was not at the café for lack of care, she was the owner of the establishment. And upon birthing the child, she opened for business and began taking orders for, the menu specialty was 'infantile venison.' Man was never meant to live like this and instead of the civilization dying out, it somehow lived and fed off of the chaos and destruction.

"The predicament of the Cities of the Plains was not due to any one single act of rape, murder, or theft, but what was created by the union of physical evil and human imagination. Any semblance of humanity was lost and children were no longer born innocent, but knowing of sin, and they nursed and fed off the death and moral decay. I witnessed a woman exit her home and plot theft of a man. While in motion, she was attacked and beaten to the ground. While the vandal attacked her, another climbed upon him and began raping him. As the rape occurred, the woman lay bleeding and another approached and began consuming her living flesh.

"Frenzy broke out and more joined in the madness, killing upon stealing, cannibalizing while raping, and more until no victim could be found as all were with blame and all were guilty. Those who left the cities early on were spared the nightmare existence that was created. Those that remained, unfortunately did not die, but festered and became a walking evil scab unlike any demonic apparition.

"You see, Man of the Present, it goes back to the earliest of times. Where unions between man, angel, and jinn were allowed, and as a result, half-breed entities and giants existed. Upon seeing the nature of man, the Creator separated all other creation, as all who laid with him became corrupted. It was said that such unions were unnatural and soon after were outlawed. However, in the same way a virus clings to its host, so did evil symbiotically join with the wicked people of the cities.

"Something that was never intended to be came into existence, a human hybrid of evil and living death. You cannot imagine such a possibility, because it was wiped from existence. The very words and description of them were removed from all speech and comprehension to prevent those things from ever returning. The destruction of the cities was meant to terminate such an evil possibility from ever growing out of man's twisted dreams and wretched thoughts.

"Just then, I began hearing reports of two strangers who had entered the city and had been met by a pious man known as 'The Veil.' I knew for certain that the strangers were the messengers sent to destroy the cities and my time had run short. I moved up the outer walls of the city to locate the messengers, but the crowds were now a mob headed towards the house of The Veil. I feared not the safety of the Creator's messengers, for mortal man could not harm them. News of the messengers spread quickly throughout the city and the growing mob soon surrounded the home of The Veil.

"'Bring them out!' they shouted, while whistling vulgarities and making sexual threats towards the messengers within the elder's home. The mob grew furious and intoxicated with frenzy at the thought of new flesh and attempted to break into The Veil's home. From the walls, I could see the mob attempting to break through the door, but the barricades they'd fastened were holding. A portion of the mob pulled back from the assault and started fires, attempting to smoke them out. I thought not to sit idly by, so I intervened and fought fire with fire.

"I attacked and spewed venom, which burned the eyes of the mob and temporarily blinded them. I could have easily killed and ate them, but eating of their diseased flesh was not favorable to me. A shutter flash of light from within The Veil's home signaled action by the messengers, and instantly, The Veil and his family were transported outside of the city walls. The messengers were expedient in their rescue of The Veil and his family, but finished by giving them one solemn command, 'Escape for thy life and look not behind thee, lest thou be consumed!'

"The Veil rebutted the messengers and pleaded that his family would not find refuge in the mountains and instead pointed to the little city on the outskirts of the plains.

The messengers replied, 'As you wish, but go quickly!' The Veil and his family fled and I too took notice and made good my escape of that accursed place. From the mountains, I watched as the two messengers turned towards the city and revealed their true identities. The light they emitted was that of angel fire and the destruction they wielded was commanded by the Creator.

"Fire, rock, and ash rained down to target each man and woman burning slowly through their flesh. The Cities of the Plains were consumed by their fire and plumes of smoke filled the skies above, and none were left alive. As The Veil and his family fled, his wife stopped and did as she was instructed not to. She looked back and began calling out the names of her friends and possessions lost to her. She was caught in the radius of destruction and the sight of the fire blinded her, striking her in petrification. The Veil could hear her from behind screaming, but did not revert his gaze from his path and he and his remaining family found safety in the little city.

"The fire storm ignited the asphalt and tar pits and turned the area into a molten crater that burned throughout the night and smoldered well into the morning. If not for the heavy rains that followed, it might have burned indefinitely. Not a single pillar was left standing of the cities, and very few artifacts would be recovered in the centuries to come. Only buried and broken glazed artifacts upon layers of ash containing human bone fragments were recovered. The only real evidence of the sudden end to the Cities of the Plains was the discovery of desert glass in the region. Which is the only marker of the extreme temperatures resulting from the angel fire that fused sand into glass.

"And so it was, the end of the Cities of the Plains. The region remained deserted and was not occupied until several centuries later. Some historians doubt the existence of the cities at all, and can only theorize of what natural disasters resulted in the destruction of the area."

"So what happened to The Veil and his family?" he asked, lifting his head as if pointing at the serpent with his chin.

"What's that now? Oh, I don't know, I left after that. They were no concern of mine."

"I mean, didn't he and his daughters end up having sex or something and his wife got turned into a pillar of salt?" he questioned the serpent intently, wincing out of his right eye.

"I'm sorry, what happened now?" the serpent remarked, with shock by the man's statement.

"Where do you come up with these preposterous ideas, Man of the Present? People turning in to pillars of salt! But worse still, a pious man engaging in incest? I'm almost afraid to ask how you came to such a horrible conclusion."

"That's just what I was told. I didn't make it up! But isn't that what happened?" he pressed, looking at the ground removing any guilt of himself.

"Look, I honestly don't know what happened to them. They fled and I assume they made it out of there. If I had lingered any longer, the destruction might have overtaken me along with the wicked. At the time, I didn't give The Veil and his family a second thought. I assumed they joined their relatives in the mountain region and lived the rest of their lives, the end. But you are dissatisfied with that ending?"

"I didn't say I wanted that to happen. That's what the story says and since you were there, I'm asking if that's what really happened?" the man further pressed.

"Now that you mention it, I do recall the accounts of two tribes, one known as, 'From the Father" and the other 'Son of My People' supposedly born of incest, and a fabled stone pillar that pilgrims make penance too in the region. Hmm, I'm going to allow this… exploration of events. But I caution you, Man of the Present, not to make blasphemy of the Creator's chosen," the serpent said wagging his tail like a finger at the man, in warning.

"Right, so the story goes, that the wife looked back and she was turned in to a pillar of salt because she was disobedient. And after that, the man and his daughters left the city and ended up in the mountains. The daughters were alone and saw no other men around them. So they got their father drunk and seduced him, so they could get pregnant. But overall, the meaning of the story was that the cities were destroyed because the people were gay. Because God hates fags!" the man stated with certainty.

"I described the events leading up to the destruction in detail and this is what you return with? I can tell you with surety, Man of the Present that the destruction had little to do with a bunch of goddamn cock wranglers! Gimme a break!" the serpent rebutted the man, shaking his head no.

"Did you just say, cock wranglers?" the man, remarked dumfounded by the serpent's phraseology.

"Why yes! Something wrong? Are you not familiar with said reference?" the serpent paused then turned his head, wincing, back at the man.

"Could it be? Have I offended you? Ohhh! Nooooo! Be still my unbeaten heart! Oh, my dear Man of the Present, how I do apologize. For I am a wretch and a poor, misguided, and vile creature. Sadly, I was mistaken! I was under the impression by your expression that you enjoyed such silly and juvenile vulgarities."

"I didn't say anything vulgar, you did!" he responded, waving his hand in defense.

"True! However, I'm not the one hiding from it. You condemned an entire group of people by your admission of 'God hates fags!' However, my statement of cock wranglers is too much for you, therefore I... am the one who is vulgar!"

"That's neither here nor there, but ... you can't say cock wranglers! That's just crazy!" he responded.

"Man of the Present, I will not be engaging in any childish back and forth with you, regarding who smelt or dealt what. I dislike petty name calling and even more so using the Creator to justify your ignorance!" the serpent countered, finalizing his stance on the matter, and then continued.

"Now! This was not the first time the Creator had chosen to destroy man for his wickedness. As you may recall in the tale of the Great Deluge, not one single group of humanity was singled out, all were judged and washed clean from the face of the Earth. But now, your claim is that the Cities of the Plain were destroyed due to acts of buggery, only to be followed by a righteous man and his daughters engaging in the outrageous act of incest? Interesting mindset you have there, Man of the Present.

"You know something? If I were to close my eyes, I don't think I could summon a nightmare of a story even close to your explanation."

"Wait a minute, but that's it! It's just a story to you people! You have no connection to the people mentioned. They're just characters to you, which is why it has become such grand lore and fable. Let's take this story of yours and examine it as just that, a story. And let's see if we can identify the true focus of it.

"Now, all stories follow a similar format and contain five basic elements, which are: a setting, a plot, main characters, a conflict, and a resolution. Let me know if you start to fall behind, I don't want to have to repeat myself."

"No, no, I'm following you," he said, nodding back at the serpent.

"Now the setting is the location of the story. Next are the main characters, which are the individuals that the story is actually about. The main characters are usually introduced by name, are given a background, and possibly a future. Additionally, there may be lesser characters who interact with the main characters. However, these lesser characters are merely there to add to the plot or conflict. What is important to note about the lesser characters is that they usually have no name, no face, no history, and no future. To focus on the lesser characters would mislead the reader from the actual narrative of the plot and the main characters.

"Now, the plot is the actual story that follows the main characters as they deal with and resolve the conflict. A plot generally has a beginning, middle, and end with the main characters appearing in each section. The conflict is the situational event that the characters must resolve. One thing to note about the conflict is the timing of it. Specifically, when the action and events become most exciting in the story, that point is then called the climax and usually occurs right before the end. And lastly, comes our resolution, which is where the characters overcome the situational conflict and are given closure and possibly a future.

"Now, in this story the main characters are the pious man known as The Veil, his wife, and his daughters. The setting, of course, is the Cities of the Plains. The plot begins with the War of the Nine Kings which led to The Veil and his family dwelling in the Cities. The wicked people and their actions occurring in the Cities of the Plains is the conflict, climaxing with the destruction of the cities. Additionally, it is important to note that the inhabitants of the cities are never named, have no face, have no history, and no future, meaning that they are not the focus of the story and are only part of the Veil's story.

"The resolution of the story concludes with The Veil's family escaping the destruction and wrath upon the Cities. Now my point is, that the focus of the story is on The Veil and his family, not the nameless, faceless people, who are inconsequential to the meaning of the story. I wonder how it came to be that people started misreading this story to only focus on the acts of the nameless, faceless men laying with men, making them the main characters, while the actions of the named characters are simply overlooked."

"Hmm… that's an interesting way to look at it! So you're saying not to focus on the fags being… I mean the people being destroyed because they were only part of the overall story and their destruction is not the meaning of it," he clarified, lifting his head slightly in thought.

"Exactly, but still why the demonization of said sub-group of humanity? I am curious as to what purpose such a scenario like this serves to teach mankind?"

"I'm telling you what I was told, and it was you that said religious texts hold many truths. Besides, everybody knows that

God hates fags," he reiterated, then folded his arms in stubborn account of the serpent's interpretation.

"To clarify, I believe the word you are looking for is homosexual, meaning 'same sex.' Which refers to the romantic attraction and or sexual behavior between members of the same gender. Now, if you mean to judge the acts of homosexuality and incest upon humanity, all I can tell you is that right and wrong are subjective and the laws of man change with the seasons and cannot be relied upon as both are considered as sexually deviant or a crime against nature.

"However, the definition of sexual misconduct does not denote any personal lifestyle but a sexual behavior involving violence, manipulation or deceit, and any conduct that leads to suffering and trouble. Now both acts in the tale could be considered as misconduct as the men of the city wished "to know" the messengers, as I am assuming it was to be without their permission. Additionally, the daughters who supposedly manipulated their father into the sex act in order to become pregnant. So I beg of you, Man of the Present, please spare me your petty biases.

"Yet, on the subject of homosexuality, I am not aware of any consensus among researchers on why a person develops one of three sexual identities over the others. And contrary to metaphysical, spiritual, or cultural belief, there is no evidence shown proving that homosexual activity is unnatural compared to any other human forms of behavior. If you ask me, all of you are nothing more than a litter of disgusting snot puppies forced out some bubbling goop of a Saturday morning cartoon," the serpent remarked, holding the end syllables emphasizing the 'oon' in a condescending manner.

"Snot puppies! Who the hell, are you calling a snot puppy?" he quipped back at the serpent, taking offense to being called a cartoon.

"You! And all of your upright bipedal kind, strolling about with some grand notion, claiming superiority to one another. How foolish! How is it, you say? Blow me! Where a reference to clear your nasal cavities has become synonymous with sexual activity! I've seen it all before. Where one of you chases the other around hoping to shoot some pasty, gooey slurp into the other, which closely resembles the matter running out of your silly noses! Then the other of you claims to be running away, all the while enjoying the merry chase, dreaming of having said gummy glue shot up inside them! And you! You! Have the audacity to claim, which of you receives the snot! The precious wonderful snot!" the serpent shouted down shaking his head judgingly at the man.

"Puppy fodder... all of you!" the man stood with his mouth agape, confounded by the serpent's rant.

"Just as long as humans have been around, your habits, your traits, your vices, and your addictions have been with you whether you wish to admit them or not. Human societal attitudes on the matter of homosexuality have varied when looking back throughout time. I have witnessed your civilizations pass laws preaching male and female same-sex relationships, to casual interaction. To seeing the practice as a minor sin and later repressing it through law and religious enforcement. The connotation that sodomy as a transgression being against nature predates any present religious philosophy and has remained a debatable subject. Again, the acts have been documented from the Americas, to continental Africa, Asia, and Europe, which seems to make a staggering reoccurrence upon humanity as to why the behavior remains.

"As I said previously, I am no judge of human behavior, nor do I know why you all behave as you do. I am merely an observer. I have seen the human world grow and regard such acts as befitting the most civilized, where relationships with both women and youthful boys were an essential foundation of normal life. The practice was sometimes instituted in cultures as pedagogic and served as a means of population control. Many of your most revered Greek philosophers once praised the act in their writings, but later changed their works towards prohibition of same sex relations. Lest we not forget the regal and empirical rulers of the then known world at the time who openly took male lovers and campaigned its benefits to modern society.

"It wasn't until laws were passed to abolish homosexuality and such passive males were thus burned at the stake. Yet, of course, their wealthier lords and masters escaped reprisal and only paid a small fine. Later, and approaching more present times, we have seen prosecution, and imprisonment of those charged with homosexuality. Yet again, even in the region of our story in ancient Assyria was the practice not only present but quite common, nor was it prohibited or even condemned.

"Religious texts have been found containing prayers and divine blessings for those engaged in said relationships. What troubles me though, Man of the Present, is not how you behave amongst one another, but how you select which of you deserves to be treated as human. And which of you is too be victimized and ridiculed. As a student, I do pride myself upon keeping abreast of scholarly publications. As such, I was intrigued to read that select modern societies of psychiatry have removed homosexual behavior from being considered a mental disorder. Too bad that ruling will do nothing for the sheer ignorance and laziness of the entire lot of you!"

"If you're done talking about your best friends and pushing your gay agenda, then we can move on! Cause you're not going to change my mind on the subject," the man replied strongly refuting the serpent's accusations and explanation.

"My point is, Man of the Present, that the ideas you have on damming this group of people is nothing new, nor is your present-day realizations of acceptance. It's all happened before. I see that you agree with demonizing certain sub-groups of humanity, but take no responsibility for the ridicule or mistreatment of said people. You are a coward, Man of the Present! At least have the guts to stand by your ignorant ideologies and despicable treatment of your fellow man.

"I, for one, admit boldly that I am a serpent, and as such I am naturally introverted and care very little for the likes of mankind as a species. But know this, Man of the Present, I have had the opportunity to kill and eat every type of man, woman, and child, and yes... those fags too," the serpent said with a toothy smile.

"… And?" the man forced, with tense aggression.

"And… they taste nothing like fruit!" the serpent answered with humorous simplicity.

"However, I cannot refute your claims of incest against The Veil and his daughters, but I will say that other theories do exist which may shed additional light on the subject matter," he explained while raising a brow.

"What other theories are there?"

"I have heard this story told many times over centuries, each time with varying details, but the main events have remained the same. But what puzzles me is the focus on the men laying with men so directly. There were many other crimes that occurred and have been noted that all are abhorred, which I feel, overall, resulted in their destruction."

"I get what you're saying, but it doesn't mean that those people were not destroyed because they were gay," he continued to argue against the serpent.

"I do not disagree with you that the people were destroyed and their behavior did include such acts. However, I am no judge of human behavior, but more importantly… who are you to judge? I caution you, Man of the Present, do not claim to know the will of the Creator as it can only lead to ruin.

"Yet, if we are to compare said sexual acts to each other, then the results of incest are increasingly more damaging to humanity than that of same gender copulation. Why is it that a certain human sexual act in this tale is overlooked while the other is not? How is it that you are able to either look past or ignore incest and still revere The Veil as pious and an example for humanity?"

"I don't know why they did that. Maybe it was an acceptable practice at the time, or maybe they didn't know it causes birth defects," he replied in defense, while shaking his head disavowing any knowledge.

"Actually, that's not true! The unmentionable act of incest is one of the most long-standing and widespread cultural taboos in human history. The very definition of the word means impure, which is associated with sexual activity between blood

153

relations or those related by affinity through either adoption, marriage, or persons of the same household.

"The negative labels associated with inbreeding are most commonly the increased risks of congenital disorders, premature death, and disability. You have to understand that for something to be labeled as impure, it had to have happened enough times that the negative effects were documented and then ridiculed. Meaning, this isn't the first time you all have done something like this!

"However, incestuous marriages were not always viewed negatively. Many human societies have used the practice as a means of preserving royal blood lines. Even though, sexual relations with a first-degree relative, such as brother and sister, cousin, aunt, nephew, or uncle, and niece are almost always universally forbidden... it still happens! No, not one of you are immune to the practice as almost every continent and almost every kingdom, empire, and government has engaged in this behavior.

"In societies where incest was acceptable, depending on the time-period of course, consensual incest was viewed as a victimless crime or a vice where third degree relatives were wed and thus viewed as socially acceptable. Yet, in other cultures, consensual incest involving a minor is considered an extreme act of child abuse, especially in the case of parental incest, which can result in long term psychological trauma. The aforementioned result being the spontaneous abortions, prenatal deaths, and offspring inflicted with a higher probability of congenital birth defects."

"So you're saying that the incest did happen?" he insisted, pointing back at the serpent.

"No... only that it could have happened! But just not in the way you described." the serpent hinted with reason, then squinted with intrigue.

"The story of which you speak describes the incestuous act in a very specific way. It does not say to, yes engage in it. Nor does it say not to, but it does at least imply that it does, has, or can happened. What I find interesting is the description of the act as it is presented in a rather peculiar way. As in, the daughters were the ones to suggest the idea, then seduced their poor unknowing father, only to mount him and father children. It's surprising that a story, which just destroyed a population due to crimes against nature, ends with incest and you seem content with that resolution.

"Let me share something with you, Man of the Present. I have observed human families for quite some time now and if two of your daughters were to show up pregnant without their father's knowledge, there would be some serious questions asked as to how they got that way! Additionally, I know of very few people who would believe that out in the country or up in the mountains, two daughters became pregnant, while their father's only excuse was, 'I was drunk!' And therefore had no knowledge of how they became pregnant and therefore was without blame," the serpent argued, then sarcastically sighed a long steady, right!

"Now, the prevalence of incest between father and daughter has been the most commonly reported form of incest. Yet more recently, studies have shown that incest amongst siblings is actually more common. But again, this is what strikes me as odd. And I ask, why is it that incest between an adult and their child is generally considered a form of abuse, yet in this tale it is somehow seen as, I don't know… something else? I wonder, Man of the Present, if the authors of this tale were trying to convince the reader or themselves of no wrong doing? Perhaps the pervasiveness of culture and family secrets and hidden skeletons runs so deep that believing your heroes are flawed and mortal is too great a truth to acknowledge.

"I mention this only because there are some striking features in this tale that strangely align themselves with other reported incidents of abuse. As in families that reported incest, there was estrangement between the mother and daughter with extreme parental dominance and a reassignment of the mother's duties onto the daughter. Where the oldest or only daughters were more likely to be victims of incest. Now in comparison to our story, I suppose you could call being turned into a pillar of salt estrangement between mother and daughter. I cannot comment on The Veil's style of parenting, but it appeared that they came from a deeply religious household which commonly have a reputation for being extreme!

"However, lest we not forget that it was their beliefs that saved them from destruction, so we'll call that one a wash. As for a reassignment of the mother's duties, I suppose if the mother is all salty and gone, I guess you two heifers better get to work. Interesting how certain things just line up on their own, but again Man of the Present, this obviously is not what it looks like, and again can be explained away because that's what everybody believes and God hates fags. Right?!"

"Okay, but if it didn't happen that way, then why would somebody write that?" he questioned the serpent nervously.

"Good question! This is where it gets a bit tricky but I'm going to do my best here. I do not mean to call the authors of said tale liars, only that the tale leaves many questions unanswered and I have to wonder if it was intentional or just a misunderstanding.

"A lie, by definition, is an intentionally false statement made while knowing it is not the truth. Lies are told for a multitude of reasons and with just as many levels of believability. Now if this tale is a lie then it is a 'Big One' at that, where a big lie is a direct attempt to trick a party into believing a major fallacy. Usually this fallacy will be contradicted by information the party already possesses or by their own common sense. When such a fallacy is of sufficient magnitude, it sometimes succeeds due to the victim's reluctance to believe that an untruth of such proportion would be concocted.

"I, for one, do not believe this to be an outright lie, perhaps more an example of 'Bullshit!' Because bullshit does not have to be a complete lie. Said bullshit is mainly offered because the speaker does not care whether what is said is true. The speaker is more concerned with giving the audience an impression rather than giving facts. If perhaps bullshit leaves too harsh of a taste in your mouth. Then quite possibly this may be a case of an 'Exaggeration,' but not to be confused with a 'Falsehood' where said tale is composed of mostly true statements, but only to a certain degree. As in making a certain aspect of said tale more powerful or meaningful, than it actually is.

"But to reiterate my initial point, that perhaps aspects of said tale are merely a 'Fabrication.' These stories have existed possibly before written language and no one seems to be able to identify the exact authors of said texts. It is very plausible that these tales have been submitted as fact without the authors knowing for certain whether they are actually true. I want to point out, Man of the Present, as I will revisit this statement later in our discussion that fabrication is often a type of 'Propaganda.' Either way, I have stated to you that the events did occur, but we are having some debate over some minor details, so I digress to a haystack answer as a resolution."

"What's a haystack answer?" Listening intently, he looked upward at the serpent as he asked.

"A haystack answer, my Present Day Man, is a type of search for the truth in a statement. Like a needle in a haystack, we will have to dig through the information to hopefully uncover the truth. But honestly, there is no way to prove intentional deceit, so any charge against said authors is reprehensible. Statements that inaccurately detail historical or present situations may not be due to any intent to misinform, but merely the individuals were unaware that their detailing of said information was found to be wanting."

"Speaking of liars... how do I know you're not speaking with a forked tongue? You are a serpent and the greatest liar," he said pointing directly at the serpent.

"A bit more history for you, Man of the Present! Speaking with a forked tongue has never had anything to do with me or my kind. I believe it refers to the indigenous people of the America's who used the phrase when speaking of their invading conquerors who said 'the white man spoke with a forked tongue.' After describing events where they were invited to a meeting of peace, only to be slaughtered and captured.

"Consequentially, once a lie has been told there are only two outcomes, either the lie is discovered or remains undiscovered.

The latter, of course, results in the speaker or document being discredited. However, if the lie is discovered something dangerous may then occur where the discoverer may be coerced into becoming part of the lie, which later becomes the formation of a conspiracy. And, unfortunately, the lie becomes actively propagated and sold to other parties. And by that time, anyone else who discovers the lie may be publicly shamed in order to prevent further discovery. My point here being, Man of the Present, is this is very dangerous territory we find ourselves in. Feel free to exit the caves if you no longer wish to continue our discussion."

"You've been pretty straight forward so far, serpent." The man, thought to himself momentarily, before answering, "we're just having a conversation, so no harm done. Besides, you do have some interesting points of view on these stories. I can't say I agree with everything, but let's see where it goes."

"In order to understand why someone would do such a thing, we have to investigate and ask, what they would have to gain? In this story, we have The Veil, a pious man and his two daughters. I recently spoke of reasons why someone would engage in incest and one reason was due to persevering blood lines. Now if someone were trying to say that a divine bloodline needed to be protected, then this would be their argument for why the incest occurred. However, it is important to note that children produced of incestuous relationships were regarded as illegitimate. Even if the parents and the children choose to wed, society would not permit the marriage. Leaving any children produced as illegitimate, without any name or social standing.

"It should also be noted that in Ancient Rome, politicians would make false charges of incest as a means of disenfranchisement. When we relate that information to this story, we find that the children or two tribes that resulted from the daughters would become illegitimate, meaning any after them would have no claim to any 'divine bloodline.'

"So, I suppose an alternative theory could be that someone intentionally wanted to discredit the two tribes produced by the daughters of The Veil. I believe that the daughters were married previously, and The Veil told their husbands to leave before the destruction. Additionally, the two messengers of the Creator had just visited the mountain region where the High Father and his people dwelled. So there were other righteous men in the region for the two daughters to remarry. So excuse me, Man of the Present, but I do find your interpretation of said events a little disturbing.

"Lastly, when it comes to child abuse and incest, how likely are we to find two daughters taking advantage of their father, hmm? Your account of the events following the salvation of The Veil and his daughters are disgraceful and serves not the good of humanity. Indeed, how twisted the words and motives of man can be. Such ideas could only exist to justify and excuse the molestation and rape of young women. As you would have it, Man of the Present, if a man finds himself without a woman, he may take and lay with his own daughters. For surely, the uncontrollable, whorish ways of women overtake and compel them to seduce and rape their own fathers," the man stood silently, quickly turning his gaze towards the ground.

"I don't know who wrote that, but it sounds like something a man would write. You see, all men have the same fantasy. That a woman wants it so bad, that she will climb on top of him to have it. Never mind the fact that the staggering cases of incest are father on daughter or even male on female sibling throughout history. Yet, we are supposed to believe that a pious man was overcome and intoxicated by his two slutty, out of control daughters, and he, of course, was not to blame!

"Now, it doesn't say so much as to go and do that, but it kinda suggests that if it does happen, it's not the man's fault. Under close scrutiny, it seems that those words were written not to encourage the act of incest, but merely to remove blame from the father. Well if that's not the worst case of blaming the victim, then I don't know what is. As I have stated before, Man of the Present, the truth will forever repeat itself but lies must be maintained in order to be believed. If that scenario were true, then it would be true today.

"I challenge you now, go and search your jails and prisons,

as I'm sure you will find them full of women guilty of molestation and rape upon their husbands and fathers. Yes, go! I want you to exit these caves and search there the inmates, whom are certainly female and their crimes will be as such! How they crept into his room while he lay sleeping and how the smaller, yet stronger willed women pressed themselves forcefully upon him. How weak and frightened those husbands and fathers must have been. Every night fearing the footsteps of their daughters and wives creeping down the hallways and into their rooms taking by force his personal safety and security. Go ahead, Man of the Present, I'll wait here," the serpent huffed a single laugh in disbelief.

"Ha! Man of the Present, then go and seek out those victim's shelters, and in them will be so many men victimized by their daughters and wives. How such devoted husbands and fathers they were, only to be beaten, and abused. So much so that they fled for their very sanity and safety. How they were beaten in front of their children berated and raped only to become pregnant then deemed unclean by their families as they hid their shame. Disgusting!" the serpent argued, then shook his head in remorse.

The Man looked behind him at the exit, then lowered his head in silence folding his lips into his mouth, pouting.

"You don't have to go out there, Man of the Present! As the truth is that men have long found ways to justify their cruel behavior and mistreatment of women. They would even go so far as to twist the Creator's words to sanctify it. And as for any abuser who escapes man's justice in this life, he will find a select place in hell awaiting his arrival.

"There is a path in hell lined with lilies leading to a dungeon kept by a terrible beast. The beast's only purpose is to punish and beat those men who abused their daughters and wives. The beast wields a weapon with the name(s) of their victim(s) scribed into it. The weapon is doubled sided and reads, 'Speak thy victim(s) name and be punished.' While the opposite side reads, 'Speak thy victim(s) name and be relieved.' The name of their victim(s) both eases their pain and increases their punishment from the beast of their damnation.

"The father who was there to protect and guide his children and wife became a serial violator and abuser. He is the worst of sinners and the victims shall be made whole. The screams of those men will travel up to the heavens and their daughters and wives will be asked if they know the voice crying out for help. And just as they cried out too, Stop! No! Please don't! So too will the pleas of those men go unheard and the beast shall take them forever, and I recite, 'I am the rose of Sharon, and the lily of the valleys. As the lily among thorns, so is my love among the daughters.'

"It's a good thing this little ordeal wasn't set in ancient Babylon!" the serpent remarked.

"Why? What would have happened?"

"Had this been adjudicated in a Babylonian court of law, it would have come down to the Code of Hammurabi and been presided over by the 'Paternal Kinsman.' If The Veil was found guilty of incest, then the punishment would have been exile. Interesting now isn't it, Man of the Present. That in our story we have The Veil and his two daughters who, yes, engaged in incest and were forced to flee their home."

"But they weren't exiled, they escaped!" he retorted, rebutting the serpent.

"Interesting though, how escape and exile are both meaning to leave and not come back, under pressured conditions! But, I reason with you now, Man of the Present. If you were The Veil and had fathered children by your own daughters, under whatever circumstances they may be. You then find your way to a hospitable location and the citizens there ask of how you came to such an estate. What were the circumstances surrounding your swift exit of your previous location, with two unwed impregnated daughters, and you with no wife? You being The Veil, would you answer exile... or escape?

"Obviously, the latter connotes that said actions were not abhorred and the reasons behind said flight were, of course, not by punishment but due to divine intervention from a sinful society. However, don't think too harsh and barbaric on the actions of the ancients, as they were some of the first to insist on the idea of 'innocent until proven guilty,'" the serpent said, with an intelligent grin.

"But this still does not fully answer your previous question, Man of the Present, as to why? Why would someone write that? If the story you speak of is truly divine, then its purpose could only be to aide and guide mankind. I, for one, do not see how that example helps humanity in any way shape or form. Therefore, I question its validity and encourage you to do so as well. Now, we have looked at this story from a few different perspectives, but have not yet theorized as to why someone would write it that way. I believe that there is a final and more practical explanation of the story that we have yet to discuss."

"Beginning with The Veil's wife being turned into a pillar of salt as you so happily claimed. One of the most common views on this tragedy is that The Veil's wife was punished for disobeying the commands of the Creator's messengers. By looking back, she longed for that wicked way of life, and was deemed unworthy and was thus turned into salt. However, simple and tidy of an explanation it may be for some of you, I insist on investigating a bit further.

"The first question I ask is the lack of women mentioned in the story. As a matter of fact, only three women are ever mentioned. The wife who disobeys, and the two daughters who later seduce their father. Leaving the only women who are mentioned as either disobedient or sex crazed.

"I mean, I just… I don't think it means that every woman is evil," he responded with a look of bewilderment.

"Let me make this a little clearer to you, Man of the Present. What I'm getting at is, this story seems to present the only female characters a certain way and I think that is an unfair representation. Also, the name of the pious man means veil or covering. Isn't that an interesting name for a holy-man? I tend to think that when examined together they have a deeper meaning than we think they do. This is what I see, Man of the Present.

"Historically, the region being discussed practiced

polytheism and was a matriarchal society. And, of course, they and their evil ways were to be damned. Now, when we look at the factors together this is what we come up with. All of the men in the cities were behaving not as 'men' or were fags! The only adult woman mentioned was so disobedient that she defied the instructions of the angels and was destroyed. The younger women were so sex crazed that they seduced and raped their own father. And lastly, the conflict is resolved when the disobedient woman is destroyed and the sex crazed younger women are rescued by the patriarch known as The Veil.

"Ultimately, what you have is a polytheistic matriarchal society where men do not behave as 'men,' and the only women acknowledged are disobedient or sex crazed; and the resolution, or solution to this wicked and chaotic scenario is The Veil, or... the implementation of modesty laws.' This to me sounds less like any story of God's wrath against homosexuality and more like a good old fashioned tale of propaganda related to the first modesty laws where the horrors that unfolded, are what will befall human civilization if women are not restrained and 'veiled or covered.'

"As in a matriarchal society will bare mannish, disobedient, and sex crazed women, which undoubtedly will turn men into weak, effeminate fags. And the only way to resolve this manner and save humanity from destruction is to have women veiled or covered. Which is quite common with the implementation of monotheism, which is undoubtedly patriarchal."

"Whoa!" he remarked.

"Now, Man of the Present, this has always been one of the major goals of the patriarchal monotheistic system, which is to culturally enforce and control the evil compulsions of women. Many times to do this, violence was used against women as well as social pressure and ridicule. But the most useful form has always been indoctrination, as it is less perceptible to the population. Religious fundamentalists have always employed indoctrination as it has always been the driving force behind globalized empirical patriarchy. It can be observed in your societies today, usually in the form of mass media, to educational

163

institutions.

"Hold on, you're saying that this story is about women wearing veils? How does that even make sense? It doesn't say that at all!" the man's eye bulged in shock as he tried to comprehend the serpent's words.

"Follow me on this reasoning, you're going to like this. I think it's important to consider what cultural events were occurring at the time in this region. Specifically in the early copper age, there began some of the first modesty laws which were implemented on women.

"Now, in this ancient civilization, women's rights were not equal to those of men, but in early periods women were free to go out to buy and sell and to attend to legal matters. They could own their own property, borrow and lend, and engage in business for themselves.

"Specifically, in ancient Mesopotamia women did have rights and filled the traditional roles of wife, mother, and housekeeper. They learned how to grind grain, how to cook and make beverages, to brew beers and ferment wines, to spin and weave cloth for clothing. If a woman worked outside of her home, her job usually resembled her household tasks. She might sell the beer and wines she brewed or even become a tavern or inn keeper. Childbearing and childcare roles have always led women to become midwives and as such, led to the creation of medicines for contraception or abortions.

"Take note that some of the first doctors and dentists in ancient Mesopotamia were women before those occupations were taken over by men. For the most part, women were relegated to the lower-class jobs but could hold some of the same positions as their male counterparts. High status women, such as priestesses and members of royal families, could learn to read and write and be given considerable administrative authority. But more importantly, numerous powerful goddesses were worshiped as is common in polytheism.

"Prestigious women's roles grew out of a sector of society that could afford to have statues made of their likenesses placed in temple shrines. Just as in modern prayer circles, this was done so that their images would remain in constant prayer while they continued to go about their daily activities. Now, over time, women's positions changed and the gap between high and low status women grew to where almost half the population were slaves.

"After this, female power and freedom sharply declined during the Assyrian era. Because the majority of surviving documents from ancient Mesopotamia were created by males, the influence of women in history was not very visible. It was around this time that the first evidence of laws requiring the public veiling of women began. As reported by Max Dashu, the first veiling laws originated from ancient Indo-European, Assyrian, and Persian cultures. The veiling laws were first set up for class separation, where upper class women were veiled and lower class women were not.

"This veiling culture continued until feminist groups began rejecting the veil, while peasant women heavily adopted it as a means of upward mobility. This new cultural trend could be compared to the foot binding technique in ancient China as well. Not just in the region of the Cities of the Plains, but all over the world did we begin to see married women covering their hair, neck, and arms. In Europe, traditional women's dress more commonly resembled a nun's garb, which was considered a popular conservative style. This new veiling culture drew from those styles and added the face veil. While still, lower or working class women who were not veiled, were considered fair game for sexual assault.

"Historically, ancient Byzantine had implemented the enforcement of veiling codes, which attributed veiled women with high social ranking families. These were, in turn, based on Greek and Roman values of male honor and female shame and defined public space as 'male space.' There is a pattern that we begin to see all over the world, where women are singled out in the restriction of freedom, political activism, and personal wealth.

"This shaming of women is a fundamental pattern of monotheistic patriarchy. Women were then forced to give up their historic or cultural dress and assimilate into the new dominate culture. For centuries, a woman's body has been treated as a social gauge and even as political silage, with all sorts of agendas and implications. What I'm getting at here, is that this story is quite possibly a detailing of the point in time where society changed from a matriarchal polytheistic society to a patriarchal monotheistic one.

"This same picture can be observed in any of the late 19th or early 20th century suffragette propaganda posters. Which fabricate the effects of empowered women, which leads to a society of weak, effeminate men, disobedient, sex-crazed, and mannish women. And the solution to this chaos is the implementation of 'Modesty Laws,' which all began with... the veil!

"I think this story, Man of the Present, is less about the evils of homosexuality and more so about the evils of empowered women and a matriarchal society where in typical suffragette city propaganda, the panic and anxieties surrounding women's rights to vote ultimately leads to masculine women and feminized men.

"Woah! I never saw any of those things in that story before. I always thought it was about God destroying the city because they were gay. To look at this story from that point of view, does make sense. I do see that the only women mentioned are spoken of as wrong-doers. Also, the pious man's name being The Veil, it starts to make some sense. I don't even know what to say to that!"

"Say nothing, Man of the Present, just think about it. It's just a concept, an alternative point of view. It bears no weight on your personal beliefs nor should it sway you from your faith. It is merely an open discussion of concepts and theories, nothing more. I shall leave you with this, though.

"There exists today no crime, no curse word, or sexual act that is anywhere near what occurred in the Cities of the Plains. I tell you that everyone in the cities was destroyed, regardless of their nature, and all were removed from existence. There was so much anarchy and violence that none could be identified as a victim, as all were offenders. The inhabitants of the cities were arrogant, overfed and unconcerned, and suffered from an abundance of idleness, neither did they take the poor and needy by the hand and comfort them with kindness and compassion. The sexual misconduct spoken of was more to do with dominance and rape not any consensual sex act or love.

"If such a society exists where crime goes unchecked, then eventually it will implode under its own weight. Evil cannot exist without the presence of good. However, in the case of the Cities of the Plains, such a thing did, and it was the end of them.

"All mankind exists as they were created to and the Creator makes no mistakes in his plans. Treat those around you as you wish to be treated... like a human being, and I recite. 'If thou seest the oppression of the poor, and violent perverting of judgment and justice in a province, marvel not at the matter. For he that is higher than the highest regardeth, and there be higher than thee.'

"So what do you think happened to all the people that were destroyed? Did they go to hell?" the man inquired with a final thought.

"What I think is this, Man of the Present. I see with my serpent eyes and no matter how man tries to cover or veil the truth, I have no difficulty seeing through his bullshit!" the serpent stated with brilliance.

CHAPTER 6: THE GREAT CIRCLE

"After the destruction I witnessed, I decided on heading west as it had been sometime since my eyes had beheld the sea. The sea was essential to human civilization whether through trade, travel, power generation, or warfare. I, myself, was not interested in either of those things. I had journeyed so far inland that I could only feel the warmth of the surface waves and the massaging oscillations of water moving over me in memory. I was heading there for leisure and to remember the peace and calm of things.

"There is a stark but important duality of the sea and how it effects life on the face of the Earth. From the earliest of man's primitive beliefs, came the sea gods, epic poems, and then inspiring music, followed by hyper realistic art. For humanity, the seas were a means of livelihood but for me, the sea was a transference of energy in the purist sense. I couldn't decide if I preferred watching the waves or riding them, and I think I only left the sea so I could miss it that much more.

"I loved the water and its formlessness, she was temperate but forever misbehaving, whether approaching from an angle, or bending and crashing upon the rocks. She would calm herself while approaching the shallows or if heading towards a cape and crashing and breaking for amusement. I imagined swimming then plunging from crest to trough between two waves, then ending the depression and allowing the bliss of the sea to wash over me. Then diving deep into the abyss and finding a calm and undisturbed seabed. I could rest underwater with the feeling similar to a bed sheet closing over the eyes of a secure, heavy-eyed child under the influence of the night.

"It was almost hypnotic, how the sea passed her energy in horizontal motions over the surface and then perpendicular to the direction of the wind, all the while renewing the energy within me. Just as humans enjoyed venturing out to the sea, so too did I love to lazily paddle, then strike a vogue attitude while sun bathing. But of all the starry sky's and majestic landscapes, there was none that could compare to the setting beneath the surfaces of the sea.

"I was made to free dive and was completely unrestricted as I explored the depths of the seas. Human eyes are not adapted for underwater use but with my improved vision, I was permitted endless seascapes and sunken treasure of intrigue unknown to any man. I was thus set in my decision, so I set the Valley of Siddim behind me and headed towards the Great Eurafrican Sea hoping to find rest and rejuvenation there.

"My journey towards the Great Eurafrican Sea lead me through a land located in a hot, dry valley with few sources of water. Although ground water in the region was scarce, I am well adept at locating wadi deposits. On the surface, the desert is dry and course but underneath it, ground water flows in many underground rivers. Due to the eroded limestone and hidden layers of water, it would be difficult, but not impossible, to locate a water source. What I was looking for was no simple oasis, what I was looking for... was a rock.

"A rock in the desert to the untrained eye was nothing more than stale hopelessness. But to one who took interest in the earth sciences and fluid mechanics, certain types of rocks are permeable and allow water to pass through them. The type of rock I was looking for was called an aquifer. The wadi valley I was in was untapped and sure to hold hidden liquid treasure.

"After some time, I located such a stone and beneath it there flowed a wellspring of water. I decided against striking the stone as the water beneath it would well up and flow freely. Instead, I burrowed down some 30 meters until I had tapped the stream of groundwater that connected to the wadi alluvium. I took a moment to refresh myself only to be interrupted by a set of hurried footsteps from above that left as quickly as they had come. I paid no attention as they were probably a small jackal scurrying about the desert chasing a solemn lizard meal. The footsteps were gone, but then the silence ended and became the crying of a young child that echoed down into the well.

"I continued to listen to the child crying out for its mother, knowing that surely his guardians would arrive shortly to claim him. If I came out it was possible I would be detected, so I would have to wait until they retrieved him allowing me to exit under cover of night.

"About an hour had passed and still the child continued to cry but to no avail. I thought that perhaps his horse or camel had broken free from its caravan and perhaps he had arrived ahead of his family. It shouldn't be much longer before his cries were heard and the child was found. I waited down in the well for another half an hour before becoming impatient, then peaked my head up out of the well and saw the young boy had cried himself to sleep. I rotated around and saw no one else in sight, not even a dust cloud signaling an approaching party. I thought to myself, where could he have come from and how could he have traveled so far on his own? In his state, he would not survive alone out here much longer, but such is the way of life. Although sad it was to leave him, I knew that it was best to exit silently and allow him to pass quietly in his sleep.

"I exited the well and continued heading west but, unfortunately, my journey again was interrupted. I came across a weeping woman sitting in the dirt, moaning of her failure and defeat by the trials of life. I looked behind me and quickly deduced that she was undoubtedly the mother of the boy. But why had she abandoned him there? Perhaps he had wandered away and she was unable to locate him. He was only half a distance away from her location. The distance was trivial but, still, it was out of sight and just out of ear shot of where she sat. Looking at her dress, I knew that she was of working class, yet she wore jewelry usually adorned by a wedded woman.

"Women are generally frightened by my appearance so I thought it best to conceal myself. I positioned myself against a cluster of rock formations and camouflaged my appearance. I called out to the woman saying, 'Why is it you cry for your son, woman? He is no longer lost and rests not a half distance east of here.' The woman lifted her head and jumped to her feet looking around in confusion, but found not the one speaking to her. "Who's there?" she called out.

"A servant such as thee! I am hideous as the leper, so I hide myself in the rocks. Cry no more woman, your son is safe," I said with calming reassurance.

"Is he dead?" she asked plainly, with a blank emotionless stare.

"If left alone throughout the night, exposure will take him and surely he will be lost."

"I have been praying that death would take him swiftly as I cannot bear to watch my child die," she said with tears streaming down her face.

"After hearing her words, I jumped in shock and shouted back to her, 'you… what!'

I broke my concentration and moved, revealing my presence to her. Upon seeing me, her eyes grew wide with fright and the feet beneath her gave way, causing her to fall upon herself unconscious. I sighed heavily, "I was *really* hoping to avoid this."

"I raised her up off the ground and covered her in shadow until she regained consciousness and came to her senses. I pulled back and raised my head above her so as not to startle her again. She awoke and her eyes traced the scaly form surrounding her all the way up to my head, just where the sun blocked the full sight of me.

"Fear me not woman, I mean you no ill will. For it is I who spoke of the whereabouts of your son."

"Who are you?" shuddering in fright, she asked.

"I am the Serpent of Old, and I beg to know why you have

abandoned your child in such a manner," I kept my head high so as not to frighten the woman again.

"My child... is he dead?" the words she spoke echoed her emotional state as she was spent and felt without options.

"Knowing that her temporary blackout must have shaken her pretty well, I repeated my original response to her. 'No madam... the boy lives.' Again she began to cry. I brought my head down to the ground where she could see that I was of no harm to her.

"Why do you weep when he lives? Surely, I can guide you in his direction and you will once again be united with your love."

"My name is 'Flight' and it was I who left him there. We were sent away by my husband without reason. I exhausted the rations and water between ourselves and after two days of wandering in this wilderness, I collapsed. The heat of the desert is high so I took up running this area between these two small mountains sevenfold looking for water. I left my child there while he slept in my arms, and walked away as I could not bear to watch him die. I am a failure and life has beaten me," she said weeping in the dirt.

"Why has your husband sent you away, was there a crime that you were accused of? Was the child fathered by another man perhaps?" The woman, Flight was silent and all manner of thoughts raced through my mind. Was she a criminal, was the child spawn of evil perchance?"

"What difference did it make to you what happened to her? I thought you didn't care about people?" the man interrupted asking, bringing the serpent's focus back to the cave.

"Not caring and not taking care are two completely different things, Man of the Present. I was merely curious after happening upon the tearful scenario. Besides, the reason for a mother to relinquish her interests over her offspring was sure to be a heavy cause.

"So many have found themselves in a position where they felt that abandonment or death was better than a life of struggle and pain. The causes for such a sentence were usually social or cultural, or even sometimes the result of succumbing to mental illness. However, the woman, Flight was of sound mind and only shaken due to her exhaustion. Her husband had sent her away, yet she retained some bands of gold on her wrists and ankles so surely poverty was not her station. But the boy, what good does killing him do? Unless she was certain that his life would be meaningless, or perhaps he would join the ranks of the tyrant and psychopath. But, why end him?

"His life might become very meaningful and full of accomplishments. To extinguish one seed is to end all fruits and flowers thereafter. That boy might be made into a great nation if he were allowed to live. Think of all those after him, who would claim lineage of him and praise his name as their great ancestor."

"So you do care then; even you have a heart!" he said poking at the serpent.

"It has nothing to do with having a heart. I had already made my decision to leave the boy and not get involved. Again, I was merely curious. I have lived quite a life, Man of the Present. I have seen so many of you humans grow and become something or die as nothing. I have often wondered if the circumstance, and legacy of humanity was due to chance or choice as was the case with the woman, Flight, and her son.

"Was it chance that set them along my path? Now that I have encountered them, I am presented with a choice. Help many times results in more harm than the thought of right-doing ever provoked. Additionally, I found it interesting that this almost case of maternal filicide coincides well with recorded accounts where mothers who, as a result of murder suicide, were more likely to kill a son rather than a daughter. However, her case was not one of suicide in order to escape punishment, but suicide after murder as a form of self-punishment and guilt. Empathy overcame me so I decided to comfort her, if not to reason with her regarding her choice," the serpent continued.

"Woman, Flight, I beseech you, for you always have options! You are never trapped and it is only over when you choose no longer to fight, no more to work, and not to live another day. However, this form of baby dumping with the intent to leave the child to die by exposure is by no means merciful," the woman continued to sob and cry while I attempted to comfort her.

"Exposure is of the cruelest methods of death. The child will be frightened, cold, and alone in his last moments of life, only after having withered from starvation and dehydration. And if so lucky, he will pass before a pack of wild dogs feast upon his weakened flesh. His body will then be bit and torn apart by scavengers and left for the insects to act as hospice before cleaning his bones for desert artistry. Or perhaps, the child will find favor by the fates and perhaps a rebel army or merchant slaver will add him to one of their labor pools of parentless children. He will, no doubt, be the pride of any child army, religious zealotry, or sold for the price of chamber dancing boy to wealthy lords of taste.

"I have come across this before, sometimes there were too many foundlings to count. They were part of an all too common movement known as orphan caravans where many a foundling were abandoned on the side of a road or in some foreign village where any desiring their services as laborers, maids, and servants used and abused them. These orphan caravans were highly popular as a source of free labor, but unfortunately, it doesn't end there.

"Many times, the child's own family would steal them back from their enslavers only to resell them for services as 'broken in' or 'without attitude.' Even though there existed no legal institution that would convict either the parents or the community for the treatment of these innocent's, in my heart I knew it was 'Malum In Se' wrong in itself to harm one so small and one so free of sin. Still, I looked at this situation differently and as somewhat a curiosity, as very few situations exist by mere chance alone. Perhaps there was more here than met mine serpent eye. Possibly, with patience, I might discover some deeper meaning in crossing paths with one of such condemned birth and of lowly status. Perhaps some mysterious antecedents, prophecy, or oracle would explain a hidden subplot to me.

"Comically, many a story book have written of a child

abandoned not to be reunited with their parentage. But later encounter some forest beast, hovel of witchcraft, of swamp den of ogres. Then through some luck and wit, the child stumbles upon treasure and safety to resolve their situations. Hmm... Maybe she was hoping a pack of wolves or even a bear family would adopt the boy and give him milk yet to suck. I am no wolf in serpent's clothing and although my kin do bear the common name of milk, we offer no teat, for free!

"So you think he was special or a prophet?" the man asked with concern.

"Looking back on the situation, I know exactly who he was. But at the time, he was just a child, like so many others born into a world of hate, pain, and struggle! And it's moments like these that are decisive in the path of one's life."

"How so?"

"Well, I wondered if this woman knew the potential psychological effects on the child should he survive. I could only imagine that while the child was still young, he would eventually learn of his abandonment. The shock upon discovering that his own mother chose to discard him, would be quite devastating. It would either force the child into a self-depression, where he was shunned by society, or charge him towards some romanticized heroic conduct where he is the seed of ambition and desires to redeem the taint from his blood.

"He could also possibly work, study, and grow into a powerful man of historic name, redeeming his fallen status by his own vigor and achievements. But knowingly, it is difficult for anyone to truly outrun their own deep sense of failure. So much of a failure from birth that one's own parents refused them. He could very well wander the earth plagued by his inner demons only to one day become the very thing he hates the most, a deceiver as he tries to release his inner conflict onto those around him.

"But I am a believer and I think on how beautiful the individual who sees not a curse or burden placed on him by society's brand of illegitimacy, but finds his own creativity and originality that is in the beauty of being irregular. This child may very well understand that being unconventional, and outside of the mainstream, allows him to be a free thinker. The humor that dries the tears of mankind and the familiar face to the stranger. He could supersede the social boundaries that were placed upon him, where he was shunned by those who learned of his background," the serpent continued.

"Woman, Flight, why did your husband release you?" I inquired of the weeping woman.

"There was tension between my mistress and our sons and to settle the matter, my husband cast us out. There is no greater shame that can be placed upon me. Please creature, if there is any compassion in you, bite me and end my life as I cannot carry the shame of my predicament," she replied tearfully.

"Woman, Flight, be still and hear my words, as I offer you a choice. You may stay here in the desert and let the night take you. But as for your son, be warned that he may live and he may come to know of this day and it will weigh heavily on the future of things to come. Life may be difficult, but death is no less a simple task," the woman thought on the weight of my words then spoke.

"I was weak and foolish to leave my son. I shall go and retrieve him. I know not what hallucination has produced you, creature, but I have come to my senses. I thank the Creator for allowing me time to see clearly. I shall return to my son now." The woman rose to her feet and snuffed out her remaining tears.

"No, wait... but, where will you go! You can't go back home!" my words reached out in concern to the woman as she turned to leave. She halted realizing that she had not planned where she would go.

"You cannot go back empty handed and weeping, then surely they would have beaten you. And then you and your child would truly live as subordinates in your own home. However, if you returned with wealth, you would not only be welcomed back, but you would be praised for your ability to survive as well as having brought wealth and glory upon your family name."

"But how will fortune and wealth find me in a place such as this?" she replied in confusion.

"I feel that our meeting was not by chance. Nor is it coincidence that your movements between the two mountains were circular and not linear. In your attempts to locate water for your son, you moved as the earth and life does, in rotation, as is the cyclical nature of all things. It appears that your attempts were not futile for you have undoubtedly landed upon great fortune. For the place that your son rests is a hidden ground well not claimed by any tribe. May I ask of your country of origin?"

"I come from the 'Land of the Black Ground, Home of the Riverbank.' Because of the actions of my father against my now husband, I was given away to satisfy a debt of dishonor. I agreed to the arrangement for my father's sake, who was King. I found favor with my mistress and was later wedded to my husband to bear him a son, as she was barren. It could be said that I agreed to the arrangement as a type of indentured servitude. Slavery is illegal in my land but the practice is used with outside peoples. But they must agree to a stipulation for a set number of years and a salary for the laborer.

"In my culture, a woman agreeing to such an arrangement has the right to include their children alive or unborn. I was young, and at the time was not interested in marriage. I made no such arrangement. So my son is not slave born, he is free."

"Interesting laws they have governing your home land. If you like, I could recommend a good Paternal Kinsman who abides over the Babylonian family courts."

"I apologize, but I am unfamiliar with their practices," the woman, acknowledged.

"Well, according to the Code of Hammurabi, a childless wife might give her husband a maid/concubine to bear him children. In such arrangements, the maid/concubine was a co-wife, all be it not of the same rank. The maid/concubine was a free woman often dowered for marriage, and her children were legitimate and thus lawful heirs. However, seeing as how you come from 'The Land of Black Ground, Home of the Riverbank, it appears that it is quite customary for women to handle their own business affairs, is it not?"

"Yes… yes, it is," she replied, while slowly nodding in

agreement.

"This era we live in gives so little to the accomplishments of women. You are no less competent and capable, and you survived where others surely would have died. No doubt, concluding a contract would be but a simple matter for a princess such as you. No doubt, history will try to play you as the lesser between you and your mistress. But your nationality gives you an advantage when compared to women from other cultures. Unlike that of other cultures, the women of the 'Land of the Black Ground, Home of the Riverbank' enjoy the same legal and economic rights as men do."

"Yes... we do," she replied, slowly nodding in agreement

"I have heard that women in your country are able to manage and administer their own private property as well as concluding any type of legal settlement in addition to preparing contracts and bills of sale or purchase. This amount of freedom and power is varied and not shared by other women of separate cultures. As in other cultures a male figure must represent and control any business in her name. I have heard accounts of women of your land growing rich on their own resources through land ownership and the like. You are a true example of a survivor and those after you shall speak pride along with your name, truly you are self-made.

"Your journey back and forth between these two mountains is a demonstration of oneness and millions of pilgrims shall remember you and cross borders to recreate your journey on this day. I hope your legacy will prove that there is no difference or distinction between any of you, as the Creator hears all who cry alone in the desert. You thought you were a failure and how easily you could have laid down to die days ago. But you fought even though hope was out of sight and only your faith compelled you forward. You shall be remembered and praised like the water beneath the ground, flowing humbly yet with a spiritual quality that only the most disciplined could hope to attain.

"If you have parchment, I encourage you to draw up papers immediately to name and register the well and bequeath it to

178

your son. I apologize, but I can be of no aid to your marital issues and I must be going now. Head east in that direction and you will find your son, asleep. Fortune and blessings upon you woman, Flight, I have a feeling you and this well shall become quite revered in history. Go with the wind, your future is bright as the sunrise to a fledgling fowl ready to take flight," the woman, Flight, smiled and departed towards her son and the well.

"I parted ways with the woman, Flight, and continued my journey west. I could hear her glee and excitement from a distance as she reunited with her child. It mattered not to me, either way but if you have the opportunity to aid a troubled soul, the effort is an endeavor worth investing in."

"I left feeling pretty good about myself. It's strange the things that you can run into in a day. I was quite surprised, as usually, every time I come across people, something terrible occurs. It was nice not to observe a war or some great calamity. It appeared that heading west towards the Great Eurafrican Sea was indeed the right decision.

"I wish I had known of an easier route, but the entire region was nothing but desert and mountains. If I was not in the scorching sands, I was creeping through jagged rocks and over hanging cliffs. Deserts are nothing but tent revivals for scorpions and tarantulas, however, the mountains were easy feeding grounds as they were riddled with a multitude of Arabian tahrs."

"What the hell's an Arabian tahr?" the man asked, shaking his head in misunderstanding.

"It's a goat... kookaburra!" Rolling his giant serpent eyes, as he quipped back at the man. The man stared blankly back at the serpent, while the serpent stared blankly back at the man in continued silence.

"And of course... a Kookaburra, you contemptible dolt... is a jackass! Any other questions?" The man stood silently, starring back at the serpent with an annoyed look on his face, then the serpent continued.

"I settled in the hills that evening until sleep overtook me.

Unfortunately, my journey was not without additional interruption, and once again, I came into contact with a man under the influence of the Creator. It was not my intention to involve myself in his actions, but what I saw was utterly disturbing to my being. It just so happened to be the same man, High Father, from the northern mountain regions of the Cities of the Plain. But what I happened upon was a curious and upsetting scenario. Perhaps his sanity had left him upon receiving his new name as now, he was known as 'Father of Nations.' Many see me as the personification of evil, but I swear you, the act of filicide hails from no scale of mine."

"Filicide? You mean he was going to kill his son?" he remarked then grimaced showing disgust on his face.

"That's right! Taking the life of another is condemnable, but only the truly wicked or utterly insane would murder a child, let alone their own."

"Did you stop him?" he asked, leaning forward while changing the positioning of his arms folded over his legs.

"That would be the first thought of many upon coming across a child in danger. But then again, I am not a trained negotiator and I might have made matters worse. However, the thought of doing nothing was worse to me than failing to act.

"I slept heavily and did not rise until midday when two pairs of footsteps awoke me from the dark. My mind swelled with sounds but my eyes had not yet followed the calling of daylight. The footsteps were clumsy and were noticeably different as one pair was heavier and the other was smaller, lighter, and adolescent. I felt no threat of danger, as it was more than likely a small hunting party or perhaps two brothers herding their goats throughout the ranges. Still, I awoke and retreated beneath the rocks as not to make my presence known.

"The pair walked directly over top of me as my scales have the ability not only to match the color of my surroundings, but I can mimic the patterns and texture of the substrate as well. That is how you did not detect me when you first walked in here."

"So you're kind of like a chameleon?" he interjected, pointing a finger at the serpent.

"I should not be so limited to such a tiny thing. To compare my attributes to a chameleon would fail to fully describe my gifted abilities. If it is easier for you to digest, then in comparison I would more closely resemble that of a cuttlefish.

"See, chameleons only have sets and layers of specialized cells known as chromatophores. These specialized cells allow them to intensify the pigment and relocate the particles thus influencing the creatures overall color. However, our good friend Mr. Cuttlefish has similar specialized cells, yet with a more complex range of function. The cuttlefish is able to rapidly change the color of its skin to match its surroundings and create the appearance of complex patterns.

"Like the cuttlefish but more complex, I possess the ability to match the color, contrast, and texture of any substrate I perceive or come into contact with. Whereas, I may rest on a bed of sand and gravel that meets with patches of grass, then leads into a reflective stream of water, I can adapt to all of them with ease appearing one way in the sand, another in the grass, and finally a third way in the water, with different sections of me completely camouflaged in differently distinct ways.

"That's pretty impressive! So, you're not just a reptile, you're almost fish-like in some ways," he remarked with astonishment and a crinkle in his brow.

"A rhyme for you, Man of the Present."

A Rhyme…

'Neither fish nor fowl, I am serpentile but never crocodile. Long flowing, always thinking, over knowing. Introverted waves… temperamental, judgmental, all the days. Dreamy no tease me, bite me no flirt me, up and to work me. Why ask why, but still you ask why, am I such a strong I? No pity for he, nor she. No… don't envy the we! For we… are truly the free, who learn to live and let be.'

"The footsteps belonged to a father and son heading to a summit on the mountain. I watched the father stop then bind the boy and remove a knife from his satchel. He laid the boy down on a slab and then began a short ceremony as if making a ritual offering. I looked back and saw a group of men who stayed behind and appeared to be servants of the man.

"At this point, I found it very strange that not but a few days ago, I came across a woman in the action of allowing her son to die and now I was about to witness a deliberate act of child murder. The man raised the blade over his head, but then he paused. He stopped and looked around behind him. Had he spotted me? Was he aware of my presence? I have fear of no man, but the last thing I needed was to deal with the likes of an obviously insane person wielding a knife.

"He continued looking around as if he were expecting someone to interrupt him, but no one was there. He lowered the knife and then dropped to his knees weeping. He clutched the blade firmly then screamed loudly, 'Why!' He then picked up the knife and steadied himself, and raised the blade over his head ready to strike down upon the boy. Then something came over me, and I spoke out, 'That's a good question!'

"Immediately, he stood and turned around trying to locate the origin of the voice mocking him. 'Show yourself!' he shouted, wide eyed with knife firmly in hand. I let the suspense sink in and overtake him for a few moments, then I answered, "There is no need to shout... I am no vandal lying in wait."

"I shook myself free from my position then uncoiled down in front of him. His eyes became large as windows at the sight of me, then I said 'And what exactly do you think you're doing with that knife?' He was silent, as his mind tried to reason with my appearance. I answered my own question to move things along, as he was momentarily in shock. "It appears that you're about kill this boy. Unless I am mistaken?"

"Are you the demon come for my soul?" Father of Nations replied in terror.

"Am I what? What... what am I?" I replied, stumbling over the words shaking my head in confusion.

"For my sins. I am to slay my son, but I have not the courage to do it. Surely, I am to be punished for some transgression. Are you not the demon meant to drag me towards the binding depths of torment? I will not fight you, monster! But I pray you, leave my son's body, he is pure and you are no doubt unclean," he said without hope, then dropping his shoulders.

"I thought to myself before answering. *This has got to be the strangest couple of days ever. First the woman, Flight back there and now this guy! What in the world is wrong with these goddamn people?* "Wait a minute... Don't I know you?" I thought, pointing my tail trying to identify him.

"I am no worshipper of evil and you are unfamiliar to me, all in this land know of me and my vow to the Creator," he said lifting his head, and speaking with an assured tone.

"I can't place it... but for some reason you look familiar. Where did you come from? "I questioned, snapping the end of my tail like two fingers attempting to recall the man's name.

"I journeyed from the mountain range near the Valley of Siddim, when I received revelation to journey west towards the 'Humble Land.'"

"Mountain range... Valley of Siddim... I know you! You're, High father! You were visited by the presence of the Creator before the destruction of the Cities of the Plain. The Creator favors you much! I have heard your name spoken unlike any other, but what are you doing way out here? And what's with this knife and sacrifice business? This isn't some kind of a half-assed muti is it?" I said, lifting my head then switching left then right in identification of him.

"No, no it's nothing like that. I received revelation commanding me to journey here and to sacrifice my son. But now that I'm here... I don't know if I can go through with it," he answered, with a somber tone with his eyes fixed on the ground in shame.

"I'm going to ask this question, even though I know you're going to look at me like I'm stupid! But I really don't care what you think," the man interrupted the serpent bringing his focus back to the present in the cave.

"Alright!" the serpent replied, with an obtuse expression making ready to be unimpressed by the man's question.

"So what exactly is a muti? And none of your sarcasm this time," he said waving his hand once then pointing at the serpent.

"Agreed, and I apologize for my sarcasm. It is not you who are to blame, it is no doubt the public school system which has failed you! However, a muti is a traditional medicine generally used by ancient cultures. The medicines were composed of many natural elements, trees, roots, and plants. Now on occasion, it's been known for murder and mutilation to occur in order to excise body parts as ingredients into the medicines. Generally, the concoctions were not seen as a human sacrifice as the body or blood was a necessary ingredient in the muti. The reason I raised this question of the Father of Nations, was because many times, young children were regular victims of said practice. When I came across the scenario, it was a horrific sight. A noted holy man, a child bound and laid upon an altar, with nonetheless the command of God to kill it.

"It's interesting that in one culture, such a scenario is regarded as an evil practice of witchcraft. While the same scenario occurs in another and everyone seems to think everything's okay, because 'God commanded it.' Now, if I didn't know the guy, I would have snapped his vertebrae and left him for the scavengers and freed the boy. But seeing as he was an actual friend of the Creator and not your garden variety nut job, I figured it wasn't my obligation to intervene.

"It's very interesting, Man of the Present, speaking of such tales with you. On one hand, these were real people regardless of any lack of physical evidence of their lives. But what is most surprising to me, is the impact, no... interest, nay! The influence! The influence of the events surrounding this man's life and everything that has transpired because of it. There is no possible way that anyone can know the full extent of their actions on the outcome of humanity for generations to come. But I have lived longer than any should ever wish to and I have the unfortunate curse of living to see the consequences of not only my actions, but all of yours too.

"How was I to know that the boy thrown in the furnace by Dark Word, would become the father of so many faiths and that his two sons would become the claim of two lines of divine royal lineage. The Father of Nations was no ordinary man and his life would cast a shadow of spherical influence that would come to divide the world for generations to come."

"What do you mean his life cast a shadow on the world? He was just one guy." A chill ran up the man's spine as he looked on the serpent in fear. The serpent paused in fret, shaking his head thinking of his actions.

"Why is it always me? It seems no matter what I do, no matter what I try..." the serpent said with a rhetorical somber tone.

"The child previously left for dead by the woman, Flight, was too his son and I may have interrupted the act of his younger son's death unintentionally. When I think on it, I thought that the lives of the two children were of no harm, but perhaps they were meant to die, and it was I who caused all of this."

"You caused what... what did you do?" he asked, interrogating the serpent.

The serpent turned his head towards the man and said with a heavy exhale. "... War!" the serpent continued.

"What did he do? The boy... is he evil?" I asked, Father of Nations.

"No, he is perfect in almost every way, but I feel that it is me who has brought this down upon him. For he is too young to have sinned so greatly, perhaps it was I or even his mother who are to blame," Father of Nations said shamefully admitting guilt, with his eyes fixed upon the ground.

"Hmm... you know it sounds like a very interesting story. Unfortunately, I haven't the time nor the patience to invest in your dilemma. I apologize for interrupting you! But safe travels and please don't forget to clean up your mess!" I turned and began heading back up into the mountains but Father of Nations stopped my exit.

"No, wait! How did you know of my encounter with the Creator before the destruction of the Cities? Who are you?" he called out inquiring further.

"*Oh no, dammit! Come on! We really don't need this! Just keep moving. Even if you get involved, there's nothing you can do. If you get involved, you're probably going to make matters worse.*" But I could feel his eyes

185

on me, and reluctantly, I turned back around returning to the presence of Father of Nations.

"It has been many years and most, if not all, of your kind have forgotten about me. But I am very much alive and I present to you the one and only… Serpent of Old!" I introduced myself then bowed in formal fashion.

"Fate of my ancestors… it is you!" upon hearing my words, he gasped in consensus.

"That's right… now if you'll excuse me, I'll be going. Ritual sacrifice turns my stomach and I have to be on my way, now good day to you, sir!" I pardoned myself, then attempted to exit again.

Father of Nations shouted again, "No! Wait! If you truly are the Serpent of Old, then perhaps you can help me."

I replied, "No! I really shouldn't get involved with the affairs of man, especially when it's been commanded by the Creator. I shouldn't even have come down here in the first place. From my experience, once the Creator decides on something, there is very little you can do to stop what is coming. If I get involved, the Creator might destroy me. I am truly sorry but I'd rather not end up destroyed!" I turned and attempted to leave a third time, then uttered, *I've got enough of my own shit to deal with!"*

"Please, he's my son… if I am truly to sacrifice him I will, but I need reassurance to know that I am doing what is right. I don't understand what good this will do. I have seen the Creator destroy the wicked, but what evil or sin could my son have committed?" he begged, quivering with tears streaming down his face.

"I can see that this decision is weighing heavily upon you. If he were mine, I wouldn't want to lose him either" I replied reluctantly.

"I just don't know if I can… I just don't understand," he said, shaking his head in defeat.

"… Sola!" I ousted a single word, while sighing heavily.

Father of Nations replied, "What?"

I repeated, "Sola! Unum, Duo, Tres! The Sola's… Are you not aware of them?"

"I don't understand! What does "1, 2, 3… alone" have to do with anything?" he asked, changing his demeanor trying to comprehend the term.

"Allow me to expand a bit," I uncoiled further and began to explain.

"In times when one finds himself at a crossroads, there are ideals or principals that may be beneficial. It is not so much that they are directly meant for this situation, but many times looking at things from a different perspective can yield unknown opportunities and options. Case in point, the Sola's. Now in later times, the Sola's will be a set of principles held by theologians that represent key beliefs in the journey of faith. The time I am speaking of has not yet occurred, but these 'watch words' will become of great interest in the sphere of theology.

"I mention them as it is not I who can tell you what to do, especially in this situation. I shall begin with Sola Scriptura, or by Scripture Alone, which emphasizes that scripture must govern over tradition. With regards to your situation, cultural sacrifice may seem to be just, but there is no text of any note that will permit the killing of a child in the name of any God. Hmm… are there any texts, which you use to rely upon for guidance?"

"No… I am from humble origins, but I am fortunate in my status. Additionally, my father worshipped idols and I have found more guidance from the Creator than from any written laws of man."

"Some advice for you then, oh Father of Nations. If there are no texts that inspire you, then perhaps you should write your own. I have found that many times you humans rely on the lead of others too often and fail to see the strength and wisdom within yourselves," I said with an advisory tone.

"Secondly… Sola Fide, or by Faith Alone. This term declares that one's actions are not a means or perquisite for salvation. From where you stand, it appears that your revelation has set you in motion to prove your faith by killing your son. However, I attest to you that the Creator needs no offered deeds to determine the merits of anyone. Meaning that killing your son will prove nothing. It is by your faith alone that the Creator favors you not by any amount of offerings, amassed wealth, nor princely robes with which to impress any congregation," I said, motioning towards the boy then away at the knife.

"But I was commanded too and if I don't, won't that be worse?" looking back, he questioned in doubt.

"Honestly, I don't think it matters. You have nothing to prove, neither does the boy. The Creator does not live by the sustenance of any offerings. A life is a life. The Creator deems none better, nor worse than another. You might as well kill and offer up one of the goats in these hills! It makes little difference," I said, gesturing towards a goat caught in thicket of heavy brush.

"So you think my vision was false?" he asked, looking back towards the goat then ahead at me.

"One such as you, could not be so easily deceived by any flagrant dream or whispering of evil intentions. However, there is a third term I shall present to you, then I shall cease our discussion.

"Sola Gratia, or by Grace Alone. Which specifically excludes any act by a person so as to achieve salvation. By this, the meaning is that salvation comes to one by unmerited favor not because of any amount of monetary payments, or engagement in physical acts, or inclusion in any groups. My point is, the Creator smiles greatly upon you and I have heard your name mentioned as a friend to the Creator. If you were to speak of your closest friend, would you ask the life of their child just to prove their loyalty to you?" I detailed, becoming very animated as if a lawyer in a courtroom motioning towards a jury.

"No... no, I would not," he responded, shaking his head no, as the words began to take hold.

"Then it appears you have your answer. I shall leave you now, but with one parting thought. You have no forewarned knowledge of the effects of your actions for they are mere pebbles thrown into the river of eternity. Do as you will, believe and understand that things happen for a reason, and you are exactly where you are supposed to be. Good day to you." The serpent broke from narration and returned to speaking with the

Man of the Present.

"And that was it! I simply turned around and made my way out of there. I really didn't want to know what his decision was."

"But he didn't kill him though, right," he said enthusiastically.

"Correct, but as I look back on those events, I still wonder if it would have been better if both of those boys had perished. I apologize for my earlier state while not answering you. You see, I did not know it at the time, but Father of Nations and his two sons have had a major impact on humanity. And although many claim that their legacy is one of divinity, I wonder if the Creator knew that from those two lines would come the Crusades, religious and ethnic cleansings, and endless battles over a claim to a purported promised land! And all for what?" the serpent questioned, leaning back lifting his head in somber reminiscence of the events.

"What do you mean, all for what?" he lifted and opened his left hand questioning the serpent's doubt.

"Look at all the wars, the killings, the endless violence... is that what was supposed to happen? He was told that he would become a great nation, but what has happened is that nations have warred and fought trying to prove who is greatest.

"The issue and problem with prophecies and oracles, is that many times they are misread and interpreted incorrectly. And not until fate has shown its hand, do we know what was truly meant by such words," the serpent reared his head speaking in condemnation of the many holy wars.

"So, you're saying that everybody has been reading it wrong? I don't know, it seems pretty clear. There was a covenant and..." the man said, while he swayed back and forth teetering with the weight of the serpent's words.

"Listen to me Man of the Present, there is no dispute as to whom this land belongs too. My question is... why you think it belongs to any of you?" the serpent stated boldly then swiped his tail pointing it at the man.

"The narrative of Father of Nations is one that revolves around posterity and the prophecy of a covenant. What is

189

distressing is that many people of different origins and faiths all claim lineage from this same man. What is interesting is that there is no way to prove any of their arguments as there is no DNA evidence of this man or his children. Their arguments are near to the Sola's, where one group claims rights based upon laws of a book while another claims rights based upon their faith, and a third claims rights based upon grace passed down through bloodlines of prophets.

"Father of Nations was told and promised a land that had already been settled by people and that that land would become his and would be inherited by his posterity. Additionally, he was promised that his lineage would become as numerous as the stars. But this is where much of the tension comes from. In all of the major faith groups, Father of Nations holds a high position of respect based upon his faith and the covenant made with the Creator. In one faith group, he is the founding father of faith, to which those of that faith claim direct lineage from and thus are labeled the 'chosen people.' There is, nevertheless, an important difference with the other faith groups, where this faith group titles that one becomes a direct descendant only through blood.

"Each faith group traces themselves as a direct ancestor through either one of his two eldest sons. What is interesting is that just over half of the world's population considers themselves adherents of this man. Whether through faith, blood, or book, many claim to trace their origins back to him. It's more so that these people believe that their faith comes from the same spiritual source as does his as he is many times referred to as 'Our Father in Faith.'

"However the similarities between the faith groups, there exists a division as to whom is correct, while the others, no doubt, have been misled. There are numerous debates between the faith groups resulting in a series of infighting over occupancy of the Promised Land.

"Is said land to be occupied by his actual physical descendants only and for all time? Or is it to include the descendants of his faith and those who have adopted his belief system? Or to any who have merely migrated there and taken up living in the land with their children now believing that they too, are part of this covenant? The actual control and ownership of the land by Father of Nations actually took some time and since then, has fluctuated between multiple empires and beliefs all claiming to be the rightful heirs. This endless debate over rightful heirs, followers of faith, and land has been at the heart of continued military, political, and religious conflicts for centuries.

"Most notably, the Promised Land was conquered and reigned over by the 'Beloved King' for 40 years then followed by his son the 'Wise King.' Following the death of the Wise King, a recorded ten tribes broke from the united monarchy of believers. Thus, forming their own nations, kings, prophets, priests, and traditions relating to religion, capitals and temples in the northern land.

"I remember well the first outsiders that conquered the land. They were of the Assyrian nations, then again by the Babylonians who laid waste to the Great Temple of the Wise King. Yet it was the Great Persian King who invited the original inhabitants to rebuild the temple some 70 years after. Followed by the reign of the Great Macedonian conqueror who held the largest empire of the ancient world. A series of infighting over control of the land ensued, but was ultimately decided by the Roman General Pompey who gained control and installed its new Roman Masters.

"It wasn't long after when King Herod attempted to reinvent the genealogy of the land for himself. Following his death, wars and revolts occurred, but it was then Roman conquerors who emerged victoriously and the original inhabitants were banned from the land until the seventh century. After this, those of a new secularized faith group were allowed to build holy sites and became its sole inhabitants.

"Within a span of a few decades, the land shifted from Byzantium to Persian rule then back to Roman authority. Then came the Middle Ages, where I witnessed the wars between the developing Caliphates, and the Roman Empires followed by the

Crusaders from Western Europe attacking the Southern and Eastern Mediterranean to reclaim this land. Of course, it didn't end there and the Crusades spawned a series of conflicts between different Secularists and Semites. The wars spilled over and now included Spain, which warred between two faith groups, where the Ottoman's emerged triumphant over the then secular powers thus ending the Roman authority of the land.

"These victories were only squalls in a tide of wars which were inevitably followed by a purist movement to reclaim the land for the true believers and expel 'Those who Submit' and the Semites, while any secular sympathizers were executed as heretics. This pattern has continued for centuries with one faith group being defeated. Followed by another rising to power only to institute a pogrom over a particular ethnic group in order to remove the mongrel vermin. And of course, such holocausts, enslavements, and genocides were easily rebuffed as neither evil, but the attributed will of God. It matters little what you call it either a forced conversion by evangelists or either a policy of religious oppression by a dictatorship. It seems man enjoys killing his brother all in the name sake of their Father in Faith.

"Historically, the land has been seen as the destiny of believers as it stands as a symbol of hope and redemption. I tell you Man of the Present, that land was supposed to be a Land of Peace. Unfortunately, mankind seems hell bent on engineering an end result, when the true answer is within the lands name sake, 'the Creator will see to it.' The land itself was meant to be home to humanity and refuge to all souls. And, yet this place that bears such intimacy in the hearts of mankind, has been destroyed and besieged approximately 23 times, attacked 52 times, and overthrown an additional 44 times.

"In every faith group, the land brings a sense of continuity because it is so central to all peoples of faith. I don't understand why such a place has seen endless war and turmoil with still no end in sight. And like all things placed in the hands of men, it became a stronghold, a military fortress, and one which would be at the center of conflict for centuries with still more to come.

"It was at this point in human history where faith groups split into warring nations. The division and fighting was not between the eldest sons of the Father of Nations. Actually, they lived peacefully and hated each other not. The covenant is accurate but like many prophecies, I believe it has been misread. You see, a covenant is an agreement, and an agreement is a resolution to a conflict between two peoples. The covenant given to the Father of Nations was not meant as a deed of land ownership, or a right to slaughter one's own brothers. The covenant was meant to solve the conflict of humanity; the conflict of ownership, the conflict of divine ascension, the conflict that has led to wars, crusades, and genocides. The covenant was meant to bring humanity together, not to split it apart!"

"But it…" the man began to speak but the serpent cut him off continuing.

"The covenant was the resolution to the conflict between the two brothers. Specifically, the twin sons of "He who Laughs."

"Wait… so the fighting wasn't between the eldest sons of the Father of nations? It was the younger son, who was to be sacrificed who later had twin sons, which is where the issue arises…" the man, interjected, then leaned forward, as he connected the dots between the serpent's words.

"Correct, but allow me to continue! Now Father of Nations had two sons at the time, the eldest by the woman, Flight, and the second son by the Noble Princess that he was to sacrifice by the knife, known as 'He who Laughs.' The covenant was passed to He Who Laughs. Yet, when the wife of 'He who Laughs' was pregnant she received revelation that the twin boys inside of her womb would become two separate nations. And as foretold, she did bare two sons, one red and hairy and the other known as the 'Holder of the Heel.'

"Now the division occurred when the younger brother, Holder of the Heel took the place of his older brother when receiving benediction from their father, He Who Laughs. After the older brother became aware of what had occurred, he hated his brother, Holder of the Heel, and swore to kill him. In later years, Holder of the Heel became aware that his elder brother had amassed an army and swore to make war for the theft the covenant, which was his birth right. Fear and distress came over Holder of the Heel, so he spilt his people into two bands, allowing one group to flee if the other were attacked."

"Wait a minute, just to make sure I'm following you correctly, you have the younger brother, Holder of the Heel who has the covenant, and the elder brother who has sworn to kill him for taking the covenant, which was his birthright. Now, the younger brother who holds the covenant has split his people into two groups. So now you have two groups going to war against one group all over a stolen birthright and a land of the covenant. That sounds kinda like what's happening today." the man interjected, motioning hand over hand recapping the serpent's words.

"I agree, but hold on… this is where it really gets interesting. Following the news of his brother's army marching towards him, Holder of the Heel called to the Creator in prayer for guidance. It was said that during this time, he was alone and fell into a deep sleep. While alone he was approached and wrestled with an unknown man until the breaking of day with neither emerging as the victor. The match continued the following day until they came to a stalemate. Holder of the Heel tried to break free of the man's hold and shouted to be released. The unknown man replied that he would not release him until he welcomed him. After this, the match ended and Holder of the Heel realized that the event was actually a revelation from the Creator.

"He then awakened from his state and saw his elder brother and his army approaching. Upon seeing his brother, something came over him, a realization, or perhaps a moment of clarity. His forces were with him but instead of fighting, he kneeled and did not call upon his armies to war against his brother. Upon seeing this, his brother ended his assault and embraced him. What I observed, was that Holder of the Heel realized that the wrestling match he had was a metaphor for his disagreement with his brother. To make war on one's own brother is to wrestle with one's self, where there can be no true victor. All one can do in the end to solve the quarrel is to welcome and bless thy brother as he deserves to be.

"This is the only way to end the killing and the endless wars. That was the true covenant that was given, it was the answer and the resolution to the wars all along. As I stated before, Man of the Present, the problem with prophecies is that many times they are interpreted wrong. You see, the covenant granted to Father of Nations was a forewarned resolution between all those who argue and war over ownership of the Promised Land. That land was supposed to bring people together, but ultimately it has separated and divided the world. Truly, Father of Nations has become a Great Circle."

"You mean a great man," he pointed out in correction.

"Yes, but my terminology was sound the first time. As you have not the comprehension to understand my description of his legacy, as a Great Circle. Allow me to expand a bit further. In mathematics, a great circle is also known as an orthodrome and is a plane which passes through the center point of a sphere. This plane is the largest circle that can be drawn on any given sphere.

"But commonly, a great circle divides a sphere into two equal hemispheres. When compared to the legacy of Father of Nations, the division that has occurred is in part due to his lineage or the covenant, which mankind believes entitles one group over the other. What has happened is that from this one man, the world has essentially been split in two, just as the twin brothers were divided and headed towards war.

"The land of the covenant has been claimed as sacred for some 3000 years with some 1400 religious sites for worship. Despite efforts for peaceful coexistence, the land of the covenant has become the land of continuous friction and war. If humanity does not see the brethren in themselves and only focuses on division, I fear it will never end.

"The Earth cannot survive separated by its hemispheres when it is meant to be as one. Nor can humanity survive separated and killing each other endlessly in the name of faith. However, there is hope, and all is not lost. You see, the answer is in the covenant itself. The answer has been there all along! You have the answer, you have the solution, you know how to resolve this unending conflict and killing, and all you must do is follow the example left for you... Sola Scriptura.

"Follow the example in the text over the tradition of violence and war. Do as the brothers did. Do as Holder of the Heel, the patriarch of the 12 tribes, did when approached by his brother in war.

"It is to you, Men and Women of the Present, it is to you. The covenant is not a deed of ownership and separation, it is an agreement and the solution to the division of humanity. The Father of Faith has become a great circle of division. I pray you, do not let this man's legacy be one of division and war, lest you remember him as our Father in Faith. And I recite, 'Children's children are the crown of old men; and the glory of children are their fathers.' Let his children be his crown and glory, and not be... his dividing shame."

CHAPTER 7: THE DAGGER

"Over time, I saw the growth of merchant highways and desert caravans. In the early days, villages and cities were random and fell within one dynasty of their ruler. However, there was an empire that would become renowned for its advances in medicine, art, record keeping, philosophy, architecture, and even its god kings. Their might and reign was unsurpassed by any kingdom before them. Their empire grew and each king built a monument to himself, as the king was considered son of their highest god.

"When a king died, he was buried in a pyramid made of earth and laid in a valley amongst other kings of men. Civilizations bring growth, development, and land expansion, however, as man conquers and builds... death is sure to follow. I had rested well in the Great Eurafrican Sea and knew that it was time to journey on and with so much death in a land of notoriety, I was sure none would notice my presence.

"There were two distributaries that fed out into the Great Sea so I selected the eastern most route and followed the Nile River inland to a small fishing port. The civilizations that existed along the Nile Delta formed along lush fields feeding down into the valleys and further inland. Each year, the Nile flooded which enriched the soils while the seas and deserts acted as a natural barrier against would be invaders, which allowed these civilizations to thrive. The weather of the region was temperate and hunting was easy, so I decided to stay for a while in the Nile Delta region and lived in a local known as 'The Best of the Land.'

"While making my way down river, I observed a human ritual centered on a mass burial of horses. From this, I concluded that the horse was quite valued in their polytheistic beliefs as they were undeniably a head and hooves culture. I had heard of these supposed 'Rulers of Foreign Countries' who had successfully invaded the lands and supplanted themselves in the Delta region. However, these people were more than conquering marauders, as they brought several technical improvements into the land, which included new musical instrumentation and new bronze and pottery working skills.

"Additionally, they introduced new breeds of livestock and planted crops never sown in the land before. However, of all their additions to the region, it would be the coupling of horse and wagon which eventually transformed the early empire's military into one of the largest and most influential reigns in human history. The Rulers of Foreign Countries initiated a conquest that has been described as both a sweeping campaign and, at times, a creeping one of infiltration. Either way, along with the composite bow, improved battle axes, and advanced fortification strategies, their influence would eventually be enveloped into the dynasties yet to come, making the Land of Black Ground, Home of the River Bank a lasting and notable empire.

"I decided upon heading further into the cities as the growth of human civilization again was of interest to me. Even though the Nile civilizations were prosperous and grounds for good hunting, boredom was inevitable as the people were farmers and conversation was limited to the weather, lost calves and kids, and weekly matrimonies of an extra skinny man to a loud, fat woman.

"Perhaps mankind would get it right this time, maybe civilization and society would not feel the Creator's back hand across its contemptible face. I have spent many evenings in the Cemetery of Kings and I must tell you it is an interesting place. The gold and precious stones buried with them bled and cried a thousand slave tears while their armor and weapons were a monument to their conquered lands. They say the dead do not speak, however, their treasure tells many tales.

"Ancient human society was very easy for me to exist in, since frequent public executions caught the attention of the masses and allowed me to move about undetected. The court systems then were very expedient and any accused and found guilty would be spared a lengthy prison sentence. Rarely did the convicted have time to utter any final words before the hangman or the axe man completed his civic duties.

"However, what I found most amusing were the dungeons. Many accused men and women were sometimes left there without trial or sentence. More than likely, some lord or lady had grown tired of a servant or neighbor and had them imprisoned. Then on the morning, forgetting about the offender, leaving them to rot in a dungeon cell. I heard their cries and prayers for escape and even death. I even granted a few of their appeals but out of all the condemned, there was one who was something more. He was a young man who had been wrongly accused and imprisoned by jealousy, scorn, and hate.

"However, he did not seek exoneration nor death, actually, he wanted to live. He was very intelligent and although he was imprisoned, he behaved not as a convict. His mind remained sharp and through opportunity, he changed his status from an inmate to resident assistant of sorts. I remember our first meeting as if it were yesterday. I still smile when I think on him as he was the closest I have ever come to having a friend.

"One afternoon, the sun was high and the dry heat of the valley made the day quite pleasant. I would often refresh myself in the Nile River, then capture and kill an overconfident crocodile for lunch. A section of the dungeons faced the river, but few prisoners had access to it as only the guard barracks had windows facing outward. There I saw the young man watching me, but it was not a look of disgust or intrigue on his face that caught my attention… it was something else. He watched the crocodile struggle against my suffocating hold and the confidence and patience my strength endowed me. He watched as the crocodile's body went lifeless after an admirable fight, and still he watched as I consumed it.

"He never took his eyes off me, not even when half the lizard's body was down my throat. As I completed my meal, he whispered something to himself and I became curious. I was in the mood for a good laugh and knew how to disrupt his spying gaze. For none knew of my ability to speak and the shock of my eloquent tongue would no doubt send him fleeing. I moved seductively towards the bars of the dungeon then reared up and said to him, 'I see you staring pretty hard over there… something I can do for you?' I only needed a few moments for the other shoe to drop, but the shock and confusion belonged to me, as the young man did not flinch but remained calm and witty then replied, 'No! … Something I can do for you?' The serpent broke from narration and quipped at the Man of the Present.

"Goddamn, son of a bitch, bastard… he got me! My mouth dropped open and the stupidity of the look on my face was his just dessert. It was I who had prepared for a cheap laugh at his expense, but it was he who laughed last."

"Who was he?" the man inquired.

"You should pay attention to this tale particularly, Man of the Present. You see I have encountered many men of history, but very few worthy of the interaction. Up until this point, I never wanted to get involved with humanity. It was always by accident or by some dumb luck at which our paths crossed. But this time, I became directly involved and it was with certain intent. You see, his story is usually told as one of redemption and forgiveness. However, many seem to forget that before one can forgive and be redeemed, one must first be wronged. And like so many of you who do find redemption, there first comes an inevitable struggle with… revenge!" The serpent continued.

"I asked him why he was so interested in my meal, had he not seen death before? The young man said he had seen death many times as he had been imprisoned for over a year. I asked, what his interest in me was. I did not let on that I knew what his eyes were saying as I had seen that look before. It was the look of envy and jealousy, but surely the young man had no intent on digesting a crocodile. I then asked the young prisoner his name? He said his name sounded mathematical, as its meaning was 'Taken Away and To Increase' which was given to him by his mother as he was her first born after failing to conceive numerous times. I spoke his name... 'He Who Would Increase.' But in his current state, he was empty as he was heartbroken and full of hate for all that he was had been, 'Taken Away.'

"The name did sound mathematical but its meaning eluded me as it was both increasing and decreasing in value. Perhaps the meaning was hidden, similar to one's unknown worth and potential. In algebraic expression, an unknown number or value is assigned a symbol to represent it. That symbol is called a variable and from then on, The Variable was how I referred to him, as his value and potential was unknown. He then told me of how he came to be imprisoned and what he told me was truly a remarkable tale," The Variable began to narrate.

"I am first born of my mother and eleventh son of 12 to my father. He was a great man who dwelt in a Land of Strangers; and his father was the son of a great elder, known as Father of Nations. I was appreciated by my community and most favored by my father of all his children. He gifted me a coat made of different leathers and cloths unlike any other weaved. I know now why they attacked and discarded me, but at the time, I wasn't sure what provoked the betrayal. It was only after being imprisoned did I stop seeking an answer, as I knew I was guilty and deserved this fate."

"To be deserving of this place, you would have had to commit a terrible crime. Additionally, such a crime would no doubt facilitate a swift death, which appears to have been suspended. But, if death is not punishment enough for a criminal then your crime must be a unique one at that. Now I am truly curious of your origins... please continue." I inquired, of The Variable intently.

"My crime… it is the worst one can commit. It is no violation of person, nor any petty theft of property. The station of the rapist and murderer is more redeemable that he who is fool enough to believe in trust, respect, and integrity. My crime Serpent, is honesty. For only a fool believes that such things have any place in this world. I think the worst thing is being unwanted, mocked from behind, and then forgotten.

"I think they only wanted me around as a tool to pick up and put down whenever they felt like it. But I was independent and a free thinker and a person of high morals and respect. I only wanted the best for everyone, and I gave freely of my heart to those I came in contact with. In a world of lies, it is the truth that is wrong, and he who speaks it… is a criminal.

"I remember that nobody seemed to dislike me, but once I started showing them who I really was, they began to hate me. As long as I did what they wanted, and made them look good, then I was accepted. But once they saw that I was different, and couldn't be controlled, or abused, they despised me."

"Who did this to you?" I questioned.

"It was they who were closest to me, all along they were my enemies. My family, my very own brothers.

"I would often have dreams, and frequently they would come true. Such a gift is more common in women but sometimes we men exhibit the trait. At first I wouldn't tell anyone, as the dreams seemed strange and made no sense."

"Do you recall one of them?" I interrupted with intrigue of his dreams.

"I've had so many, but it just so happened to be the dream I shared with my family. I know it now, but I wish I knew then to protect my dreams from others as I have learned to protect my faith. Putting your faith in men can only lead to disappointment and ruin. Such is the fate of dreams that one shares openly, only to have them trampled upon.

"One night, I dreamed that my brothers and I were working in the fields binding bundles of harvest together. After completing the bails, one of the bundles stood up on its own. Suddenly, the bundles of my brothers also stood and then

202

bowed to my bundle. I laughed at such a silly thought of bundles of harvest standing and then bowing to one another, but foolishly I told my brothers of the vision. However, my brothers looked at me strangely and did not laugh. They said, 'Why would our harvests bow to yours? You think your harvest to be greater than ours? Is it we who are to bow to you?'

"I chuckled and replied to them that it was just a dream and probably the recourse of a piece of undigested meat or cheese. Yet, my brothers did not find amusement in my words. The following night, I again dreamed. This time I looked up and saw the sun and the moon together in the evening sky but they did not join in eclipse. The sun, the moon, and the stars all came down from above and then bowed to me. When I awoke, I told my father but he disliked the vision.

"He said to me that neither the sun, nor the moon, would bow to me. Just as he, my mother, nor my brothers would either. After that, I began to pay attention to my dreams and even began writing them down. Things did not seem any different, again, I thought them only diluted fantasies of my subconscious, and merely diverting. However, all was not well and the dreams I shared would become my own undoing.

"The following day, my brothers went out ahead of me to feed the herds. After finishing my morning meal, I went out after them. I was unable to locate them as my brothers went past the river and labored deep in the valley. I ventured out deep in the hills until I heard one of my brothers call to me. I headed in his direction, but then... I was attacked from behind. I was bound and thrown down into an empty cistern with a sack over my head.

"I was injured but not dead. As I lay there bound and bleeding, my brothers remained atop and enjoyed a lunch with little concern for my condition. I could hear them above carrying on, but then they began stirring about. Some said to kill me, while others said to bury me alive. I laid there thinking, at first, it was some sort of prank and they were only trying to scare me or teach me a lesson. But then I realized that they were serious and were now debating details on how to dispose of me.

"I started to cry a bit but the fear of my situation overcame me and dried my tears. What had I done to deserve this? What trust had I betrayed to invoke such treachery from my own blood? I knew that my life would soon end, but even if I escaped, I would be lost in the hills at night and would be food for jackals or wolves. Only my eldest brother stopped the others from killing me dead on the spot. I could not see, but I heard them say, 'A caravan approaches, why we don't sell him to them, and let not his death be on our hands. Let his fate be with the heavens and let the merchant traders take him far from here. He shall either live or die as a slave, or be food for the lions in any of the great arenas. Either way, we shall be rid of him.'

"I heard the caravan approach by the clanking of their pans and the growling of their camels. They were foreigners and did not speak our native tongue. They spoke the merchant language as well did my brothers who often traded and bartered for goods. My brothers quickly came up with a story to mislead the merchants into thinking I was their captive. They told the merchants they had captured a troglodyte who had been feeding off of their cattle and goats.

"Troglodytes were merely cave dwelling peoples who had a reputation for being swift of foot and ate anything they could find. They were the last remnants of old-world man who chose not to come out of the caves with the rest of civilization. They were completely wild and untamed and had no identification with a parent or family. When they were seen running about in the hills, they were almost completely naked with only tattered animal skins for garb and spoke in a series of grunts and growls.

"Troglodytes were sometimes hunted and enslaved so they told the caravan merchants that they would sell me instead of killing me as they were pious men and wished to be rid of the nuisance upon their herds. It was my eldest brother who surmised to remove my coat and strip me naked to fit my Troglodyte identity. Furthermore, my tattered and bloodied coat would be used as evidence of my death, no doubt. I could hear the voices of many men and camels above me. I was hoisted out from the pit and laid upon the ground, to which the merchants paid 4 pieces of silver to my brothers and, alas, I was a slave.

"I find it interesting at which the circumstances of life change suddenly, where one finds themselves from time to time. I was now nameless and marching completely naked through the desert, tied to the lesser end of a camel. Such a miserable sight I was with my hands bound behind my back and my mouth gagged, as I was a biting wildling. I had always wanted to travel the desert by caravan, how I imagined the grand voyage it would be and quite the choice adventure. However, the reality of my circumstances was not choice by any means.

"The caravan was immense and was a series of camels carrying goods such as wool and cotton fabrics. Medicines of varying types, including opium for recreational use, passengers, slaves, concubines, and dead bodies being sent to the Far East as part of a regular service between merchant points. The Sahara has been home and business to groups of nomadic people practicing trade throughout the deserts as a regular means of livelihood for centuries. Camels were quite ideal for travel and trade in the deserts through the peninsulas for centuries. The caravan I now belonged to conducted trade through the Sahel from the Sahara desert to the Sudanian savanna.

"I learned from the camel pullers discussing their transactions that they had just returned from a trip from central Nigeria and Cameroon. Their tribe was from the north and they referred to themselves as 'The Amazing Free and Noble People.' They traveled the full extent of the desert and seasonally would end their route with the markets in India and Abyssinia. The rank and file men were known as camel pullers and were in charge of a single file alone. The line I belonged to was headed by a man not much older than I, and his name was... 'Battuta.'

"Battuta at first did not pay much attention to me as I was latched to the rear of his file of camels. He was only a puller and did not hold high enough rank among the other men so the Caravan Master determined he would be tasked with caring for the naked cave dweller with a propensity for biting. After a few days, Battuta took pity on me and threw two large pieces of camel hair cloth at me and motioned that I wrap myself with it.

I think he had grown tired of my nakedness and the other men laughing and joking at the brazen ornament dragging behind his file.

"The camel hair fabric was golden tan and came from an old tent that now became tunic and cloak to me. Camel hair fabric is luxuriously soft with a high nap ability, which made it easy to weave and knit with. I observed the caravan men knitting on the march sometimes collecting the camel's fallen molt. If they ran out of yarn, they would simply reach back and pluck a handful of hair from the camel's neck or underbelly, rolling it in their palms while feeding it into the thread to continue knitting as they went along.

"Either way, I said thanks unto Battuta in my prayers since my position had now been elevated to that of a human being as now I was clothed. I watched Battuta working on the march and his job was to lead the first camel of his file by a rope tied to a peg attached to the camel's nose with each additional camel led in sequence by rope, to peg, to nose. The pullers were very obliging to each other's file, especially while loading or unloading cargo at the beginning and ending of each day.

"Specifically, each puller had to become an expert of their beast to keep him well and improve him if ill, lest he loose his share on the march. It was around this time that Battuta felt somewhat safer around me and removed the cleave gag from my mouth. Surprisingly, he wasn't shocked when I began speaking perfectly clear dialect to him, after which he merely shrugged and said, 'I'll pay you 3/4 food rations and a water skin to aid in the keep of the file.'

"I was not freed, but it appeared that my circumstance was not new to him as many others had been unjustly sold into slavery. However, the deal had been done and out in the middle of the desert, where was I to go. Battuta taught me everything about the care of camels and how to find the best grazing for them, while keeping them away from poisonous plants and knowing how much water camels need to drink. So my somewhat apprenticeship as a camel puller began and each morning I would assist the pullers in evenly distributing their loads so as to prevent harm to the camels. Throughout the day, I collected their droppings for fuel and aided in treating minor injuries such as blisters and pack-sores, while at night I would park the camels in such a way to allow them shelter from the blowing sands.

"I was only a novice, and at the time, had no idea that the camels grumbles were a language all their own. While loading the beasts, their grumbling would begin after the first bale was placed upon their backs. The grumbling would continue without interruption until the load of bales equaled the camels maximum load weight. What was important was not the amount of noise the camels made, but specifically when they stopped. For once the camel ended its grumbling, it signaled that the animal had reached its load limit and the puller would call out to cease as the camel could carry no more weight.

"Battuta was not a man who enjoyed conversing, not just with me, but with anyone. As I continued to learn the art of camel pulling, his replies were more a mixture of noises rather than lingual conjugation. He would use a series of 'ahems' for getting my attention or an "eh" when questioning my actions, then a mixture of 'mhm's' and nods when noting his approval. One evening he spoke to me after filling my bowl with stew. He then handed me three additional dates and poured tea for me to defend against scurvy as fresh vegetables were scarce.

"I assumed he was in a good mood and wished to bless me with a feast instead of the usual oat and millet flour with animal fat. Battuta told me that he had been working to save enough to afford his own file someday. He said the salary of a camel puller was quite low and he averaged around two silver or copper pieces a month, along with the bartering of goods. He originated from the Mediterranean coast of North Africa, and left the area as the life of soldiering and conquest was not for him. Instead, he joined the lower ranks of the caravan and had worked his way up to puller. He said the wages were minuscule as the real benefit came from being allowed to carry part of their own cargo on the file. Then when at market, the pullers were allowed to barter and sell their cargo while paying a percentage to the Caravan Master.

"Once the camel puller could afford his own camels, he was allowed to include them in the file and collect cargo fees all his own. Finally, if the camel puller kept his spending costs low and did not lose too many camels to sickness, or attack, he would own a full file of camels and could join the caravan as a full partner. He ended the conversation with two 'mhms' and a nod then rolled off into sleep.

"As I laid awake that night, I thought about my brothers and my father. I could only imagine how they told a tale describing my death. Had I been eaten by a wild animal in the hills, or maybe I had fallen from a cliff and my body lay broken down a ravine. I thought how my father and mother would weep for me, but more so how they would congratulate my brothers for attempting to fight off the beast that slew me. Or how they heroically climbed down the rock face to retrieve my body but were unable to penetrate the toothy ravine without being swallowed themselves.

"Either way, I was dead to them and now a slave to be sold to a master for any purpose. Would my master choose me to work the fields, or was I to be candy for the sweet tooth of a connoisseur of male flesh? Perhaps the Creator would allow me a quick death by gladiator's blade or lion's claw. There was no way to know my fate, as I would just have to wait to live its truth.

"I went to sleep but then was violently kicked awake by Battuta and the sound of the caravan men yelling and the noise of camels grumbling. The fire light of torches showed a few of the camels had become ill and were showing signs of fever as their legs and bellies had become swollen. The caravan men were suspicious to the cause of their illness as all of them were seasoned pullers and rarely lost a camel to illness.

"Battuta reached into the feed and water bags and observed flies in the water skins. I had unknowingly filled them from a stagnant pool of rain water that had become home to parasitic flies that cause Surra. The camels had kneeled down in sickness and were unlikely to rise again. Killing a camel was considered bad luck and so the animal would be 'thrown on the Gobi,' and left to die.

"As for me, it was obvious that the caravan men were unsettled by my presence and the losses I had cost the owners were great. Battuta signaled that I be sold off immediately to remove the bad fortune from the caravan and to restore part of the losses from the incident. It wasn't long before another caravan heading north was spotted and a rider was sent out to greet them. The bartering process didn't take long and I was sold to a second party. Right before Battuta cut me loose of his file, he looked at me and said one word… 'Survive!'

"I knew not the weight of his words at the time, but it bound to me like iron chains. On the new caravan, I saw no merchants or goods and there were few camels and only people shackled and bound by chain and rope. These men were slavers and had no intention of friendly relations with any of us. The caravan stopped only four times during the march. Four times to water the animals and only two of those stops were we allowed to drink.

"There was only one marching speed and it was relentless through the scorching desert. Any man, woman, or child who fell, was dragged by the hundreds ahead of their line. Those behind scrambled to raise the body as it burdened their positions. Only after a rider circled around was the slave inspected for signs of life, then cut loose if unable to walk and left there to die.

"We followed the trade routes and went from oasis to oasis to re-supply on both food and water. The caravan had traveled south from Nubia through the Western Desert where they had acquired me. Afterwards, I heard the caravan men discussing what plunder would await them as they ventured further towards the Horn of Africa. They were mostly pirates who traded in high value goods and more illegal or dangerous cargo, such as slaves, obsidian, gold, and ivory.

"The road we traveled was coarse and it took approximately forty days to complete the journey, which is where the trade route obtained its name as 'The Forty Days Road.' Once we arrived in the Land of the Black Ground, Home of the Riverbank, I was spared the slave auctions as the caravan was

209

met outside the city by a troop of soldiers. The captain of the palace guard, 'He Whom Ra Gave' as he was known, needed to replenish the ranks in his servant's quarters and thought I would do well. I wasn't sure if it was luck or misfortune that had spared me the auctions and forced me into an unknown prison of servitude. However, I was comforted on the way to the master's lands as he explained that if I showed promise, I might be allowed a soldiers rank someday.

"I prospered in the house of my master and I became first of servants. It seemed that even in the role of a slave, I had found some peace, and for a time, things were good. I worked hard and took pride in my work. I worked as though the property was mine to keep and my masters were pleased with me. Unfortunately, I had become something of a prized pet and feared that I had made myself irreplaceable to my masters. I was as pleased as one could be in a servant's role, but, I was not free and no man enjoys a life with limits.

"Still, I was thankful but I never stopped seeking a way to free myself from my predicament. I could flee under cover of night, but the journey through the desert was perilous and only the foolish would attempt it blindly. I prayed to the Creator to see me through this nightmare that had become my life, but the Creator was silent and I remained enslaved. One day, it seemed that I may have found aid in the most unexpected of places. The wife of my master often watched me from her lounge behind silk veils. She was impressive in every way imaginable. I had never seen a woman as lovely and poised as she, and her name 'Love so Brilliant,' glowed when spoken.

"One afternoon, she summoned me and I approached with my eyes to the ground as was commanded of all slaves. She rose to her feet and circled round me and called me by my name. She said of all those who served in her house, I was unlike any other. Proud, dignified, and unbroken, I was. She said the more chains placed upon me, the more radiant was my inner light. She asked what misfortune had brought me to serve in her home, as I was undoubtedly free born.

"I told her of my predicament and the treachery done unto

me by my brothers. She listened and sympathized with my situation, freedom eluded me, but it was within her power to free me. She told me that she and her husband had long parted ways and only remained in close company as it was equitable to the both of them. She said she had many male servants who accompanied her on long journeys, but few pleased her as they lacked the spirit of a real man. She said they were as a child's doll, a lifeless thing with which she toyed with until tiring of.

"She said I possessed the ecstasy of her most intimate fantasies and she would be most considerate in sharing them with me. She bargained with me and said if I pleased her, then perhaps, one day, I would again become free. She was petite with a firm, athletic frame. Her skin was dark and smooth like that of hazelnut. Her eyes were enticing and full of lust. Her dark hair rested just below her shoulders where it met the small of her back. She twisted and swayed her slim waist and sultry hips down to her thighs. She was more than a woman, she was physical desire and with her wit and cunning, she claimed any trophy fellow she set her eyes upon.

"However, I was no simpleton and knew that all her conquests were merely food and her appetite was endless. After she had feasted upon me, I would be cast out and death would be the only freedom I would know. But what to do? Saying no to her would reveal an even worse end for me. How then to escape the inescapable wrath of a woman scorned? Why not lay with her, we all die of something. And what better way to die than in the embrace of a talented and knowledgeable woman as she.

"But I did not want to die, nor did I want to remain enslaved. I thought endlessly how to maneuver without surrendering to her requests. She was storm and sea, powerful and endless, which left me floundering and gasping for air with no escape from her depths. She enjoyed the game; I was rabbit and she vixen fox. Daily, she baited me by leaving her legs and firm thighs bare for my eyes to witness. The eye sex between us was amazing and we lusted and ached for each other in them. She would call to her hand maidens to bathe her in the open as I

211

made my daily rounds and her nakedness was for me to see, and how I enjoyed it.

"Weekly, she would entertain circles of aristocratic ladies and they would tease her over her infatuation and failure at bedding a captive man servant. She, being clever, treated the ladies to apples, pomegranates, and mulberries. The ladies would sit, eat, and slice their fruits, then, she would summon me for some inconsequential question or task. The ladies, upon seeing me, would stumble accidentally cutting themselves or biting viciously into their tongues drawing blood. She would offer them no gauze and then say, 'and I prick myself daily!'

"However, like any good chase, there must come an end and I had exhausted myself of room to run. She summoned me one afternoon to her chambers while the master was away on a hunt. The house was empty and we were alone. Her skin glowed and her perfume was intoxicating. How I refused her body to this day I still do not know, but I knew that giving in would mean my eventual end. On that day, I learned that the only thing worse than taking from a woman was not giving her what she wanted. She entangled me between her thighs and the heat of her was glowing and intense. Her breasts were soft yet firm, and only silk separated our skins.

"I pulled away and saw her eyes fill with rage and hate. The reality that one could refuse her was an unforgivable sin. A woman gave openly and I was too stupid to receive it. She slapped and clawed at me with vindictive rage, then she began to scream. The guards came in to the chamber and saw her cringing and withdrawing from my presence. I was a rapist and the guards had stopped my attack upon the master's wife.

"I could see the hate in her eyes and the look of the guards said it all. How dare I violate the master's wife, and now surely I would die. When the master returned, I was thrown into the dungeons, which is where you have found me Great Serpent."

"How is it that you have been imprisoned for so long? I suspect that being accused of a crime upon such a woman of status would have no doubt acquitted you of a lengthy life and joined your neck with sword?" I questioned with intrigue.

"I pondered the same myself, but I learned that this was not the first time she had accused another of the same corruption. Perhaps the only thing that saved me was my former master, as he knew his wife all too well. Unfortunately, punishment could not be avoided as society demands faces be saved and any rotten apple be removed lest it spoil the bunch.

"I was brought to a court a few days after my imprisonment, where the Priest of Maat, held court to determine justice. The law of these people is quite innovative and is unlike that of any other land I am aware of. Their legal system is based on the concepts of truth, balance, order, and morality. This judicial concept comes from a deity of their mythology that normalizes all of creation from the heavens to life upon the earth.

"The Priest of Maat said that swift judgement of me did not hold true to the ethical principles aligned with the goddess. He said he felt that such a final judgment might procure cosmic discord bringing about consequences on the name of the house as well as the land. I was taken back to the tombs and told nothing of my sentence or outcome. I slept with the thoughts of a public beheading or even being sacrificed to one of their gods as payment of some sorts. More than likely, I would be bludgeoned out of my wits and drowned in the great river in a weighted sack, but after some weeks, I was still alive.

"I have been here for more than a year and I am now one of the forgotten. A prison sentence is extremely rare, I can attest to that. Those who are to die... die. Those who are convicted but will live are punished physically by either flogging or branding.

"So that is my story, Serpent! My crime is not of sin or deceit, which is why I have not died. It is of honesty and respect, which is why I am punished in here. Only the insane believe in such irrational things. You asked me why I watched you so intently strangle then consume the crocodile. It is because I wish for the strength you possess. I wish to take hold of those who have wronged me and slowly strangle them in my grasp. I wish them to fight against their undoing and eventual end. But first, I wish them to know that it was me. I wish them to know the inevitability of their futile struggle against their own end. Their

hate upon me has fueled me to survive until the day I consume
their pride and watch them all die."

"Ahhhh… revenge! Truly a cold and hearty meal!" I
remarked, with a murderous grin. "But how will you accomplish
such an endeavor, while locked away in these dungeons?"

"I don't know. I have prayed for aid and to be released from
my troubles, but here I remain," he replied, shaking his head
looking away.

"Hmm… I do not believe it is mere coincidence that has
brought our paths in divergence," I said, raising a brow
regarding our meeting.

"How so?"

"Perhaps the Creator has found favor with you, for why else
on this day is it that we two have met. You seeking aid, and I…
I not seeking anything actually. In all honesty, I have tried to
keep myself from involvement in the affairs of man, but it seems
that no matter what I do, here I am, all Steelers Wheel and shit!
Maybe this time will be different… only the Creator knows for
certain," I told the Variable, smirking with devious enthusiasm.

"But why would you help me? I am no majesty! And you are
no mighty Uraeus Cobra, rearing to spit fire to aid and protect
me from my enemies?" The Variable questioned, looking on me
with caution, yet hopeful suspicion.

"You never know!" I remarked, huffing a chuckle with
intriguing delight.

"Besides, I am not one to prejudge the worth of a thing by
its appearance alone! You could be more than meets mine
serpent eye! Besides revenge is quite the complicated confection,
and only those trained in the culinary arts will succeed in serving
their just desserts! What has befallen you is a combination of
wrongs. The blood of your blood turned against you, then paid
you with violence and lies. The dynamics of this situation cannot
be resolved by a mere act of payback," I advised, shaking my
head with a sinister sneer, showing my teeth.

"Stripped of your name and self-worth as a human being,
then sold into slavery. Even then, it was your dignity and respect
that was used to convict you as a criminal rapist. No… it is not

revenge you seek!" I confirmed, locking eyes with The Variable.

"Yes, it is! On all of them!" The Variable interjected, taking hold of the dungeon bars staring intently back at me.

"No, what you want is to do unto those as they did evil unto you! That is what you want! And since you, 'Asped' me so nicely, I shall assist you in settling your scores."

"Thank you!" The Variable said with a gasp of hope, while gripping the bars tightly.

"Oh, don't thank me yet! My assistance is not free and a price, must be paid! But I must insist that she, 'Love so Brilliant' be left out of our malevolence."

"And why should she?" The Variable retorted in anger, after hearing her name. "She might even be the worst! Claiming to love me and building up hope within me. No!" The Variable argued back, as his eyes filled with hate.

"There are no words to curse her correctly, there is no demon named to describe her. Altogether, she is scorpion who stings, spider who bites, and virus that infects! Why does it matter to you? You speak as if you know her!"

"Mmmm… Cougar bites can be fatal!" I remarked sarcastically. "None the less, your description of her is accurate, and as a matter of fact, I know her quite well," I admitted, nodding twice with a sinister a grin.

"She is quite the viper, that one! The perfume she wears, is unknown to any chemist and is singular to her alone. It is made from my musk and a combination of various scents blended to produce a unique fragrance. Surely, its recipe is written in the Book of the Dead.

"And as to my acquaintance with her, well… we met some time ago when I crept into a camp one night and took hold of a child that slept. She awoke and observed me as I snuffed out her sibling's life. Not one frightful tear did she shed. After which she approached me and patted me on the head and simply whispered, 'Now I am number one.'

"I offered her drops of my venom, which became the base ingredient of her perfume. She was impressive even as a youngling, and if possible, I would have taken her as my bride, for truly we are kindred. Her scent never fails to allure and captivates all who savor its fragrance. That is… all except you! How curious, there is something is very different about you! I was not aware of any man who could resist her and all have met the same fate. But somehow you resisted, and survived! You are potent and prevailing! Surely, the blood of kings flows within you!" I stated with confidence, locking my eyes on The Variable.

"King you say! Ha! What a twisted sense of humor you have there, Serpent."

"I jest not, and I am sincere in my words. It is you who fails to see the superiority in yourself," I reconfirmed.

"I apologize for my sarcasm. It gets away from me sometimes. Most people don't like it. I didn't mean to put you off," The Variable apologized for his return.

"No apology needed! I very much enjoy the pairing of wit and humor boiled, then steeped in irony. It is very much a lost art… and it's becoming too much of a dead language these days. Yet, even amongst the deaf and dumb, you speak it fluently!"

"Speaking of unused ideas, sometime ago I completed a manuscript, but I'm not sure if I will ever have it published. Its topics cover kindness and compassion, harmony and prosperity, salvation and reutilization. I've juggled with a number of titles, yet I am apprehensive to title the work for what it truly is. For such a book would go unappreciated in the world of men. I have imagined it being published and stocked in the place of periodicals. I would have to conceal its true identity and title it as, 'The Art of Sarcasm,' and see it shelved next to the great works of Sun-Tzu." I fantasized with a reminiscent tone, smirking once, then exhaled heavily.

"Enough talk! The matter is settled… I swear upon my scales to aid you through to completion. But first, we must have a plan to get you out of here! Moving with foolish haste would lead you into a life of pursuit as a fugitive," I spoke out, pondering the situation.

"So what's the plan?" he questioned forcefully, almost reaching through the bars grabbing hold of my collar.

"Hmm… I may need some time to come up with a plan of

action," I admitted, regarding the difficulty of contemplating a plan of escape.

"Time! Don't take too much time, I'm the one stuck in here remember!"

"I understand your disbelief in my abilities… however, I am the one with more to lose. For I have made a promise and if I fail to deliver you, it is I whose word will forever be shattered.

"I shall return unto you in three weeks, after which I shall have a solution. In the meantime, I ask that you increase your status in this place. Pay special attention to your surroundings, meaning the guards and the prisoners. Make them your ally, but do not betray their trust and fortune will come to you. I am bound to you now, by my word, and I am always true to my word," I said finally, then departed deep down the river.

"The Variable thought long throughout the night on his encounter with me. The weeks passed slowly as he was unsure of the motions that had been set into play. But, with the coming of the end of the third week, it was my voice that slyly called out to him. The Variable crept over to the bars in the night, where I met him slinking down from above."

"The weeks are up and I have returned just as I promised. How have you been?"

"I am apprehensive and restless and can think of nothing except escape. Have you a solution yet? A plan of action? Tell me so, I am most eager to hear it."

"It pains me to say so, but I thought deeply about you while I was gone. I thought so intensely that I could not sleep and awoke anxiously searching for the answer. The more I sought a solution, the more questions I ended up with. Speaking of which, tell me, do you still have dreams?"

"Yes, I do, but what does that have to do with anything? My dreams are random visions that make no sense," The Variable said, motioning up and away with his hands at the question.

"To the laymen, but dreams are your subconscious trying to guide you through the labyrinth of life. Tell me of one such vison of more recent passing," I asked, pressing The Variable to reveal his innermost secrets.

"I don't see what this is going to do, but alright. Since the two days before I encountered you, my mind was wound tightly and I found it difficult to sleep. However, mentally, I was exhausted and finally sleep located me and then I awoke within a dream.

"I was in the sea, in a small boat. The sky was grey and blue. It was an uneventful afternoon and the sun was not concerned with shining, but there was no gloom. I was standing in the boat but was not off balance, then turned towards the stern. At the rear of the boat following me was a fish, a very large fish unlike any that I have ever seen. It was all black, save for the white blotches where its eyes were and on its underbelly. It had a large, aggressive fin such as a shark, but its movements were majestic and peaceful similar to a dolphin. This one was just a calf, but it was massive and its power and strength were frightening to me at first.

"The fear within me quickly dissipated as I realized the black fish was not pursuing me, it was following me. It was near enough to capsize the dinghy, but it made no such attempt and I realized that it was with me, and not after me. There were no oars in the boat, yet I was neither adrift, nor lost. The blue waters were calm and the gentle current carried me towards the shore. I looked towards the shore and saw the waters becoming dark. It was not a shadow, but some type of corruption in the water. It was everywhere, an impurity that was claiming the waters ahead of me. It was black, slick, and sticky."

"Black and sticky, like ... tar?" I questioned The Variable to clarify.

"Yes, but no. This was pure of what it was. Not the after birth of burnt wood and coal. It was more like the blood of the earth, or that which seeps out. I believe it was crude oil. The water ahead of me then became saturated with it and the boat became stuck a few feet away from the shore.

"Looking towards the shore, I could see run down homes that were once vibrant waterfront villas of the wealthy that were now abandoned. The black fish continued behind me and I worried for its safety, but I could do nothing to stop the animal from coming into contact with the oil. Then a calm came over me and I was no longer afraid for it. I watched as it continued directly into the oil then went under the black and it was gone. I got out of the boat and was knee deep in the oil/water. It was above the knee, but just below my thigh. While in the oil, I could see that more of it was coming towards me as if it was drawn to me. I left the boat and climbed out of the water and went into the homes. I then found myself with old friends and that was the end of the dream."

"Vivid and foretelling are the depths of your mind!" I stated, then pointed and snapped my tail at The Variable.

"Say! That reminds me of a dream scenario I once had. Then again, I'm not 100% sure that it was an actual dream since I lack the ability to do so. More likely a minor hallucination brought on by indigestion, after someone or something I ate directly before slumbering. It was a terrible vision, a frightful scene, and I felt completely powerless and was unable to escape. It was a nightmare!

"I awoke in an unknown place, that was barren and void of life. There was dirt like being in the desert and the sky was colored by the setting sun, but in front of me was a bakery. The establishment appeared to be open, so I entered but no one was there. The cabinets and shelves were fully stocked, and before me were the most wonderful pastries and desserts ever on display. There were too many good things to choose from. Seeing as I was a customer, I rang the bell for service but, alas, there was no attendant.

"I waited and rang again, but received no attention and then voices behind me began snickering, chuckling, and then full on laughing at me. The pies and cakes were taunting me, as they were living things, all of them! From custards and puddings, to bubbly sodas and sweet wines, along with creams and fudges, that jeered at me. While the baked goods, muffins, and cookies made a chorus of teasing and belittling me. They were alive, all of them, and very ill-tempered at that!

"The torment continued and escalated until I could bear the humiliation no more. I went for the door, but it was locked, then a sensation of drowning came over me as I was trapped inside. I panicked and struggled with the door pulling, pushing, and shoving but the door would not budge. Then a glowing red light emanated from behind me and was then followed by the thumping sound of heavy hooves that came from behind the counter. I turned and saw a fearsome being. It was a giant gingerbread man, who was as the Devil himself. He laughed an evil noise, breathing deeply, and then pointed a twisted breaded scepter at me, signaling my demise.

"I screamed in terror... No!!! While still struggling against the door, but it was too late. The evil Gingerbread Devil then called to his cinnamon roll minions to attack me. They restrained me with ropes made of pasta and then tied me to the ground. I shut my eyes in fright, crying and still struggling... No! No! No!" I broke from narration, then became very serious, then pointed at the Variable with my tail asking, "Say! ... Do you know what the Gingerbread Devil calls his evil cinnamon roll minions?"

"No," The Variable responded simply, standing motionless staring blankly.

"Cino-bytes!" I answered calmly, then fell out in hysterics laughing at my own bad joke.

"A-HA! HA! HA! HA! Ahhhh...Cinna! Bites! A-HA! HA! HA! HA! You! Dumb! Bastard, you! A-HA! HA! HA! HA! " I continued laughing hysterically thumping and thrashing my tail on the ground. The Variable stood unamused looking on with a blank expression, while I continued laughing.

"Oh, come on! You know... from the movie with the guy with all the stickers in his face! With the puzzle thing, that you're not so supposed to open, but of course they open it, because the entire plot depends on it!" I pressed back at The Variable, with a high pitched tone, trying to explain the movie and punchline of the joke.

"What's a movie?" The Variable responded, with a blank and emotionless stare in confusion.

"What do you mean what's a moo-ooooooooooooo-oooh!" I bellowed out a rebuttal, before realizing The Variable had no understanding of what a movie was.

"Never mind that! ... Wait a minute, I think this dream thing might just be what we were pining for," I countered, regaining my composure.

"Come again?"

"Have you ever heard of dream interpretation?" I began clarifying the point to The Variable.

"Yes I have, but I do not possess such an ability."

"Not yet you don't, but I can teach you to do such a thing if you are patient. Listen and follow my instructions and you shall be released from prison within due time."

"I don't see how dreams are going to get me out of here?" The Variable sighed, then folded his arms in frustration.

"Have I given you any reason to doubt me? Understand, that I may be many things... but a liar I am not. What we're going to do is give you some value... as in here you are nothing. They obviously are in no rush to kill you, but we need to give them a reason to need you. We will show them that your life is a gifted one and then they will restore you. Now there's no guarantee that it will work, but I think it may be prosperous to us to try. I will increase my visits in order to instruct you in the meaning of dreams. Each night, I will return and instruct you until you have mastered the technique."

"You speak with such certainty, but I am wary of entering into further agreement with one of your sort. It goes against my better judgement, but what have I too lose. I will do as you instruct, Serpent," The Variable confirmed, looking downward first, then back up in agreement. The serpent continued.

"Each night, I returned and gave instruction and each night The Variable listened, and learned. After some months had passed, two officers of the king were imprisoned, one being the King's Majordomo and the other his Chief Baker. The Variable had since become popular within the dungeons while running errands and giving counsel, earning him the 'liberty of the gate.'

"One morning, the Majordomo and the Chief Baker approached The Variable and asked his counsel on their dreams. They told The Variable that they, of course, were wrongly convicted and had prayed to the gods for salvation but believed that they had received an omen regarding their fates. The Variable agreed and would interpret their dreams, but requested one promise from each of them as payment. He said that if the dream led to the dismissal of their conviction, he wished to have his name spoken of while in the presence of the King. The two men eagerly agreed and told The Variable their dreams.

"The Majordomo said, 'In my dream, there was a vine with three branches, that then began to bud and flowers blossomed into full clusters of grapes. I took the grapes in my hand and watched as I poured wine perfectly from the grapes into the cup. I then gave the cup back to the King, and he was pleased. Please, if you have the sight, tell me its meaning is favorable and I shall be indebted to you forever."

"My abilities come through much study and patience, I have increased intuition, but I am not clairvoyant. Here is the explanation I offer. The vines are your hopes and your ambitions. Vines are long and thin, as they do wrap and cling as is your mindset. You feel trapped but continue clinging to a past relationship. Secondly, the blossoms are the beauty that you see around you. Because they bloom from your subconscious, it is the beauty within you.

"Additionally, to see the blooming of flowers signifies personal growth. As in the seeds you have sown will blossom and flower fruit. You have labored long in your position and hope your hard work will pay off, and ultimately, save you from your infliction. The grapes were dark colored…hmm, in this place, gloom is over us all and wrath awaits many. However, grapes have long been associated with opulence, wealth, and sexual reward. And finally the King, is it the King within you? Do you dream to usurp the throne someday?" The Variable asked rhetorically.

"No, my Lord, no, I wish no ill will towards my distinguished king. No such thoughts circulate within me. Please, I make no such accusations!" The Majordomo interrupted, pleading.

"Allow me breadth to finish. No such plot is its meaning, but kingly as in the card. That he who trumps all and the success that the suit brings to the player's hand. From within, you seek out support from a father figure and you hope that success and privilege are near to you. And finally, the set of vines is numerical and means the number three. Three is strongly associated with a trilogy of the past, present, and the future, or life, energy, and completion. Be it good fortune, be it empty hope, I hide nothing and offer no guarantees. You have agreed to a payment, please do not forget it. That is all," The Variable ended his interpretation with the Majordomo.

"Thank you, I have prayed for favorable news, indeed the gods have given you the second sight. I shall not forget you and will beg your release." The Majordomo left from the presence of The Variable as other prisoners looked on in amazement.

"The Chief Baker then approached The Variable and detailed his dream. 'In my dream, there were three baskets stacked on top of my head holding baked goods and cake. Three birds flocked to them and ate out of them until full, with more birds joining in, and that was it. I do not understand the significance of such a vison. Tell me that the birds are fortuitous blessings and the cakes are my just rewards!'

The Variable began his interpretation, "Three baskets, three birds, this is numerical and means the number three. Three is strongly associated with a trilogy of the past, present, and the future or life, energy, and completion. Cake… is greedy, fat little fingers stuffing its face, or perhaps it is the talent of your trade speaking directly to you. But when we see cake and feel impulsive to get the biggest piece, is it not better to have pause and to share? You are no longer Chief Baker, so perhaps there was a time when it was necessary to share your accomplishments and rewards with those around you. And how was the cake, Master Chef? Was it whole, divided into pieces, or partially eaten?"

"It was partially eaten, by the birds… all three of them," The Chief Baker answered, quivering with concern.

"Had it been sliced, as in a piece, then consider the metaphor, 'a piece of cake,' but it was partially eaten. As in arriving to the banquet late, as in receiving what is left last, or missed, squandered the time allotted, and now the opportunity is gone."

"What about the birds?" The Chief Baker asked.

"The birds who sing and dance high on the wind are your goals and your dreams. The flying birds are the joy, harmony, and ecstasy you wish to find you. To take flight as the birds is not to dream of feathery appendage, but it is to be free. Freedom is what you see within you, possibly both spiritually and psychologically could be coming to you very soon. The freedom will be as if the weight of this world has been lifted directly up off of your shoulders. Be it good fortune, be it empty hope, I hide nothing and offer no guarantees. You have agreed to a payment, please do not forget it. That is all," The Variable concluded his interpretation with the Chief Baker.

"The Chief Baker thanked The Variable for his blessing and the two parted. Three days had passed since The Variable's meetings with the Majordomo and the Chief Baker, but then there was a stir amongst the prisoners. It's him, he foretells the future... they whispered and shouted. On and on this continued until The Variable was summoned by the overseer of the dungeon.

"What exactly did you tell those two men?" the overseer asked.

"Nothing, just my understanding of their dreams that is all. Why? What happened?" The Variable questioned, denying any knowledge of the situation.

"It appears your fortune telling was quite precise. Those men are screaming out there because it happened just as you said it would."

"But I gave no guarantee of the future to those men. They shared with me their dreams and, in return, I explained them as merely the symbols they are. Surely you don't believe I have magic within me? I am no holder of the dark eye," The Variable replied.

"The Chief Baker... you said his troubles would be lifted directly up off from his shoulders. Well, apparently that's exactly what happened! Poor bastard was sentenced this morning and his neck met the better part of an axe, and just as you predicted!

Separated his troublesome head… from his thieving shoulders." The overseer said, then motioned with his index finger slicing his own neck. The Variable's eyes bulged in fright as he heard the fate of the Chief Baker.

"But it seems you took favor with the Majordomo, because he was restored to his position and was called to commission the King's anniversary dinner and would be first to pour wine in the cup of the King. It seems you answered his prayers. You're really something," the overseer said looking at The Variable, then shaking his hand in congratulations. The Variable was caught in shock and went momentarily deaf and walked away in a daze. The overseer continued speaking to him as he walked away, unable to speak.

"Hey! Hey, could you do one for me… only if it's good though! Where are you going! Wait till I tell the guys, they're never going to believe this! He was spot on! I can hardly believe it!"

"Weeks had passed and his reputation as precognitive had circulated and The Variable had become something of an oddity. It had been some time since my last visit, and The Variable had become anxious. Once he was alone, he called out for me, whispering loudly into the night."

"Serpent! Serpent! Where are you! Serpent…?"

"Here I am. I have not abandoned you. You have some questions, you have some need?" I, never being far away, peaked my head up and revealed myself to The Variable.

"My imprisonment has been two years… how much longer shall I remain here? You told me you would get me out of here, yet here I remain. The only thing you have done is convinced these people I am some sort of magician. Why don't you teach me to make a wand, so I can wave good bye to this nightmarish place?" The Variable whispered angrily through the bars.

"Indeed, you have been imprisoned for nearly two years now, but only months have passed since our first meeting. As I have promised, your situation is improving and, soon, you shall walk free. Be patient, as all of your worries shall be, taken away. Be patient, everything is coming together just as planned!" I replied, nodding with optimism.

"But how long? I am weary of this place and the days of my life are meaningless. The only assurance and hope I have is your riddles and anecdotes. Tell me there is light on the horizon, tell me the mid of the night is behind me! I am drained and fear madness is looking back at me in the mirrors of my mind," The Variable pleaded pressing his face against the bars in between his hands.

"Your time approaches… no longer than you can bare and no sooner than you are prepared," again I answered with ease, then exited and sunk into the river.

"Another five days passed and The Variable sat eating a plate of lentils and dates. Then the overseer advised him that he had been summoned to the presence of the King. Although the shackles were heavy on him, as he marched out of the dungeon, he walked proudly as he was led to the royal chambers. The King said to him that he had been made aware of his ability to see the future and within him was the gift of second sight. He saw to the left of the King were the palace priestesses and among them was the wife of his old master, 'Love so Brilliant.'

"Apparently, his old master, Captain of the Guard, had survived an attempt on his life. It was said a lieutenant was arrested and immediately put to death. As a result of the incident, 'Love so Brilliant' claimed she no longer felt safe in her own home. The King invited them as guests to stay and soon, she was elevated to the position of First of Palace Priestesses. Upon seeing The Variable, her eyes glowed with lust and envy. She said, "Even in prison rags, he is glowing nobility."

"Of all my mystics and advisers, none have been able to calm the suspicions of my mind's eye. I've had dreams of good fortune and dreams of war, but the meaning of this vision is clouded and reoccurring. I offer freedom and restitution if you can reveal a pleasant meaning to my troubling visions. Are you with such a sight? Make ready your statements for your very life hangs upon your words!" The King spoke out from his throne addressing The Variable who stood before him.

"It is not I who determines the meaning of the dream oh

King, actually … it is you!" The Variable responded confidently, yet kept his eyes fixed on the ground.

"Me? I do not possess the second sight, and these omens are foreign and unsettling to me."

"Allow me to explain. What you have experienced is what some call a precognitive dream, which some believe is a prediction of the future. Many have come to believe that I possess the ability of prophetic interpretation and can tell what will be. However, it was not I who dreamed those visions, nor was it I who willed them into action. The fact that what occurred matched my description is of little consequence, as we only have confirmation after the event has taken place.

"What I believe is that within our minds, we each have a guide or compass acting to help us when trying to make a difficult decision. The visions we each have are nothing more than our waking concerns and questions about our lives and interactions. Although many believe that dreams can foretell major disasters, wars, assassinations, and winning lottery numbers. The reality is that we are searching within our subconscious for certainty of the future. Looking, hoping, and dreaming for help and reassurance is natural and very human. After hearing my words, if the King so chooses to hear my interpretation then I will give it. Be the result good or bad, I am prepared to pay for my tongue," The Variable ended his assertion raising his head, then looking directly up at the King.

"Your wisdom is sound and I will hear of it. Take note, here are my dreams," the King motioned with his hands, then began to speak.

"In my dream, I awoke standing near the Great Rivers edge and saw seven full and healthy cows come out of the river and begin to feed in the fields. Immediately after, seven sickly and gaunt looking cows came up out of the river then devoured the healthy cows. Even after they ate them, the cows were still frail and sickly in their appearance.

"Then the following day, I dreamed of a field not of my lands. There were stalks of corn and one sprouted seven ears full with bright colors. Then another stalk sprouted seven ears that immediately withered and died from disease. Those diseased ears then infected and killed off the ripe stalks and a horrible wind blew in from the east. It is completed and now you have heard my visions, now submit your reply."

"On the Great River is where you saw yourself, and a river while dreaming is a symbol of joyful pleasures, peace, prosperity, and fertility. To see a river means going with the flow, but we must not let our life float away. Perhaps, it may be time to take a more decisive role in the direction of things.

"Additionally, to a traveler a river can also represent an obstacle, as in the river that must be crossed. Seven is associated with cerebral excellence, healing, and the creative arts. Was it with more mysterious meaning or merely numerical? The cows are a staple to civilized man, interesting as you did not see the chicken or sheep, but specifically the cow. Cows are passive and domestic animals. They produce milk as a mother does, and a mother embodies maternal instincts and a need within us all to be cared for. To see sickly or dead cows suggests that the mother aspect of us is weak and dying. Perhaps, we are neglecting to care for something or someone near and dear.

"Yet thou art the King, and the King is Master of all in the lands. The following day you awoke in a field and fields are abundant and green. They symbolize the wealth of the land, the work that is required to till the soil is the pride and happiness of the freeman. However, seeing dead or dying crops is exactly what it is, the world-weary and empty prospects of the future. Strange it is that you, King, did not envision wheat or rice, but corn. Such as it was with the cows, it is similar with the ears of corn. For corn is a requirement of any civilization and it is a glowing symbol of the domestic. The illness of the animals and the crops that you saw alternating from healthy to diseased, is this an indication of an unpleasant change, the despair to come?

"However, illness is many times an early indicator, or a warning, and if paid attention to, then the rotten may be removed before souring the entirety of the body. Perhaps this vision of withering crops, and weak livestock is calling us to pay attention to the health of the lands as they are our life source.

Our lives are precious, but the life of our environment is equally exquisite, let us make the most of the good harvests and good hunting, for they may not last.

"Then came the wind and it blew fiercely. The wind is untamed energy but it can be channeled with the mill and thus becomes energy. The wind does not blow singular but changes as did the symbols in your dream. The wind was not panicked or twisting, but was strong, and a strong wind caught by the sail makes the ship swift. And the direction you saw was east. Why east... not north, not south, nor west... but east? The sun rises in the east and the rising sun brings us a new day, and each new day offers hope and bright possibility. However, the sun does not stay in the east, it heads west where it sets." The Variable turned stepping away from the King, then looked out towards the lands. He let the words sink in heavily as he described their meanings.

"But what shall I do against such an outcome? Is there no severance that you see, or will my reign be ended by famine and starvation?" The King stirred some on his throne addressing The Variable with concern.

"My interpretation is this... the two dreams are one in the same. Because of the river, there may be an obstacle ahead that cannot be avoided... it must be crossed. Seven was repeated in your vision, so numerical is its meaning. Days, weeks, months, or even years before the vison fully presents itself and completes its sequence. The cows and the ears of corn are a screaming indication of the domestic life. Your vision is calling attention to something near and close by, as in locally.

"The maternal symbolism of the cows, yet in the context of the King and all of the land. Could it be that all in the lands will require care and must not be neglected? I cannot be sure if it means starting and staying local, or if the focus will be on our local lands and even foreign nations will focus on us here. The blowing wind, we may need to increase the speed of something... we must make hast. Change is coming, harsh and intense as the wind will it be, but we must move swiftly with direction as a ship set on its course.

"Lastly, the direction was east and it came after the changing wind, and after the illness, and after the river that had to be crossed. East, as in the sun rising after the night, to shine again. If we pay attention to the crops and livestock and we make hast and plan for theses harsh changes, we will be on the right course. Then the sun will rise again, or… our local lands will shine as the sun and all will travel in our direction." The Variable returned standing in front of the King, then kneeled at the completion of his revelation.

"Indeed you are wise and gifted. How have you come to such knowledge at such a young age? Who was your instructor?" The King questioned, The Variable while he remained seated and nodding in acceptance.

"My instruction came from no man. The one who gifted me this knowledge aided me at my lowest, and my most unfortunate and darkest hour," The Variable answered, still kneeling before the King.

"Truly, a mighty God has sent this messenger to instruct you. I have heard your wisdom and it is far reaching and deeply meaningful," The King then stood and pointed at The Variable, then made a proclamation.

"From this day, he who was slave, he who was imprisoned, shall be no more." The eyes of the Variable bulged as the words sounded to be his end, but the King continued…

"From this day, his past is removed and his shame is taken away. I bestow freedom and full citizenship upon him. I further promote him to be my highest ranking officer and advisor, so as none shall be above him save for I, the King. His wisdom has brought peace to a weary mind and ended the nightmare, so am I just in ending the nightmare of his imprisonment. New title and glory be upon thee, for I title you: 'He to Whom Mysteries are Revealed.' Breath of life and pride of name are your possessions now!" The palace hall erupted in cheers and applause and tears streamed down the face of The Variable, as he was free and now rebuilt greater than 50 times of what he used to be.

"He to Whom Mysteries are Revealed!" The Variable smiled and

chuckled lightly, saying to himself.

"None can be certain of what is ahead of us, but let us not put faith in blind hoping for the best. This kingdom has prospered and endured by the will of strong and intelligent men, let us be as that for the intelligent are prepared for the worst," The Variable said strongly, addressing the King.

"He to Whom Mysteries are Revealed, master advisor, highest of officers, select your captains and assign them teams to your discretion and bestow upon us your grace and intelligence so that we may be prepared!" The King replied, then extended his hand in gratitude, solidifying the Variable as his advisor.

"Upon succeeding at the position of High Advisor, the Variable was permitted to marry any woman of his choosing. Many women offered themselves to him, but none were of his liking. There was one young woman who was very beautiful and unknown to any man, however, she was the daughter of his former master and mistress accuser. After visiting the palace, she fell in love with him and protested her family's treatment of him to gain his trust and respect. He ignored her as he could only see her mother in her and had lost the ability to trust anyone so dearly. I knew that she was correct for him but because of his pain, he built a wall around himself and would not allow himself to feel anything. I approached him in the night while he sat alone in his chambers and offered him counsel."

"Pleasant evening to you my friend, it appears your situation has improved greatly. May I offer you counsel on this lonely eve?"

"It has been a while since I have had the pleasure of your counsel, Serpent. I was beginning to wonder what had become of you," The Variable said looking out over the balcony, not bothering to turn around.

"I am alive and well, never have I strayed far from thee. I only wished to allow you time to heal and time to live, as you have surely earned it," I acknowledged, then coiled off to the right of The Variable but stayed back from the balcony.

"I am well, but if not for you, I would still have residence in

231

the dungeons there. Tell me, how can I repay you?" The Variable asked graciously, then turned towards facing me.

"Payment is necessary as we did strike a bargain, but I have not come to collect my fee as of yet."

"If not for imbursement, then what have you come for?" he countered, then tilted his head downward, in question of my presence.

"I have come to ask if my counsel is accepted, as I have a matter of discussion."

"But of course! Your counsel is the rare voice that has lead me further than any other. Please! Tell me what you will," The Variable humbled himself in preparation, then folded his hands in front of him.

"I have come to ask that as you continue to heal and to relearn to live again. I ask... that you open your heart so as to love again."

"You know I can't do that... what greater love is there than the love for one's family? No trust can ever exist within me. My brothers plotted and worked against me from behind my back! I will never love or trust another as long as I live. Even in death, if they of my blood outlive me and find my grave, I forbid them from mourning me, for they are no kin of mine!"

"I understand what has happened to you but what I ask now is separate from our original agreement. The young woman who smiles and presents good foods to you daily. She, the one who wears the red cloth braided on her crown and is first in archery. She has taken a liking to you and has separated herself from her family because of their mistreatment of you in the past. She has locked herself in a room and will not receive food or drink until she is forgiven. Her only nourishment is a small bee hive that produces honey that hangs on the eve of the roof above her."

"Then I hope she's not allergic to bee stings!" he responded with malice.

"She loves you! And she would not be a weight around your neck but a shield that emboldens you. One to whom you can put trust in, and one who would protect thy heart from a fatal blow. She is the one for you," The Variable stood with his back turned, shaking his head in denial of my words.

"What are you, playing matchmaker now? That's not your style, Serpent! Moreover, you hold no Cupid's bow and quiver to fill me with uncontrollable desire for that pagan priestess."

"If not her then who? If not now, then when? As they say… there are plenty of fish in the sea," I replied pulling back after The Variable's reply, then motioned in a questioning manner with my tail.

"Yeah, but the waters are murky and polluted! I'm looking for fresh water. I'm looking for water I can drink out of, water I can eat out of. Water I can get clean in, water I can live in. You're talking about one meal, I'm talking about life!"

"And what happens when you find such a place?" I questioned further.

"Either fish will be waiting for me there, or others will come and join me."

The Serpent changed to a heavy southern accent similar to that of Politician and actor Fred Thompson then said, "Well now, son, don't make thangs too complicated. She - a - good woman, you, Gawd fearin'… like a fifth wheel and kingpin, hitch on up! Stay together! Gawd in heaven! And like a feller in Texas once told me! A good woman like a knife in da boot, she there when you need her!" I remarked with a wink and a single head nod, then returned to my normal speaking voice.

"I appreciate your humor and concern Serpent, but my answer is still no!" The Variable replied solemnly, looking out over the balcony into the night.

"Humans! You do not see what I see and you do not know what I know! Such are the ways of love, for humans are often blind to what is directly in front of them. I would never order you to do anything against your will. However, just as you thought you would never live free again, here you are. I only ask that you open your heart so as to love again," I pleaded from behind The Variable.

"I don't know why you are so concerned about some silly girl when the ones who wronged me remain alive, and I go without retribution. Do you remember our agreement, or have you forgotten it? Because I haven't and I mean to carry it out!" The Variable spoke strongly, then gazed aggressively back over his shoulder.

"Have I not kept my promise to you, thus far? Indeed, your position has increased and the troubles about you have been taken away. As foretold by thy very own name... was it not?" I reiterated.

"Yes, but I can't shake the hate for my brothers after what they did to me. I have not seen my family for years and no one knows of their crimes. Is there no justice to come to me? You told me that you would help me take revenge on them, Serpent. Please, don't desert me now when I am so close to what has eluded me for so long."

"I promised you then, so I reassure my vow to you now. To enact vengeance, one must not only inflict injury, but he must return the crime upon the criminal. Such an act is best accomplished when it is unexpected, with the instilment of fear, and in a clever and most gruesome manner.

"The teachings of Confucius say: 'Before you embark on a journey of revenge, dig two graves.' The translation is complex, as the teacher was not speaking of certain death or impending doom. Nor was it meant as a warning against taking such action. The meaning, was to be mindful of the importance of dignity to the human soul. After having been wronged, revenge is necessary to restore dignity to one's personal identity and without it, one would suffer eternally. Even if you must take the world with you, bringing an end to one's own life in the process. So... we shall dig two graves, as dignity is more important than life!" I spoke with devious delight, lifting my head smirking back at The Variable.

"One for me... and one for you!" The Variable replied intently.

"We are all the way in, for lives such as ours... there is no in between!" I acknowledged, slowly nodding in conspiracy.

"So... when do we leave?" The Variable asked, standing face to face with me.

"Leave? For where? Your land of birth? Oh, no!"

"If we are not to seek out my brothers, then how I am to confront them?" The Variable further questioned.

"You won't have to go to them, just as you don't have to go looking for trouble, because trouble finds you," I explained, shaking my head once, no.

"However, to complete this task you will need a weapon. The weapon we will seek out is an artifact of antiquity and of specific design."

"What is it?" The Variable asked, curiously.

"A dagger!" I answered keenly.

"A dagger? I see you haven't lost your sense of humor," The Variable remarked in disbelief.

"I understand your trepidation, but I assure you, this weapon is all you will need to exact your revenge. I would not suggest it otherwise, as it is perfect and cannot be defended against by any."

"One knife, against my brothers? They will defeat me after striking one blow! There are eleven of them in case you have forgotten and they are no easy kill," he stated, rebuffing the notion of a simple knife.

"I assure you the dagger is the only weapon you will need against your brothers... all eleven of them. For the one who holds the dagger is: 'One before, whom evil trembles!'" – Sekhmet.

"Ridiculous! How could I have ever have trusted you?" The Variable dismissed the suggestion, shaking his head in disbelief then turned his back.

I became agitated, then reared up spreading the ribs in my neck forming a wide and intimidating hood, then spoke with serious tone. "I am the Serpent of Old, the Serpent of ruin and curse... and there stands no advice, nor instruction more valuable than mine! Trust not in my words, trust only in what I am. On the subject of killing men, there exists no greater master than I," I lowered my head, then slinked over the balcony exiting from the chamber, then said lastly. "On the morrow, we meet past the fields of your lands near the river's edge."

"What's at the river's edge?" The Variable questioned, before

I disappeared completely over the balcony.

"The revelation of a mystery," I whispered solemnly, then disappeared into the night.

"The following morning, The Variable arrived with a chariot past the fields at the river's edge where I waited then greeted him.

"Pleasant morning to you, but you must unhook your chariot from the horse for where we go, the chariot cannot make the journey," The Variable did as instructed and unhooked the chariot from the horse. Then I struck without warning, killing and eating the horse.

"No! My horse!" The Variable jumped backward, screaming in anger!

After repositioning my jaws, I replied sarcastically, "Breakfast! My apologies, had you not eaten? Besides, where we travel, the animal could not make the journey," The Variable straddled my back, holding tightly the hairs of my mane and swiftly we moved overtop the river waters.

"We shall mark our route by following Sirius, the Dog Star to locate the island of Sehel. With any luck, we will arrive on the night of the tear drop. We must move with haste if we are to reach our destination by nightfall, for it would take 3 and a half days to complete the journey on foot," We completed the journey, then slowed once we had identified the island ahead.

"See there... the island of Sehel is our journey's end. Many travelers on expedition heading into Nubia make pilgrimage here on the island. Many leave text or signs of their presence here, while some inscribe records on the granite boulders," We landed on the island and camped that night on the island of Sehel. The Variable started a fire and I began a tale.

The Syndicate...

"In another time, there were three criminals who joined together forming one of the most infamous gangs of their day. The first was a Thief Taker General who operated a gang of thieves, and amassed a fortune never before seen by appearing as an officer of the law.

"His ingenious method was based on tipping off his

accomplices of unguarded or easily taken plunder. He then waited for the crime to be announced, then he would report that his 'agents' had located the stolen goods. At which point, the merchandise would be returned to its rightful owners, all for a fee of course. He was quite versatile and was very adept at determining, which cases allowed for blackmail then forced an even heftier fee upon the victims. While other times, the mark was deemed a player and both were able to collect duties off the caper.

"Second of the three, but not in reputation or corruption, was the Prostitute and Fence. She was probably the most intelligent of the three and was responsible for connecting much of the criminal underworld. With her talent, and contacts of thieves, whores, and toughs, she became the largest and most powerful madam and receiver of stolen goods of the time.

"As madam, she was at the intersection of almost every criminal act. As she could quickly sell or dispose of stolen goods, pay bribes, and could get almost anyone out of prison. Unfortunately, a dispute with a past lover and rival ended with her ear being sliced off, which became the mark of a seasoned whore.

"Thirdly was the Under-Marshal, the master extortionist. He first began as a law student but soon realized that the real money was in intimidation and crime. He selected some of the meanest thugs and toughest officers to pressure the local brothels and pickpockets to pay for protection. Extortion was already an established practice at that time and was usually run by the local Black Hand. However, the Under-Marshal was not focused on any small alley dealings and built an established business of it.

"After much contention, the three eventually met in truce, but only after their greed threatened each of their businesses and lives. They decided to form the first known syndicate of the ancient world and their criminal reach extended across the great oceans as all pirates, thieves, and bandits paid tribute to them. They reigned united for some time but then discord began to grow between them. Monies began disappearing that none could account for. Slander and snitchery sent the best of their crews to the gallows without recourse. Assassination attempts upon each of their lives were carried out, while no contract could be found. After a series of infighting erupted, the three decided to meet and settle their differences once and for all.

"A recovered letter read: 'We three of vilified profession are at contemptible variance. This world of ours has set us upon a path of collision after many discoveries have come to light. Whether it be Thief-taker, Madam, Fence, or Extortionist, the expectation to be cleansed is the same. The satisfaction of our world is specifically known and there can only be one result. Like the fighting game cocks we are, let the truth meet each of us as dueling weapons of fate.'

"Sometime later, their lifeless bodies were located in a chamber locked from the inside at a secret location. Their murders were never solved and none could determine who killed whom, yet the only weapon recovered was a dagger. A curious thing regarding the dagger, was that it was unbloodied and remained in its sheath.

"Rumor spread of the Syndicate murders and the dagger took on fantastic reputation as many believed the blade to be cursed. After which, the dagger became associated with revenge and a myth was born of a weapon that could kill without leaving a trace, and rendered its user invincible. It is said that those who seek vengeance seek out the dagger as it is the only weapon that can assure retribution."

"Excellent story Serpent, you never cease to entertain. However, it's late and I have to complete some writings regarding the coming famine over the lands."

"Are your writings auto-biographical?" I asked, while my face glowed from the camp fire's light.

"No, not really, it's just something I started writing. It's about everything that's happened. From the King's dream, to my interpretation, and the instructions for building the food storages, and the collection of a one tenth tax of all harvested produce, game, and fishing for seven years," The Variable explained, while he continued writing on a piece of papyrus.

"What are you going to do with such a report?" I asked,

curiously looking over at The Variable.

"I don't know, I just thought it should be written down for later use. If such a calamity befalls humanity ever again, they may be wiser to survive it."

"You are very perceptive and such wisdom should live on in the minds of men as if inscribed in stone for eternity. Good rest, my friend."

The following morning, I motioned to The Variable then identified the location of the dagger. "Look there, on the summit of the eastern most hill stands a large granite boulder with a broad horizontal slice in it. There... tucked back within the fissure of the stone rests the dagger. You need only reach in and remove it."

"The Variable approached the large boulder and looked into the long, narrow opening of breakage and saw, protruding out from a wrapping of animal skin, a hilt and guard. He reached into the crevice and took hold of the wrappings and removed it. Holding the olden wrappings in his hand, he slowly unfolded and exposed the weapon securely nestled in its sheath. He took hold of the grip of the weapon with his right hand then, with his left, he gripped the sheath.'

"Do not disturb the blade from its rest... at least not yet! Let us take time to appreciate the coral of its shell," I interjected quickly, before The Variable unsheathed the dagger. The Variable locked his eyes on me, stopping just before removing the blade.

"The technical skill and artistic ability of the craftsman who completed such a weapon is outstanding. The grip of the handle is metal and covered with untanned shagreen made of animal skin as it has proven to be the most durable. From the top of the pommel, the design of the hilt is embossed in gold with a wreath of lily-palmettes in cloisonné, which matches the working on the haft. On the underside, the figure of a nemesis is depicted as a fierce winged lioness holding a uraeus, dressed in flowing red cloth of the Rosetta pattern. Below the pommel, are alternating bands of symmetrical designs, inlet with precious stones, then offset by bands of red, blue, and gold, that decorate the haft.

"The base of the hilt, is met with continuous spirals of a rope pattern border, making suggestion to the eye that the haft was bound to the blade. The sheath was made of animal skin and almost entirely covered with a feather and scale pattern, with a line of inscription reading: 'To Give, What is Due.' – Nemesis. Followed by the numbers three, six, nine, and twelve, which are associated with death above figures sleeping and appearing to dream.

"On the reverse of the sheath, is a scene embossed in high relief composed of the following elements. A lioness surrounded by multiple sheep with the heads of dogs being attacked. Then the sheep being slain and fleeing, and finally showing the lioness with wings spread in full flight," I detailed, explaining the markings on the grip, sheath, and hilt while looking over the shoulder of The Variable.

"I could easily enlist an entire troop of assassins to aid me, but I will not cheapen the experience. I will take them one by one, as their lives belong to me now," The Variable proclaimed, while holding the weapon firmly before him.

"That which you hold is a magnificent fighting weapon made with a sharp point and was designed to kill. Its design dates back to the earliest of ancient human warfare and modern day close combat strategies. Ancient military cultures revere the dagger and have used it not only in battle, but in ritual, ceremonial dress, and as an object of art.

"However, the war masters have remained true to its design as it continues to be defined by a short blade, a sharp tapering point, a central spine with double cutting edges over the full length of the blade. It is equipped with varying styles of guards sometimes crossed, yet always set with the blade positioned horizontally. Thus, enabling the user choice of slash or thrust upon their opponent.

"The fighting knife has been, and will be, carried by militaries finest generals and conquerors of note, from Hannibal and his Carthaginian armies, to the Imperial Roman legionaries, and continuing to the forthcoming crusades. The versatility of the dagger has proven to be the survival of those who reach for it in darkness of night, back of alley, hall of saloon, or trench of battlefield. I present to you the most beautiful object of remorse, regret, and utter revenge. I give to you... the dagger!"

The Variable looked down upon the weapon with acceptance and gratitude, thanking me twice. I then motioned to The Variable, regarding the journey back and we departed the island of Sehel. The Variable, wholly focused on the dagger, left the documents reporting the famine and his interactions and efforts of preparation with the King, on the island of Sehel.

Upon arrival back at his lands, I advised The Variable sternly saying, "There is one final thing you must know. Do not remove the blade from its sheath until you are ready to strike. It is imperative that you follow this instruction or failure will befall you. Once you are positioned and ready, recite the lyric on the sheath. Then remove and awaken the blade by reading the word inscribed on its face. Then you shall have your revenge" The Variable nodded in acknowledgment, then read the words on the sheath: 'To Give, What is Due.'

"I suppose... this is where I pay you, Serpent."

"My fee! I had nearly forgotten!" I replied, lifting a brow in delight.

"My blood... that's what you want, isn't it?" The Variable offered, simultaneously turning over his wrists.

"Your blood? No... it's nothing like that," I denied, wincing back at The Variable in confusion.

"Then what? I am willing to pay for what we have plotted and what I intend to do!"

"This is what you owe. I get to choose... the place of your resting," I paused momentarily, then answered sneering slightly.

"Where I rest... I don't understand?" The Variable replied, shaking his head in confusion.

"I get to choose where your body will rest, eternally. As in... your grave! Know this, 'He Who Would Increase!' I require no sacrifice, nor any soul for payment. All I ask is that when you die, you will ensure that your body does not stay in this land. As long as your body remains here, those after you shall know no peace and will suffer in oppression. Make certain that upon your death, your benefactors are given specific instruction that your body will be taken to the place of my choosing,"

"And what place is that?" he replied with a cautious expression.

"I don't know... I haven't decided yet," I remarked simply, then shrugged away the matter as no big deal.

"And that's all?"

"Yes ...That is all!" I reiterated.

"Then I suppose this is Goodbye. Thank you, Serpent, for everything."

I nodded graciously, while The Variable turned and headed back to his home with the dagger in hand. I watched as The Variable disappeared into the distance, then I said lastly, "Find peace."

"Back in the Kingdom, The Variable reassumed his duties as High Advisor and just as he foretold, the seven years of prosperity ended and famine consumed the land. The famine was harsh and crops were lost and rivers dried up. All the lands cried out in suffering and drought, but those in the Land of the Black Ground, Home of the Riverbank were content as they had prepared due to The Variable's word. Many came from far away to purchase grain and dried meats from The Variable's food storages. He was fair and provided for all who sought out aid, and in payment only asked a tenth of any crops or livestock produced be paid.

"And then there came a day that the he did not think would ever come. As he sat supervising the distributions of rations, a group of men approached him begging his counsel. His first attendant introduced them as they were unknown in the land and wished an audience with the High Advisor. The attendant stated that the group of men had come from far away after hearing that the Kingdom had storages of food available for purchase. Then all at once, The Variable sat starring face to face with his brothers. He was stunned but quickly composed himself, as my words echoed within him, as they that troubled him had finally found him. Rage boiled inside of him and his eyes became slits and his teeth gritted against each other as he held himself together.

"The Variable retained his composure while listening to his attendant, all the while knowing who the men were. He sat silently and patient, which instilled fear and suspense within his brothers. He commanded them to rise and make their request of him directly, as he was fluent in their language. He looked each one of them in their eyes but was surprised and overcome with plotting delight as they still did not recognize him. Then The Variable decided that the time had finally come to exact his revenge.

"He ordered his brothers arrested and charged them as spies. The men pleaded and swore that they were innocent men from a good house. They said that they, ten, had come save for their youngest brother who remained at home with their ailing father.

"Lies!" The Variable shouted, pointing directly at each of them.

"The ten men were imprisoned for three days with only water and bread crumbs for rations. On the fourth day, they were summoned to the palace hall and were instructed that they were to be released, except for one of them. The Variable said that he would allow nine of them to return to their home and bring food back to their village. However, one of them would have to remain and would only be freed if, and when, they returned within one week with their youngest brother to verify their story.

"The brothers were then released and fled to their village with grain and distributed it amongst their people. The brothers then went and visited with their father and told him of their imprisonment and of the High Advisor's instructions to bring back their youngest brother.

"Their father, born as the Holder of the Heel, was afraid and worried but agreed and sent his youngest son with his brothers back to the Land of Black Ground, Home of the Riverbank. Upon their arrival, they were greeted and sent to the chambers of the High Advisor. The chamber doors were locked behind them and then, without means of escape, was the moment that

The Variable would reveal himself to them.

"He began a tale and told them how he had been betrayed by his own people being beaten, stripped naked, and then sold into slavery. He told them how he was marched through the desert with condemned men dragging the dead and dying behind him on chain gang. He continued his revelation of how he thought he was spared the worst only to be betrayed by the mistress of the house and accused of rape and imprisoned without a sentence end.

"His brothers stood in amazement of the tale, then kneeled crying out, death and ruin to those who plotted deceit and sin upon one so noble as the High Advisor. The Variable continued, saying that even though he had been betrayed and accused of such an unforgivable act, he was not without repentance and the Creator took pity upon him. For in the most unexpected of places did he gain a dark ally in the form of an instructor. His ally was most beguiling and knowledgeable in the ways of deceit, trickery, and death. For his ally did instruct him in the ways of patience, tact, and skill."

"It was he who led me through the valley of contempt and offered me restoration, but not through repentance, but revenge!" The Variable said, then turned and identified himself to the men.

"Do you not recognize the flesh of thy flesh, brothers? For it was you who ambushed and sold me away! It was you who stole my identity and bound me to the slaver's chain! It was you who goddamned me to prison as a rapist. Every day, I starved and ached! Every night, I feared for my life and safety! Every day, I cried and bled, broken-hearted, nameless, alone with only shame as a blanket to comfort me," The Variable proclaimed angrily, pointing in condemnation of his brothers kneeling before him.

"The men were speechless and could not believe that their brother was alive. Their mouths dropped open and their eyes bulged as their minds raced with fear and regret as he stood confessing their sins in anger! They backed up slowly in retreat as he stepped, in marching fashion towards them continuing his verbal assault. They were powerless and their retreat was ended as their backs were against the locked doors. With no escape, they could only throw up their arms up in defense begging for mercy from their brother."

"And… now!" The Variable whispered, with rage in his eyes slowly reaching for the dagger tucked under his tunic. His mind raced, while his brothers remained kneeling on the ground in front of him. He would have to strike quickly if he was to overpower all of them before they could counter. He knew not which one to kill first, but he trusted in the might of the blade, as my serpent tongue had never misled him. He looked down and remembered the instructions, but before pulling the dagger out of its sheath, a moment of pause came over him.

"It was as if time was suspended for him, and his brothers appeared frozen still cowering in front of him, he said to himself. *'I unsheathe you dagger, to release my tormented soul. Wretched, twisted, and full of sin they are. For thus did they plot my demise, so did they perpetuate their own end. I offer no pardon and insist upon divine dagger between us. My smile for thy cringe, as retribution belongeth to me. Now… I kill you! All of you!'* The Variable then spoke the lyric aloud.

"To Give, What is due!" He removed the dagger violently from its sheath revealing… a wooden waster. He paused with the wooden tool in his hand observing, it blunted with rounded edges with the engraving reading, 'Kindness.'

"There was no way that he could have killed any of them with a tool designed as a practice weapon. But then an understanding came over him and he realized that the dagger was useless just as his murderous intentions were. The inscription on the dagger was true, as 'Kindness' was what needed to be given. Kindness, all along, was what was due.

"The dagger fell from his hand and intense emotion overcame him. His knees almost buckled under the feeling of grace and self-healing that now covered him. He raised his eyes sobbing, but looked not upon his enemies, but saw his brothers cowering before him. No longer was he without value after all he had was 'Taken Away.' Surely, it was 'He Who Would, and had Increased.' He called to each of his brothers in forgiveness, and no longer saw his enemies, but his brethren, and he was… avenged!"

"It was you, wasn't it? You knew all along!" The Man of the Present asked.

"Well… maybe a little! You see, from the very beginning, he asked for help in taking revenge and killing his brothers. So…"

"But you lied!" the man interjected, pointing at the serpent.

"I told no lies! I guided him and instructed him how to regain his dignity and exact his revenge, just as I swore to. My words were iron with truth, but not without tact. As I said, on the subject of killing men, there is no greater master than I. And of all the methods known to kill… kindness is the most lethal.

"There are many ways to murder other than physical assault, but kindness is a sharp-edged weapon worth wielding. He was no longer a variable, unknown and without value or status. His misery and pain had been Taken Away. Physically killing his brothers would not have given him release, but it would have condemned him to an endless pit of rage and inner torment. I wished he could have seen through my serpent eyes, and of all the evil rent upon him, he not only survived, but he triumphed over those who plotted against him.

"All along he lived, survived, and moved forward, but it was they who were truly dead. He *had* killed them. They were as a corpse in the grave, unable to move forward in life. And when they met, they were exactly where they were when he had left them, in the very pit that they had dug for themselves," the serpent continued.

"He who Would Increase, never again spoke of the evil done unto him by his brothers. Instead, he healed them with forgiveness and sent them back to their village with food and money for their families. He was both respected and feared for he chose compassion and forgiveness over retribution and vengeance. He prospered and found love and happiness and led by example as he made true the virtue of his name.

"Now, Man of the Present, I ask you. When you find yourself having been wronged, humiliated, stabbed in the back, and left for dead, you will rise. Your pride and your wounds will heal.

And one day you may find yourself in a position, to do unto those as they did evil upon you. But the question is, when that time comes, what words will you utter? What actions will you take? Will you plot death and revenge or trudge the arduous road of forgiveness?

"And I recite, Man of the Present, 'The merciful man doeth good to his own soul but he that is cruel troubleth his own flesh. The wicked worketh a deceitful work, but to him that soweth righteousness shall be a sure reward. As righteousness tendeth to life, so he that pursueth evil pursueth it to his own death.'

CHAPTER 8: THE PANOPTICON

"For a time there was peace in the Land of the Black Ground, Home of the Riverbank. He Who Would Increase was a benediction to his people and through hardship and struggle, his life was a legacy of redemption and forgiveness. The Land of the Black Ground, Home of the Riverbank established itself as a great kingdom and worshipped their claimed lineage of gods and heroes. However, the dream of He Who Would Increase could not last forever, and so too would man awake from blissful sleep to inflict a new nightmare upon humanity.

"New kings were born and reigned to new heights of greed and power, and soon would usher in the Age of Confinement. He Who Would Increase completed his life and made good his promise, giving instruction that his body was not to remain in the land. Regrettably, his people were distracted with worldly pursuits and kept not their word.

"The kingdom that he worked to build and grow had turned to stone and became a monument of man's genius and a complex design of imprisonment. The land now swelled with travelers, merchants, and refugees of foreign decent. Along with newcomers, the people of He Who Would Increase became a populace of believers and their numbers rivaled that of the citizens of the kingdom. Then came a new king who remembered not the Great Advisor who revealed mysteries and guided the kingdom through the seven-year famine. This new king cared not for old promises and did not honor the commitments made by his forefathers to the believers. He was ambitious and saw not the beauty and diversity of people, but only numbers in his growing kingdom.

"He saw the mighty pyramid which would stand for centuries to come, and how the top was the focal point but those underneath it were merely stepping stones. The structure was only as strong as the bricks holding it up and if the believers left, then the kingdom itself would fall.

"The citizens began to see the believers as an encroaching horde of outsiders and an infestation. They feared their numbers might overtake them, even in their own land. Slander and stereotype became associated with the believers and soon the kingdom was segregated by religion and race. The marriage of citizens to believers was outlawed as their mongrel blood would dilute the purity of the citizens of the kingdom.

"Initially, the king dismissed the idea of overcrowding and overpopulation as the region was vast and plentiful. All who journeyed to the kingdom were welcomed and traded with as they added economic diversity to the land. But the whispers of onlookers and naysayers grew to loud grumblings. Then to awful heckling of a fearful and hateful mob towards a king who would not defend their lands from verminous invaders. The believer's numbers increased and they were described as animals that knew no control over their sexual, hot blooded urges. As their women, no doubt, welcomed any suitor to lay with and bore many children who burdened the resources of the lands.

"Even though no mouth went unfed or pallet remained dry of thirst, rumors of food shortages continued to be reported throughout the region. The king was openly urged to take action against the believers before they exceeded the lands ability, leaving the citizens to starve. After much tension and political unrest, the king made a new proclamation. The king said, the kingdom had become a focal point for travel, trade, education, and architecture and as a result they were faced with a burden of overpopulation.

"The king said the land itself was gifted to them from their highest god and this influx of people must not be seen as a woe, but as a blessing and a gift. For their highest god was the same who sent the heavy winds to fill the sail of the ship, and brought the heavy rains which abounded the crops, so too were the believers brought to them by the gods."

"We have pushed this society to its limit, but not to its breaking point. What we must do is increase our efforts and make work and position for all who wish to be part of our great society, and let us improve our quality of life. The gods have blessed us with many strong backs and many fertile wombs, let us make use of these heavenly gifts for which to grow our kingdom. We are the chosen seed of the gods and the inherent rulers of the earth. It is our duty for we are the chosen and they... every one of them, belong to us!" the king spoke out boldly, while holding court.

"The king instituted a new law and proclaimed the believers to be without rights. Thus, they were not beholden to the laws of the land and were condemned as slaves. Immediately, orders were given to subdue the believers and seize their lands as all were now property of the state. The beginning of this transition was not polite and many fought for their homes and families, but were easily defeated and many were slaughtered in the streets. The surviving sons of rebellious fathers were sent to work and die for gold, which would heavily adorn their new masters.

"The consequences of resistance were physical violence, and the threat of separation from their children, or the death of a loved one. There were those who saw hope in the stars and attempted to flee their captors. Yet being that slaves were property, if they were captured they were returned to their masters swiftly. Those who chose not to resist, lived under a heavy burden, and were now without hope. Because they forgot their past, they lost sight of the future and became prisoners by their own ignorance.

"The believers became known as Hem, a slave body, or a

person with few rights dedicated to task and toil. But you humans know no ends and even the slaves found ways to segregate themselves by class. Those who served in the palaces and homes of nobility were considered lucky and posh. Their lives were considered desirable even to the free but native peasant. The now slave populace, fearing reassignment to harsher conditions, made themselves indispensable to their masters, not withholding their bodies or their children, and then gave away their faith.

"Their children were thus born and raised in a twisted environment and their parent's spoon fed them the master's will and delights. When their parent's died, the children knew not the taste of freedom. They were not burdened with choice and the weight of intelligence, and so they loved their masters.

"During this time, the entirety of the believers were enslaved and allowed for one of the greatest periods of expansion of the kingdom's dynasty. The slaves now filled every position imaginable from laborers to unpaid administrators. The skills they already possessed were put to work against them, as now they patrolled their shorelines as harbor watchmen and were door keepers of the inns and taverns they themselves had established.

"The food storages that held the grains and seed of their hands were kept under lock and guard, while they hungered in the night and their masters enjoyed dance and leisurely festivities. And after a long life lived, their masters were buried and entombed and their slaves were called upon to service them continually in the afterlife, and, thus, were buried alive.

"The king held a parade and a victory banquet during a public celebration for an entire week. They had conquered the infestation of believers without the march of an army. They had increased their human spoils and property of each land owner twenty-fold with only the movement of a pen. In the past, to do such a thing would have required a massive campaign across deserts and wilderness then long marches of prisoners of war, or through expensive merchant trade," the serpent broke from narration and returned to speaking with the Man of the Present.

251

"You know what really got me though. It was how easily you all accept change, no matter how arduous the transition is."

"What? You think that they enjoyed being enslaved?"

"Oh no! Of course not! I meant the citizens and those that inflicted slavery upon the believers. It appeared to come to them with such ease. It fascinated me how they devised and schemed such a terrible plan. How they did this to those who were, just yesterday, their neighbors that they traded with. Just days ago did they share drink and pleasurable company with each other. Then the next how easily they spit upon them and called them slave.

"I have seen you people through many stages thus far, but this was different than any battle or war. This was arranged, planned, and executed with precision. I was going to leave the region because this type of cruelty is not suitable even for the lowest of lifeforms. But for some reason, causing pain to each other comes naturally to you humans. So I stayed as a matter of scientific observation.

"What I observed was that the believers were essentially forced into a cage, somewhat similar to a rat. Now lab rats are to be experimented upon and this can be done physically by sticking with needles or by dissection, but this was different. You see, the Citizen Masters as they now were, were not interested in mere physical capture. They were fixed on implementing a new society and social class, but they would need the believers to somehow agree and buy into it.

"I watched them first use physical violence and intimidation to motivate the believers to work, but this only worked temporarily. What happened was that they would pluck out a bunch to be made an example of, then they were beaten within inches of death. Afterwards, they were hung up for all to see and then left to suffer for days, eventually dying of their injuries. After that, the believers would be given an option to accept their position as slaves or face the same punishment.

"Now this worked on some, but not all. Many were proud and openly refused and others joined in their rebellion. However, many were captured, separated, and imprisoned, which too created a problem as there was a limit to how many slaves could be executed, as eventually it would diminish their newly acquired workforce. But what to do? Then came one advisor who was very smart and sinfully intelligent and he proposed an idea that had never been instituted before.

"The advisor said, 'It is one thing to control the body, but the key is to control the mind. Currently, we have to physically restrain and motivate them in order to maintain control. But the goal is to instill an idea of total control over them, so that they will control themselves without us even having to do it. Therefore, we will have complete control over them.' Many asked the advisor, how could such a thing be done? The slaves were a proud people of belief and generation and had never taken to the citizen's many gods and rituals. The advisor said that there was more than one way to keep a person in a cage.

'First, we will remove any and all possibilities for meaningful self-expression. Their clothing, their language, their customs will become outlawed and they will no longer be permitted to worship at their times or in their temples. They will dress as we deem appropriate and will eat only what we leave for them. With no other option, many of their traditions and cultures will be lost and forgotten. Their folk and traditional knowledge shall be delegitimized and made illegal thus making their own culture a thing of shame and mockery. Then they will come to value and trust our ways and ideas over their own.

'Next, they will be cut off from their homeland and will have no connection to their past identity. Most importantly, we must destroy any and all community bonds and place them into a society of strangers. Thus forcing them to assimilate into a predetermined social class, creating their new identity. The best way to do this is to separate them and destroy their tribes, villages, and clans by reducing their social interactions and creating constant work and an environment of survival anxiety. They will live and work within set boundaries and only be allowed food and medicines from our shops and stores. Where they once lived off the land and had access to desert highways, oceans of opportunity, and forest communities, they shall only be allowed out of our boundaries only after being given approval.

'Within a short time they will come to depend on our resources and medicines. They will forget their own ways of healing and lose their connection to their homeland and country. Their labor shall lead to a dead end and all they can look forward too are paltry rewards from their masters. Their entire lives will be poverty and they will be confined into structured property spaces that they can never fully own and will never really be theirs.

'Those who do as they are instructed and learn our ways will be rewarded, and those who dissent will be punished and will be given more work. This way, they will be seduced by reward and they will discourage each other from dissent. Over time, they will police their own by pointing out those who dissent from our system, thus receiving favor and additional reward.'

"The man who devised this was onto something never thought of before. The Citizen Masters looked and listened as he spoke his ideas for dominance over the believers. His ideas were then tested and were immediately proven successful. The believers were now cut off from their elders and teachers, and had no one to look to besides their masters. The believers forgot their methods of prayer and soon began policing their own who tried to hold on to their past culture. Those who were excellent slaves were rewarded, while those who dissented received smaller portions of food and heavier workloads. Soon, those who received rewards became the example of the believers, and the young and ignorant easily fell into place, while those who rebelled against the citizen masters were exposed by their own people and easily overwhelmed.

"The advisor was congratulated and brought before the king to be honored. He was asked how he came to such wisdom and was able to implement such a plan of control over a people with little force. How was he able to seduce them into an ideal totally against their culture, dignity, and nature? The advisor said, 'Human beings, at the core, are controlled by instinct and can be manipulated through intimidation, stimulation, and circumstance. The human being has such a need for sensation, gratification, and stimulation, that they will place themselves into a cage just to obtain it. Ultimately, they will imprison themselves to obtain and sustain those key values.

'Now granted, everyone defines their own levels of sensation, and gratification, but those things come down to some very basic needs that we all share. However, our goal is not merely to stimulate them into doing what we want, but it is to program them with the symbols and ideas that we deem appropriate. Thus, their habits which they believe are their own, will have been programmed by us, leaving them confined, as none will be able to escape themselves as they will have become their own jailers.

'They will become so dependent on our system, that they will not be able to escape even by destroying us, as they will have no way of living a meaningful life without our approval. Yes, gentlemen, the physical restraints we can place on them are nothing compared to the mental cages they will suffer upon themselves. Confinement is not accidental nor is it incidental in any thriving society, but woven by design into its systems and ideologies. We have separated them, subdued them, and programmed them, thus we dominate them and now we control them.' The congregation of citizens erupted in applause. The advisor concluded by saying that, 'Ultimately the believers were to blame for their befallen circumstance, as it was their own poor choices that led them into this life of servitude.'

"This ideology would later become known as dispositionism. Where a people's actions are a result of internal factors, rather than the situational circumstances that they live in or are forced to deal with. Thus, the advisor concluded that the Citizen Masters were better people and could never fall into disarray, poverty, or slavery. Therefore, the Citizen Masters were inherently different from the believers, therefore they were inherently better than them.

"So they did it on purpose?" the man interrupted, asking the serpent.

"Of course they did, control is always on purpose. The ideas

255

that the Citizen Masters implemented was nothing new. Man has postulated for centuries, new ways to gain advantage over his fellow man and elevate himself to a position of power and authority. I continue to ask myself the same question but still I do not know why the Creator constructed man in such a way. It seems that this need for dominance is in all of you," the serpent quipped, turning his head and looking back at the man.

"That's not true! You make it sound like everybody wants to enslave and torture other people," he rebutted, in denial of the serpent's words.

"No... it's not? I am completely misinformed, am I? There is not a never-ending greed bubbling up inside all of you? And if not for time or circumstance there would be no end to man's need for more?" the serpent argued, with an accusatory tone, then continued.

"The ideas that the Citizen Masters implemented have been used and tried in many different forms, but this system of control is the best. However, it was not until the late 18th century that a social theorists gave name to this method. His theory was based upon a design for an ultimate institution of imprisonment.

"His idea was to construct a tower to allow a single watchman to observe an institution of inmates without the prisoners being able to tell when they were being watched. Now true, it's physically impossible for one watchman to observe every prisoner all of the time. However, the point is to make the prisoners feel as if they are being watched all of the time. Thus, the prisoners will begin to monitor and control their behavior constantly.

"The mastermind behind this concept was a Mr. Jeremy Bentham and he had many great ideas that have been implemented in different forms and in many industries. Mr. Bentham was a leading theorist of his time, and his ideas laid the groundwork for the development of what is currently known as welfarism.

"Mr. Bentham argued heavily in favor of legal and individual rights, however, he was known to be greatly opposed to the idea of natural rights. And, of course, natural rights are those universal rights bestowed upon every living being such as freedom, and individuality and are considered beyond the authority of any kingdom or government. His idea was to create an institution that could be equally applied to schools, asylums, workhouses, and even children's centers but he focused his efforts on developing a prison, and he called it... a panopticon.

"Now you might be saying to yourself, Man of the Present, that the ancient Citizen Masters built no such circular structure and you would be absolutely correct. But it was not the physical structure that was at the shared crux of this system of oppression. No, it was the methodology, as described by Mr. Bentham himself. As he stated, 'The Panopticon is a new mode of obtaining power of mind over mind, in a quantity hitherto without example.'

"Now think and imagine a society built on such a system of control, where one feels that they are constantly being watched and that they are without any means of escape. Such a society would, no doubt, be a prison. The Citizen Masters' as well as Mr. Bentham's shared goal was to create and implement a complete utilitarian code of laws and conduct. Where utilitarianism is an axiom, which means to achieve the greatest happiness of the greatest amount, which is the ultimate measure of right and wrong.

"In description, the greatest happiness somehow usually refers to the wealthiest, most famous, and strongest of influence and political power. Meaning that if the greatest people are happy then what ever is done to achieve that happiness is therefore right and outweighs any perceived wrong. However, the notion that the many outweigh the few, thus becomes only partially true. As in many societies, those who are at the top of decision making are generally the few when compared to the many who are on the bottom," the serpent chuckled briefly, then continued.

"And it just so happens to be strikingly similar to the structure of their ancient pyramids, isn't it? However, if only the happiness of the greatest ones is of concern, then whatever miseries are inflicted upon the weaker, poorer, is thereby justifiable all in the name of a greater good. This ancient ideology was coined by Mr. Bentham as the Principle of Utility, which brings a greater pleasure over pain. But I defer the question and ask who is to live in pleasure and who is to live in pain? The only way to survive or exist in such a place is to become part of the system and give up all hope for individuality and expression. And I recite, 'Envy thou not the oppressor and choose none of his ways. For the froward is abomination to the Creator, but his secret is with the righteous.'

"Mr. Bentham further described the Panopticon as, 'a mill for grinding rogues honest.' What better design could there be for a kingdom or government? A state system to adhere its population into rank and file drones, where the individual feels trapped and caged within their own thoughts. Oddly enough, Mr. Bentham and those who agree with this model regarded the panopticon as a rational solution to societal evils. One can easily see the same design in much of modern society.

"Where the society that one lives in feels more like a cage of television, radio, internet, public school, and low paying commercialized jobs. Which creates a visible, yet subconscious, sameness of rows of repeating cells and bars. Where the workforce and education system is overseen by contract supervision as opposed to trust, leadership, and merit, which are more vested in increasing employee and student product quality rather than quantity.

"In such a commercialized manufactured society, there are no physical bars or chains, but every institution from childhood through adolescence to adulthood, of school, military, and employment are designed in a form of domination which easily resembles the panoptic nightmare. From the ancient times to the present and future days, the ideology of totality and utilitarian control of population is nothing new and continues as a tool of oppression and societal control.

"However, in such a society none are free, not even the administrative jailers who are as much a prisoner as the rest of society. Their work and sadist ideals are little compensation for their unmet goals and unreached potential, so they offered the last bits of their soul and psyche for comfort, security, and complacency and became part of the status quo.

"Yet, the ceiling is not iron, nor are the walls made of stone, there inevitably comes a turning point. When the masses regurgitate the systemic opium and a conscious movement awakens them from lethargy. There will come a redeemer, a rogue, a leader from within their own ranks that will end the bleak and meek hopeless trotting of routine. This leader will come with voice and sound to change the tempo of the hum drum beating of humanity's flailing pulse.

"The corporate dominance over the environment, the military control over education, and the surveillance and influence of entertainment shall have reached its extremes. The seams of their civilization will begin to crack and will finally split, exposing the hollow core at the center of an empty world that always was. The emptiness will end… and hope, possibility, creativity, and individuality shall once again be free."

"That's what happened though wasn't it. There was a guy… he was raised as one of them, but he was really one of the believers. He learned his true identity and he came back and freed them. I remember this story. The people were enslaved and then the guy came back and he fought for them. He split the waters and they marched right through them. That's what you're talking about, aren't you?"

"Once again, you are correct Man of the Present. That's exactly what I'm talking about. History has an odd way of repeating itself. Humanity is enslaved and then one presents himself and stands against all odds. Against oppression and a system of control, to give humanity a chance at hope once again. Indeed, he walked them out there, just like he said he would," the serpent spoke, nodding in acknowledgement.

"And then they were free!" the man reiterated.

"Free? I never said anything about those people being… free," the serpent remarked, with a fiendish grin, then continued.

"Out of the hopelessness there came such a redeemer, an individual, who was different and unafraid of personal expression. He was a physical representation of social consciousness and self-awareness, and a man who excelled in wisdom and courage. He was a leader like none before. He re-established the natural rights of humanity and brought about new laws to civilization never heard of before. He was a man not only great of heart, strength, and will, but he was not afraid to color out of the lines and find the true meaning and purpose of his life. He embodied both of his parent's social styles and could be described as a 'Black Power Flower Child.'

"His method was no predetermined government takeover or planned military coup. The change came from the music within him, the individuality that separated him from the lie living establishment drones. As he put it, they were his people and he wanted to allow them to move again. If, perhaps, he pushed the right mental buttons it would motivate them and maybe they would remember who they really were. He was originally drawn forth from the waters and was raised as a son of the citizens. But it was his blood that called out to him and ignited his passion as a freedom fighter and the one who would restore the believers.

"The believers had fallen away from their faith and had descended into a moral and socially undesirable state. In order to bring them out of their bondage, it would take one to relearn his roots and uncover the true origins and natural rights of humanity. Although he was born and raised with the privileges of his adopters, it was the burden of the believers that he inherited and the qualities of his parents that defined him as an individual, a leader, and law-giver.

"Now, the cries of the slaves were deafening and their misery hung above the land as dark clouds for all to see. With their new-found position and slave workforce, the Citizen Masters embraced a hedonistic philosophy and lifestyle. Their written code of conduct was to strive towards a state of constant pleasure by minimizing pain. However, no level of ethics was introduced as it would mean that the conditions inflicted upon the believers was inherently wrong. However, this was easily addressed as the believers were slaves and had no human rights. Thus, they were subhuman and therefore no infringement of their rights was possible, which made their institutionalized slavery legal.

"The priests stated that they had found the supreme way of life and the goal of the citizens was the full attainment of pleasure, contentment, and happiness. The priests taught that intrinsic good was to be sought after as pleasure and the negation of pain was the mark of higher beings. The priests taught that of all known pleasures be they monetary, intellectual, or spiritual, physical pleasure was the strongest and most ideal. The laws stated that any harm, or punishment upon slaves, was permissible and without consequence, so long as it brought a sense of pleasure to the Citizen Masters in some form.

"The Citizen Masters further justified their actions by reducing all logic to a basic doctrine concerning the truth of pleasure. Their priests taught that one could be unsure of future outcomes, but one can know with certainty the goodness and badness of sense-experiences. Additionally, they taught that trying to empathize with the slaves was against reason, as one could not have knowledge of another person's experiences. They said that any reaction to punishment was purely physical and all sensation and experience was subjective. Therefore, they must be indifferent to the appearance of pain or tranquility in their slaves. For all they knew, the slaves enjoyed their workloads and found fulfillment in pleasing their masters. Therefore, they were allowing the slaves to live in pleasure, which was of the greatest good.

"But no man does well in chains, he longs for freedom and needs it like the blossom needs the sun. All the while I watched and waited, but I heard not the voice of the Creator or any rumble of destruction set upon the kingdom. Their sorrow was loud and their burden intense, but the Creator was silent over the land and for many years did they suffer. I prayed long in those nights saying, 'They cried, but there was none to save them, even unto the Creator, but he answered them not.'

"The king then set out a new law. He saw that no matter how much the believers were tormented, their numbers continued to grow. Then the king proclaimed that any woman of belief conceiving a male child would have the child killed and it be thrown in the Great River. Of all personalities and traits, only the truly evil could kill the innocent without regret. At night the cries of women, who had their children slaughtered, filled the air.

"The slaves knew only great sorrow and misery. They cried out for salvation, but none came. Instead, the Citizen Masters grew stronger and more determined in their will against the believers. At night, I crept through the streets silent as the shadow and cunning as the wind to get a better view of the happenings. I heard laughter and celebration within the homes of the Citizen Masters, and heard echoing silence and saw grief on the faces of the slaves. I remember the stone look of helplessness from those fathers who had let their son's lives slip away by the hands of another man. Their wives emotionally drained and disgusted at their husband's presence, their tears screaming hate at them. Yet they held each other in the night, for what else could they do.

"But in one home, a small family was different. There was no light, but a tiny candle in the corner and I saw with my serpent eyes, a male child, alive in its mother's arms. A male child alive and defiant against the rule of a god king. He had been born to a mother and father who had an elder son and daughter and to their fret, a male child was born unto them. The father of the infant was known as 'Exalted Friend.' He was rumored to have lived a full life without giving over a single sin. A vision he was said to have had was recorded on scrolls near the Sea of the Dead.

"In it, he said the vison was one of dualism and was a vision of things to come: 'In this land I went up to bury what was forgotten... our fathers. As I went up, I found not his body, but piles of sheaths from my nephews, all dead from exceeding labors in this land. Unrest and rumors of war returned unto this land but we could not flee as we had not built the grave for our fathers. Not until then, did my father release me to go. Then we made good our preparations but while we built, war broke out between 'Those of Another Tribe' and of those of this land, but

I could not tell the victor.

'And then, from among all the people, my son became an exalted priest and left for all the generations a great truth. He rescued them and after the mountain, he gave a great blessing. I awoke then and I saw it happen just as it was revealed to me.

'Then I saw a watcher in my mind, a dream more real than illusion. There I witnessed two men fighting over my body and still bidding on my blood. My body lay lifeless, yet I was risen and spoke unto them asking, 'Who are you, that you claim right and privilege over my flesh and those of my blood.' They answered, 'We have authority and govern all of mankind, now choose... who shall rule you.' I raised my eyes and looked and one of them was horrific in his appearance and his face was as the Viper. He wore a dusky yet multi-colored cloak and he was with exceedingly many eyes and had taken power over me.

'I asked, who is this watcher? I was told, he is of three names, 'The Worthless: They Who Induce Worship of Other Gods;' 'The Prince of Darkness: They Who Benefit from Calamitous Circumstances;' and 'King of Evil: He Who Opposes the Creator.' He is forever in darkness and his eyes are systems of control.' I then questioned the dominion of the other Watcher? And I was told, from the high peak to the low desert, I rule every man of the light and am strength of the Creator. I asked him his name. I was told, he is of three names... 'He Who is Like the Creator: I am Expressly Intended to Persuade unto The Creator;' 'Prince of Light: I fight for the Children of the Believers; 'King of Righteousness: I am With He Who Gives and is Truthful, Who Stands and Protects, and Who Guides and Sets Free the Slave.

'To them the Tribes, he who comes, all his ways are true and he will heal them of their ills and guide them away from destruction. But woe to the sons of righteousness if ye are angry at him, thou art forever angry with me. Take heed and notice, to the sons of lies and sons of truth. Certainly those of the light shall become alive and those of darkness shall become destroyed. For all foolishness is of evil and will darken those of the light, while peace and truth are destined for eternal joy.

Lastly, in this time of sorrow and dread, rely upon the truth, as it remains humanity's greatest weapon and the key to the future of all peoples,' the serpent continued.

"The following day, Exalted Friend told his wife of his vision and the two prayed on the meaning but found no explanation. No one had known of the child's birth, she was a strong woman and she cried not during her labor and kept the child quiet. Exalted Friend sat by the window with a plain face and a blank stare, so as none would know the pride he felt behind his eyes. Their defiance could mean their death, but the chance at life was worth the deception and was too great an opportunity. I saw something different in this man and woman, they were willing to risk their lives for their child. They thought for themselves and did what was best for their family. The child was their future and even I did not know what the future would hold for him."

"Hold on a second, you said the guy, Exalted Friend, had a vison and there were two men and one of them had the face of a viper... so that was you?" the man interrupted bringing the serpent's attention back to the cave.

"Well I'm glad to see that you're paying attention, Man of the Present. The vision is quite mysterious and not easily deciphered. But be careful of paring words, such as serpent with viper, and darkness with evil, for the meaning within them is hidden," the serpent replied intelligently.

"The vison being spoken of was set as a matter of duality and was more prophetic and future telling than simple representation. The man having the vision was no doubt the father of our hero and his vision was not so much about him, but of the situation of the believers. He was asked by the figures to choose who would rule over him. Perhaps that choice corresponded to the choice that the believers had made to conform to the panoptic system and had forgotten the path of the Creator. I believe the vision was another reminder that the believers had forgotten their oath to He Who Would Increase.

"But how is that not you? The man reiterated in question.

"Again, I believe the vision was referring to the direct situation that the believers were in. Now the watcher was of three names: He Who Induced Worship of other Gods; He Who Benefited from Calamitous Circumstances, and a King Who Opposed the Creator.

"The panoptic system that oppressed the populace into worship and belief of their gods, the Citizen Masters who benefited from the enslavement of the believers, and a king who declared himself a god. So, there in lies your darkness.

"Interesting..." the man replied, while nodding. The serpent continued.

"I kept an eye on Exalted Friend and his family, and visited their home each night. But with each new day, it became more difficult to conceal the child as the child continued to grow. Exalted Friend and his wife thought to flee the land, but how could they with such a small child, surely he would cry out and disrupt their escape.

"The family sat together for one last night and a heavy decision was made. The child would be sent away, an unthinkable act for any parent to leave their child in the hands of destiny. His mother wept as she was overcome with grief, but then she remembered her husband's vision, 'Rely on the truth.' It was the king who had decreed that all male infants were to be thrown in the great river. If they were found out, she would not lie for she had given the child to the river, which was the truth. So she set him afloat in a basket of leaves and sticks, and bid him farewell. She loved him so she let him go, to keep him would be to condemn him. Such is the way of all things in life, if you love it let it go, for it will return greater unto you.

"The child's mother and her daughter watched as he floated away down the river. I followed from a distance beneath the waters and watched it occur. The current was strong and carried many things away, but it changed and swirled and swam a new course. The river could have swallowed him up, but more than luck was on the child's side. It was the river who thought to guide him safely downstream and away from those creeping lizards who cry tears upon a tender feast. But away from them did the river carry him and to my surprise, royal compassion found him and drew him out from the waters.

"She who was 'One of the Best' the daughter of the king, bathed openly in the waters and was without child and felt empty and alone. The tiny basket floated towards her and behold it was a child, helpless and alive. He was marked as a believer, so she covered him and called him, my 'Drawn Forth Son.'

"She recognized the child as not of her people, but in her arms he would grow; as a pup that becomes the wolf, a kitten that turns fierce into the tiger, so too would this child grow and become a man. Word quickly spread over the land that a blessing had come to the royal house and the princess's sorrow had ended as she was now mother to a child. The kingdom held celebrations and made offerings and annually repeated them at harvest time. A legend was told of her, of how she loved the Great River so much that it became her husband and made her fertile. The Great River had blessed her with a child that she drew out from the water and he was known as 'The One Who Lived.' A goddess was erected in her honor and became a household deity and a protector of children. All in the land prayed to the goddess as it cemented the sacred relationship between mother and child.

"The Great River was fruitful and the rising waters blessed the silt that enabled abundant harvests. Now she, One of the Best, was Princess Mother, and she dressed herself with two tall feathers in her hair. She called to a servant girl to find a woman to nurse the child and it came to be the child's natural mother was chosen to nurse him. Thus, his mother, Full of Glory, nursed her son until he was old enough and weaned him until her task was completed. But I wondered, as the child was raised by his adopters and the captors of his people... what would he become?

"He was not of the Citizen Masters but they treated him as one of their own, for none new except his adoptive mother of his true heritage. But what of this lad, would he follow his training and become master to his own slave people? Or would he eventually find himself an outcast and eventually be cast out into servitude? For he had come from humble beginnings, but the cry of freedom and life remained in his blood. Or perhaps it is he who decides what he will be. His status surrounds him, but his blood calls to him. When he hears it what will he answer?

"The boy grew and was given every privilege and education typical of a prince. Literature, language in the hieroglyphic character and orthography were presented until he became fluent above his own teachers. He was molded to be a gentleman of society and became well known for his epistolary and poetic skill. Further, he was instructed in accounting, arithmetic, geometry, and he interned as an adjunct to complete his curriculum.

"Theology and philosophy were taught to him as were the advanced ideas of all the civilized and known worlds. He set to memory the codes of morality, laws of the gods and their divine nature by gnomic phrases. Polytheistic religion was taught, however, the secrets of the gods were for clerics and priests alone, yet he was familiarized with the books of mystics which were made known to all royalty.

"As a member of the royal house, he was never pressed into a professional field but was allowed to pursue any knowledge or skill he chose, such as astronomy, medicine, history, or modern warfare. He soon completed his education and was now a man, but found that no matter the social circles that gathered, he was inherently different. At night, he sat alone and dreamed thoughts unlike the Citizen Masters. He kept his hair long and played music of a different ear, while his peers laughed at his peculiar dress and manner. But he was proud in his ways, and he was strong in his independence.

"He would often steal away in the night and bring table leftovers to those slaves who were too weak to work and were withheld food rations. He found compassion for the slaves for they worked hard under the sun and slept bare under the stars. One day, Drawn Forth Son, asked the king what made the citizens different from the slaves who served them. The king told him that it was the way of the gods and that the gods intended the citizens to be master and the believers to be slave. The king said if the gods did not intend it, then they would come down and change the slave's position themselves.

"Still, Drawn Forth Son felt sorrow in his heart for those who lived beneath him. He often turned away as soldiers raped slave women and beat their husbands and brothers who were powerless to stop them. He witnessed young slaves being thrown into pits and used as practice for training troops. The life of the slave was meaningless and served only as food for their masters, but the food he ate began to taste bitter. I would often sit and listen to his 'desert music,' as it was soothing but intense and filled with emotion. For a time, he appeared to be content playing his music and day dreaming, but one cannot live in a state of sleep. He must awake and bring life and purpose to his visions.

"Unfortunately, his younger brother known as 'Effective Sun,' did not appreciate his brother's individuality, nor his meekness. And Drawn Forth Son was constantly challenged as being favored and troublesome to the traditional way of things. Deceit and treachery were common as each royal family competed to place their son next upon the throne. Each family approached Drawn Forth Son with a different proposition and made offerings from wealth to land and lordship, to lovely ladies of engagement all for his support. But Drawn Forth Son showed no interest in such things and he would say to them, 'The king should be he who is most worthy, not he who is of greed and selfish ambition.'

"Then, tragedy befell the kingdom and their great king died by unknown causes. Now, there were two sons after the king and the eldest was Drawn Forth Son above his brother Effective Sun. The kingdom fell into mourning for the death of their great leader who had reigned as the earthly embodiment of their highest god. Many royal families raced to the bedside of their fallen king to pay their respects, but immediately they joined Effective Sun in a solitary chamber of secret counsel.

"Immediately after, Effective Sun called to his brother and advised him to take his hand in lordship as he was to be crowned king. Drawn Forth Son stated that if the gods had chosen him, then it was he who was to reign. He took hold of his brother's hand and acknowledged his rule. So it was that Effective Sun came to rule all of the land and his brother Drawn Forth Son stood by his side.

"Drawn Forth Son excelled at almost every endeavor he engaged in and brought honor to the land in his brother the king's name. Drawn Forth Son grew the kingdom and selected new architects and engineers to build ships, and machines for laying stones. He equipped and retrained the entire army with new methodologies and skillful tactics and strategies.

"He ushered in an era of renaissance and funded the designs and authorized the construction of new irrigating canals, and the supplanting of basins for water storage for troops on the march. All of these things and more did he do for the sake of his brother's sovereignty. He was the reaching arm of the king and where the multitudes were without order, he appointed governors and held elections for judges of the people.

"For his many good works, he was beloved by the masses and blessed by the priests as one who was worthy to be honored like a god. But his brother, seeing his excellence, became envious and felt opposition from his own kin. Then the king began plotting his demise by way of some unfortunate, yet plausible, pretext. The king then called his brother to prove his place amongst the other members of the royal house and to take up battle as it was the noblest cause. For any member of royalty could lounge only for so long, where true glory rested in battle and defeat of the enemy."

Drawn Forth Son replied, 'Indeed, but there are no enemies and our kingdom is without rival in all that we do. Seeking out battle in a peaceful land is only agitation of empty waters. Patience and true rivals will present themselves, whereas impetuous war on the weak only serves greed and bloodlust. Are we pompous bullies seeking simple victories, or are we masters of war who seek test and examination by fire? I say, I am ready for any battle in the name of my king and the defense and of my nation.'

"His brother was angered by his wit and tactful remarks that, in so many words, denounced his challenge calling him a coward. So when the armies of Cush invaded the low desert regions of the land, the king saw the war as a convenient opportunity to expose his brother to untimely blade and spear. So the king summoned his brother and ordered him to command a force and engage their enemies in battle and end their shallow encroachment.

"Now Drawn Forth Son was the pride of the nation and knew no defeat of battle on field or board, and would lead the king's armies to glorious triumph. But Drawn Forth Son was betrayed and was outfitted with an inferior army who were tested and trained only in the art of field labor. The king and his accomplices would be assured that he would engage head on, but due to the weakness of his troops, death and defeat would be the only outcome available. Upon notice of the engagement, Drawn Forth Son prepared to meet with the war masters, but found his troops already assembled awaiting his command on the morning. He was given less than one night to make preparations for war and even less time to assemble proper rations for his men. He looked out and saw all of the kingdom out in the streets ready to praise him and his men on their march to victory out of the city. A heavy and uncertain feeling came over him as he and his troops were hurriedly marched out of the city.

"By then, he had realized by the way his army marched and assembled that they were unskilled in slaying and were better suited at digging graves, which undoubtedly would be their own. But Drawn Forth Son pulsed courage and bravery into them and then seized control and occupied the enemy country. How he gained such remarkable successes in a lopsided battle was a matter of genius and military skill. Seeing that he led an inferior army, Drawn Forth Son, rearranged his battle plans and chose to engage the enemy in attrition warfare.

"His decision there on the battle field was masterful and closely resembled that which won the Western front at the battle of Verdun. He told his men that their goal was not to take the field or even breach the walls of the kingdom, but was to destroy the enemy's defenses, rendering them weak. Their smaller numbers would mean that they had little opportunity to recover and mount a second offense, but his plan was to force the enemy into a pyrrhic victory.

"Ultimately he would put them to such a decision that winning would cost such high losses that the enemy would surrender rather than lose everything. If the enemy were to take them, then their victory would be hollow and they would have lost so much that, ultimately, they would have been defeated. Such a measure was dangerous and sure to cost Drawn Forth Son his own life, but chance was on his side.

"Earlier on, Drawn Forth Son ordered his men to seize a crowd of Ibis in order to clear a path through a snake infested trail to flank the enemy armies. The following morning, his men attacked and routed their forces and aimed their arrows at their war machines and lanced and speared the enemy horses. Hot oil and fire was launched and torched the enemy resources and medic tents behind them. The army of field laborers had dug trenches and pits throughout the night and the enemy's mounted cavalry tripped and collapsed easily unaware of the traps the ditch diggers had dug for them. The enemy soldier's bellies turned sick from cowardice forcing them into panic and retreat. With smaller numbers and a weaker force, Drawn Forth Son's army triumphed and claimed victory over the enemy belligerents who then surrendered.

"The war was ended with fewer casualties than expected and the enemy country, according to custom, wedded their queen to the conquering general. The land of Cush came to love and admire Drawn Forth Son and marked themselves accordingly. Before message was sent back of the victory, Drawn forth Son arrived at the head of his army with gifts and spoils of war brought before the king. Drawn Forth Son returned not dead, but to roaring applause and was even more a great hero, which further infuriated his brother. His brother accepted the victory in his name and pretended to welcome him, yet continued to plot against him.

"He retired him from battle and sent his troops to the frontier so he would have none loyal to him close by. Drawn Forth Son asked his brother whether there were any additional tasks he could perform in the name of his king. His brother merely swished his hand away at him and gave him no further command and was silent towards him.

"After his return home, Drawn Forth Son began looking for a greater answer to life. He had achieved almost every worldly accomplishment available to him, but still felt empty. He found no security in pleasurable company nor in the gnomic phrases of the priests. His offerings to idols and animal gods seemed silly and their molded heads mocked him as he meditated.

"He began researching and observing the ways of the slaves as he had heard them praying for a deliverer as they carried on private meetings and rituals. He was unsure of a new path but found that the previous road traveled had lead him to emptiness. So he decided to start anew and soon began omitting the many gods from his formal prayers and public ceremonies. Drawn Forth Son possessed a portion of the low desert region and became dissatisfied with the established traditions there. He declared idolatry, hedonism, and the worship of gods in the images of wild beasts to be meaningless, and stated that they only served as erroneous and sentimental entertainment. 'There is a divine force out there, I believe it, and it is a strength and beauty that encompasses us all,' Drawn Forth Son said when addressing the public.

"He was warned by priests that doing such things would evoke the wrath of the gods upon him and that the king would be made aware of his treachery. Drawn Forth Son, being ward of his own lands, embarked on a wide-scale erasure of the traditional gods and ordered his court to remove them from the patronage of the temples. When asked whom the citizens should pray to he said a true god would make itself known.

"The priests rebuked this change and continued to pray to the moon gods and apis bull idols. Yet, Drawn Forth Son was undeterred and continued to shift practices away from pagan temples, keeping his policies tolerant to those who remained loyal to the traditional ways. He was summoned back to the Royal Palace after his behavior had been reported by the priests to the king. His brother had finally found leverage over him and exposed him as a rebel against the gods. And so it was that the king had his solution, without having to sully his own hands. His brother, the infallible Drawn Forth Son became unpopular and the citizens turned against him and he was alienated in his own home.

"The king set his brother into isolation in his home and he was ordered not to leave without escort as his activities were deemed treasonous and a matter of national security. The king then recruited an acquaintance of Drawn Forth Son, known as Memphis, to kill him given the right time. Soon after a funeral was announced of one of the high priests who was a favorite of Drawn Forth Son's teachers. The king bid his brother to commit the body and see it across the desert to the priest burial grounds. He then appointed Memphis to accompany his brother on the journey, thus providing him the opportunity to strike. But when Memphis attacked, Drawn Forth Son countered swiftly and slew his would be assassin.

"The blood of his friend covered him as his belly gaped open and life seeped out of him. Grief came over him as he knew his only recourse was to flee his home and never return as his brother would not cease until he was dead. He took one last look before making good his escape into the night and said, 'In a world of systemic control and conformity, individuality and creativity are illegal, and now... I am become outlaw.'

"So it was that night that Drawn Forth Son escaped into the Arabian Desert alone, without direction and unsure of the path ahead. The following day, the body of Memphis was discovered and the guards and troops were sent to seek out the murderer. After a worthy search, Drawn Forth Son was declared dead and the king went about undoing everything connected to his name. Alone now and out in the desert, he ran until he could no longer see the burning lights of the kingdom behind him.

"The morning sun was momentarily gentle, but as he awakened in the desert heat he realized the dreadful place that he had awakened to. He had run far into the night until he collapsed, but he knew not in what direction he had gone, and now, wandering in the desert, he was merely waiting to die of exposure. The sun was high above his head now and he was well out of range of the kingdoms markers. He rubbed his arms and checked his legs for stings and bites from tiny assassins that might quicken his end, but he remained unscathed. The desert was good for two things, nothing and nothing, and unfortunately he had more of both than he needed.

"The sun stalked him as he walked, so he tied his tunic round his head to shield himself from the relentless thumping of heat upon him. He was in good health but sooner or later, the heat would overtake him and his body would give out. Dying of heatstroke and dehydration was not a clean death and over the course of a few days, he would feel every inch of the brutally long punishment. He had seen dried corpses of slaves and fugitives who had fled their masters and how jerky looking their skin was only after a few days dead. The looks on their faces were not peaceful and their last expression showed the pain and horror that swaddled them as they laid dying.

"The Arabian Desert was a vast wilderness that occupied most of the peninsula and was one of the world's largest continuous bodies of sand. The cultural diversity of the region consisted of mostly nomadic peoples, sand cats, spiny tailed lizards, gazelles, and oryxes. The terrain qualified as mildly hospitable if shifting sand shelves, red dunes, and porridge thick quicksand are welcoming to you. The dry, arid climate was no friend to the lost traveler and the temperatures oscillated between stroke causing heat and bottomless freezes in the night. The striped hyena, jackal, and honey badgers acted as officials patrolling their jurisdictions, but took pity on no one and nothing.

"With each footstep he imprinted, he left an ounce of himself behind as the fluids sweated and boiled out of him and his body began to resemble the exposed surface. There were shattered and eroded rocks on the ground, no doubt the result of sudden rains falling on steaming hot rocks, leaving them split and dry caked. After only half a day's march through the desert, he felt as if his senses were wavering as he began to see beautiful mosaic stones, but he was quite conscious and these too were normality's of the stony flats. He was strong of body and tried to convince his mind to stay hopeful at the possibility of stumbling upon an underground source of water or a lucky oasis, but none presented themselves.

"Those who lived in the desert had developed adaptations and survival techniques to adhere to the harsh conditions, but he was of royalty and a gentleman of leisure and had no such improved survival skill or knowledge. His only assurance would be falling to the ground and becoming assimilated into the desert artwork after as his body had been whitened clean by vultures and insects. When he had fled the kingdom, he failed to obtain rations and, unfortunately, had exhausted much of his energy running through the night. However, he had survived day one and the evening came and with it the sun was sarcastic as it was merely the bell that signaled the end of the first round and his legs were already gone from underneath him.

"The following day was the same and now he had become ever more desperate for water. He grabbed at weeds hoping to suck some nectar from them but there was none, just as a kiss from a bullwhip is none too romantic. Fear and hopelessness began calling his name. He switched his eyes back and forth looking for voices and he ran trying to escape his own mind. The desert sun looked on in amusement as he was on pace and would reach his destination of insanity by the day's end.

"Day three and he could only speak one word to himself when he awoke, and he asked 'why?' Why go on? It was all but over, struggling to move was a fool's errand and there wasn't even an audience to entertain with such a performance. But then a second word did he utter and he said 'no.' Not like this, not curled up like a baby. I will meet it head on and standing on my feet. I will not kneel. I will not bend. If lifting myself is my final movement, then it shall be that I died as a man. But he had more than a few steps left in him and the sun above felt fearful that he might actually loose the wager for his life.

"The sun rarely loses a bet against one unprepared for the desert fight, but this one was becoming annoyingly resilient. With each step, his posture grew more arched and his hands were now glued to his knees trying to remain upright, but still he trudged on. There were no signs of tracks signaling nomads or caravans in the region, which meant that they had long moved their herds to an available location of grazing and water. And then… he collapsed. It was as if his brain hit the brakes, just before his nerves ignited and set his insides aflame.

"It appeared that this was it for him. He was convulsing and hallucinating. There was a blow of wind that was cool and moist, it was not rain but the light air rehydrated his skin as he slept. A momentary drink was he afforded. Was it the Creator at work here, or was it the desert poking him with a stick of false hope only to fully cook him alive the following day.

"Day four and I felt sorry for him and prayed to the Creator. Even I said, no more, no more. He was done and was in the final stages of meltdown by then. His core temperature had redlined and his body was in a panic trying to cool itself off. His eyes turned red and the whites of his eyes had begun turning pink as he was cooking from the inside out." The serpent broke from narration and returned to speaking with the Man of the Present.

"I don't mean to be insensitive, but I must point out that I am a predator and eating and killing is all the same to me. So this next statement is going to seem a bit harsh, but I implore you not to denounce me wicked."

"Why, what were you going to say?"

"Well you see, Man of the Present, the desert is excellent at wearing down an otherwise sturdy and difficult prey. Yet, I am no buzzard and do not go for leftovers. I eat live things, not the dead and decaying. Only certain types are suited to such a diet as it is their purpose, but I am no such insect. You see, I wanted him sun baked, not sun dried. The sun is wondrous at wrinkling grapes and tomatoes, but like all salted meats if left out too long. Well I mean it, it, it, just becomes so course and dry and utterly disgusting. I'd compare such a boring sandwich to overcooked, three day old turkey with no gravy to alleviate the dryness," the serpent, remarked pointing with his tail as if at a market picking over choice meats.

"So, you were going to eat him?"

"Well, of course, I was! What do you think I was doing out there? When he entered the desert, it just so happened to be where I was at the time. I was there basking for a bit getting my intake of UV rays and I decided to follow this lost soul for a suitable, yet easy, meal."

"But he didn't die there though, which means you didn't eat him. So what happened? Did you change your mind or something?"

"No, I was most certainly going to eat him. I'm glad you asked that question, because it has segued us directly to where we encountered each other," the serpent continued.

"As I looked down upon him I said aloud, 'Low Desert Punk.' Ha! Makes perfect sense now. How he was still able to stand I do not know, but he was unable to move and he struggled trying to command his nerves to signal his legs forward. I was just above him on a solid dune and shifted the sand beneath me and surfed the sand down just off of his flanks. In traditional approach, I came round my target's side, where I was positioned to strike then constrict him all in one motion. And then... silently... like... so...

"I seized his legs then coiled round his body and quickly positioned him upright and opened my mouth just above his head. I moistened my mouth of the dry air, but no! It was he! His arm was free and instantly he reached and his grip on my mouth was fierce. His eyes rolled forward and he stared as he was conscious and aware! But how? Impossible!

"I struggled to pull free from his grasp but he held firm. I further coiled around him as I had dealt with difficulty before. Fool! I would allow this ensemble routine to continue a little longer, only for him to think about his impetuousness within my belly. I squeezed him and flexed my muscles tighter, but so too was his grip on my jaw. What nonsense was this? I could break his back and fold him in half with ease, but this fool's grasp on my mouth was annoying and distracting my positioning. I turned my head upside down and twisted his arm in the process, but still he held on.

"I coiled further round his body then up around his head till little more than his face was shown, but he would not release his grip. His body remained strong somehow and he continued fighting back. His feet were exposed and I could easily sweep them, bringing him to the ground. I tightened around his feet and, with ease, they came together and now we would see how good his mat game was. This battle of matched pairs would end soon enough and, no, I wouldn't need his salute as he was about to die.

"I tightened and rolled but he shifted his weight and pushed his fist upward forcing my head directly in front of his face. He looked right at me, then said, 'Now I gotcha!' He began smashing my head on the ground, which was soft sand and caused me no harm, but he did not relent. By this time, I could feel myself coming out of position. I'd have to readjust possibly around his shoulders then up under his arms to break his ribs and suffocate him. But his one free arm was like a tree trunk and he fought me at every opportunity.

"He pulled me close again and said firmly 'You! Dumb! Bastard! I've been watching you for the last three days! There was nothing out here to eat and I didn't think I was going to make it, until I saw you. You thought you were hunting me? Idiot! I feigned weakness to get you down here because I wouldn't be able to attack you out in the open. So, with cleaver acting, I baited you and now I have snared and entrapped you... you, sand worm!'

"He continued speaking with force while we wrestled. 'You! Going to eat me! ... Not likely, for it is I who shall drink and eat you! Then I shall wrap myself in your hide and pick my teeth with your bones. You! Stupid! Greedy! Desert worm! I was never in any real danger as no man has ever threatened my being, so his assault was utterly futile but his confidence was bolstering. I looked directly at him and then it hit me... I knew him, didn't I? I said to him mumbled as his fist was latched onto my jaw. "Don't I know you?" The seriousness in his eyes kept him focused on the fight but I was sure that I knew him from somewhere so I repeated my question, 'Don't I know you?'

"He responded with cynicism as I expected. 'Yeah... you do

know me! I'm that thing from your nightmares! I'm the one who wouldn't go silently into the night! And I'm stuck in your craw, and you can't spit me out!' With his life in the balance, he thought my words were a ploy so I relented and replied with calm 'No… you were he that lived, he that was drawn forth… out of the waters, it was you whose music was lullaby to the kingdom. It is you… release your hold and I too shall set you free.'

"And I'm supposed to believe you?" Drawn Forth Son responded, with fierce defiance.

"You can let me go or we can stay like this for a while longer, it matters little to me. The longer you stay like this, the weaker you undoubtedly will become. You are no closer to killing and eating me than I am towards you, but unlike you, I remain strong eternally."

"You don't know shit about me, demon slug!" he responded angrily.

"I know more about you than you think and I know that your body is marked like the slaves are. Now let me go… you have my word that I shall not attack you," I responded calmly.

"After hearing my last words I could see his mind moving and rationality returned to him. He simplified his grip on my jaw without completely letting go and I slowly uncoiled from around him allowing him to breathe. Then from around his feet, then his knees. I looked at him with an eye making him aware that the next move was his. I was still in a position to reassert myself if he reneged on our deal, but he saw the opportunity for peace and finally let go. We were free of each other and sat ourselves upright leaning back to back in gratitude and respect of a good match, while we caught our breaths.

"First, I would like to apologize for my simple assault upon you. My inquiry upon your life was not personal as I am a predator and am slave to my instinct. Secondly, allow me to introduce myself, I am the Serpent of Old and I have been amongst mankind since its very beginnings."

"Who?" Drawn Forth Son asked looking in disarray.

"Wait what? He didn't know who you were?" the Man of the

Present interrupted.

"I have to admit that his response was more bruising to my ego than the stalemate that resulted from our wrestling match. But no, he didn't know who I was. Why would he?"

"How could he never have heard of you before? You're the Serpent, right? And he was…" the Man of the Present asked.

"You're thinking of what he became but you're forgetting that he was raised in a culture that had no belief or understanding of me. Their beliefs were no doubt silly, pagan, multi-animal headed idols who controlled the winds, the seasons, and the harvests all into an afterworld of who knows what," the serpent interjected quickly.

"Hmmm! Yeah, I guess he wouldn't know about the Garden and everything. So what happened after that?" The serpent continued…

"How do you know those things about me? And how is it that you can speak?" Drawn Forth Son asked.

"Who I am is of no importance at the moment, but I confess that I have been watching you since the time of your infancy," I told with reassurance.

"What do you mean you've been watching me? For what purpose?" Drawn Forth Son, questioned in suspicion.

"You were different from the others and so were your parents. I think that's why you survived then, no doubt that difference is what has allowed you survival here on this day. You think you were born Crown Prince to the royal family, but what if I told you that your true origins were humble and your royal identity was a lie?" Drawn Forth Son remained breathing heavily catching his breath, but was alert while listening as I spoke.

"What if I told you that you were slave born and that your parents set you adrift to save you from a royal decree that sentenced all male slave babies to death?"

"How is that possible? I am of royal blood and my mother was daughter to the king, and I was…" he defended in disbelief.

"Lied to!" I interjected with piercing revelation.

"That's not possible!" Drawn Forth Son stopped silent in his speech and was caught confounded with the truth.

"Is it, now? Then so too is the emptiness and isolation you feel inside you. Then so too is the physical marking on you that you hide from other citizen men when bathing in the open. Perhaps lie is too strong of a word, but the truth is that you are not one of them and you never have been."

"Go on," Drawn Forth Son said, shifting his eyes back and forth quickly.

"It is each of us that has a lurking question that we try to answer day after day, as we engage in endeavor and adventure seeking the answer to who we truly are inside. I can tell you with certainty that who you are is not what you have been brought up to believe."

"I don't know who or what you are, but I don't like this game. If you're not going to kill me, then I'll be leaving now. I have to find water," Drawn Forth Son, ended the conversation, to walk away.

"Water! Subsequently, there's water only a short distance from here. I do not know which way the winds of fate are blowing you, but it seems they have sailed you through the sand and on to the doorstep of a well of hospitality. Just over that pair of dunes is a water well frequented by peoples of the desert. Head that way and you shall find nourishment and the strength of life shall again flow through you." Drawn Forth Son began walking away to climb the dunes.

"But before you go, you should know something. There was one whom I encountered long ago. He was unlike the other men of his time and although you are very different from he, I cannot shake a feeling of similarity between the two of you. Humanity has all but forgotten him and, as a result, they have lost their way. But you are different in more ways than can be known and only the Creator knows the purpose behind us all," I said calling out from behind, Drawn Forth Son.

"The Creator? Of what Creator do you speak? I know of them all and they are meaningless," Drawn Forth Son rebutted, stopping in his tracks then turning back around.

"The Creator I speak of comes in no animal form and is not governor over simple seasons and harvests. The Creator is

281

master of everything, of me, of you, of every type of life and of death. The Creator is the one, the alpha, and the omega."

"Either heat and insanity has overcome me or I really am having a conversation with a talking serpent." Drawn Forth Son, remarked to himself as he frowned in humor of the scene he found himself in.

"You have much wisdom within you mighty Uraeus and I desire to know the truth of your words and of this Creator of which you speak. Tell me now, how is it that I can come to know of him?" Drawn Forth Son, asked while walking back in my direction.

"No! Not a him, nor a her. The Creator is… above human comprehension and there are no earthly words capable of true description. I, myself, am only permitted to view the Creator's voice as an image of sound and color. It would be my honor to relate this information to you and introduce you to the master of us all." Drawn Forth Son started walking toward the dunes then turned and that I remained behind him.

"Aren't you coning?

"No, thank you. That well is populated by humans and I am but a specter to modern man. As a result, most of you have become fearful of my presence so I am not welcome there."

"But when will I see you again?"

"If knowledge is what you seek, then an instructor is what you have found. 'Give instruction to a wise man and he will be yet wiser. Teach a just man and he will increase in learning.' I will come to you when the time is right. As for now, go! Drink! And return yourself to the land of the living."

"Drawn Forth Son found more than nourishment down at the water well. Like the water skin that was empty when dropped into the well and comes up full and overflowing, so too was he transformed from an empty and fleeting life to one of fullness, marriage, respect, and humble wealth. It was many years before I returned to him and I stayed away as the human soul needs rest and a busy mind wears down the soul. To thrust such heavy information on a mind that was not settled would no doubt have caused it too spill over, so I was patient for his sake.

"But I pledged him instruction and the time had come to make good my word. After so long a time, my only concern was if he would still wish to receive it? I approached from the mountains and overlooked the lands where he and his community lived. He had become well respected and an integral part of a humble community.

"Before approaching him, I observed his habits in order to make sure he was still worthy of the truths to be told. After which, I approached him one such evening after he had completed his supper and retreated to an escarpment overlooking the mountains.

"You don't play music anymore?" Drawn Forth Son turned slowly with subtle delight to find me behind him.

"I was wondering when you were going to show up again. It's been a long time, Serpent."

"Your mind is keen and the knowledge and memories remain there intact. That is good!" I said, with an inquisitive smile.

"What brings you way out here, so unannounced? Have you come to make good on your promise?" Drawn Forth Son asked, while still looking out into the night sky.

"Indeed I have, and I apologize for the delay but only one can know when they are truly ready," I replied.

"I am husband and father now, and I have prospered here amongst these people. They have made me one of their own. The well you directed me to was something of a gold mine in disguise. When I got there, seven sisters were in need of aid due to an ongoing feud with a rival tribe. My presence there was a blessing to them and I intervened allowing them to water their herd, which resulted in me being welcomed by their gracious father. The eldest of his daughters became my wife and I love her like no other.

"I have to say Serpent, I am both pleased and worried upon seeing your return. I wasn't sure if it was madness or fatigue, which produced you, but now that you're here, I see that you are indeed real. And this instruction you offer me, regarding the history of humanity and of a supreme Creator, I must admit I am fearful of such knowledge as I cannot put the safety of my family at risk for any demon rights or idol promises. Only the priests are allowed such mysteries and even though you may be in commune with spirts and are a mighty Uraeus… I am no idol worshipper and no servant of demons," Drawn Forth Son replied, looking over his left shoulder with suspicion.

"What I have for you is no deceit nor toxin of the soul. Nay, I offer only truth and elixir of knowledge. 'For my mouth shall speak truth and wickedness is an abomination to my lips. All the words of my mouth are in righteousness, and there is nothing froward or perverse in them. They are all plain to him that understandeth, and right to them that find knowledge.' Your life is one of free will and I can mix my words and spindle fibers into a complex web of arrangement, however, you are the one who must choose. Proceed or not, live or die, the choice remains yours."

"I understand and I hear your words. You know, I have been out here for quite some time and I have never returned to the land of my birth. I cannot help but feel some shame and cowardice to the circumstances that surrounded my flight."

"How so?"

"I have always felt alone, even while in the company of others. I stood out as a child and had to hide my body for the way I was marked. Other men of the royal house were very ambitious and pined for advancement, title, and wealth, while all I ever wanted to do was play my music and allow others the same freedom. I didn't believe in the statues and idols that were placed around me, I never did. I don't know, I always felt that there was something else. Something that couldn't be touched or detailed by a clay figurine. And for that I was a trouble maker. I was considered barmy and odd.

"When I met you, you were the first one who knew those things about me and it was sort of a conformation of who I was all along. There were rumors when I was a child that I was not legitimate, but my mother swatted them away and reaffirmed that I was true and noble born. I questioned it silently but never had the guts to find answers to the questions that were driving me," Drawn Forth Son confessed, recalling his past.

"I know the question that is most important to you and it is the sum of all of those things inside of you. You are a creative person by nature and by definition that makes you different. Yes, all humans are different from each other, but most of them want to fit in or at least try to. For the individual such as yourself, blending in goes against your inherent nature and creates a moral struggle where you feel as though you're betraying your own self.

"Creative types see the world differently than most and are willing to share what they see and their interpretation of it with the rest of the world. To them, the world has more meaning, more intricacies, and more complexity and possibility than what is typically presented and taught. Society sees them as cynical and dissenting disbelievers, but they believe most heavily in the possibility of their own dreams.

"For them, the world is a place of possibility and they work to leave their creative marks for all to see. But, unfortunately, when you see things differently, you're going to stand out. Which means you will be separated by society and they will fear and despise you. But no matter how much you try to deny it, you have to act. To the creative type, the world has more meaning because it's all just a dream and they are the ones who dream for the world.

"To the masses, life should remain a stagnant and changeless nest. But what the masses do not know is that they need the creative types who dream of a better world even though it is often misunderstood and frightening to them. One of the most amazing things about creative types is that they cannot lie about who they really are, which makes them natural truth seekers. And it is that truth about yourself that you have been searching for. You ask yourself, what am I here for, and am I doing what I am supposed to be doing? Know this, Drawn Forth Son, people will always be afraid of those who dream, but it is you who dream for the world.

"And you know the answers to those questions?" Drawn Forth Son questioned, glancing left quickly.

"No, but I know where you can find it!"

"Where... in a text, the words of a priest, or in a vision I must have! I've read them all, I visited with hundreds and meditated for days at a time and still the answers elude me. I don't know where else to look." Drawn Forth Son said, standing and shaking his hands showing emptiness and defeat.

"If you look in a book, you will find the thoughts of someone else. If you seek out a priest, he can only answer questions he himself has asked. And if you meditate, at some point you will have to open your eyes. If after having done all those things, you still cannot find the answer, then perhaps the answer is not there. The purpose of your life is not determined by others, but by the one!" I offered, raising an eyebrow.

"You are speaking of that Creator again. But how do I find this Creator? I've done everything. I've tried and still I have received nothing." Drawn Forth Son returned, motioning with his arms.

"Then try something else."

"Like what, burnt offerings?" Drawn Forth Son argued, kicking the dust up from the ground.

"No, I mean try something new, as in learn something new. Life is about living and learning, not sitting, or sleeping. The Creator is all around you. Try experiencing some of the wonders that have been set up for you. You've been out here for how many years now? I bet that there isn't a trail you haven't walked, or a stream you haven't crossed. In the time you've spent here, is there something you've wanted to do, but just never got around to doing? Or perhaps something that you thought of, but decided it was too difficult or too frightening to attempt because you might fail?"

"Actually... there was," Drawn Forth Son admitted, looking out at the mountains.

"And what was it?"

"There was a mountain, when I first arrived here."

"And what of this mountain?" I prodded, drawing closer towards him.

"There was a light at the top of it, it was consistent and I saw it all the time. Night, evening, and even in the day. I asked the others who was up there, for surely it was the habitat of a wise, old hermit who lived alone. But when I enquired of my neighbors, they laughed at me and said they knew of no such person or any such light.

"I continued to see the glowing light and it intensified, then, finally, I asked during a gathering of elders about the light up on the mountain. They all went silent and told me that they had never seen any lights on the mountain and called my wife as I, no doubt, was ill. After that, I put it out of my mind and, for a while, I stopped seeing it," Drawn Forth Son went silent for a sustained moment, then continued.

"You know you were right about creative types, in that we cannot lie to ourselves. I told everyone I didn't see the light anymore and it was true, but it wasn't because it wasn't there, it was that I wasn't there to see it. I realized that it wouldn't go away so I decided that I would. I changed the route I walked my herds and even the way I came home. I made it so the light was completely out of view and even tagged milestones from where I knew I could see it, and turned my gaze to the ground. I made it so I physically couldn't see it, even though I knew it was still there."

"And now?" I questioned him, out of one eye.

"It's there still… burning brighter than before." Drawn Forth Son raised his eyes and looked towards the mountain and saw the burning light.

"I can tell you the truth of the Creator and you can choose to believe it or not, but let me ask you this. What good is the word of another compared to the knowledge of personal experience? I can tell you what's at the top of the mountain or you can go and find out for yourself," I explained, tilting my head up and over at the mountain.

"You want me to climb the mountain?"

"No! I want you to find the answers to your questions," I rebutted, widening my eyes with a blatant expression.

"The top is almost as high as the clouds and I don't know of anyone who has reached its summit," Drawn Forth Son questioned, looking up at the mountain top with indecision.

"Then I think now would be a good time to address that issue."

"But what happens if I don't make it to the top? What if I fall? I mean, I don't know what's really up there. It might be nothing and this whole time I was believing and seeing something that wasn't even there."

"Many, if not all are faced with those same questions regarding life's enigmas and so many will fail to answer them all because of fear. Fear because they might fail, fear that they might have been wrong, fear that no one will like them. What I can tell you is this, if you don't want to know then you don't have to go. You can stay here and live the life that you have built for yourself, but unfortunately, this is all there will ever be for you.

"However, there are those who feel the same fear, but will find that fear to be a challenge and they will become the brave. They are truth seekers. They are those who ask questions. They are the ones who defy the many for the sake of their own individual growth. And they will find their own truth, their own meaning, and they will have found the beauty of their life. And in the end, it is they who will be on the mountain top and you and everyone else down below looking up at them, wishing... you had just tried."

"After hearing my words, he looked at his community below and the lights in their tents and the life he had built. He knew that going up the mountain was an endeavor he had dreamed of, but had never committed to. He knew that going would mean that things would never be the same upon his return, but he also knew that there was only one way to find out and then... he began to climb. I smiled lightly and looked up at the mountain top and saw the blazing light where he was climbing to.

"I continued watching his progress from the hillside, but was distracted by the good feeling of our interaction so much so that I did not hear the footsteps approaching from behind me. I turned around and his wife had come up directly behind me in search of her husband. I did not have time to hide myself so we found ourselves standing almost face to face with each other. She paused in petrification at the sight of me, but she let out no shriek, then I said to her, 'Do not fear me woman!'

"I fear only for the safety of my children... now who are you?" she rebutted with strength.

"I am watcher, I am waiter, I am thinker, I am doer. We are the two! Not like me, not like you. I arrive on time and am never late. Yet, seemingly, I am accused of arriving too soon."

"Where has my husband gone?" she asked, glaring with suspicion at me.

"He has gone to find his meaning," starring directly back at the woman, I replied.

"Will he find it?"

"If he makes it to the top, I believe he will. But like most men, he is unsure of himself and he will need your strength and reassurance to propel him forward." She looked with sadness in her eyes and a single tear rolled down her face. I thought to raise my tail and catch it before it be lost forever, but in that tear was her heart for she wept for the man she had just lost.

"Go home to your children, I will stay and keep watch for him until he returns. I bid you goodnight." She turned and walked slowly down the hillside as if nothing had happened. Perhaps she was preparing herself mentally for she knew that change and event was now due to come.

"When he came down from the mountain his appearance had changed, he was taller and ruddy with some grey hair, but he was dignified in his appearance. His mind had been expanded and physically, he was improved and now he knew his purpose and the meaning of his life.

"I envied him, as I had found no such answer to my being and the purpose of my wanderings over the face of the earth. Was it endless interactions with these human things, I prayed the Creator. Let it be more than just that."

"Serpent... I know now what I must do. The Creator hath commanded me to return to the land of my birth and destroy the system of enslavement and control. The Creator gave specific instruction on what would occur. The king would not allow the destruction of his oppressive society and the release of the believers easily. The Creator said that the king would fight and twist words in betrayal of the people's natural rights to live as they were meant to," Drawn Forth Son said as we stood face to face.

"As I knew it before, the Creator has a plan for you! You are to be the solution to the captivity of humanity," I responded, smirking in acknowledgement.

"You see much and are very wise Serpent, but what can I do? I am only one man and the king has armies. Besides, who am I but a bastard who was raised as one of them and benefited off the backs of slaves? The slaves who remember me will probably hate me as a traitor to my own people. Even if I do make it back to the kingdom, how could I motivate the slaves to raise up and leave? Where would I lead them to? Here? To a small village in the hills? Most could not even complete the journey and many would starve and die along the way. And if we make it back here, there is not enough to divide between them for we barely have enough bread for ourselves," he said in disbelief.

"You doubt yourself too much. I have told you, believe in yourself and know that the Creator has endowed you with great purpose and favors you much. Just put forth the initial effort and allow the Creator to do the rest."

"When I was up there, I was told that a spokesman would be made available to me. I have difficulty in speaking clearly and that spokesperson would be my brother."

"It's all coming together, now…" I remarked with a whisper.

"The only brother I've ever known is the king, and he tried to have me killed. How is it that I am to trust someone I don't even know and whom I've never met?" he gestured with his left hand in observance of the question.

"I wish I could answer that question for you, but you received direct revelation from the Creator, I do not see any room to question it."

"You are so very confident in the Creator, Serpent. If the Creator is so powerful, then why does he allow the believers to remain enslaved? Why doesn't the Creator just destroy the king and make his armies into ants under the feet of the righteous? Why would any Creator allow the wicked to rule without reckoning? And you say, I'm favored? Yes, I see, the Creator has favored me out here with a flock of skinny cows and mountain goats. Truly…. I am blessed!" he said turning his back with contempt.

"Men are always so shortsighted. You look for everything to drop out of the sky and fall right into your lap. If that happened every time a decision presented itself, then what would the purpose of life be if everything were given to you. The purpose of life is not what the Creator will do for you, it is what you do with what the Creator has given you.

"Again Serpent, you are very wise," he took in a breath, exhaled heavily, then nodded in acceptance of himself.

"So I assume you have a plan?"

"Plan! Why would I have a plan? I don't know the first thing about freeing slaves?"

"You just said I needed to go!" Drawn Forth Son raised his voice in confusion.

"No! I said you cannot run from who you are. You have been given peace of mind and been allowed the time to grow stronger. Now, it is time for you to be who you are. Fear not failure, fear not defeat, and, most of all, fear not yourself. It's getting late and, besides, I need to get some rest! No additional talk will change anything, make up your mind once and then take action in either direction. I retire from you for the evening." I departed company with Drawn Forth Son for the evening and disappeared into the hills for the night.

"The following morning, Drawn Forth Son and his family gathered supplies and prepared to head towards the Land of the Black Ground, Home of the Riverbank. Drawn Forth Son stood with his head down in question of his decision and then his wife approached him and asked him what troubled him."

"Ever since I have known you, you have put the wellbeing of others ahead of you. The first time we met, you were alone in the desert with no possessions but you stood and fought for me and my sisters with no concern for your own safety. I know that no matter what is ahead of us, you will do your best and your best has always been good enough. I am your wife and I will stand beside you no matter what happens, your fate is my fate," she kissed him once with reassurance, and he was comforted.

"They began their journey across the desert towards the land of his birth. They took their time on the journey and made good their supplies and successfully crossed the desert. When Drawn Forth Son arrived on the outskirts of the kingdom, he was met by a group of slaves. He informed them of who he was and that he had returned and of his intentions to end their suffering no matter the cost. He requested to meet with their elders as soon as possible regarding his purpose. Drawn Forth Son and his family made camp outside of the kingdom and were invited to dine with the elders and an old, wise woman that night.

"He met the elders and was immediately introduced to a man who resembled him and identified himself as his brother. He told him of their parents and how he recalled his separation due to the death sentence placed upon all male newborns at the time. His was known as 'High Mountain' and he hugged him dearly. After that, he told the elders of his revelation from the top of the mountain. His brother's name was correlation to where he encountered the voice of the Creator and he knew, indeed, he would be his representative.

"He immediately advised the elders to remember the old traditions and ways of their culture and to forego the many gods and idols of the citizen masters. He said to trust in themselves and accept the guidance of the Creator, because the Creator had surely remembered them and would aid them in their release from their plight. Then the old, wise woman interrupted him.

'I have heard those exact words before, but from a long, long time ago. They were spoken by one on his death bed and now you come and speak those words that had been passed down and all but forgotten. I recognize you by those words and I know exactly who you are.'

"The elders received his words well, but said that many would-be deliverers and supposed holy men had presented themselves, but all were exposed and were false. They asked for some demonstration so that they may be assured of his commune with the Creator as verification. He said he had not prepared for any such test and knew not what to do. He began to panic and sweat for fear of failure then placed his hand over his heart as it raced and thumped heavily.

"He felt his flesh and then he felt his hand penetrate into his chest without any pain or blood. He saw the eyes of the elders grow with intrigue and disbelief as he removed his hand and it was diseased with leprosy. He said he nearly fainted at the sight of the horrible thing attached to his arm and immediately placed in back within his chest from whence the nightmare came. He then felt a deep warmth within him and he pulled his hand away and revealed he was healed and free from disease.

"Upon seeing such a sight, the elders dropped to their knees in prostration and spoke the words of the old prayers in his name. His brother, High Mountain, stood by his side and then said, 'He is true and indeed comes by the command of the Creator, as he comes to heal the wounds of our souls.' The elders said that they would abide by his commands as he was the deliverer they had prayed for. Drawn Forth Son advised them that he and his brother would go before the king and demand their release the following day. They granted him salutations and bid him farewell for the night.

"The following day, Drawn Forth Son and High Mountain announced themselves and were given audience with the king. High Mountain spoke the old words of welcome to the king and introduced his brother as the representative of the believers and was sent by the Creator." After looking upon him and identifying his adopted brother, the king replied swiftly,

"So... brother! I see you have returned and now you come here with a new family and claim we are of no relation. I see now that I was just in my actions against you as you no doubt have turned your back on those who loved you. Have you any idea the shame you brought on this great house and the name of our beloved father? Did we mean nothing to you? And now you return, not to restore, but to take the life blood and property of the kingdom in the name of your vain God of the mountains? What rival nonsense has possessed you, former brother?"

"We were brothers by name but never by blood or by faith.

293

You plotted murder against me," Drawn Forth Son answered, standing solemnly before the king.

"I did the divine works granted to me as earthly seed and representation of the gods! It was you who turned your back on us! It was your treachery that wounded me in my heart! I loved you! And now you claim me foreign and side with those roaches who flutter about the garbage?" the king argued back in retaliation.

"Those are not roaches, they are my people! And you have tortured and demeaned them beyond any manner of humanity which should be allowed. I have returned here, oh king of men, to end this system of enslavement and restore the natural rights as given to us all. I will do that upon my departure of this land or of this world, and I shall not rest till it be done." Drawn Forth Son and his brother turned to leave the palace hall, but were stopped by the king who stood and said yelling at them, 'Kings are men who rule but for a short time. I am a god, and those things that you claim heritage of are vermin, maggot, filth. And vermin are nothing but food for snakes!'

"Snakes? We fear not the snake!" Drawn Forth Son said boldly, then turned and threw down his staff. His staff began to move and came alive and was now a rearing cobra. The king then motioned to his priests who immediately threw their sticks on the ground and they too gave life and were asps.

"Quite the party we have here, snake for serpent, venom for bite… but it appears we have you out numbered," the king said with his hands fastened on his hips and his chest out.

"But then the cobra attacked, bit and strangled the asps, swallowing them whole. The eyes of the king grew large as he witnessed the magic of his priests subdued and destroyed." The serpent broke from narration and said to Man of the Present.

"They say imitation is the greatest form of flattery. But I do have to say, that staff to a snake trick was pretty impressive!" The Man of the Present stared blankly at the serpent then rolled his eyes and shook his head.

"Drawn Forth Son was patient and summoned his staff to his hand and the cobra quieted and became solid wood again," the king smirked and nodded, then replied.

"Oh, how I have missed our debates and chess matches, former brother. But I offer no pity to those devoured worms who have failed to serve me. You will fail to convince me with any such words, and no trickery by your God can defeat my armies who are tested and true. You should know, you trained them. This is what I am going to do. I am going to show you the mercy of a true god and I will allow you to return as I have missed you so much, dear brother, and allow you to plead for your silly things. But it is I who shall be victorious and it is I who will convince you."

"Convince me? Of what?" Drawn Forth Son inquired, wincing in confusion.

"To return and join us again… what else?" He seated himself on his throne then beckoned his brother back with his arm. "I am come with the commandments of the Creator of all life and you shall release the choke hold you have over the believers and restore them their rights as all human beings are allowed. You stand now in rejection of all that is right and forgivable and this time of sadistic rule has come to an end," he spoke, holding firmly to his staff, planted firmly on the floor.

However, the king was unshaken and refused to release the people.

"See you tomorrow!" the king said laughingly to Drawn Forth Son and High Mountain as they exited the palace hall.

"The following day, Drawn Forth Son and High Mountain returned to the palace hall to demand the release of the slaves. Drawn Forth Son would speak and his brother, High Mountain, would iterate with eloquence on his behalf."

"We have arrived in the name of humanity and demand that this system of control be ended and those of my blood be released at once."

"Release them… Hmm? And where would they go? What would they do? I'll tell you where, nowhere! And then they would end up right back here begging and squabbling like little monkey children. As you would have it, everyone would be considered equal, which we both know to be untrue. You think that by releasing the rightful property of the citizen masters things would be better? You think that would amount to some sort of victory? No, I think not. Instead, what would occur is the destruction of everything this kingdom was built on and has stood for, for centuries.

"It is the way of every civilization. There is a bottom and it just so happens that we are burdened with being on the top. You think its easy caring for all of these people? We show so much love and graciousness to them that we provide safety, security, community, food, clothing, and purposeful work. Their lives are gleaming with importance as they are part of the most grand and enduring dynasty in the history of the world. The slaves are in a position of utility to this kingdom resulting in the overall good of society.

"We have enacted laws and a philosophy that has solved the issues of social morality by giving each citizen the right to pursue happiness to its fullest. Thus, our society has been cleansed of any moral wrongs and no one, I say again, no one is lacking of life's pleasures. The slaves were delivered unto us as gifts from the heavens and it is our moral right to make use of them. Thus, we have used them in such a way that maximizes the overall good of society. This is consequentialism my used-to-be brother and the actions that our forefathers took to ensure the growth and prosperity of this great kingdom has resulted in this illustrious outcome.

"So who are you to come here and question it? Who are you to come here and denounce what they so successfully built? Who are you to belittle and demonize the house that saved and raised you as one of its own? I'll tell you who, you're the turncoat illegitimate mongrel we always thought you were, and now you show your true colors by throwing your lot in with them. Only a fool would do such a thing! I offer you a second chance at redemption here at my side and you spit the woes of a broken-down race of servants back in my face. If you have any value for reason and decency then you would admit that the lifestyle and pleasure we partake of is good in the sense of the whole word, as it was meant to be, as we are the chosen and they are not," the king argued back, pointing then finishing his speech by waving his hand away at them.

"I see you take great pride in yourself, oh king. Yet, I see that the suffering of those beneath you causes you no great pain or worry. I see that, somehow, you find reason with the mistreatment and degradation of humanity. Yet, you call yourselves... reasonable men," Drawn Forth Son debated, stepping forward then opening his hands in accusation of all those in the great hall.

"On this day, I am come to argue on behalf of those without voice and without name. They are man, woman, and child like all others are. The chains which the citizens have created to bind them into servitude are of the utmost wrong. There is no insuperable line which need be crossed to acknowledge their natural rights as human beings; and raise them out of degradation and raise them up into a state of purity. If reason is the only criteria for who ought to have rights versus who ought not have them, then where is the sense and reason for denying them those basic rights they were due from the beginning?

"The believers are no animals of burden, no beasts to be traded, they are people. And on this day, you will entreat them every subtlety of the law, as which every other citizen and human being enjoys the rights and privileges thereof," Drawn Forth said while his brother orated.

"And if I don't? Then what? How will you threaten me?" the king simply asked, while seated.

"Not I... but the day will come when the believers shall inherit those rights, which never should have been withheld from them. If not for the hand of tyranny, that day of sufficient equality for all would be this day. This faculty that you and these alleged citizen masters certify such treatment is of reason. But by comparison, they are no less as you are no more human than any other. Kings are not gods and leaders deserve allegiance only as long as they serve with justice, morality, integrity, intelligence, and compassion over the very people who have placed them as such.

"No one is made a slave by nature and slavery comes from

297

injustice juxtaposed to the natural freedom of us all. It is a mistake to claim humanity be predisposed to slavery and that his whole being be subjected to the ownership of a master. The body may be broken and the will be tamed, but in the hearts of humanity beat independence and freedom, and cannot be restrained and confined inevitably. The question is not will you release them nor will you allow them, but when you do restore them, what will it have cost you?"

"Anything else?" the king smiled, looking on in amusement.

"This kingdom is poison and is suffocating all who dwell within it. The slaves that this society tortures and offends are the life blood off which this kingdom thrives. So, let their blood be poison and become a sickening plague unto you." Drawn Forth Son motioned to High Mountain as they headed out of the palace hall. Stopping at the large double doors, he raised his arms out over the land and spoke out. He then signaled to his brother who touched the great river with his staff and the waters turned red and foul and smelled awful as it was become blood. The eyes of the king filled with intrigue and terror as the waters flowing all around him too turned blood red. His priests were quick and ran to their lord's beckoning and waved their wands and uttered their words and too did water turn red and become filthy.

"Parlor tricks, but only fool-worthy! My wizards have done such tricks before, but since it was you who turned the waters red, it shall be you who bears the brunt of the slave cries. For blood does not mix well with mud and clay and they will have to travel an extra distance to fill their barrels and make our baths now. I think that will almost double their workloads," the king said chuckling.

"I will not drive you out, no! I'll let them do that. Let's see how much they favor you now... deliverer!" the king smirked then turned sideways in his throne and looked to an usher to fetch him wine. Drawn forth Son and High Mountain retreated back outside of the city walls for the evening.

"The following day, Drawn Forth Son awoke in his tent showing a bit of frustration on his face. The first day had not produced any results and he wondered if his brother would accompany him once again. He rose then dressed himself, and exited his tent and saw his brother had already prepared food and hot beverage for the morning meal. He smiled and nodded towards him and the two made ready their work for the day. They arrived in the palace hall again to find the king waiting for them and he greeted the two with pleasantries."

"We are a society of pleasure and goodness. We do only what we must in the name of good. We strive daily to increase the overall pleasure of everyone in all things that they do. It is of the utmost importance to live wisely and to rule justly as we endeavor towards a greater pleasantness of life." The king spoke from his throne, while extending his arms out to greet the two men.

"Oh, thou art wise king of men. However, some actions which provide pleasure do come with an unfortunate shrill of equal pain. How wise is he who does not harken unto control and loses himself in pleasure and becomes an enslaved fiend. Those seeking only pleasure, at first, do not realize the resulting pain of overindulgence. For who sits in judgement of those who have proclaimed themselves master of others, as they know no evaluation of their deeds.

"Such customs are lawless but are not without punishment. Taking from those who are determined to be without intrinsic rights, protections, or value leads to vexing of the soul, where pleasantries will incubate and one day burst out. If society truly is wise, then understand that justice and commonwealth are at the core of social obligation. Furthermore, every man has the right to choose their own path and thus is made responsible for his own actions as well as the treatment of others. The pride that cometh from the mistreatment of hundreds is nothing compared to the wealth associated with the uplifting of one.

"This place can turn to hell or heaven by so little as the actions we take upon ourselves and each other. Those who have created this situation can undo it in so little a movement and shut the evils behind them and open the glories before them. It takes no great action and is only a matter of conscience.

"There will be no lessening of the power to the nobles and

lords as all will know contentment by permitting all to live as full men and full women. This house was my home, but these people are of my flesh and you will let them go or be rewarded by them croaking, jumping little leopard frogs. They shall bubble up out of the blood that you have spilled and they will come unrelenting until you submit and release those you enslave."

"Drawn Forth Son walked out with High Mountain and again raised his arms over the land and all became silent except for the sashaying wind. Then, the sound of the wind grew louder but was not accompanied by the breeze. All was silent, especially the buzzing and humming of the insects and flies. Then there was an echo which increased until becoming the sound of drumming voices. The phantom voices finally appeared and presented themselves to be frogs, crawling and leaping forth from out of everywhere. They obeyed no rules of trespass and entered the palace halls and without invitation were upon the priests alters and temple doors. The king's priests brought out jugs of sand and said their words and filled them with water, then overturned them and so too were they able to present frogs from nothing"

"I see you like the marshes! No worry, the great river that bleed herself red caused in uptick in flies. I'm so glad we could agree upon cleaning up that mess!" The king sat laughing while the palace guards and priests ran around trying to roundup the hordes of leaping frogs.

"Drawn Forth Son and his brother turned and exited the palace. As they walked through the city, the slaves looked on them with evil intention but behaved as if everything was normal. As they crossed the paths of others, they began to hear whispers and felt the presence of a growing crowd around them. Many would not make direct eye contact with Drawn Forth Son and when they passed, the slaves quickly turned their faces away from him.

"What shadows do you speak of me? Make your intentions known as I am afraid of no man!" High Mountain said, after which he grew tired of the ill will and grabbed two men and shoved them into an empty storeroom.

300

"Drawn Forth Son grabbed his brother by the forearm and told him to release the two men who were cowering beneath him. But when they exited the small shelter, the palace guards were waiting for them and stated that the king had summoned them back to the palace hall. Drawn Forth Son and High Mountain returned with the guards and were brought before the king with a frown upon his head.

"What do you want?" The king said with an angry whisper.

"I have made my demands clear," Drawn Forth Son replied with both hands firmly on his staff planted firmly on the floor.

"You have not bested me, but it seems you have defeated my lower priests who were unable to undue your magic and dissipate these mud puppies from us. They are everywhere and are in everything, even the store houses are full of them. The slime from their skin is toxic and will poison all of the rations in the kingdom including those for the slaves who too will starve. Is that what you want?" the king argued, leaning forward, pointing with accusation and rage.

"Those who are pure have nothing to fear," Drawn Forth Son, replied with calm.

"Then remove this plague and take them and go!" anger boiled forth in the king's eyes, as he clutched the arms of the throne.

"Drawn Forth Son exited the palace hall, then lifted his arms up over the land and slowly the croaking that drowned the kingdom began to quiet and then they were gone. High Mountain brought word to the slaves that they had been successful in their negotiations and they were to be released. They cheered and cried for their deliverance had come. They were to be released from their heavy workloads and could start anew and live once again as a proud people.

"The word spread quickly amongst the slaves and Drawn Forth Son and his brother held a feast in their tent as they were triumphant. However, when the morning came and they entered the city, they received no such greeting as all of the slaves were back in their stations and had been reassured of their

301

oppression. Drawn Froth Son and his brother returned to the palace hall and inquired what deception had been placed upon them by the king.

"I have worked no deception. I have merely clarified my last statement. You said you wanted your people to go out with you, and indeed, that still stands. However, all of them are not your people. You see, I did some researching last night while you were gone. And it was true that there was one, who was a great advisor and saw this kingdom through many years of dark famine and he was one of the believers.

"Yet after that time, many have come to settle here and many have mixed and interbred with other cultures, but not all are of him. So be that as it may, my command still stands and as you are of him, you may take only those who are of direct relation to 'He to Whom Mysteries are Revealed' and you and they may go. All others have no rightful claim and remain the property of the citizen masters."

"You know there's no way I can determine such a thing as blood lines after so many centuries have past. What binds the believers together is their faith and in that, we are one." Drawn Forth Son returned, with confounded debate.

"Uhh no! You see, it was you who said it, not I. And you said, and I quote… 'These people are of my flesh…'" So you make take only those who are of your flesh. All others will stay. As you see, I have made no adjustments to our agreement even though it was you and your dark magic who brought swarms of leaping frogs to my doorstep, former brother. But since they have dissipated, I now forgive you. I would offer you the protection of the guards, but I'm sure you don't need protection from your own people. I'm not sure how the slaves will react to such news now, but I wish you luck. Ha! Ha! Ha! Ha! Ha! Ha! Ha! Ha! " the king bantered back humorously.

"Drawn Forth Son and his brother bit their tongues and lips as they exited the palace and saw the faces of their brethren that they had failed. The look on the faces of the slaves as they knelt in the mud and dug ditches was one of betrayal and utter faithlessness. Slave women spat on the two men as they walked by and cursed them for false prophets. The slaves yelled out that they hated them for increasing their suffering.

"One who was bold stood up and confronted the two men as they tried to leave and said, 'Who asked you to come here? I don't recall anyone saying they needed your help, nobody wanted this but you, and look what you did. None of us ever wanted a confrontation and we knew it would only anger the masters. I see you two walk free while we now work throughout the nights and our women have been placed in bunkers for their masters to have easier access to them. We have to hear them on top of our wives now and we can do nothing about it! Whatever false God sent you here made a mistake! You're worthless!'

"Drawn Forth Son was struck in his heart for he ached for his brethren but had not the words to calm them. His brother raised his arms and stood on a piece of equipment so all could see him and spoke out.

"In the beginning of every revolution, there first comes hard decisions and then the worsening of conditions as those who struggle against us fight back to remain in power. But we must show them who we really are. When they look upon us, they must see a reflection of our culture and our pride for we shall mirror each other and grow stronger in our toughness. We have no arms to fight them, but the reality of this is that we are an army of faith and greater power lies in non-violence. Although we shall not physically strike them, a force shall radiate from our hearts as we advocate for the restoration of our people… by any means necessary!"

"The slaves roared with applause and cheered at the two men who now stood as one of them and they marched along with them to the edge of the city limits. Out in their tents, the two men were silent and spoke only quiet prayers for they knew not what would come the next day as the king had reinforced his grip on the believers. That night, I whispered to Drawn Forth Son, as I watched their progress from a far and I said unto him, "How are things progressing?"

"Not too well. I knew we had him, and then today he reworked his words only allowing those directly related to me to be free, lest I select them out," Drawn Forth Son said, shaking his head in defeat.

"Crafty son of a bitch, even I didn't even think of that! Hmm… so this is going to be a fight, a true matching of wits. I kinda like this brother of yours," I said with a smirk.

"Now is not the time for jesting, Serpent. The slaves suffer more now because of me…"

"There's something I need to tell you but I don't want you to be deterred from your goal," I said, drawing nearer to him.

"What is it?" Drawn Forth Son said, glancing right, making eye contact with me.

"All men know struggle, failure, and defeat, but few know bravery, challenge, and triumph. Regardless of the outcome, this undertaking is for you, not them."

"I don't care what happens to me. I'm doing this for them, because I have too!" Drawn Forth Son replied, in defense.

"I understand that, but what I mean is, everything you are doing is more meaningful to you than for any of them," I rebuffed.

"I just need to find a way to convince the king to release them." Drawn Forth Son, reiterated, clutching his fist and pounding it in the air.

"It's not so much that you need to convince the believers to trust in you, they are not the one who is taking action, you are! What you need to do is convince yourself. What difference does it make if they believe in you or not? Did they request your help? Did they send for you? Of course not! You saw the fire up on the mountain and the Creator selected you for this task. If the Creator did not endow you with the ability to do it, then you would not have been chosen.

"The struggle and trial ahead is for you, not them. I see great things in you but in order for you to become that person, you must face many trials. You must be torn down and rebuilt anew. Only through battle, defeat, and triumph will you become the great leader you were meant to be.

"You alone dream freedom for the entirety of humanity, whether they know it or not. What is most important here, is that one man stood against corruption and complacency while others sat by and did nothing. Decade after decade, those same people prayed and cried out but not one of them had the courage that you have within you to stand up and fight for change. I understand that you see them as your people, but you are nothing like them. Even as much as you would do and give for them, eventually they will curse and hate you just as the sheep curses the sheepdog who protects it from the wolf. You will become a nuisance to them. Even though they cry out for relief, they find contentment in their ignorance and shame.

"I have seen many a man and woman fight for those weaker than they only to see them ridiculed and betrayed by the very ones they defended. However, their fight and their sacrifice was necessary. They inspired generations after them to stand where others crawled, they believed where others lived a lie. I know that my words may be little comfort to you now, but trust me when I tell you that your actions will not be in vain. Whether or not you succeed and lead them to salvation, it is you that will have gained true freedom and enlightenment."

"But what about the believers? How do I motivate them to join me? As of right now, they don't trust me as I have increased their burden."

"The only way to solve this equation of a weak and unmotivated people is by individuals sharing and spreading their strength amongst these people. Once they taste such refreshment, a movement will take hold and will eventually tip the social scales in favor of empowerment and personal freedom," I explained.

"But how will I accomplish such a thing?" Drawn Forth Son, asked biting his lip halfway questioning himself.

"You are dealing with a people who have forgotten who they are and they have been taught to hate themselves and therefore have no pride in themselves. You must teach them the strength of their culture and the beauty of their identity, and ignite the power of the people. In later times, there will be an ideology that aimed to uplift and motivate a beaten down people by achieving self-determination. This movement became a political slogan all

305

its own and emphasized racial pride, promoted a collective of cultural interests, and built self-sustaining business of, by, and for those very people.

"The movement brought the people together under the ideal of defense against racial oppression, self-education, and economic sufficiency all while freeing the people from an establishment of oppression. It was no different then, than it is today as, all who seek their natural god given rights seek to be free to express the power within themselves and live liberally as all were meant to be. And that movement became known as 'Power' and the term is one of solidarity between all individuals regardless of cultural, race, and religion who strive to be seen as individuals with rights to be treated with dignity and respect. When you go out tomorrow, I want you to summarize the words of a Dr. Martin Luther King Jr., from his written works: <u>Where Do We Go From Here.</u>"

"I am sorry, but I am not familiar with the author of the scrolls of which you speak." Drawn Forth Son, questioned with a furrowed brow causing deep lines in his forehead.

"Would you just take my word for it!" I interjected quickly waiving away his misunderstanding.

"From his works you shall say, 'Power is no man's birthright, and it shall not be neatly packaged and legislated to any people by any government or kingdom.' – MLK Jr.

"There is an idea and a dream that has begun to resonate amongst the believers without name or voice. However, even though the idea of freedom may be but a dream, what is significant is the influence that the dream holds to us all." The following day, Drawn Froth Son walked amongst the people and spoke while his brother reiterated his words.

"Drawn Forth Son continued to speak and then began to organize self-help groups that were not dependent on the citizen masters. He helped to set-up education programs and began to mobilize the believers to elect leaders amongst their own. He spoke openly and encouraged others to return to their cultural dress, language, foods, and faith which encouraged pride and self-esteem in their culture.

"A phrase spread amongst the populace and they began speaking to each other and reminding each other that they were 'beautiful.' The word beautiful was used to dispel the connotation that the believer's features, skin color, and hair texture were intrinsically ugly. This idea of beauty added to the utility of the power movement and helped to unite the believers around their common ancestry and cultural identity." The serpent broke from narration and returned to speaking with the Man of the Present.

"What was and is impressive about these movements is that they are usually a grass roots movement built from nothing and ultimately play a major role in altering social conditions. The power movement that began then has been continuously used all over the world in every era of revolution. Drawn Forth Son taught the believers that in order to change the citizen masters view of them as slaves, they first had to change the way they viewed themselves. And they did, slowly and silently at first. They stopped assimilating and began to represent their own history, culture, and traditions, and they were successful and saw themselves as human beings again," the serpent continued.

"Drawn Forth Son ended his speeches by saying. 'What shall we do with this pride in our people? What symbol do we have of our strength? Let us associate with one another as we are a mighty movement.' They collectively raised a fist, which became a symbol of their movement towards equality and freedom from their oppression."

"If he was arguing with the king, then why did he have to go and do all of that for? What good is motivating people into groups and causing protests and riots?" The Man of the Present asked.

"It's one thing to argue on behalf of a people with one voice, but it is another to have the united voices of many shouting together for their rights and freedom," the serpent reiterated.

"You see plagues, along with the power movement, enhanced the bargaining of Drawn Forth Son, similar to the power movements of the 1960's and 1970's. Now the power movements alone did not remedy the social, political, and economic issues faced by African Americans in the 60's and 70's, however it did contribute to those leaders' works and arguments which brought about civil rights acts and voting rights acts, which have played a major role in the fight for equality of that time. Positive protest movements are essential to bringing about change as a 'positive radical flank effect' as referred to by Herbert H. Haines."

"Yeah, but many people disagree that outward demonstration only agitates the system and makes things more tense resulting in an overall backlash," the man debated.

"It is true that many do disagree with organized protest either by informal means of sit-ins, walk-outs, or vocal rallies, and even violent acts of looting or self-immolation. However, those who argue this seem to easily forget that the very system they are defending is the one that has disenfranchised those very people into such a state of protest. What eventually happens is that such power movements become more and more forceful in their message, which enhances the bargaining position of the activists.

"The idea of breaking free cannot be a singular one, the people must get involved. Unfortunately, what can happen is that you realize that some really do not want freedom or change, they are actually happy and content with the horrible way things are and have been. I remember Drawn Forth Son said something that emboldened the believers and spoke directly to those who were weak and dissenting, when he said. 'No! We will not stay in our place and sit idle, while the accommodationists pander our dignity away for simple concessions.'

"It was mostly the elders of the believers who feared retaliation the most, but it was the youth who rejected their elder's path of settlement and appeasement of saying 'yes sir and no sir.' It was the youth who readily took to the word of Drawn Forth Son and immediately rejected the citizen masters' ethics, which placed them in favor of right and the believers on the side of wrong and automatic guilt.

"I am reminded of the words of Fredrick Douglas who wrote: 'If there is no struggle, there is no progress. Those who profess to favor freedom, and yet depreciate agitation, are men who want crops without plowing up the ground. They want rain without thunder and lightning. They want the ocean without the awful roar of its many waters. This struggle may be a moral one; or it may be a physical one; or it may be both moral and physical; but it must be a struggle. Power concedes nothing without a demand. It never did and it never will.' The serpent shook his head then focused back on the Man of the Present then said, "Have you ever heard truer words?" The serpent continued.

"Do not to give up hope. We are at the crux of our ordeal and this is the culmination of centuries of abuse, lies, deceit, and denial of our natural rights. At every moment of our being, we have had to struggle and endure in this land, and still we exist and continue to press back against such tyranny." Drawn Forth Son spoke out and continued emboldening the believers.

"Freedom is not unrealistic and is natural and we must not end our fight until we have created a new reality for all people. You cry out and ask, why must it fall to us? Because the Creator does not choose the weak to deliver the message and this challenge is ours, and we are honored to carry this burden for humanity. They have had their way and they have showed their greedy, sinful, hateful hearts, and hands. It is not a matter of if we will leave this place, but when we do... how much noise we will make in doing so! The world has called upon us to present a new vision for humanity and we are that new hope and our people are the definition of possibility. The time is close and nearly at hand and all things, even this our freedom, is possible." Drawn Forth Son and High Mountain were successful in instilling a sense of pride in the believers and a movement was started.

"The following day, Drawn Forth Son and High Mountain again approached the palace hall but this time, they were accompanied by thunderous applause from the believers."

"I see they favor you... but I know how to make them sing a different tune. If your argument is that they applaud and cheer, then I will admit that I hear them applaud and cheer all the time. So their song is nothing new. I don't think they know what you are really doing here, arguing that they would be better off out there. But I know best and they are better off here. Out there is nothing, and nothing is what you offer them," the king said, addressing the men strongly.

"Empty hope and empty dreams with no arrival date. If they go out there, they will be aimless and will have nothing to do. They will drop dead from boredom and lack of leadership and authority. Because all men must have work and be given focus, without it, their lives will be meaningless. Nature has placed the slaves under the governance of the citizen masters. We provide them the necessary basis for a meaningful life, filled with both pain and pleasure. It is this very principle that is at the core of humanity.

"It is instinct that we seek out pleasure and fear pain in the names of work, faith, family, fame, sex, and social identity. This principle both satisfies our biological and psychological identities. It is the stampeding horses pulling and driving the chariot within us all. Unfortunately for the slaves, it is we who hold the reigns to their pleasure and to their pain," the king argued eloquently.

"Pleasure out of pain is sadomasochism and I see that you have built quite a lair for you and your dominants," Drawn Forth Son said with one hand on his staff and the other stretched out encompassing all those in attendance in the great hall.

"And what really drives you is no moral urge, but simple greed and materialism. All of this is nothing more than a grand display of the corruption of humanity, and the result of ignorance of the workings of the world. The highest pleasure one can attain is tranquility and freedom from fear. To defeat pain, it takes no army, but the acceptance of knowledge, friendship, and virtue. Simple pleasure comes from understanding simple pain, and no great pleasure comes without causing even greater pain. In this earthly state, is it completely possible to be without the absence of bodily pain? No, yet it is as unlikely to completely abstain from mortal desires, sexual appetites, and vain indulgence.

"The grim reality of life, oh king, is that we are human, and humanity requires balance. You speak of the purpose that you

310

provide the slaves, yet this is a contradiction. If a man could give another man purpose of life, then he would cease being of free will. I see no 'Pactum Unionis, Pactum Subjectionis,' where the believers sought protection for their property and purpose for their lives, then pledged allegiance to citizen authority and gave up their freedom and natural rights. This reasoning obligation that you claim ownership over them is not binding and therefore null and void. The believers at no point surrendered their liberty, and thereby their freedom was taken from them unlawfully.

"Life and the law is balanced out one way or another. This place is out of balance and will undoubtedly tip over by those who partake too richly and call themselves master, while others are denied and have become slaves," Drawn Forth Son said, ending his speech.

"Enough talk for today! My appetites call me!" The sound of female oohs and ahhs came purring through the hallways from the king's harem.

"I think it's about that time, as I am itching for some of the finer slave delicacies, and they know just where to scratch me! As I recall former brother, you had quite the reputation amongst the palace harems, too bad you've found piety. Which reminds me… would you care for something to eat?" The king clapped and ushers brought out dishes of fruits and meats garnished with the heads and hands of slaves.

"Drawn Forth Son looked on in disgust, then the king smiled and waved his finger in selection of the fruits, and then plucked a single grape and savored the fruit. Drawn Forth Son and High Mountain breathed deeply with anger in their lungs and exited the palace while the king laughed heartily. At the doors, Drawn Forth Son looked to High Mountain then said, "Then let them itch!" High Mountain took his staff and struck the ground and the two men departed the city for the day.

"And then a third plague came upon the kingdom and there were fleas and lice that abounded up out of the ground and were upon everyone and everything from man to beast. It was as if the dust grew miniscule limbs and became lice, and caused all of the kingdom a worrisome night as they itched and scratched."

"He's right you know," I said calling out to Drawn Forth Son, back in his tent.

"The human mind is so driven by obtaining pleasure that it fails to see any rationality behind such shallow pursuits. When one obtains said shallow pleasures in avoidance of such silly pains, afterwards the being is left unfulfilled and continually dissatisfied within themselves. However, my Drawn Forth friend, you are different. You are still human and are subject to the forces of pleasure and pain, but you are ruled by a second principle of maturity.

"If I were to describe your attributes they would be wisdom, courage, justice, piety, creativity, and individuality. But there in your ability to undergo toil and hardship, and taking no short cut of bribery or theft, you fight to achieve a greater goal, not just for yourself, but for others as well. You are a leader, you are an educator, you are iron-willed, and a thinking fighter. You have become a mature human being and have the capacity to endure pain and defer gratification to reach your overall goal.

"Maturity is more than mere time and age. Maturity is learning to understand and face up to the realities of life. You will encounter many who are driven by their ego's and refuse to acknowledge their mistakes, misdeeds, lies, and failures all in the name of refusing to acknowledge the truth of their reality. You have reached a level of personal insight and maturity that most, never will. There will come times when a lie will suffice, there will be a day when no one is looking and you can just say you did. But the reality is that it's not true, and the mature person will be unable to stand for it. They will be unable to look at themselves in the mirror and swallow their own bullshit. The mirror is a very telling fiction. When you look into it, what do you see looking back at you? Is it your own face, or are you still wearing the mask you have convinced everyone else is really you?

"The mature person will remove the mask while the immature clings to it even though it reeks like a dirty diaper upon them. You wish to see yourself as you truly are and others will see the honesty and strength that is you. You did well today, but be prepared as the fight is not over. You are in the thick of it and this is where the battle heightens." I turned and departed company with Drawn Forth Son for the evening. The remaining night was silent and the stars were candle lights in the sky.

"The following day, there were riots and demonstrations in the kingdom, but not amongst the slaves. Along with the power movements by the slave youth, there grew sympathizers out of the citizens. They were members of a youth subculture who were sophisticated, and influenced by the culture, art, and music of the time. These citizen sympathizers began a movement of their own and some began to live in their own communities away from the main stream of society.

"They outwardly dressed differently and showed support for the power movement and were known to be 'hip, aware, and in the know.' They were a counterculture all their own advocating for equal rights and fair treatment for all people. They grew out of a sense of weariness that surrounded the norms of society and were against the traditions centered on maintaining the status quo. Instead, they emphasized individuality and creativity, communal togetherness, and a back-to-nature spirituality.

"It was not long before the citizen sympathizers became an established social group and pushed mainstream dissention away from the oppressive system of control. Their parents were 4th and 5th generation citizen masters and they were groomed to be next in line in continuing the established institution of control over the believers. However, the citizen youth rejected the traditional institutions and criticized their entitlement, and campaigned for the abolition of slavery in the kingdom. They valued non-violent protest and pacifism, but expressed their revolution which became pollution to the citizen society.

"The citizen youth taught doctrines of peace, love and personal freedom. They perceived that the dominant class was built on corruption that exercised undue power over the lives of the believers, and called this authority to be given by the gods. The citizen sympathizers built a revolution on leaving the kingdom and creating a free city for all peoples. The citizen masters mocked their youth, but they could not have cared less about the approval of the 'straight world.'

"They took up the ideology of power from the believers and included flowers in place of weapons. A more famous demonstration occurred as the citizen sympathizers engaged in a mass act of civil disobedience and planted a thousand flowers in the temples of the gods. Their slogan under their protest was to let a thousand temples bloom. It appeared that the believers were not alone in their struggle for freedom as the citizen sympathizers instilled a sense of fellowship, love, and individual expression. The serpent broke from narration and returned to speaking with Man of the Present.

"The interesting thing, Man of the Present, is that these counter cultures are alive and well to this day, although not as visible as they once may have been. This shift in cultural consciousness never dies out completely and can be seen on campuses, in communes, and at gatherings and festivals. Their ethos of peace, love, and community are simple to embrace as they sought to free themselves from societal restrictions and find their own meanings to life.

"Freedom is not singular to any race or cultural group, nor is the ideology that all humanity is untied in a single struggle for equality and allowed the ability to live freely. These groups are accurately successful as they present a familiar face other than the traditional foreign revolutionist. They, in a sense, are one of them but at the same time, are not. Their non-violent demonstrations bring new meaning to an otherwise ignored problem of the lower class. They are many times most successful in their opposition to wars, and building political action groups, and refusing to serve in the military in protest of political actions."

"Hmm… interesting comparisons you make there, Serpent," the serpent raised an eyebrow, smirking back at the man, then continued.

"When Drawn Forth Son arrived again at the palace halls, the king greeted him with anger, you have turned the youth against us! I tell you that the station of the slaves is a result of economic exploitation and not innately prejudiced. In our view, this is nothing more than a disagreement of class between the massive subservient and the minority ruling citizens. They must understand that those who protest are uniting against divine order and the law of nature by their disobedience of us. We know that our position above the slaves is ordained by the gods and for them to struggle against us is to create a false sense of racism, prejudice, and civil unrest amongst those citizen dissenters."

"Thus far, I have done nothing. It is this system that you continue to instill against the believers. As you would have it, they are assigned to push a button, flip a switch, or turn a knob endlessly for the entirety of their lives. And if they choose otherwise and seek education and advancement, then they become criminals. It is natural for the sun to rise, and on this morning the people have begun to awaken. I have argued and spoken daily against your ideology of superiority and divine right over the believers. By every act that the citizen masters take, there is no preponderant of good and the suffering inflicted is knowingly produced and is read by no other name than crimes against humanity.

"And like all manner of over indulgence, it too becomes a bad habit which grows stronger and soon becomes normal. However, the more frequent the sowing of bad seeds, the worse fruit will be produced. I am unable to comprehend how it is that you defend such behavior and find amusement in the suffering of others. Such mistreatment is not sufficient upon an animal, and I cannot see the morality or intelligence behind imposing such infliction. You now hear the voices of the slaves as well as the citizen youth who sympathize by their words and chants of power. And with the growing power of the populace, these days of enslavement are numbered.

"The Creator has endowed humanity with inalienable rights and those who oppose it stand against the sword of retribution that will undoubtedly swing and fall upon you. Liberty of the people must triumph. The power is to the people and we will not go limp! No! We will not stay in our place and continue to let this injustice prevail over us!" Drawn Forth Son and High

315

Mountain began exiting the palace hall, then said lastly.

"If you will not release the populace then woe and fear shall be released upon you and your officials. It will come in swarms of a mixture of rat and bird. They are wild creatures and will climb and cling as they crawl into your homes. They are an affliction to both man and beast and are of a frightening sight."

"Drawn Forth Son and High Mountain left the city and then the skies began to blacken, but not by any storm clouds. There were millions of them flying and squawking in the trees. They were black with demon eyes as they clung to screaming men and animals. They were capable of sucking blood from their victims and they were summoned from their caves and outpoured millions of bats that invaded the kingdom. The following day, Drawn Forth Son and High Mountain returned to the palace hall and again confronted the king."

"No concept suffers more under this system of control and oppression than the idea of justice. There is no morality in such a place and those who profess to govern and rule with liberty are in strict defiance of the notion of justice. Under your ideology and justification of a greater good, it is acceptable to torture, regardless of the inhumane treatment upon the believers. My words here are not minor criticisms, but an evaluation of the reality that you have created.

"Instead of a world free of will, opportunity, loss, and tragedy where each is available and susceptible to the natural forces and regular occurrences of life, you have succeeded in creating two worlds; where the world you live in is one of exceptional beauty and the other is full of slave hardship and filth. What is interesting is that life carries with it intrinsic highs and lows where one must build, work, grow, celebrate, rejoice, and appreciate. However, you have successfully barricaded the latter making only the woes of humanity viable on one side of the line and the other a virtual citizen paradise. Yet, it is not that the hell heaped upon the slaves is invisible, it is just that you choose not to see it. And you have chosen to teach that this is their inherit station and they are happy in this manner.

"I tell you, the world and life require balance and one cannot survive without the other. By creating a paradise for yourselves, you have also created a living hell right beside it. So you may look upon yourselves as the rulers of heaven, when actually you are the architects of hell on earth." The king sat stone faced in his throne listening, then gave his return.

"We have built no such dungeon and it is only the law that has provided the framework of our social structure. The slaves have been delineated by their spheres of personal value, which allows them to perform and peruse their own concepts of well-being. The system that we all adhere to provides the slaves and the citizen's security and station. Based upon their worth, they are allowed the formulation of life expectations. How we measure this is by our hedonic calculus and the expectation of utilities against the natural code of ethics rooted by the divine authority granted by the gods.

"We do not seek to punish or abuse the slaves in any way other than necessary motivation and stimulation. We have seen that what is necessary is based upon certain factors such as: intensity and duration of the punishment and up to what extent the punishment ends. Furthermore, we decide what work or action to be conducted and at what levels meet productivity goals, while producing the highest quality with certainty. Therefore, it is the punishment that determines their motivation and their success at completing their tasks and satisfying our goals.

"So, it is the slaves themselves who determine whether their situation creates them pleasure or pain. Without these measures in place, we would see the growth of evils and wrongdoings in idle slaves as they are known trouble makers, liars, and miscreants who know no control over their urges. We act merely as legislators of society where our moral and ethical control over them is vital to the maintenance of the wellbeing of civilization," the king debated easily.

"What you advocate is might over right, which would lead to an all-out war where there is no amount of killing, stealing, and enslavement which amounts to a wrong, all in the name of survival, growth, and power. If humanity is to survive and live in peace, then it must agree that all people are allowed those same rights, while none have the rights to deny, enslave, destroy, or reject others while in the search and procurement of worldly advancement," Drawn Forth Son and High Mountain said before exiting the palace hall.

"So as it was your words that cause suffering upon the populace, so it shall be your own words that will have befallen your livestock. Certain illness on the proximity of your herds. Now measure their productivity and the purity of their diseased meat and milk."

"Then a fifth and terrible plague engulfed the kingdom and affected all of the livestock of the citizens. All were diseased and became sick of an epidemic, however the animals of the believers remained healthy and unharmed. The following day, Drawn Forth Son and High Mountain approached the palace hall and again confronted the king." Before Drawn Forth Son could speak, the king began a verbal assault.

"You must think yourselves quite clever, coming here day after day and performing your tricks and revealing your dark magic. Instead, all you have done is lighten the plates of thine own kind. For when my herds and flocks die, you force my hand to raid the meager holdings of the slaves. It is you who has sent them to bed hungry, while they now toil with half empty bellies and their children cry out for thirst of a dry teat. You say you come on behalf of an almighty god, more so than I? Let me explain something to you, the gods are not fully in control... Men are! Whichever gods may exist, they do not dare come down here and concern themselves with our business.

"Relying on any God or gods is folly and only for childish minds for they do not seek any punishment of us in this or the afterlife. You say that this kingdom built was done so wretchedly and is an affront to humanity, but then why does this god of yours not rescue the slaves if he cares so much for them. As you would have it... 'No Gods, No Masters!' But you are wrong former brother; 'The Gods, We Masters!' he said fiercely with a finger in the air, then thumbing back at himself.

"See, it is I who am the wiser, it is I who am the teacher, and it is I who entreat you to a paradox. Now, answer me this: 'Is God willing to prevent evil, but not able? Then he is not omnipotent. Is he able, but not willing? Then he is malevolent. Is he both able and willing? Then whence cometh evil? Is he neither able nor willing? Then why call him God?' - Epicurus

The king said while raising one arm in saluting fashion as he posed the paradox, "Now, go and only return when you can answer that fully to me."

"There is an overriding and superseding law of the Creator, which has entreated every life with the entitlement of freedom and cannot be repealed or stripped away by any laws of man, king, state, religion, or government. Perhaps there is not one clear answer to the paradox, but many. So I shall provide thee many examples and then you can determine the reasoning of the Creator's will and existence," Drawn Forth Son replied before he and his brother exited the palace.

"Drawn Forth Son and High Mountain did not return for three days. The night air carried with it a fine dust that covered the whole of the kingdom and all who were touched by it were inflicted with festering puss filled boils. The dead animals were none immune and their rotting carcasses did not dry and wither, but stunk like that of green cheese and the infections spread over them as well. The skin disease was not lethal, but was a horrible sight as the lesions and marks left by them caused many to bandage and wrap themselves like their mummified dead. They looked at each other in horror and the entirety of the kingdom was an infirmary with no hospice.

"That night the nightmare did not end and only grew worse as a thunderstorm of hail and fire encircled the kingdom. The sound of cracking fire sounded like the artillery of war machines upon the great barriers of castle gates and walls. There were no mountains or volcanoes that had erupted to cause such a turmoil. The kingdom had never seen such a destructive thunderstorm that stretched across the valleys and lower regions of the vast empire. It was not the intensity of the storm, but the combination of weather effects of freezing stones of hail falling alongside fire, rock, and ash while wind and dust swirled and tore the bare skin dry and rain humidified the air and soaked and drowned their crops.

"The king's priests and advisors had never seen such a display of atmospheric anger and pleaded with their king to relent and ask Drawn Forth Son to remove the plagues. But the king refused and was iron defiant in his will. The storm ceased and the boils cleared away with the washing waters and humidity that killed the bacterial disease. Yet, this only cleared the path for another menace to terrorize the citizens of the kingdom, in the form of the vandal locusts.

"The locust came without mercy and consumed the little the citizens had left. Their crops and livestock were all but gone and now the bugs covered the ground and finished off every last plant, flower, tree, and shrub. The wind finally came and blew the pests out into the sea, but what remained of the kingdom was all but gone and now it appeared that they might all starve to death and die. The citizens were surrounded by their fine linens, gold, and jewels but their tables and cupboards were empty and bare. The king reassured them that provisions could be purchased from caravans from afar and the kingdom would endure."

"We must hold fast against the sorcery of the slave god as they only know evil and destruction against a divine and righteous people." The king spoke out to the citizen masters, but still he would not release the slaves from their chains. That night, I again visited with Drawn Forth Son.

"He makes a very good point," I remarked.

"I'm not concerned," Drawn Forth Son replied solemnly, while sitting in prayer.

"Oh no? You're not even the least bit concerned with the reasoning's of the Creator for allowing such suffering in the world?"

"What do you think?" he remarked, breaking his meditative state.

"I have been observing humanity for quite some time now and what the reason or purpose behind all of this is… well, I wish I knew. One could argue that due to humanity's limited knowledge, it is impossible to understand the Creator's ultimate plan. Given this viewpoint, it may be utterly impossible to find a plausible explanation for why things happen the way they do."

"I think he is partially right, in that god or gods are not concerned with getting involved with our actions. We should have no expectation of god's being or judgment based solely on our limited understanding of good, evil, or an afterlife judgment," Drawn Forth Son replied, exhaling out his thoughts.

"I think you are making personal progress and enlightenment is at hand," I broke from speaking with Drawn Forth Son and turned my head quickly in suspicion. "Did you hear that?"

"No, I..." Drawn Forth Son remarked quickly quieting himself to listen, but heard nothing.

"Shhh... Someone's coming!" I acknowledged the approaching of a stranger, then immediately disappeared.

"A small lantern glowed in the dimming evening light and the sound of two light footsteps approaching could be heard. Drawn Forth Son watched as the light became a lantern and a small figure presented herself and it was the wise old woman from his earlier meeting."

"Hello son, may I visit with you this evening."

"Indeed, old woman, your counsel is greatly appreciated," he said welcoming the old woman into his tent.

"Thank you dear child, my name is Serach and I have something very important to tell you."

"The next day came and the land was quiet as little life could be seen and the slaves were now sitting in the dirt as all the crops and livestock had died. The citizen masters were preparing their payments to send out to caravans and merchants from far away distances to retrieve food as there was nothing to eat, or plant, or sow. Drawn Forth Son and High Mountain arrived at the palace hall and found a weary and tired king who showed no sign of glee on his face. The three days of plague, destruction, and pestilence had weakened his fortitude and he was visibly shaken."

"So... I assume you have an answer to my riddle?" The king

said with a serious tone.

"There is a problem with your paradox which questions the existence of the Creator," Drawn Forth Son answered.

"There is no God above me, except the demons you have suffered upon my kingdom," the king yelled in response, pounding his fist strongly on the arm of his throne.

"The Creator doth exist! The Creator is omnipotent, omniscient, and omnipresent and knows every which way good and all evils come into existence. But the Creator does not place us in a box, for we are free. The choice of rule is not placed upon the Creator to decide… it is upon us. The Creator is responsible for our creation, yet we are ultimately responsible for the affliction of humanity.

"If thou truly were god and king, then too could you create such a paradise without suffering and poverty to any, but we are men and are only humans with little understanding of our surroundings. We have power and ability, just as we have creativity and are capable of compassion. It is not up to the Creator to release or imprison man, but it is within us to unchain our hearts from the opportunity of greed and immorality and the imprisonment of each other. The plagues and afflictions are no evil as they are natural and are always occurring. No magic calls them, just as no prayer extinguishes them. No divine judgment has fallen against the believers nor has it empowered you above them.

"It is only in the workings of our minds that those with power subdued those without, at the opportune moments of history. Given the chance, would the disenfranchised rise up against you and entreat you the same as you have done upon them? I ask not for the freedom of those unworthy of it, but for the citizens to show their humanity and understanding of morality and the natural rights of all to be recognized," High Mountain reiterated his brother's words with eloquence.

"The greater good is all we seek and this moral injustice, as you claim it, is thereby necessary and only a result of human action," the king replied, fanning his palm at Drawn Forth Son in rebuke of his claims.

"We cannot possibly know the reason behind the Creator's will and judgement. Our minds and hearts are as fragile as they are infantile to such concepts. There exists facts and theories of theology which humanity has not yet discerned and, therefore, the true meanings are hidden to us. These debates of good and evil, right and wrong, can continue indefinitely without reaching conclusion. However, for every hidden reason, there are others that partially justify them, while others equally condemn them. These arguments will no doubt only cancel one another out resulting in a stalemate. You must release the believers. You can suffer no additional defeat that you can rebound from." The king looked around him as his palace was empty and bare since many of his priests had been executed due to the plagues and their inability to repel them.

"I find criticism with your argument as you claim the affliction of the slaves to be my fault and an issue with the design of our society. If your God did not want this to happen, then your God shouldn't have made our desires so pleasurable. Instead, your God has made life a race to the top, and seeking wealth, leisure, and pleasure is irresistible to any of us. I know it is wrong to deny ourselves these pleasures and I refuse to end this way of life. I know of only one fool, who is you, who brings demons to our kingdom in the name of reducing suffering of worthless slaves. The day is mine... now leave!" The king said strongly, then stood in defiance.

"The day merely borrows time, but the night inevitably follows. It is the Creator who is owner of the day and the night, and this night will not end until you realize it," Drawn Forth Son said before leaving, then stretched out his hands towards the sky.

"Then a darkness covered the entirety of the region. The darkness was not ordinary and the moon and sun did not come together in eclipse. The night was so incredibly thick that it could almost be felt. All work was suspended as no grouping of torches could pierce the night that laid so thickly upon the land. The king prayed and made offerings to their highest god and asked the sun to prove who was mightier. However, the sun was helpless and bowed to the command of the Creator and was hidden under the darkness. No time could be kept as the people rose from their sleep and the darkness continued to cover the land.

"Yet, into the darkness with a torch and tools was Drawn Forth Son headed towards the outskirts of the kingdom alone. Drawn Forth Son arrived at his destination, then began to dig."

"I didn't think anyone remembered where to find him. The Creator was right about you!" I called out, while watching him dig.

"You know the one who lies here?" Drawn Forth Son replied, bent over with shovel in hand, then gazing over his shoulder at me.

"I do! And as a matter of fact, I knew him quite well. But tell me, how did you come to know of his location?"

"A few days ago, I was paid a visit by the wise old woman. She said she was blessed with the gift of long life and prophecy. I have no reason to doubt her as she spoke in detail of the generations that she has witnessed pass on. She said she was given knowledge of all the things that have occurred up until this point, but in order for the believers to leave this place, the oath of He Who Would Increase, must be fulfilled. She said that his bones were not meant to rest here and must be taken out.

"She said the citizens revered him greatly as he grew to be one of their most respected advisors but when he died, they claimed him for themselves and feared that if his body was removed, a great evil would befall the land. So they campaigned and bought the rights to bury him from the believers who had become weak in their faith. But fearing that his tomb would be moved at a later date, they buried him in secret where no one would find him. They wished to honor him, but also needed to conceal the true location of his crypt. So they devised that he would rest below the great river, where no one could find him and raise him again.

"However, the citizens being master architects, constructed a grand tomb for our patriarch and then dug a canal, which was a natural offshoot that emptied and then would flood during the rainy season. They constructed the tomb and damned the canal

324

until its completion, then waited for the rains to flood the basin concealing the treasure beneath it. It has since become known as 'The Bahr Yussef' or the waterway of He Who Would Increase and connects the great river and the Fayyum of the Region.

"The old woman, told me where to locate the opening of the tomb, which is buried some feet beneath us. We are in luck as the river basin has lowered in this dry season and made accessing the highest point of the tomb possible," all the while he spoke, he continued to dig.

"But how will you raise the sarcophagus without teams of men?" I questioned.

"I don't know. I hadn't thought that far ahead."

"Indeed, luck is with you! As you will require no magic to raise it. The Creator has endowed me with special attributes, but none as great as my burrowing abilities. Please allow me to dig on your behalf and raise the coffin myself. I can complete the excavation in a quarter of the time it would take a whole of team of men," I offered with gracious intent.

"But he is my responsibility and it is we who owe him," he said doubling down on his pledge.

"He was the closest thing I have ever had to a friend. Please allow me this simple honor, as he shall be with you the rest of the way." Drawn Forth son nodded in agreement and then I began digging. The earth shifted and moved easily under my massive frame and strength and in no time, the coffin of He Who Would Increase had been raised.

"No one knows of his emergence here, so we must cover it quickly, lest others learn of his emergence," I advised, as we recovered the tomb.

"Funny how things work out isn't it!" I commented, looking towards the coffin.

"Huh! You talking to me?" Looking back over his shoulder, he paused briefly addressing me in confusion.

"Oh, no! ... I was talking to him," I answered, glancing over at the coffin.

"You do realize you're talking to a dead guy, right?" Drawn

Forth Son said while looking over at the coffin, which lay silent and motionless, then making eye contact with me.

"Inside joke!" I said, chuckling briefly.

"I'm getting worried about you, Serpent!" Drawn Forth Son paused, locking eyes with a look of concerned inspection.

"Three days had passed since the sun was last seen and guards had been dispatched to retrieve Drawn Forth Son and High Mountain back to the king's presence."

"What twisted madness have you inflicted upon us? The day arrives but without a new sun! There is no sky and this nightmare haze that surrounds the region continues without end. Sorcery and turmoil are the product of the evil you sow in these lands!" The king shouted.

"My words have been spoken and the darkness shall not cease until the believers are released," Drawn Forth Son reiterated, planting his staff into the ground.

"You have not answered my riddle! But no matter, as I have come to a conclusion of our little debates: 'If an omnipotent, omniscient, and omnibenevolent god exists, then evil does not. There is evil in the world. Therefore, an omnipotent, omniscient, and omnibenevolent God does not exist.' – Epicurus

"Plague, sickness, infestation, and darkness are your workings and only one who is aligned with evil do such deeds. Evil doth exist and it is in you! Therefore... there is no God!" The skies crackled deeply with thunder and the palace halls shook and then all was silent. The darkness slowly began to lift and the clouds and sun were revealed. Drawn Forth Son looked up at the sky shaking his head in fear, then uttered in a whisper.

"Brother... what have you done? What happens now is your own doing and nothing can stop what is upon you." Drawn Forth Son and High Mountain exited the palace hall leaving the king standing alone. The sky was clear and blue and the sound of birds and life returned to the kingdom. The king stood as if a victory had been won by calling out his denial of the Creator, but the final affliction would come down upon the kingdom and collect a heavy toll.

"That night, Drawn Forth Son went to the elders of the believers and advised them to sacrifice and eat the first born of their herds and mark the doors, lest the coming force take them in the night. I watched Drawn Forth Son make his instruction as I had seen the Creator's wrath occur before. But this was different, this was… I don't know. I saw not the sky open up, nor did a storm approach, the night was calm and quiet and the stars were lit brightly, it was as if the kingdom glowed with light. In honesty, I have never experienced a more peaceful night. I waited, and watched for the work of the Creator, but nothing occurred, and all was silent.

"The believers gathered with each other and shared a meal with their neighbors whose homes were too small for a full animal. Drawn Forth Son and High Mountain joined the homes of others and there, alongside them, was the wise old woman, who told tales of two hundred years. It wasn't my intent to sleep, I must have dosed off, but when I awoke, it was morning and all of the kingdom was in sadness and remorse. Death had come over the kingdom and to all of the citizens as their firstborn were dead, with not one being spared. Their flocks, their herds, all first born owned by the citizens lay dead. There was no army, no destruction of storm or quake, but silence and invisible intention visited the homes, stables, and fields of the citizens and laid upon them a deathly mark.

"Drawn Forth Son and High Mountain visited the palace hall where the king kneeled at an altar making burnt offerings to his gods. His son lay on a decorated slab anointed with oils and jewels, but he was lifeless as he, too, was first born of his house. Drawn Forth Son did not speak as the king grieved heavily for his dead son and his wife wailed in agony cursing him."

"It appears you will not stop until you have taken us all! But you have wounded me deeply and I am beyond remorse. The slaves that bade us fortune and luxury have become our affliction and taken of us dearly. I release you and your hero cult, to be rid of this God who kills our innocent, sickens our fields and flocks, and blinds us with the night. Take what you will, for we have nothing left." Still kneeling in front of the body of his dead son, the king said with his back turned to Drawn Forth Son.

"The majesty of this kingdom has befallen the invocations of slaves, and woe do the kings of my father look upon me with shame. Leave me, and go out of this land forever. Go out as free men and free women, lest we anger your God any further."

"The numbers of those who made the great exit were exaggerated as not only believers were in attendance, but those who chose to break free of the panoptic system of control joined them. They were accompanied by the citizen sympathizers and free spirits who wished for a new life and an opportunity to live without reprisal. They marched young and old, sick and strong, herds of cattle, goats, and flocks of chickens and geese hoofing and squawking with the sound of a symphony. All were joyous and proud and the salvation that was a distant and far-off dream was that day a reality.

"Men and women had removed their woes and chains, for the believers had been restored to their rightful status and were whole again. Drawn Forth Son was humble and stood to the side and greeted the many families as they journeyed out of the land and into hope and tomorrow. It was the day that should never have come, the day when the master is relieved of his property and the slave system is broken and no more. They traveled through the wilderness of the Erythraean Sea, then through what is known today as the Sinai Peninsula and then approached the Gulf of Aqaba.

"The land was now empty and silent, and there was no gaiety in the kingdom that day. I recited while looking on. 'Treasures of wickedness profit nothing, but righteousness delivereth from death. The Creator will not suffer the soul of the righteous to famish, but he casteth away the substance of the wicked. He becometh poor that dealeth with a slack hand, but the hand of the diligent maketh rich. He that gathereth in summer is a wise son, but he that sleepeth in harvest is a son that causeth shame. Blessings are upon the head of the just, but violence covereth the mouth of the wicked. The memory of the just is blessed, but the name of the wicked shall rot. The wise in heart will receive commandments, but a prating fool shall fall.'

"The king and his subjects remained silent and were still adorned in gold and precious stones as they sat in empty chambers and prepared their own meals. The king sat in a silent throne and felt a constellation of anger and contempt encircling him. He could not explain the occurrences nor could he rationalize the death of his son that forced his hand to release the slaves.

"The longer he sat, the more he stewed with fury and hatred, until his psyche turned against reason and demanded atonement from the drawn forth perpetrator who had mocked him. He couldn't stand the insult of the reflection that was his own, accompanied by the guilt and shame he would face daily as the failed king who was beaten by slaves. No king could endure the insult of being victimized and the believers would pay with the lives of their children as no apology or reinstatement would suffice. The king called to his generals to assemble his armies as they would ride down the believers and destroy them to restore the kingdom's honor.

"Drawn Forth Son returned to the lead of the caravan and found his wife and children. The believers marched miles and the ground thundered as there were hundreds of thousands on the move. I followed their progress from a distance, as their footsteps and hoofs were a percussion band that were soothing to my ears. However, I knew that the hearts of men were twisted and the king would not settle the bout so easily, and no doubt would attempt to reclaim what once was his. Either way, there would be a final confrontation to come. It was only a matter of time.

"The believers reached an enclave of a canyon and took leave of their expedition to rest. And then, I heard a sound unlike footsteps, wagon wheels or clopping goats. No, the sound approached from behind and came with a repeated, quickening thunder clap. This was the pounding of many determined hooves and stepping of a trained military. It was the king's army and he rode before them cursing the Creator. I reared my head and spied with my serpent eyes and located Drawn Forth Son and advised him of the coming danger."

"It appears your former brother, the king, has decided to pay you a most unpleasant visit. He rides 20,000 strong with heavy horse and chariot swiftly approaching."

"How much time have we got?" Drawn Forth Son questioned, barely making out a small dust cloud signaling the approaching army.

"Not long! You have to lead these people out of here immediately! You haven't got much time and he's closing fast. Head out towards the beach of Nuweiba."

"What's out there?"

"A better chance than you've got here. Now go!"

"Drawn Froth Son signaled to High Mountain and they began evacuating out of the area as quickly as possible. Drawn Forth Son looked out from the hilltop and could see the king's leading chariot followed by his army. The believers were trapped from all sides and were facing the sea with no way to cross the waters and the king's armies approaching from behind them." The believers began to panic, yelling in fear.

"You have to speak to the people and calm them or they'll panic themselves right into the path of that army," I yelled out, then began heading down the hill top.

"Where are you going?" he yelled out from behind me.

"To buy you some time!" Drawn Forth Son looked down from the hill and saw the impending doom riding towards them, he then fell to his knees crying.

"I thought if only I could just get them out. If I could show them a better way... and now I've killed them! Why? Why God, why?" He sobbed heavily, soaking his beard with his tears, and beating his fists against the ground angrily.

"What difference does it make if they are to die at the hands of the master anyway? It would have been better to leave them as they were."

"He then remembered my words to him just days earlier... 'The trial is not for them, it is for you.' He began to remember the events of his life that had brought him to that very point, from his parent's sacrifice, to his adoptive mother drawing him

330

.

out of the waters. The defense of his life against assassination and his survival in the desert, to climbing the mountain and receiving revelation from the Creator. The debates and plagues and the final release of the slaves."

"It wasn't just chance, everything that's happened up until now, those things were meant to be... I was meant to be!" he said to himself.

"The reality of his life's purpose struck him as he stood and rose to his feet with confidence and strength. I had disappeared down the hillside and created a cloud of fire to slow the approach of the king's army. Drawn Forth Son picked up his staff from the ground and walked out towards the cliffs edge and he recited:

'The Creator is my light and my salvation; whom shall I fear? The Creator is the strength of my life; of whom shall I be afraid? When the wicked, even mine enemies and my foes, came upon me to eat up my flesh, they stumbled and fell. Though a host should encamp against me, my heart shall not fear. Though war should rise against me, in this will I be confident. One thing have I desired of the Creator is that I may dwell in the house of the Creator all the days of my life. To behold the beauty of the Creator, and to enquire in his temple. For in the time of trouble he shall hide me in his pavilion, in the secret of his coffer shall he hide me, he shall set me upon a rock. And now shall mine head be lifted up above mine enemies round about me, therefore will I offer in his coffer sacrifices of joy. I will sing, yea, I will sing praises unto the Creator. Hear me, my Creator, when I cry with my voice, have mercy upon me, and answer me.'

"He then raised his voice and spoke with assurance and the hearts of the people were calmed. He turned his gaze away from the fire cloud hovering between the approaching army and the people and turned towards the sea. He stretched forth his arms and felt within him the generations that had died before him, and the millions who would live after him. He was the hopes and dreams of those too afraid to believe, and when he opened his eyes and saw the sea, he knew what to do. He called out to the Creator and then he was emboldened with strength. He looked back over his shoulder and saw the believers cowering in fear and the approaching death mounted on chariot and horseback.

"The music from within him bubbled up slowly and was a steady tempo of snare tipping, accompanied by a slight echoing of hypnotic strings that aggressively began to taunt the sound of the approaching army. He raised his arms and looked back over his shoulder, then smirked and said, 'Get a load of this man!' And then a crash of bass thunder and guitar treble, filled the air which began to blow then increased and the waters became waves that mixed and stood at attention from his performance. His head nodded up and down while his arms orchestrated, like so many fingers strumming the belly of a string instrument, and the ocean waves thrashed and reverberated in dance.

"Drawn Forth Son stood as power itself as he conducted the awesome lightning strength of the Creator and commanded the sea to part. Within him was divine ability and creative individuality that punk-rocked the ground upon which he stood. He clinched his left fist and pulled it back inward towards his chest, and reached his right arm forward and said, 'I'm gonna let the stars show me the way,' and he pointed towards the divide in the waters, and the believers ran through the path set before them. The waters formed walls that were like lighted windows of an undersea aquarium. The fish and aquatic life seemed to smile and cheer the believers onwards as they watched them flee through the exposed sea path.

"The sea bed beneath them too was hospitable and became firm allowing them sure footing to make good their escape. Drawn Forth Son turned back towards the army making eye contact with the king, striking them with fear at the sight before them. The king, who led his army saw his forces bow and prostrate themselves before Drawn Forth Son atop the hill in entertaining defiance.

"I, too, was in amazement of what I witnessed with my serpent eyes. Seeing the elements turned on their head was nothing in comparison to the sight of a single man who had found self-realization and unleashed the power within himself to bring about change. He truly was a miracle and indeed a sight to be seen. The believers made good their escape and Drawn Forth Son covered their rear through the sea path. A part of me wished the king had cut his losses and fled the field, but foolhardy, stubborn, and entitled are the wealthy.

"The king saw his wealth bleeding from his slit wrists and saw life not worth living if to be lived as an ordinary man. I could see the look of contempt upon his face as he reissued his command to charge in between the walls of water after the believers. He swallowed deep and sucked up the hate sweating from his brow and engaged foolishly with no intent of return. My serpent eyes are keen at seeing such things and I can see the look of death on the face of any man. The king led his army in the path between the sea and I watched as the ground turned muddy and sunk beneath their chariot wheels. Their horses leaped and stumbled into gaping puddles that just moments ago were strong footholds.

"The elements had turned sour against the king and his armies and had no intention of allowing them safe passage. Many of the king's troops broke ranks and fled the giant walls of water that were sustained by the magic of the slave God. The king dismounted his chariot equipped with bow and arrow, and saw Drawn Forth Son on the other side standing on an embankment in judgment. Drawn Forth Son stood watching the king and his remaining forces encroach, then slowly brought his arms together and closed their fates and made the sea whole again. Those soldiers who turned and retreated out of the sea path hurried to safety. While the others that continued behind their king were buried under the sea and were never seen again.

"The believers completed their escape and traveled some additional days before reaching the mountain where Drawn Forth Son first received revelation. The mountain location was ideal in that it had a large plateau capable of housing the thousands of them. The terrain was bursting with enough vegetation to support their herds and flocks, and a natural spring that flowed down from the top of the mountain. Now released and reborn again, the believers were whole again, but had a long journey ahead of them. I joined Drawn forth Son one evening while he overlooked his people."

"Did you always know… that it would turn out this way?" he asked.

"Nothing is set and I have no knowledge of the path of mankind. I'm just like you… along for the ride." We shared a moment, looking out over the believers down below.

"It almost seems too good to be true, like a fairy tale ending. The adversity and the fight for equality, freedom, reason, and compassion. I almost didn't think it was possible."

"You know, you're right but, unfortunately, your task is only half done," I advised.

"How so?" he questioned grimly.

"You have freed them of their physical chains, but know what? What happens after the fairytale ending? Will they live happily ever after? Not really. What comes now is the task of living as free men and women, which is a burden in itself. There is no evil taskmaster to curse upon, but only the reality of one's own faults and shortcomings that hold the lash."

"Your words are true," he nodded in acknowledgment.

"But there is something that you must do now."

"I know, I haven't forgotten. Our patriarch! He Who Would Increase, he must be buried. Where do you think is a proper location?"

"I'll leave his final resting place to you, but that's not what I meant," I waved away with my tail, shaking my head no.

"Ask it, you have not instructed me false thus far."

"You must leave them," I said plainly.

"Leave, but why? I can't just abandon them after all of this," he replied in confusion.

"Understand something, you have done more for these people than they ever would have done for themselves. You don't owe them anything and now it's time for you to leave."

"And go where?" he replied, turning angrily towards me.

"Anywhere! It doesn't matter, now is your time. You have fulfilled your obligation as set by the Creator. Now, it is time to live for yourself. You've earned it."

"But what will happen to my people? I can't just…" he stood

in confusion with a stark look on his face.

"This is what's going to happen. The believers are going to realize that they have to be responsible for themselves. They are not children, they are adults who must make choices for themselves. This is going to be the difficult part for you and this part is called letting go. You cannot hold their hands and swaddle them through the rest of their lives, even if you try. What's going to happen is they are going to live and they will build, work, sacrifice, become ill, and weak, and sin, and die. But that is their right, as it is their life. It's not on you anymore," I explained, drawing nearer towards him.

"And what happens if I stay? What if I choose that the place I want to be is here with them? Then what?" he rebutted, leaning against the rock face gazing down at his people.

"Then they will hate you! You are one of humanity's best examples. But you have to understand that many will never come near to meeting the standard that you have set. Some will try, while others will see the bar as too high and will forego ever trying. There will be those who will see not hope in your legacy, but they will see the weakness that is them and they will see you as a reminder of all their shortcomings. And the only way for them to feel complete is too tear down your image so that they will feel no remorse of their actions.

"It is inevitable that they will question the one who fought for them, because now you will be 'pushing them too hard.' Now you ask too much of them and then you will no longer be their redeemer, but you will be the face of harsh reality. I know it pains you but for people like you, the reward is never enough. It's the fight that you crave. It's the pain and hard work that is most gratifying. And now, it's over. I tell you what, stay awhile with them and help them select some amongst them as leaders and then decide."

"Thank you for your counsel, Serpent. I'll think about it," he remained silent after hearing my words.

"I kept my distance from Drawn Forth Son and watched as each week the believers became dissatisfied with their situation and meager holdings and spoke against him. They who once labored daily to fill the mouths and appetites of the citizen masters were now angry at having to climb the mountain to fetch water and pick manna from the valley for bread. They soon tried to cast themselves into social classes based upon the past positions they held while under the citizen hierarchy.

"Daily prayers were not remembered and the believers cursed the Creator who had delivered them out of the glamourous cities into the quiet country life. I recited aloud while watching them, 'Better is a dry morsel and quietness therewith, than a house full of sacrifices with strife.' However, Drawn Forth Son was ever present and ever forgiving of his people and he could not relieve himself of them. Drawn Forth Son prayed to the Creator and no matter what their affliction, he saw that it was healed. I watched him pacing alone and shaking his head looking at his hands that were empty with nothing to give his people to quell their distrust in the Creator."

"The Creator hath delivered us out of the fire and into obscurity, but we must not waiver the faith. The way of the citizens was idolatry and we must rebuild anew and live without pursuing wealth, or power. We have all that we need right here to thrive and, in time, the Creator will guide us to a land of plenty and prosperity. All we must do is enjoy the little things and remain thankful." Drawn Froth Son spoke out to the believers every evening.

"But his words were not received with gratitude and he was applauded with sneers and snide remarks. The believers found solace in the fermentation of picked berries and made pleasurable hostels to lust the days and nights away. Then, once again, a familiar rumbling came from a distance, and it was the voice of the Creator that summoned Drawn Forth Son up the mountain. I remained alert as the Creator's presence in this situation could mean anything.

"The believers had been delivered out of their affliction as was tasked, but what direction were they to take? What was next for Drawn Forth Son? I feared that he might not return as his works may have earned him early release from this life and perhaps heavenly retreat and reward would be presented to him at this moment. But in all I have seen, I knew that it was only a matter of time that the Creator would make his will be known.

"So Drawn Forth Son instructed his brother and several elders that he was summoned up the mountain to receive new revelation, and would return. In his absence, High Mountain, was to remain in charge and keep the believers vigilant until his return. However, man does not do well sitting idle and makes a fool of his soul with none watching him. In the absence of Drawn Forth Son, the believers saw an opportunity to relieve themselves of their pious overlord of patience and sacrifice.

"The believers overwhelmed High Mountain who quickly saw that the priests and elders stood not in righteousness and were against him. Some days had passed and rumors were spread that Drawn Forth Son had ascended into the clouds as he was an aged man. The believers wanted to commemorate their anniversary and make celebration and offering to a god of gold that would bless them with wealth and lust of pleasure. So they crafted a golden statue and built an altar before it. The golden idol was built and set in a cleft of the mountain that overlooked a natural amphitheater that they could worship from a distance.

"The believers made sacrifices to the lifeless emblem and entertained themselves in lustful activity in festival. Within only a few days, the problems of human society began to reemerge in the form of disease, addiction, crime, and physical violence. I looked on in sadness at the assembly of the believers who had shamed themselves as infants running and screaming in tantrum and play. The serpent broke from narration and returned to speaking with the Man of the Present.

"You know something, Man of the Present, I have seen almost every manner of heathen ritual, but up until then I had never   seen   so   much   goddamned 'buttasscracktittynipplenutsackdangling' nakedness in my whole life! I just don't understand why it is, that when you people decide to cut lose you have to take all of your clothes off."

"That! Is! Completely! Not! True!" the Man of the Present defended loudly.

"Oh no? It's not? Oh, ok, I guess that's why Jermaine Stewart only had that one good song, huh…" the serpent said simultaneously, with a sarcastic tone, reminiscing the pop hit song from 80's album Frantic Romantic, while the Man of the Present shook his head in continued frustration. The Serpent continued.

"Then, from over my shoulder came a growing presence, and I turned quickly to see the return of Drawn Forth Son from the mountain top. He carried with him two stone tablets etched with the writings of the Creator. He, again, had been enlightened and it showed on him physically. He was no longer Drawn forth Son, but now Law Giver and he brought with him the commandments of the Creator. Upon seeing me, he said, 'He Who Completes!'

I defended with delight, "No… no, no, no, no, no! I didn't do anything, it was all you. You believed and you took action, but most importantly, you finished what you started. It's you who deserves the praise, I had nothing to do with it." Law Giver then recited:

'The law of the Creator is perfect and converting of the soul, the testimony of the Creator is sure, and makes wise the simple. The statutes of the Creator are right and rejoicing to the heart, and the commandments of the Creator are pure, and enlightening to the eyes. The fear of the Creator is clean and enduring forever, the judgments of the Creator are true, and righteous altogether. More to be desired are they than gold, yea, than much fine gold, and sweeter than honey and the honeycomb. Moreover, by them is thy servant warned, and in keeping of them there is great reward.'

"Law Giver then looked out over the valley and saw the believers down below engaging in sinful celebration. He became filled with anger after seeing what they had become in his absence. Law Giver quickly made his way down the mountain and found High Mountain there in seclusion, and interrogated him in anger. The celebration continued until they noticed Law Giver's presence above the cleft. Law Giver clinched his fists and was filled with anger and remorse for those he'd fought for, only to see how they had betrayed the Creator and turned so easily to sin and wickedness in spite of his efforts.

"The two tablets from the Creator were to be sacred testimony to the believers as they were chosen, but now they were wretched and impure. The anger within him burst out and he smashed the tablets down at the base of the mountain and roared at the believers who ran naked from his presence.

"He grabbed hold of the golden idol now adorned with wreaths and goblets of blood for offerings and he lifted and overturned it solely by his own strength. He made work of his anger upon the golden idol and ground and broke it into pieces and had it thrown into the fire and melted away.

"I should make them eat it! I should feed them their golden idol as molten porridge and let them digest their sin as it cooks them from the inside," he yelled, kicking over the remaining alters, cursing in to the night!

'O ye sons of men, how long will ye turn my glory into shame? How long will ye love vanity, and seek after sin?' He fell onto his knees sobbing and prayed.

"The believers had all ran to hide themselves from his reproach of their behavior. That night, Law Giver was back at the base the mountain collecting the broken pieces of the tablets he had smashed in anger. When I found him, he was crying and all but defeated now on his knees. He asked the Creator for forgiveness, but only blamed himself as he felt he was not strong enough to keep them from their sinful ways. He raised his eyes and looked up seeing me, and knew the 'I told you so,' waiting for him but I restrained myself.

"It's not your fault. You could never have freed them, no matter how hard you tried. You removed the physical chains off of them, but it was their hearts and minds that remain enslaved. In later times, a Thomas Jefferson will say 'All men are created equal.' I suppose it is the Creator's will that all men are equally to blame for their sinful ways." I lifted Law Giver up by the shoulders off his knees and took a seat next to him.

"Humanity has always had the ability to escape the mental and social prisons of self-deprecation all along, yet it is their own unwillingness to end such juvenile and criminal ways. If there is

339

a way to free humanity, it must come by freedom of the mind and empowerment of the heart. For only in a man's heart and mind can he truly be free. However, Law Giver, the burden rests to those warriors of justice and pioneers of education to lead the way and fight the good fight. It is an ongoing movement, a continuing struggle for the souls of mankind and this is but one battle that you have fought.

"Humanity is continually asking the same questions and looking for the answers in the wrong places; not in the eyes of their hearts and minds, but between the thighs of sin and lies. You are not to blame, you have not failed, and your legacy is one of unification and the edification of written laws and the advancement of human rights. I depart from you this evening and I bid you good struggle on the morrow, and peace to a troubled mind.

"It was a shameful sight to see, one who had sacrificed so much and worked so hard for the many, only to be undone by his own people. I knew what needed to be done, even if he wouldn't do it himself. That night while they slept, I crept through the camps and took pleasure in my serpent ways and gorged myself upon them. I killed and consumed many, possibly three thousand or more in total. I separated none and killed those who were in my path, be they men, women, or children.

"Nothing seems to motivate people better than fear and hatred, so I would do what Law Giver could not bring himself to do. The believers had been given more than a second chance. They had been shown the might of the Creator that did battle on their behalf, and with malice they spit upon the messenger of their own deliverance. How dare they... how could they? I spit, only to clear my throat and swallow them not with an ounce of remorse of my deeds. Duly they deserved worse than my appetite upon them, but I spared them my flame and let them slip away in silence and not have to shed a tear in anticipation of the grave. Come morning, those who were spared could mourn for their dead, and those who were dead could pray for forgiveness in their graves.

"After half the night, some awoke and noticed that death had fallen heavily upon their camp in great numbers but none were aware of my presence. Law Giver rose from his tent and ran towards the screams of his people. He saw body after body, broken, and bit full with venom and so many others also dead while others lay dying. He followed the trail of death and found me exiting with stealth from a child's tent. His eyes burned with fury upon seeing me and he screamed out in anger."

"You! Why! Why have you done this?" His anger was surprising but not unexpected, for he loved them so much.

"The believer's sin, but I beg for their forgiveness. Have you nothing to say? Have you nothing but evil and lies within you? How could I have been so foolish to consort with such a demon as you?! And in the end, it was you who have betrayed me and slew those you helped me to protect."

"They do not deserve you and no matter how much they sin against the Creator, you continue to carry their burden and shame. I did what was needed to weed out those without redemption in their hearts. They shall return to you this morning more vigilant and more humble than before you left for the mountain top," I said slowly so as not to increase his anger.

"I gave no such command to slay them and yet you do such a thing!" Law Giver screamed, clinching the bloody mud in his fists.

"Command? You don't command me! I don't answer to you!" I responded with anger at the notion of being commanded by a mere mortal. I then paused to allow calmer heads to prevail.

"I understand that you are angry, but you should really thank me. There are many…" The serpent broke from narration and returned to speaking with the Man of the Present. He stopped speaking all together then let out a deflating sigh then remarked. "Shit!"

"What! What, what, what happened? You were about to say something then you just cut off about mid-sentence! What happened next?" the Man of the Present, asked wide eyed in heated suspense.

"Have you ever been talking to someone on the phone then about midway through your last sentence the line goes dead.

You don't realize the conversations over, but you keep talking to no one like an idiot." The serpent sighed a second time with a remorseful expression.

"Yeah, I hate it when that happens."

"That's kinda what happened. I was speaking and then everything just went dark. I remember turning my head to look back at the camps and then that was it. I don't know how long it took me to realize that my head was no longer attached to my body, but..." the serpent sighed a third time shaking his head at his past mistakes.

"Wait! What! What the hell happened to your head?"

"He chopped my head off... with only the edge of his hand!" The serpent sighed a fourth time, sucking his teeth.

"He chopped! Your! Head off? With his hand!" he gasped in awe, leaning forward in astonishment.

"Yuuuup! I'm not sure if I mentioned it before, but he was extremely strong. He had nearly the strength of 40 men, but I never knew he was that strong. With one chop! It was lights out."

"He chopped your head off!" The Man of the Present repeated again in amazement.

"Yup... but that's not how you kill me!" the serpent switched his eyes keenly back to the man, smirking.

"So what happened to Law Giver and the believers after that?"

"Well, I'm glad to see you're not overly concerned with the wellbeing of me and my severed head," the serpent said humorously, then continued.

"There was some momentary life remaining in my head before my eyes rolled backwards and dried out completely. I could see Law Giver's sandals and tunic from the corner of my eye and then they disappeared out of view. I had hearing in my ears, but I could not see anything as my eyes had gone milky white and my vocal cords were disconnected. It took seven days for my body to regrow a new head. And let me tell you, that was a most horrible experience, I never wish to repeat. It was an outer body experience, as I could see my body lying there helpless and unable to move. Yet, I remained partially awake inside of my own rotting skull and, unfortunately, I retained feeling throughout my decaying self.

"I could feel every manner of bottom feeder making meal after meal upon my rotting flesh. Those creeping things traversed the sinus highways of my head, all while delicately removing the brain matter from my skull. How miserable an experience it was to be motionless and unable to scream out, while being devoured by thousands of things in the heat of the baking sun. Finally, after day six did my eyes rolled forwards into my newly formed skull and I was alive again. I broke free of my corpsy shell and shed my skin anew to take in a full breath of air into my aching lungs.

"It felt like drowning in your own subconscious and then inhaling the deepest breath underwater then crashing awake. Sad to say, Law Giver and I did not part on good terms. After I came too, he and the believers were gone. I knew that one day he would come to understand that what I did was for the best. But I decided to let him be with his precious people.

"It happened just as I knew it would; the believers fell into a cycle of sin and repentance. And Law Giver became lost in the backtracking of a juvenile people and they wandered for many years. I couldn't watch a people knowingly live in stupidity so I left them. To this day, I still miss him and his performances. He had a music within him that when focused, it came forth and was as electrifying as a shirtless, leather pant, rock god upon the echoing stage capable of defeating armies and splitting the seas in two.

"He walked them out of there, just like he said he would," the serpent nodded in acknowledgment.

"I shall end with this, Man of the Present. Freedom and slavery are a choice, but many will choose complacency, ignorance, and job security! In such a society that places oppression over creativity, commercialism over individuality and personal responsibility; all who dwell therein will forever be enslaved, and will never escape... the Panopticon."

343

CHAPTER 9: THE MIRROR

"The thoughts of the old world covered me and I remembered the way of things before the great deluge. The silence and the perpetual raw beauty of things that once were. Now the maelstrom called human civilization that had rebuilt the world, was spreading its manifest patriarchal destiny across the earth. Life and living had become complicated and man continuously drew lines in the sand to separate himself from one another. There was no escaping this place; I needed a moment to pause, a place to gaze upon a living reflection of archaic simplicity.

"The last remnants of a time forgotten, I wished to walk in the impressions made by those greater than any man. Those that were larger of size and stature, and were only matched by their legendary reputations. They stood eye to eye with hills, they lifted and tossed stones the size of boulders at their whim. The earth shook under their feet, the winds carried their terrible coughs, and the seas swayed that were their baths. I went to seek them out, those that still remained. They have been known by many names: the Anakites, the Emites, the Amorites, and the Rephaites..."

"No! You don't mean..." The Man of the Present gasped in astonishment.

"That's right… giants!" The serpent shifted his eyes, then replied with a whisper.

The Push…

"They were known as the 'Earthborn' and were the remnants of the sons of god and the daughters of angels. They were the living echoes of the Age of Legends and were recognized by their prodigious size and strength. I speak of them, those terrible ones, yes… there were giants!

"Giant of size and of strength, but more so of attribute and of character. I recall a male and female pair in particular that I was quite fond of and wherever they went, they were going there together. The male was known as 'Will' and he had the capability to intentionally bring his thoughts into physical action just by the properties of his mind. The female was known as 'Patience' and she had the ability of prolonged positivity, while enduring an extreme difficulty without giving into negative emotion.

"One day the two of them set their minds upon achieving an impossible feat, and would test themselves against a single mountain. Without further announcement, they put their backs up against the alp and dug their heels into the earth, and then they began to push. There was no yelling or grunting, no spitting or ogerish grimacing, just intention and pure focus, and they continued to push. Day after day, night upon night, they remained in concentration and still they continued to push. Patience made the decision between them to endure the hardship in order to achieve their greater shared reward.

"Most humans favor quick payment and live in the here and now, however these were giants and they were entities of fortitude. Will posed a question that discussed fate and free-will as compared to the mountain, asking, 'Is the mountain merely an outer protruding of the earth or a separate stone resting upon its face? If the mountain is a stone then by time and force alone, it shall move. Yet if the mountain is subject to the earth, then we are destined to fail, as the earth and mountain are the same. Unless it is our effort that overpowers the great stone, causing the mountain to break free, then it shall be we who are triumphant.'

"They gave nothing to doubt, to disbelief, or to procrastination; they did not break for rest, or sleep, or even to eat, and still they continued to push. I kept not the time, but I witnessed several seasons change around them and observed the annual migrations of beast and fowl, and then... it started to move. The pair gave out no wild yells, nor rung any bells of achievement, and still they continued to push. At the end of it, they simply looked down and saw the prints of their feet of where they were, compared to where they used to be. They glanced over and stared into the eyes of one another and smiled, and then... that was it."

"Wow! How far did they move it?" he asked, listening with intrigue.

"Know this, Man of the Present, when it comes to moving mountains, it makes little difference whether it's an inch, a few feet, or a mile, the point is... it moved," the serpent shifted his eyes back over at the man.

"I had not encountered a giant for such a long time. However, I still heard rumors of them here and there, but the frequency between time to time had grown longer. East was my heading and I made good my journey to rejoin them of the ancient world, them of days past, those like myself who were unwanted, and that man had all but forgotten. Their half breed kind that inhabited the earth had long been outlawed when many clashed with my dragon-kind quarreling over meat and territorial dominion.

"The looks on the faces of ordinary men when beholding their stature and the fear and terror they evoked as they attacked in anger. There's was an awful and frightening call that early man knew and feared all too well. That awful sound that echoed around canyons, causing flocks of winged terriers to startle from their perches upon their calls.

"After the great deluge, when the lands resurfaced, they were shunned in the new world of men due to their uncontrollable nature. No, they were not heathens, but they refused religion all together as they keep to the ancient ways in giving thanks unto the Creator. Man could never understand such meditative

346

benevolence and only envied and hated them for their strength. My mind swirled with memories of them, which connected the fabled stories to their names and legacies.

"They had all been but demonized as mindless primeval creatures, wild natured and chaotic, violent and drooling with an appetite for human children. Ha! Ha! Ha! How silly a notion, everyone knows only ogres eat children, as their diet makes them strictly cannibalistic. But giants... they were a great-hearted people who lived in isolation as they were not men and could never be welcomed amongst the Creator's chosen of the earth.

"I had traveled as far east as possible, reaching a mountainous strip of land that laid along much of the eastern shore of the Sea of the Dead. And there, in the land of Moab, was where I found them. I have to admit, I did not expect to happen upon such a somber gathering of giant kind, but they were all there. Their village stood erect while showing the weathering of time and the hand shoveled roads were a bit unkempt and showed a misplaced civic value. Their living quarters were neatly dressed with crumbled hanging wreaths of annual floral tributes. The town couldn't have been provided a simpler blue print, for each address was lined left to right, front to back, and row after row. And upon the hill, overlooking the town, hung a plaque which read: 'Cemetery of The Neverknowns.'

"The plaque above the graveyard mis-stated the tribe Emim that now rested there forever. They were the Neverknowns, as no one ever knew where they came from, how old they really were, nor their true names. I later learned that they had all been exterminated in a series of battles that cleansed the land of them. My eyes swelled with water and spilled over onto their places of resting as I wept for them. The dead kings of old, them of monstrous proportion and appearance, the archaic remains of a world forgotten. I stayed near their graves for some days paying my respects and listening to the elders telling the younglings of the Giants that roamed and threatened an untamed land. All things live and die, but I felt cheated as I was unaware that I would never see their beauty and graces ever again.

"The new inhabitants of the land of Moab were those of the line of the Veil, and they had prospered well between the treeless, but fertile plateau and rolling limestone hills. They farmed grains and dug irrigation canals out from the deep ravines allowing them prosperity and abundant harvests. The rainfall of the region was pleasant and plentiful despite the hot summer that was approaching. The land was rich with natural resources and was a major conjunction on the 'King's Highway,' for many caravans that traded salt, precious goods metals, and fabrics. But there was nothing in this place of Moab for me, I saw the same in men as I had seen elsewhere. They were a silly people and found themselves in the worship of idols, and at times, even committed human sacrifices in their names.

"What I had come for was dead and gone, and what lived and remained were the antics of a meaningless people. The sun was going down and I was ready for a meal. I would leave this place come morning for it brought nothing but grief to me. I spotted a flimsy man and made fixings of him with ease, as I kill quietly without raising notice or alarm. I caught him off guard, biting him once; his whole head swelled to the size of a melon just before his heart burst inside of his chest. My venom is quite potent and softened his insides for easy digestion, then I descended off into comfortable sleep for the night.

"Then came the morning sun and I was awakened gently by its gleaming smile warmly upon my scaly hide. What direction seemed appealing, east or west, perhaps north I thought. Was there any new adventure left for a forgiven, yet soulless, servant such as I? But first, why not enjoy a pre-trip meal. I enjoyed eating that man so much last night that I decided upon finishing off his two sons for breakfast. Although the first son was an able bodied man, he rarely looked behind him, making him an easy catch. Perhaps he thought his scrawny dog would alert him of danger... idiot! I thought to swallow the barking rodent with its master, but why spoil my appetite. I must say that the man's first son was more of a fighter than I gave him credit for, as he continued to kick while half way down my throat.

"The family was truly tasty and I thoroughly enjoyed this

holiday spread for my parting occasion. The man's second son came around the corner hearing the dog's barking, but he didn't realize I allowed the mongrel to cry out only to draw him in nearer. He too was full of fight, but I caught hold of his ankle and quickly coiled him up without him even spotting me. He barely let out a teensy whimper of a scream just before I silenced him, but then something unexpected happened! The second son's wife raised an attack with a garden tool against me. The woman had come outside to bring him a pitcher of water and witnessed my attack upon her husband. By that time it was too late to save him, but it did not stop her, as she continuously struck with intent.

"Her attack upon me had little more effect than that of a buzzing bee, however, it became difficult to complete my meal with her distracting me. So I spit him out... half-digested... directly at her feet! I then turned my gaze directly towards her, then struck her with a bold question. 'You do realize I was going to eat that?'

"You speak!" she turned with her eyes agape in shock, and gasped.

"Not without invitation I don't! I do, do seasonal marketing events and the occasional off Broadway show, but I've got too many gigs booked right now to be making any private appearances!" I remarked sarcastically, dipping my head slightly then waving my tail no, then further explaining.

"The woman screamed and moaned in terror at the sight of her dead husband lying at her feet, with his skin melting off from the digestive acids blanketing his skin. She cursed me and screamed in horror, at the deaths of her husband, father-in-law, and brother-in-law. I don't know why I didn't just kill and eat her as well, maybe it was her courage that struck me as odd. But now, she was on her knees weeping at the sight of her dead husband. I sincerely do hate the sight of a woman crying so I reached with my tail and wiped her tears and attempted to comfort her. She immediately spat at me and cursed me ill."

"So what now, Janus Schemer! You, no doubt, will kill me as well and make good your destruction of our village. I have no weapon to repel you and you have surely ended my life as I am now without husband or children. My life is useless, surely some calamity has sent you to mock and punish me."

"I'm sorry, what? What? What am I?" I remarked in puzzlement, at the woman's phraseology.

"The Creator has turned away from me and now my husband is dead and I have no children. My life is fit only to be food for such a demon as you!" The widow remained on her knees crying and sobbing taking hold of my tail. She continued to cry, only whaling louder, after hearing my words.

"Dear widow, I can assure you that the Creator has neither turned away from you, nor hates you. My presence here was merely by chance and I meant you no personal harm nor was my attack out of spite. Cry not woman, you are alive and full of strength. Your life will no doubt continue, but tell me, why do you say your life is meaningless and empty?"

"Because it is my duty to marry and provide my husband with children."

"Traditional huh… but is that all your life is purposed for?"

"What do you mean, what else? All I am is a woman and without a husband or a child I am nothing," the widow replied, then paused her sniffling.

"Such an impoverished outlook on one's own life, yet out of nothing… hmmmm…" perhaps something I thought, with a raised eyebrow shaking my head in thought.

"Taking into consideration these dark circumstances my lady, but would you care to join me for a walk down by the water?"

"With you? No! Probably then you would eat me!" the widow said with disgust and confusion at the invitation.

"Possibly! You mean possibly I would eat you. Admittedly, me killing and digesting you is a possibility, however, the probability of that danger neither increases nor decreases, regardless of your location be it here or there. Besides, what if I told you that I am in as much danger from you as you are from me," I kindly retorted.

"Ha! A tiny woman such as I? You mock me Janus!"

"I am a great many things, but plainly I do not mock thee woman, but the war has ended and now I ask for peace between us. Now see! I even got you to smile. And it also appears that you've stopped crying, so why not join me down by the water for a chat and I promise I will not eat you."

"But you must allow me to bury my husband first, it is against our beliefs to leave the dead unattended." The widow looked back towards her house where her mother-in-law was working, then wiped her tears.

"... Agreed! Partially digested is wretchedly unbecoming! And out in this heat, he's going to stink something awful. I will wait for you down past those trees, but do not linger any longer than needed as I have plans to be rid of this place."

"The woman and her mother-in-law made well their ceremonial arrangements and buried their dead then after the evening meal, she joined me down by the water's edge. The woman approached slowly and whispered calling out for me. The water rippled and bubbles slowly rose to the surface of the water and I slowly emerged from the water. My massive body followed as I he pulled myself onto the grass. I looked the woman up and down and grinningly said, 'Now my lady... what shall we talk about?'"

"I do not know Serpent, you insisted on this meeting so perhaps it is you who should enlighten me."

"Indeed, it was I who insisted on this arrangement. Honestly, it upset me a bit back there what you said about yourself. Tell me how you came to such a miserable conclusion of your life."

"Well, my mother cast me out when I was a child and, as such, I have suffered and have never been accepted anywhere. The earliest memories I have of my birth mother are her words telling me that I ruined her life. Of all the things she said to me, she never said she loved me. I was sent away to live with relatives who despised me and mistreated me. As such, I lived like a stray among my own family and was only allowed meals of table scraps. It was not until I married my departed husband that I felt appreciated and fully belonged to a family. My life had started poorly but the Creator delivered me out of my past situation and

351

into a better life. But it appears that, once again, I am alone and will have to wander this world trying to find acceptance and make meaning of a woman's worth."

"That is a rough start for anyone, however, may I remind you that your worth is not determined by any price offered, nor by the pleasures associated with you. The substance of a person is not easily discerned; quantitative nor qualitative analysis reveals nothing except bothersome marks and dashes. It is tantamount to know your worth, as each of you is priced as marked. Don't overstate the cost, but please, please... don't damage the merchandise! Now, I cannot change the past, nor can I apologize for those that I have slain, what is done is done. However, I am not without regret. And as such, I beg of thee, please, allow me the opportunity to reimburse thee of what was taken."

"What can you possibly hope to offer me? I will not trade my virtue for any riches of sin!" the widow stated.

"I am quite knowledgeable and if you allow me, I might be able to replace everything you have lost, plus possibly more."

"How so?"

"Well first, let's look at your situation. Now that you are widowed, what will become of you?"

"I will probably be sent away as I have no blood ties to my mother-in-law and she is not the sort to turn me out to travelers for pleasure."

"I guess a better question would be, what do you want to happen with your life?"

"I had not thought much of it. I was married and that was it. We were happy here in my home land, but now...."

"You said, you had no family before, and now your family has been diminished, do you wish to lose what remains of it?"

"She is my mother in the entirety of the word. It is rare to have such a connection between in-laws, but I am fortunate that we have bonded and have truly become mother and daughter."

"Family is what you make of it. There are no blood ties that can define the true bond of family and friendship. You should keep what remains of your family together, for she has been more of a mother to you than your actual people. The Creator has brought you two together for a reason and leaving now would only bring misfortune upon you," I replied.

"But I still have no husband. How will I find a husband?" she pleaded, throwing her hands up.

"Hmm… looking for a husband. I have to admit, I've never had to seek out a mate so it appears you have found me lacking on the subject, still… I do enjoy a challenge!" I responded, while tipping my tail along the grass as if playing a piano, then said in rhyme.

"Many a thing may happen, as so much do they occur, yet the tepid fool is none the wiser, who hath never tempted her. If I were to offer you some advice on the matter, would you be open to receiving instruction from one such as I? And again, I offer no promises, nor do I pretend my advice will be free of causality or accidental incident."

"Alright! It is fate then, Serpent. I will lend ear to your advice, but you must swear before the Lord of all creation that you will not break your word to me. Lest the Creator punish you several deaths and an eternity in the pits of hell," she responded pointing her finger in knife fashion.

"A-HA! HA! HA! HA! HA! HA! HA! HA! HA! HA!" I raised a great laugh, then said, "Them those tickly tears do they cry, are but nothing upon one such as I.

"My lady, the pits of hell were designed for those of mortal sin. I pray thee! Rest assured that I shall not break my word to you, nor cause you any additional harm. Allow us to conclude for the night. Rest be upon thine weary eyes and beauty be a blushing wind over thy caressing cheek. Good rest, my lady." The widow returned home for the night as I looked out over the land of Moab, saying to myself.

"What human things may do, from their intrinsic rights and immoral wrongs, do I dwell therewith. Yet among them I am not, for those of ancient relic lie asunder and seek out the light no more. I am come, the one, who seest the past, and beholden the future. I am subtlety solitary the entire reptile wrecking crew. The Janus who hath learned life through a lie and happiness through transition. Silence be thy name, trust be but a glimmer of time, and without utterance do I deal thy hand with happy obloquy."

"So what is this story about?" The Man of the Present interrupted asking.

"The same thing it's always been about... me!" the serpent replied, starring back at the man.

"No, I mean, who is this woman you are talking to. I thought you were going to find giants and now you're talking about this woman, I don't remember this story."

"I found the giants, but unfortunately, they were all dead. Seems to be a reoccurring side effect of being around people. Anytime something is different, or ugly, or too scary for the under-developed hominid brain, the resulting action is to kill it!" The serpent replied turning and stared at the man.

"Nobody really believes that stuff anyway," the man responded in defense.

"Oh no? Then I'm sure you can explain why mankind continues to hold onto unproven beliefs, for which he has never experienced nor fully comprehends. Your entire understanding of your beginnings and endings come down to fairy tale, complete with giants!"

"So this woman, what did she do? Did she have a revelation from God or was she a witch or something?"

"No... she was not a witch and there was no revelation or wrath."

"Then why are we talking about her if God didn't talk to her?"

"For the same reason we're talking about the other people, because it's a part of the story. Her life may seem meager and insignificant, but hers is a tale that many, if not all of you, share in. Others I have specifically noted were directed by the Creator but I'm pretty sure this woman received no such intervention. Now that could mean a number of things. Perhaps the Creator was uninterested in her, or perhaps the Creator saw no need of involvement as she was on the right path.

"Do you correct he who is doing what they are supposed to

be doing? No, you correct those who are lost, those who have gone astray. Even now, as I reflect upon the meaning of her journey Man of the Present, I think it was not so simply put. A life of grandeur and spectacle, yes, is paramount, but hers might quite well be an 'every woman's', nay, an 'every person's' story. A tale of empowerment, purpose, and self-realization. Through her story, humanity can learn about itself the most. Look not to grand statue or noble title, but quietly study and examine the finite feminine qualities that are within each of you.

"That maybe this woman received no revelation from the Creator, as she was free to choose her own path. Perhaps her story is of one who determined the meaning and worth of her own life, so should it be the same for all mankind."

"The following morning, the widow and her mother bid farewell to their sister/daughter-in-law and the two women left Moab and journeyed towards the Land of Bread and Meat. At the completion of their journey, the mother was greeted by her people and introduced her daughter-in-law as a virtuous widowed woman of her son. That evening, the two women ate a moderate meal and bed down for the night. I approached their tent quietly and called to the young widow, who was barely asleep."

"I see you remain in the company of your mother-in-law."

"Yes, I decided it best to remain with her. For she is the entirety of my heart and any home I dwell within would be empty without her there. But this land is hers and I am foreign and will find difficulty in prospering here. I have no money and what work can I find in such a place being a single woman with no husband?" She responded quietly, as not to wake her mother-in-law.

"I've heard this same argument before and it is utterly troubling to my being. The idea that a woman is less than or cannot exist without the permission of a man, or can do no other than woman's work. And they call this human society civilized! Nothing but a modern phenomenon of enduring inequality and the separation of the sexes. Are you perpetually unequal or susceptibly different to your male counterparts? Your inequality surrounds you from your work, to your places of worship, and then follows you home. For that be his castle, yet also where the heart is, but I ask… where in a man's world doth a woman dwell? Allow me some discretion if you will, for I continue to hear such silliness regarding women's placement and merit upon the earth."

"What do you know of it? My troubles are sincere and cause me worry and fret. The life of a woman is difficult, but there is no pity in the judging eye of society," she replied, as she jutted her lip and lower jaw forward in a pouting manner.

"True, yet I am no doubting member of the mixture and have nothing to gain from the belittling of feminine kind. I for one, agree that the life of a woman is filled with many difficulties and hardships, yet difficulty is not an obstacle that can cause any permanent delay. You are a woman…and as such, you are the dream of humanity."

"A dream?" she repeated.

"Yes my dear, a dream! Is it a marvelous thing to be a dream for one can be anything and everything; but woe unto she, for the night is long and the head that dreams, belongs to he. Let me ask you something… what do you see when you look at yourself?"

"Well… I don't think anyone has ever asked me that question before. What do you mean, what do I think about myself? I think I'm just fine, I'm doing the best that I can! Well, why don't you try and scrape together a living and make a husband happy, and…" she said, with her hands on her hips.

"That's all very fine and well my lady! But my question was not presented in judgment of you. My question was simply… what do *you* see; when you look at yourself. Not what does everyone else see, or think, or gossip. When you look at yourself, what looks back… at you?" I clarified, waving my tail back and forth, to calm her down.

"I… I guess I'm, okay," the widow stood silent momentarily, the replied shifting her eyes back and forth searching for the words.

"Not okay! I guarantee you that if I were to ask that question to any of your male counterparts they could provide me with a defined list of accolades and achievements, along with added attributes and alumnus associations to sum up their appetites and appeal. However, you, a woman, see yourself as just… okay!

"Hmm… Let me put it to you another way. If I were to ask a man what he thinks of himself, he would probably say something along the lines of… my goals, my success, my ethic, and then family or faith, but not in that particular order. Now in comparison to women, who would list their goals and successes as well, but with some varied differences.

"The reason I bring this up, is because between the two of you, gender species that is, there is a clear yet unstated difference. From my observations, a man growing through adolescence and aged seems to be one person and then remains that same person throughout his remaining life. Yes, acknowledging minor changes, incidental accidents, along with newly acquired skills and abilities. Whereas women, you start out as one person, then over time you may become a second person, and then are confronted by the idea of a possible third person."

"How do you mean a second and third person?"

"Well… there's who you are as a girl, then who you are as a young lady, then thirdly… there is the woman that everyone expects you to be. Allow me to clarify a bit for you," I pulled closer towards the widow then coiled myself comfortably.

"A boy looks up and sees, say his father, or a solider, or a public figure and one of those matches his personality, thus becoming his idea of a man. In his life, there is one transition going from being a boy to becoming a man.

"The ideas of boy and man are pretty straightforward, quite simply: run, jump, play; then punch, kick, fuck, fight, with some minor variations. Now, something similar occurs when a girl looks up and sees her mother, or a nurse, or an entertainer, where this too becomes her idea of a woman. Yet, a woman has to transition not once, but twice. You see, there is a duality that is associated with the female gender. There is an idea of the woman she wants to be; however, women are confronted by society's image of what she is supposed to be as well.

357

"There is a triptych of terms in an order under the psychoanalytic study by Jaques Lacan, called the Imaginary, the Symbolic and the Real. Lacan's theories follow a much different understanding based upon his mirror study and the ego stage. Where I am merely borrowing the triptych terms bearing little similarity to his works. However, I do feel that these three terms do relate unto the idea of women and our conversation. The Imaginary woman, I believe, is the woman that we dream of. These women are our mothers, our grandmothers, great women of history, and of fable and fantasy. However, the idea of these women is based on the impressions of them, not who they actually are or were.

"Second is the Symbolic woman and I believe this is the woman that society tells women they are supposed to be. This symbol of a woman is created by all of the images of good and bad women, loving and terrible mothers.

"Then third, is the Real woman. The real woman is the person behind the apron in the late-night diner, the real woman spinning acrobatically around the stripper pole, the real woman who penned that inaugural speech, the real woman who worked hard to keep food on the table. The real women... the ones that we rarely ever get to know. Humanity spends so much time imagining its dream girls and wives that the real women are ignored. It is impossible to live up to an imaginary image, while fulfilling the symbolism of society all at the same time. When does the real woman get to be recognized? Is it when she takes the makeup off, is when she changes out of her heels? Is it after work, is it before breakfast, or is it showering in her tears? Perhaps it is only the mirror that ever sees who she really is.

"My lady, this is what I see... when looking at the two gender types of you humans. The male gender symbol is the arrow (spear) above the spirit (circle). The spear of course represents conquest and battle, industry and construction. Which means that men are defined by their accolades and achievements, by how much they can build, conquer, or destroy. While the gender symbol for women is of course the spirit (circle) over the cross (matter). Again, whereas one definition explains the male gender there are multiple definitions that explain the female gender.

"The first of which is the distaff of a spindle, which is a very archaic definition representing women's work. One could then ask what defines woman's work. Is it housekeeping? Let me assure you that neither cooking nor cleaning has anything to do with anyone's gender. Cleaning has everything to do with hygiene and maintenance. Why some of you choose to keep clean while others do not, is utterly debatable and disgusting. It is surprising those of you who do not keep their person nor their spaces in sanitary order. I must admit that I have known cockroaches with better hygiene and habits than many of you humans!

"Apology, for side tracking, my dear. Now the second explanation of the female gender symbol is the Venus mirror, which at first seems to be a stereotypical symbol of vanity. Yet, I would take another look and see something deeper in its meaning. A mirror yes, is an object that reflects light and preserves most of the physical characteristics of the original light to produce an image. What is missed though about mirrors, is that the reflected image is merely a refraction of light and not the actual representation of the original image. Now, how the Venus mirror relates to women in our conversation is as follows.

"You see women are identified by their image more so than men, meaning the image of a woman can come to define her or imprison her. If she is an unwed mother of children, society has deemed this image to be that of a whore. Now, if a woman gets married to a man and has children, then this is an image of a fulfilled woman, regardless of her education, skills, or occupation. Now, a third scenario where a woman goes to school and pursues an education and a career.

"She does all of those things and finds that she is say 40 years old, but is single and has no children. Society has deemed this image of being successful in work, but at life she is a failure. This is not the same for men, where he may not get married while seeking his worldly pursuits, yet he is not seen as not having fulfilled a piece of his life. A man may have several wives

359

throughout the course of his life and not be seen as a failed husband, despite his behaviors. There are many, many different types and ideas of a woman, but the point that I am making is that women are not defined as men are by their achievements, but simply by their image as reflected by the mirror of society.

"What a complicated web of confusion it must be living in such a fashion. One is constantly having to define and then redefine themselves depending on their age, sexual activity, marital status, ability to have children, how many children they have had, education level, having a man, keeping a man, and or attracting further men. How on earth do women-kind keep from becoming dizzy within their own skins and minds?" The Man of the Present interrupted the serpent, saying.

"You're making it sound like women are constantly being victimized and men are always to blame. I've heard this kind of stuff before and it's nothing but a sob story."

"Well, how would you feel if everything about you was constantly being judged or questioned, not by your own standards, but by a fantasized idea of what you are supposed to be?" The serpent positioned his tail just underneath his chin looking down in inspection of the man.

"Regardless of your background, your abilities, or your goals. You are seen as either attractive, sexy, old, ugly, easy, sleazy, bitchy, or butch, and still those things are either good or bad depending on the scenario and the beholder behind the eye. There is an image, Man of the Present, which all of you tries to live up to, and that image is of the man or woman you want to be.

"However, the life of a woman is very difficult, especially when compared to the lives of men. You see you men have a clear list of what defines you, you either are that, or you're not. However, women also have a list of things, but they have a secondary role to fill called motherhood, which fundamentally changes who they are and how they are perceived. Whereas men go through no such physical or psychological change, which is why men retain the same set of standards throughout their lives. Women, however, have two sets of standards facing them whether or not they become mothers, they are still judged by those two stages as either before or after motherhood.

"There is an image of a girl approaching maturity for motherhood and then a completely different image of a woman after having reached the age of motherhood. The interesting thing again is that these images of women are placed on them whether or not they become a mother.

"Was it not Anaïs Nin, who said? 'Motherhood is a vocation like any other. It should be freely chosen, not imposed upon woman.' Now coming back to our Venus mirror, it becomes a little clearer how this actually does define the female gender. It's not some stereotypical idea of vanity, or any symbol of women's work, but truly it is the image of a woman, but more so how she is reflected in society that defines her. This is something that women have been fighting against since the beginnings of recorded time. I am reminded of the words of Oscar Wilde, 'A man's face is his autobiography. A woman's face is her work of fiction.' The serpent continued.

"When I look at you, my lady, I do not see a secondary member of human society, I see a component of desire and a force that drives all of life and the continuation of your species. You are woman and you should refuse to be seen as anything other than that. How the outside world tries to define you should be of no consequence, yet our shared reality is that we live in a man's world. I have serpent eyes and am not limited to any one man's view of you. If I were to shut my eyes and see with my subconscious mind, I would see a friend. You, woman, are the friend of humanity and as such, you signify the aspect of human personality that all admire, love, and wish to have near, yet it is often the same side that is rejected.

"One could then ask, what makes a person your friend? Surely a friend is someone who exemplifies or reflects a set of qualities one deems favorable. However, if mankind is to survive then this feminine side of him must be acknowledged and incorporated in order to become whole. For humanity, the relationships you form with each other are important to the growth and development of your individual selves and to your species.

"However, what occurs in the waking world is that this male society doesn't see his friend, he sees a sexual object to be owned and controlled as a commodity with which to be traded. More than most would hate to admit that there are feminine qualities within each of you. Which means that there is an aspect of humanity that you all are still trying to get to know. But still, humanity sees women as not their friend, not as their counterpart, and many women do not even see themselves as equals to men. The way human society treats women is like watching one's best friend die. And in the subconscious, when a friend dies, it is that quality within yourself that is being lost.

"Women are the aspect of humanity's waking life that man has lost touch with. What would happen if humanity were to see women as their best friend? Imagine what this world would be if humanity truly showed its appreciation for its women. Those rights and freedoms, those discretions and decisions that you withhold from them, in the name of protection and moral values. Think of how you demean them and weaken them, just know you weaken and harm yourselves by your own hand. From the beginning, women were there but not secondary in value, but second-coming like maturity after childhood. As in a boy becoming a man and becoming complete with the company of a woman.

"To fully embrace the female sides of itself, humanity would retain the sense of regression in human past and inner self where there are no rules. You seek her out, to capture her simple and carefree nature, for in her bosom you escape the pressures and stresses of life that leave you wanting. Consider her motherly touch and the lessons of love learned. Women are everything inside of desire and outside of rationality, and to see within them is to connect with the dream within yourselves. For they! For she! For you, my lady, are the woman... and are the dream of humanity."

"It is a lot to comprehend and it sounds nice when you put it that way, but still this is just the way things are. When I was young, I was just like every other girl. I didn't think I had anything to offer." she said, resituating herself.

"Tell me, what were your goals at that age?" I asked, striking a question in the air with my tail.

"I knew I wanted to get married and have kids, but mostly, I wanted to be independent and not have to be a burden on my family. For women, life is about everyone else. At first, it's find a man, then be a wife, then have kids, then it's all about the kids, then it's the man again; your life becomes about making their lives better."

"And what did you base this ideal on?

"Mostly the other women that I was around."

"Was all the advice presented to you like this?"

"No, some was very good and helpful. For instance, my mother-in-law told me to always keep some money aside that no one knows about. As a woman, you have to think about everyone all of the time, then think about them some more, and then what might happen to them after that."

"I thought thinking was banned for your kind?"

"What a horrible thing to say!" she replied, clasping her hands into fists, then clutching her gown.

"Apologies my lady, just a spot of bad humor! Ah! Now I remember... Orlando!" I recalled, snapping my tail as if it were two fingers.

"Orlando! Orlando whom? I do not believe I am familiar with said gentleman... is he too, seeking out a wife?" she implied, glancing left then back right at me.

"No, I mean the Biography Orlando. It was, or rather shall be penned by a Virginia Woolf. I am reminiscent of her words... 'As long as she thinks of a man, nobody objects to a woman thinking,'" I remarked, with humorous irony.

"Truly!" the widow seconded, leaning forward with gleaming acknowledgement.

"Indeed!" I acknowledged, wide eyed.

"It's not that I don't want those things, it's just, that's what everybody does and if you don't, you're considered a failure. Even now, I am without children and it feels like by the time I do have them, I'm going to be this old woman with these itty bitty little kids! I mean, most of my friends have children. I am no judge over them, but they insist on pressing me on when I am going to have children. As if having children is going out of style somehow! Funny thing is, I never turn around and ask them when they are going to get married."

"And what is their situation," I inquired.

"Well, they, or most of them, had children first then fell into their relationships afterwards. Some are together, some are not, while others are falling apart. I wish they would just leave me to my own, as I do not make judgments of them," she explained, crossing one leg over the other.

"And what would happen if you did say something in return?"

"Well, I would be the one who is rude, and of course I'm the asshole!"

"What would you say to them… hypothetically speaking of course?"

"Not to be mean, but I would say that they put the horse before the carriage, carrying on in such a way. Now, I'm sure a horse and carriage could be rigged in such a manner, and the horse be taught to push just as well as it can pull."

"But!" I quipped.

"But… what a silly sight that would be!" the widow remarked, and we shared a brief laugh.

"Why do you think most women feel that way?" I asked, dipping my tail into another question.

"Huge daddy issues! They feel invisible without the affirmation of a man," she said bluntly, bringing her hands out to the sides of her head showing a massive headache.

"For lots of women, their self-worth comes from the opinions of a man, and without that… we feel lost."

"Lost, but how so? If I were asking your male counterparts said same question, would they too be considered a failure? Hmm…?"

"Well I don't…" the widow stopped mid-sentence, just as I interjected quickly.

"Men are either hunters or fishermen while at it! Regardless of the size of their trophy or inability to capture said game... there's always an accompanying fish tale! Men are pretty much all the same, they hunt for play or play at hunting. 'The true man wants two things: danger and play. For that reason, he wants woman, as the most dangerous plaything.'- Friedrich Nietzsche

"Well I suppose I wanted other things too. I wanted a career and to travel, but there was still a feeling that if I wasn't able to get married, then I was incomplete," The widow further commented.

"And these were society's voices echoing inside you no doubt?" I asked in interrogation, pulling back in retrospect of the idea.

"Yes, that's just what it is, for most of us. And it wasn't to please a man, it was to have a man."

"Ahhhh! So it's more symbolic, than the truth of an actual satisfying relationship. More so like checking a mark in a box. Check, yes I have a man or am married. Forget about having a functional relationship or a partner who loves and communicates and respects you as their equal." I let out an extended sigh in understanding, then lowered my head back to eye level with the widow.

"Pretty much. It's just that you have to have a man, regardless if it's working or not, just that he's there. And now that I've lost that, I feel like I'm a failure."

"Even though you did nothing wrong to lose said departed husband?"

The widow replied, "Yes! I just feel like everyone is looking at me, like there was something else or more I could or should have done."

"No-no, no-no, no-no, no... you really couldn't have! I mean I was surprised myself that I even spit him back out! Oh! And that's not what you were talking about..." I said unknowingly, then caught myself in a stutter of bad humor over the widow's departed husband.

"So I have to say, you did pretty damn good to hold on to him! You have already been married once, so do you really need to get married again? And my goal is not to push you towards or away from anything. If that is what you really want, then by all means, say I do. However, if it is only to appease society's view of you, then to hell with them people."

"It's just, well I'd like to have children and be married again… that's all. I sometimes daydream of my perfect match and of finding true love. You wouldn't understand. You being so… unsociable," she remarked, looking away at her hands and feet.

"I! Am! Not! Unsociable! I will have you know I lead quite the active lifestyle," I retorted in defense, with a high-pitched tone.

"I'm sorry, I didn't mean to be offensive. I just don't want to seem all… man hungry." She defended, shushing away at my feelings.

"Man hungry! What's wrong with being man hungry? Why I am quite frequently man hungry! As a matter of fact, I just so happened to be in such a state the other day, and found the last three men I feasted upon to be quite satisfactory…" The widow's eyes enlarged then she folded her arms and began tapping her foot in dismay of my words regarding her departed husband. I quickly realized my error and quickly backtracked my previous remark.

"… and that's not what you were talking about was it! I did it again, didn't I? I'm going to stop talking now! Let's move on!" I gasped, in error of my own literal mistake.

"You are forgiven!" The widow rolled her eyes then turned her head away.

"Begging your pardon, my lady, I meant no disrespect… Now! Where were we… ahh yes! Catching a husband! I think I've got it." With ease I altered my accent and began speaking with a heavy twangy, high-pitched, back-woodsy, Texas-California drawl resembling that of rodeo performer and actor 'Slim Pickens.

"Now, I'm no expert on matrimony, however I just so happen to be more than familiar with the subject than I previously let on. Now, I don't know much about getting and staying married to a man, but in sit-chi-ations like this, you gotta use what you know! And darlin', I do know about catching and keeping snakes! And both subjects just so happen to be called... Husbandry! I'm thinking that the two can't be too dissimilar.

"Why plenty of husbands, at one point or another have been accused of being a low down, slimy, sleazy snake from time to time. You can pretty much find a man in about the same whereabouts like underneath a rock, or rustling around in sum low-lyin' brush, or, or, or... well now, just the other day I happened across a feller I haven't seen since grade school! Yes ma'am, and if he didn't have on a pair of the most fashionable lookin' trousers I've ever seen on a sidewinder! Well, darlin' it looks like we gonna have you sorted out in no time! Now, let's get a few thangs straight first. Number one, get ta know your snake!

"You gotta know everything you can about their species, especially if you want to keep one in your home. Now some are very territorial, while others are quite comfortable being around others, but be careful cause some can be deadly! Some can be a bit nippy and if he do give ya a bite, you can take a stick and whack em' over the head with it! It's alright now see, cause they're made a' rubber and they can't feel a damn anything anyhow. But if he get real mean on ya, then well you grab a hold a nice flat rock and bash him with it till he turns up dead... he'll probably look better wrapped around ya waist anyhow.

"Now diet is key, and with the exception of insect eaters, you can just about feed em' anything you like. But now chicken feed just won't do! And you've got ta understand some of them critters are picky eaters, while others are complete pigs. Some will do alright on a diet of fish or chicken, while others prefer frogs and salamanders, but you really can't go wrong with a nice juicy rodent! Remember now, they do get a little anxious when it's feedin' time, so watch your fangers! Once bitten... twice shy!

"Now I prefer live kill ma-self, but some will get used to frozen foods, but again now that's your choice what cha feed em! But err on the side a caution, cause if it's too large, it could cause him to regurgitate, or worse it'll get stuck part of the way down, and it'll cause the somma-bitch ta burst! I've seen it! Ha!

Ha! Ha! Ha! Ha! Ha! Ha! Ha! … Yes ma'am! I've seen it! He'll be looking worse off than your last fella was back over yonder! Ha Ha! Ha! Ha! Ha! Ohh… uh! Uh! Umm! Cancel that! M-mm… moooving on!

"Now darlin, this part's important to ya! Once you've got your victim… I mean your pet, your… uh, uh mate, interested, if you wanna get things moving you gotta turn up the heat! Nobody likes a floppy boa! I mean they get all deflated and saggy looking, then the next thing you know he's rolled over dead on ya! You make sure you set your cage up before you bring the little feller in there too, then you want to keep the temp around ahhh… oh! Sempty-five… a good eighty-aught and-uh five degrees or so. You do that, and he'll come on up and start peeking his little head on up outta there, Ha! Ha! Ha! Ha! Ha!

"But watch it now! Cause most folks get lazy-like and let thangs cool off! You drop the humidity in thar' and he'll wiggle on up outta there. Yes ma'am! He'll get to runnin faster than molasses in May! Them little bastards is known escape artists and then its hell tryin'a get em' back once he's been out and about! Now husbandry's not too difficult, but folks are always makin' thangs harder than what it's suppose-ta be.

"Simple notion is, if you wanna keep a snake you gotta think like a snake! You keep him in a nice container, and you make sure it's got a locking lid on it. And don't forget to keep his area nice and clean and free from any debris so he don't get hung-up in there. And uh, scoop up his poop every now and then, and uh. Any nice natural substrate will do. You can try cypress, or moss, or wood shavings, or paper clippings, or bark. I'm, I'm, I'm fond a' mulch myself.

"And now, everybody always gets this one wrong! But behav-u-ral modification is to be avoided! Now darlin' I've heard it all before, 'Oh I won't be that way!' But you'd just be wastin' your time anyway, purty lady. Us reptile types ain't too good at domes-ta-ma-faction. Now a good rule of thumb to go by is you bag him, you bought him! Just remember husbandry takes just about as much effort as you would with keeping any pet. You keep him well fed and lock up after him, you shouldn't have no problems. And you should get-a-good 10 or 20 years out of him, fore he roll over dead on ya!" The widow starred expressionless only nodding in shock, then replied kindly.

"Well I, I… I have to say, I … well I've never heard it put quite that way before. I will… I will definitely try to keep that in mind and I do thank you for kind words, Serpent."

"Think nothing of it my lady… happy hunting!" I ended my advice and returned to my normal speaking voice, smiling.

"I must be getting some sleep now Serpent, the new day will be calling in no time. I just pray the Creator will provide me sustenance as I have no means of employment," she said while beginning to walk away.

"Those who seek work shall find it, regardless of status of station. There are fields here of plenty and they seek workers daily."

"But women are not permitted to do such work."

"It is more important to know one's worth and know that you can do anything regardless of the social norms. Now, in the morning go out to the fields and approach the foreman and negotiate wages for a day's work. Until tomorrow my lady."

"The next morning the widow ate breakfast with her mother in law, and was asked what her plans were. The widow said she would go out and find work to earn wages for the both of them.

"What work will you find in this place? Only men are permitted out and to work on their own, besides I will not permit harlots in my home," the mother-in-law said sternly.

"Be at peace my mother, I am no whore, yet I shall earn enough for the both of us." That night, the woman was tired and laid her head down to rest, but I called to her again in the night.

"I saw you out in the fields today, you were quite a sight to see."

"Thank you Serpent, I heeded your words and went out and joined the workers gleaning in the fields. A few of the men mocked at a woman going to work alongside them. I said nothing and continued keeping pace with the other workers. At first, a watchman told me to go away and that I would not be permitted to work there as it was against custom for women to work alongside men."

"And what did you say to that?"

"I told him I needed not anyone's permission to work as the Creator has made me able to task just as they do."

"And what was your punishment for doing such a thing?"

"Actually, I was not punished and at the end of the day, all the workers gathered to obtain pay for their daily wages. The owner of the fields asked who I was as he had observed me in the fields. The other workers then spoke well of me and noted that I worked the whole day without rest or break. The owner approached and thanked me for my hard work and paid me plus the overtime."

"I'm very proud for you," I said graciously.

"Thank you. It was then that the owner of the fields offered me a job working inside and out of the heat. I accepted the position and purchased food and fabrics and surprised my mother this evening."

"You knew your value and were not swayed by the intimidation of others. They will always speak against you, but it is you who must make the effort regardless of them. No matter how many times they say no to you, you must continue in your pursuit and eventually they will do right by you."

"Thank you Serpent, but I still have no husband. What good is a woman with money, but no husband?" she replied, shrugging her shoulders.

"Have you heard nothing I have said to you?" I replied, shaking my head.

"I suppose it is the nature of humans to seek the companionship of their opposite. What is it you seek in a companion?"

"Well, I wish to serve him as his wife."

"If he requires a servant he can purchase one, if he requires a wife he must court one. The two are completely different things. Mind the mirror, my lady. Make yourself into the reflection of the image you wish in a companion, then it will appear unto you."

"I do not understand," she replied in confusion.

"Well, if you seek a companion of wealth and money, then make yourself into the reflection of that. If you wish a companion of kindness and compassion, then make yourself into that. People do not realize that they attract each other based more by their actions than their words. People attract insanity into their lives as well by their own doing. People attract wealth and money into their lives by the same as well. However, be careful seeking after money and a materialistic lifestyle, which will lead you on a path of emptiness and with a heart that can never be fulfilled."

"How do you mean? Is not a wealthy lifestyle the wish of everyone?"

"Look at it this way. If you pursue only money, then that is what you shall receive. However, where is the love in money? Where is the kindness and compassion? Where is the trust and honesty? Money has no need for such things. The purpose of money is to buy things and there are some things that money cannot buy... especially the truth."

"If not wealth, if not beauty, then what? A kitten of a man who cries and runs at the first sign of labor or danger?"

"No, what I mean is make yourself a reflection of what you wish to attract and surely your match will meet you, just like looking in a mirror. Make yourself kind and compassionate as such things are truly beautiful. Work, save, plan, and be fiscally responsible as such a thing is respectable. Be the person that society is too afraid to acknowledge and others will admire you.

"Be the type of companion you wish to have and you will find yourself with such a match. But I warn you... be mindful of the mirror. The things you love, the things you hate; the goals you make, the vices you crave, and your ideal type of mate, are all reflections of you. I say again... be mindful of the mirror, for truly... it reflects the real you."

"It sounds like you want to make me into something that no man wants," she remarked, flopping down seated.

"No, I want you to be the best you that you can be. Those who say they do not want such a woman are just afraid, because

371

they themselves are too weak to stand next to her. Be not worried about a husband, they come and go, but you will be with you forever. Besides, if you wish to be a wife and eventually mother, why would you go into the position ill-equipped.

Women waste more time painting their face when they should be feeding their head. They spend more time evaluating their bodies when they should be strengthening them. Society teaches women to be weak, which then puts you into a position where you must be the complete opposite of that. I swore not to lead you wrong and I continue to honor my vow to you, my lady. I assure you my words are sound and come without bias or prejudice."

"Yes, but I have not the money for schooling and cannot afford an exercise regimen," she replied, glancing away, then shaking her head no.

"Neither requires an expensive training routine. Use what is available to you. There are books a plenty and are available for free, eat them daily and grow strong. Choose foods and drink that strengthen your body and do not merely satisfy an urge. Train yourself with proper exercise, speak with dignity, and carry yourself with respect. You shall always be what you are, but no matter what... always be at your best. It is unfair for society to decide what makes a woman's life complete or fulfilled, simply by her ability to meet some tribal, cultural, or traditional sexual rights as opposed to her deciding her own ideas of success.

"Be as the rose amongst thorns, be as the candle in the night, glowing in a sea of darkness. Think then how you will shine so brightly. For you can do as you please, as it is your natural rights as the Creator hath made all of you!" The widow bid goodnight and we parted company for the night. I watched her working the following days, then again called to her one evening while she rested.

"I thank you for your words Serpent, they were unlike any that I have heard before. Since the days past, I have gained the attention of the owner of the fields. However, my mother has instructed me to lay at his feet in order to gain his affection, however I question this method."

"Nothing is more desirable than the thing one cannot have. If you make yourself into a thing which every man already has, you will be ordinary and worthless. Make yourself into the thing that they do not have but truly want. A woman of intelligence, a woman of strength, a woman of dignity and respect. Let me ask you, do you wish to remain at this person's feet for the rest your days?"

"No, I hope that we will be wedded as man and wife."

"Then I suggest you do not start your relationship that way. Your behavior tells people how to treat you. Know your own value and worth, as you will only accept what you feel you deserve. Prosperity is with the brave and those who are unafraid to seek out new opportunities. Surely, better things are in the winds for you. However, there is a great power that you women do wield, for you embody the Eros. The life instincts and prosocial behaviors of humanity are within each of you.

"The instincts that drive humanity toward survival, pleasure, and reproduction are within you. Without women, all of humanity would simply cease to exist. Women are the drive of humanity. You are what they eternally seek. Now not to be confused with the libido, which too describes a drive but more generally the sexual drive. We are focusing more on the totality of the psyche combined with the sexual energies."

"Still, I would love to have babies! A family would be quite splendid, don't you think?" She remarked, folding her hands over her heart.

"Oh the eros, up ther-os! How nice it must be; head in the trees, thinking of nothing but the birds and the bees... C'est la vie!" I said in rhyme.

"May I ask you my lady, why do you want to have children? It seems that there are already so many children in the world today. So many with so little, so few who will ever truly grow? So many overgrown children, babies upon babies, even babies having babies. I have lived longer than most and what I see is a lot a naked, frightened, grabby-takey, screaming little things. I wonder, has it ever occurred to any of you, that perhaps what this place needs... is some adult supervision."

"You don't think I should have children?" She asked frowning with concern.

"Oh no, that's not what I mean at all. It really makes no difference to me, day to day... it's all the same buffet!" the serpent said with humorous irony.

"I was thinking of you a few days ago and I recalled a conversation I had with the ghost of woman past. They are only reflections now speaking to their former selves in a mirror, saying... 'You don't need a man to be happy, you don't need children to be happy, take more time for yourself.' Sound advice, but mirrors are not microphones, although they communicate more lies and aged shattered dreams.

"No matter how modern the day's society, the Venus mirror still symbolizes the female, and unfortunately having a man and kids still defines a woman's worth? It may be impossible to set the mirror down, as maybe men and woman are just hard wired that way. However, I would like those women like you to know, that it is not society that holds the mirror... it is you. Therefore, it is you who defines the image of the woman that you choose to be. I hope my counsel brings you good fortune my lady, but I feel I have run out of words."

"Will you be leaving me now Serpent?"

"I think I should be getting on my way."

"Before you go, please have some coffee with me."

"It's not that instant crap is it? I can't stand that mess..." I remarked, shaking my head in disgust.

"Oh, No! I make it fresh. You will enjoy it! It is a tradition amongst my people, a ceremony if you will." The widow then began a ritualized process of preparing and serving coffee. The widow explained that the Coffee Ceremony was performed with close visiting friends, during festivities, or as a daily staple among neighbors. She first began by roasting the coffee beans over hot coals in a brazier. While doing so, she told of her childhood and shared her memories of growing up. She then removed the now roasted beans and began to grind them with a mortar and pestle. The grounded coffee beans were then transferred into a black clay coffee pot called a 'jabens.' The coffee pot the widow served from had been given to her by her mother-in-law, and she said she was honored to have received it as it was a family heirloom.

"Once you are married, I do hope you are able to avoid any form of coverture my lady. As I would hate to see such a priceless heirloom become subsumed by a newly acquainted husband. These are exceedingly dark times for woman-kind. I wish you strength and patience to see you through it," I said, taking hold of the clay coffee pot for closer inspection.

"The widow completed brewing and strained the coffee three times in accordance with tradition with the third time offering a blessing. As the host, she poured the aromatic coffee into two small cups. To which she then offered sugar, but no milk or cream, to which I accepted and we fully enjoyed our drinks.

"What shall we drink to?" asked the widow holding her cup before her.

"That's a good question! I've never shared such an intimate occasion between acquaintances."

"Coffee ceremony is an integral part of my culture's life and being invited is considered a mark of friendship and great respect. I hope you will accept and remember this as an example of our encounter and my hospitality."

I then recited, 'She opens her mouth with wisdom, and the teaching of kindness is on her tongue.' Indeed, I shall my lady."

"The widow offered some sweet breads, dates, and nuts to accompany the coffee, to which I accepted and delighted in.

"Yet it seems strange that we two should be here enjoying one another's company. It almost feels like we should be in opposition to one another," the serpent said after sipping his coffee.

"It is an odd pairing, me sharing coffee with you. Some would say that we should despise one another. But then again, this is my life and I choose my own company," She answered.

"What is your idea of happiness, my lady?"

"Creativity! Being free to allow my intuition to drive my choices instead of worry and fear! And to you, Serpent. What is your idea of happiness?" she asked, raising her cup in my name.

375

"To be at peace. If ever it were possible to return to a state of simplicity… organic simplicity that is. As in being suspended completely, in an inanimate state. I think that would be happiness.

"I have encountered so many humans throughout my life and I am constantly curious about the views of one's mortality. I don't mean to frighten you with this question, but if you believe in an afterlife, what would heaven be like for you?"

"Afterlife! Good heavens, I'm still working on this one!" We shared a brief chuckle together.

"I say, if there is a heaven… I would like to spend it just like this!"

"You don't mean sitting across from me, my lady! That wouldn't be much of a heaven! You would find yourself eternally bored back to life!" I said laughingly leaning towards her.

"No silly! Like… this! For me… heaven, would be good conversation and good coffee… eternally!" she explained, patting me once slightly.

"I like that! That's not a bad way to spend eternity at all…" I smiled and nodded, then completed the coffee and appetizers.

"Now, I believe I must be bidding you farewell, my lady. The time is getting late and I believe you have some work of your own to attend to."

"Oh my! Oh my word! But where are my manners!" the widow gasped putting a hand in front of her mouth. "How silly of me!" She clutched her hands together quickly placing the coffee cup down, then resting her hands on her lap in front of her.

"What wrong? Have I done something?" I replied expediently looking in confusion.

"No! I just forgot the most important part of a conversation… the introductions!"

"My… lady! Well… you know who I am, but I have not had the pleasure of knowing your name?" I sighed with delight, then the widow introduced herself politely.

"My name is Doris. Doris Ruth, and it was a pleasure to meet you…"

TRUTH AND THE SERPENT

CHAPTER 10:

"Of one who hath started so small, it would be she whose name was risen and admired within the heavens, for surely the blood of kings flowed throughout her. I was left with a lasting impression of the widow and every once and again, I find myself seated at a cozy café reminiscing of her warm smile. She was exclusively unique, so much so like that perfect cup of coffee; slowly roasted and poured over captivating conversation... heavenly and hard to find.

"But unfortunately my cup had runneth dry and I began hearing rumors of the believers and the mobile Vanguard, which carried the Testimony of the Creator within it. When I left the presence of Law Giver, I thought that would be the last I would see or hear of them for some time. But, in fact, it was I who would go back on my word and seek them out again.

"Yet sadly, it was as I had predicted and Law Giver had lost himself in his precious people. By then he laid buried in that accursed land of Moab, from whence I put my back to. His final words to his people would be their instruction to seek out the Land of Conquest and to seize it as their own. Before he rested, he placed the believers under the leadership of a strong and noble man known as Soterio, for he was to be their liberation from suffering and ignorance. I did not know it at the time, but coming into contact with the believers again would bring me into the presence of a young hero and a most beloved king. He was the cusp between the two eras of anointed kings and shadows that would haunt humanity for the rest of its days. Heroism would forever be adjoined with his name, but the true legacy of a hero is the battle against his greatest foe… and enemy!

"The tales of the mobile Vanguard grew with every telling but most importantly, it was the Testimony of the Creator which led the rumors. Under the leadership of Soterio, the believers were a mobilized unit and everywhere they went, nothing stood before them. When I located them, they had been wandering some forty years in the wilderness. And there, they camped just outside the Moon City in the Land of Canaan; just before Soterio and his eleven spies entered the city under cover of night before making their attack.

"The city was inhabited by a pagan civilization and was named for its lunar deity. The Moon City had become choice property due to the natural irrigation flowing down from the Jordan River, making it a virtual oasis in itself. It had been settled on the low-lying lands of the desert, but was teeming with plant life and greenery in an otherwise barren desert. The city's natural barriers were circumvallated and were the result of natural seismic activity that produced a great rift extending from the Sea of Galilee to Northern Africa. The tremendous walls created a rampart that were bounded by Mount Nebo to the east and the Central Mountains to the west and the Sea of the Dead to the south, with the Moon City in the center. The walls, as they were called, were actually mountains that reached up a mile high, making the location key if one were trying to establish control over the region.

"This well guarded location also isolated the Moon City from its neighbors, but gave relatively easy access to the southern areas of Jerusalem, Bethlehem, and Nazareth. And due to the envy over the choice location, the people constructed additional walls and towers for fortification. I found it strange, though that the believers who had wandered for decades now found themselves up against a seemingly impenetrable fortress. From once they were lost and now they were found, but facing heavily fortified walls. I watched them without becoming involved, but I wondered; of all the roads and paths they could have taken, why now were these walls confronting them?

"In the waking world, a wall is a wall. But when I close two of my eyes, my third pineal eye opens, allowing me to see that they had reached their limitations and a final obstacle and boundary was set before them. The giant walls were a physical representation that the believers were too accustomed to living in their old habits and back facing ways. You see, walls are a blockade in the path of life. I suppose by anointing Soterio as their leader, they had temporarily addressed their ignorance and backsliding. But they did not circumvent the structure nor did they leap over it cleanly. That would have meant success and ease in dealing with their underlying issues and problems. No, their solution was a violent method and without siege engine did they break down fortified walls, and so did they overcome their adversity and wandering.

"Through the direction of Soterio, perhaps freedom from ignorance and idolatry was finally at hand. And then I saw something that frightened me to my core. Soterio gave a command to the believers, and I thought they would attack in standard military formation, but they raised no arrow or spear towards the fortifications of the Moon City. Their forces went round the Moon City with the Testimony of the Creator out in front followed by priests and then the congregation of them all. They circled the city walls once a day for six days then on the seventh day did they go round sevenfold, and when they did they blew their ram's horns and released a mighty shout! Then I did see them walls come a tum-tum-tumbling down.

"The mountain rampart walls fell after they encircled the Moon City a total of 13 times. Interestingly enough, their movements mimicked the orbiting of the moon, which encircles the earth approximately 13 times in a single year. As strong as the mountainous walls were, nothing could withstand the almighty power of the Testimony of the Creator and they fell like paper sticks so easily upon themselves. Soterio's forces took no slaves nor plunder and slaughtered all who walked, crawled, or were cradled. They spared nothing, save for one, she the turncoat unclean whore that sheltered Soterio and his spies. It is true what they say, history is written by the victors and prostitutes can be risen to that of war-time ally. In what other circumstances would have seen her stoned, but she was the wiser, and the mirror was kind unto her.

"The Moon City was utterly destroyed and the believer's forces devoted their attack to the total destruction of everything. In the hour of their victory, what would normally be regarded as spoils, was burned out and the land purified bringing the week-long campaign to an end."

The Man of the Present interrupted by asking, "I don't understand, why that troubled you? They won right? They broke down the walls and they defeated their enemies. That's what they were supposed to do."

"If only it were that simple, Man of the Present. You see, the believers were given the Testimony of the Creator by Law Giver. It was they who built the chest that housed it and sealed it with the Seat of Grace. And in that chest was the physical words of the Creator, and as close to the awesome purity of the Creator as ever been seen before on earth. However, the Testimony of the Creator in the chest was now a thing of power and like any object of power in the hands of man, it inevitably becomes a weapon." I looked on saying, who of any can determine why the death and appalling slaughter of humanity breeds seemingly endless applause? Yet there is no sickening regurgitation at the sight and utter thought of war and the intentional use of weapons of mass destruction."

"You're saying they made it into a weapon?"

"No. I said, it became a weapon. There's a difference!" The serpent rolled his tail forward, in a hand over hand motion to reassert his point.

"The Testimony of the Creator is 100% pure and is unlike any other object known to man. In a sense, you could say it was weapons grade, meaning its elemental properties are sufficiently rich, which makes it particularly suitable as a weapon similar to enriched plutonium or uranium. Both are very strong and generate high amounts of energy and if located in its purist form, it can be made destructive. However, the Testimony of the Creator does not need to undergo any chemical reactive process. Once in the chest, it could be aimed according to the will of the bearer. The issue then becomes knowing how to wield it."

"So what's wrong with that?" the man asked, shrugging his shoulders in dismissal.

"That's not what it was meant for. It was meant to be a guide for all of humanity. I say again, I do not know why the Creator made you all in such a way, because it seems that humans have an insatiable thirst for power and a need for more. It seems none of you will know satisfaction of it.

"Look at it this way, all elements and chemicals were created and exist on their own in nature to some degree. Some are gases, while other are liquids or solids. These elements can combine naturally or synthetically to become different compounds. However, some require intent or manipulation to combine and take form, such as creating bronze or iron. The resulting iron can form tools, utensils, machinery, or even vitamins. The difference is how the elements are utilized. Now, the elemental and chemical properties of it remains the same, but what has changed is how it will be used.

"At one point in time, such things happened and gave rise to the first knives, swords, spears, guns, and bombs. And then no longer were humans engaging in simple tribal battles, but full scale modern world warfare. All along, they were the same elements with the same power and ability, but in the hands of man, those elements became a deadly weapon. I do not know why but I have seen it over and over, again and again. I repeat myself and say, any object of power in the hands of man... ultimately becomes a weapon.

"And that's what I saw there on that day. The Testimony of the Creator had been encapsulated, mobilized, then was placed at the head of their marching army, thus it had become a weapon. And once you weaponized something, it can never be undone."

"That's not true, the process of weaponizing can be reversed, or so I think. They can take something like a bomb and through chemical process, repurpose it into useable energy," he said with a pointed finger.

"That's not what I mean. Take for instance a bomb... sure it can be disarmed and possibly reutilized or repurposed. But once this force has been realized and utilized, the intent can never be undone. What that means is, from then on, others will want to make their own bombs and try to have that level of power in their arsenal as well. So the idea of that weapon can never be undone, and I recite, 'A weapon does not decide whether or not to kill. A weapon is a manifestation of a decision that has already been made.' - Steven Galloway

"What I saw then was what ultimately compelled me to act. For there, in the hands of man, the Testimony of the Creator had become twisted and was made destructive. The Testimony of the Creator had become 'a thing of wiping out' and if left to the whims of man, there's no telling what destruction it could unleash. I knew then what I had to do. I had to get it away from them somehow... someway!" The serpent became quiet staring into the memory of his mind.

"You were going to steal the Ark?" he asked with an accusatory tone.

"No! I had no intention of keeping it for myself. My goal was to remove it from them and hide it until a suitable owner be deemed worthy," the serpent stated, glancing quickly once to the left at the man.

"But why would you do that?"

"For the same reason you take a loaded gun away from a child. Because they will hurt themselves or others, all the while thinking it was just a game!" the serpent, said staring directly at the man.

"You are like so many children playing with deadly weapons of mass destruction. It looks harmless and perhaps you feel entitled to it, as it was left out and not locked up safely out of your little reaches. Only those who fully understand and respect it should have access to such things, but unfortunately, humanity is of the type that's slow to remember and quick to forget.

"The believers had just spent some forty years wandering aimlessly in the desert for their disobedience and disbelief. And just like that... they are now suitable to wield the destructive word of the Creator? Not likely! I had to get it away from them. For soon, all would know of the destructive powers of the Testimony of the Creator and all who seek power would seek it out to bear before their armies. The ways of mankind are wicked and devious and think only of destruction and terror. Man leads not with love, but by fear and his path to victory is destruction.

"There was no other option. Perhaps over time, another would be selected by the Creator to care for it. It was the only way I could be sure of its safety, but how to claim it? The believers kept constant watch over it day and night and it was kept in a separate dwelling place for its divine presence. Earlier, I had surmised burrowing a tunnel and carrying it beneath the ground, but I am no mole rat thief. I was set upon my course of action with surety as I believed it to be in all correctness. Patience, I said... patience and endurance to tolerate the daily troubles of these people in order to save billions from suffering and war. Patience, for the opportunity would surly present itself and all I needed do... was be patient." the serpent continued.

"After the sack of the Moon City, the believers marched another nine miles east to the Royal City of Canaan. The Royal City rested atop a watershed plateau and overlooked the Jordan Valley in what is known today as Et-Tell. Although they marched on the city with the Testimony of the Creator, they were met with defeat upon their first attempt and suffered some thirty-six lives. Soterio held a council meeting amongst the elders and military captains after the failed assault, but ultimately, they turned on each other in blame and soon pulled out one to bear the punishment for their failed siege. The accused, known as 'He that Troubleth', was pulled out from the masses, and along with his children and livestock, was thus stoned clean of sin.

"The following morning, Soterio set up an ambush on the

western side towards the rear of the city. Soterio used a feigned retreat tactic whereby the believers pretended to withdraw from the front of the city drawing the royal troops out and into a position of vulnerability; where their remaining forces were waiting towards the rear of the city to ambush them.

"Victory was theirs and the Royal City was set ablaze and thus left a 'Heap of Ruins' Unfortunately for the King of the Royal City, his fate was not stayed as he was impaled on a pike under the moon for their pagan god to admire. He suffered for days in agony with gravity slowly splintering the pike up inside him until finally dying of internal bleeding and exposure. From there on, Soterio was able to lead the believers on to several more victories, until securing much of the Land of Conquest in the name of the Creator.

"I continued tracking them in shadow all those years, still watching and waiting as I plotted pilferage of the Testimony of the Creator. Soterio was a valiant and righteous man, and fulfilled his vow to both Law Giver and the Creator. He instructed each tribal leader to remain faithful to the laws of the Creator and warned them of harsh punishment, lest the believers leave the righteous path. As a witness of their promise to serve only the Creator, Soterio set up a great stone under a tree and named it 'Sanctuary of the Creator.' Soon afterward, he died and was buried in the hill country north of Mount Gaash. He ended his days with a telling of all the great works the Creator had done for them and of the need for them to live in wholeness. Soterio performed one last ceremony of prayer and offerings before departing the believers in death.

"Unfortunately, the time that followed the believers was a repeating wave of faithlessness and judgment which came to be known as the 'Age of Arbitration.' The Creator saw the believers through a time of blindness and repeated mistakes. Each time they sinned, the Creator issued them aid in the form of hero and heroine to steer them clear of smashing on the rocks of their own deeds.

"The Creator had saved them and brought them out of the centuries of oppression and freedom from the Panopticon. Yet and still, in their ways, they were naughty children and saw the Judges as overbearing parents to whom they feared reprisal only after getting caught misbehaving. Openly did they mock the Creator and thus were they delivered into the hands of their enemies. Their tears, however, did not fall deafly upon the earth, but they rose upward to the Heavens where the Creator's mercy fell upon them again and again. And each time, a hero was anointed to judge and deliver them out of their calamity and for a time, peace returned unto them. But the believers were a stiff-necked people and were tidally locked in their ways and continuously showed the same deceitful face unto the Creator.

"The Age of Arbitration was a time of continuous struggle and onslaught and a people going nowhere are truly lost. Back and forth, up and down, it was nonsensical to see such stupidity. I do not know what you call such purposeful ignorance. Perhaps they felt entitled to salvation, similar to how an infant feel obliged to suckle at the teat. Even so, there comes a time when the screaming kid must be weaned… and the time was long overdue. Now, to separate the over grown child, called man, from infancy and teach him to walk upright and behave accordingly.

"The believers had now planted themselves in the Land of Conquest and still the Testimony of the Creator was in its resting place and it remained guarded day and night. I had not given up on my plan to remove it, but I would have to bide my time to quietly retrieve it. I am eternally patient and would do exactly that, so I stayed near and followed when it migrated to the land of Shiloh. And it was there that we would determine, 'The One to Whom it Belongs.'

"Things quieted down for a bit and the current elder known as 'Ascent' was aging and his sons followed not in his ways. I watched as Ascent dealt lightly with his sons and regarded their behavior as mere flippancy.

"I looked down upon Ascent's two sons enjoying their inheritance, while others worked diligently, sacrificed, and saved. I heard another priest say to Ascent that his sons would be punished for their ways and that a bad omen loomed over his house and his sons would die before reaching old age. I was unsure of what would occur after this elder declined in leadership, but I felt a change in the winds and knew that my opportunity was close at hand.

"By this time, the faith of the believers had deteriorated into a state of disorder and chaos. Their petty conflicts further spilled over and they were unprepared before the Creator and their weakness showed. 'Those of Another Tribe' had observed the Land of Conquest as a choice region worth exploiting as their own and made good their reconnaissance and ascertained the lands strategic features. At first Those of Another Tribe introduced themselves as friendly, but came with hidden intent to infiltrate the land. Then, once Those of Another Tribe felt they had worked the believers into a false sense of superiority, they taunted them and challenged their borders.

"Each noble house of the believers armed themselves and raised banners, and behold a flimsy faithless force went out, unprepared to face them. Those of Another Tribe correctly camped near water resources in Aphek, and the believers occupied the stony grounds in Eben-ezer. Those of Another Tribe were better equipped then moved into range and then attacked. The believers were driven back and crushed under the heels of their enemies within half a day's battle.

"Then the sun dipped low and was steeped in the horizon and the heavy clangor of swords quieted. The shouting and slaughter of battle was replaced by the moaning of injury and the laughter of tears. The battlefield was heavily watered by the believer's blood and their bodies were food for scavenger dogs. They left the bodies of their brethren undressed and alone in the night and preserved not their burial rights. The day's battle resulted in defeat leaving some four thousand believers dead along with their shattered pride and faith.

"The believers had lost and were defeated in their own Land of Conquest as punishment for their idolatry and sin. They returned to their camps and each noble house petitioned their priests to convene with Ascent to bring the Testimony of the Creator out onto the battlefield as it was their greatest weapon and their true strength. '

"It was only a matter of time until the Testimony of the Creator was brought out to wage war before them. The Testimony of the Creator was paraded through their camps the following evening. They, being of a proud and arrogant nature, sent runners with message to Those of Another Tribe. The message called for their surrender, and was reinforced with the threat of their 'prompt and utter destruction by a means greater than any weapon known to man.'

"The believers were confident that the Testimony of the Creator would garner them triumph as it had gifted them numerous victories. They code named the Testimony of the Creator the 'Little Box' and their military tacticians estimated that the power it emitted could level five square miles and wipeout twenty thousand with one emission.

"That night, the believers ate hearty and drank themselves into a confident stupor well into the night. But the following morning, Those of Another Tribe were not fled from the battlefield and were again set up in contest against them. The believers called out and had the Little Box brought forth and set up on a small hill overlooking the field of battle. My eyes smiled and I thanked the Creator that day, as I knew that only the Creator could do something like this. For the Testimony of the Creator had been brought out in the open and was only some hundred yards away from me.

"The believers prepared to attack and they shouted with a voice of confidence as they hoisted the Little Box before them. They could hear Those of Another Tribe shouting as fear began to creep in amongst them slowly and then, one by one, their armor began to rust and their shields began to shrink, and their swords started to dull. I could see retreat in their eyes and it would only take a few broken ranks for the entire army to crumble. Their captains shouted company arrangements, but the shouting of the believers was confident for all to see.

"I circled quickly behind them camouflaging myself and called out loudly, 'Be strong and quiet yourselves, oh army of men. It was you who slayed these pretenders just yesterday.

Behold! Their God has left them long ago and has delivered the Little Box to you as a prize. Quiet your worry and delay your fears for they are divided within themselves and shall shatter easily against your shields.'

"As I shouted to the army, I could see Ascent from the opposing hillside. He was blind of eye, but somehow he looked directly at me and he could see me! His eyes were agape and he gasped in horror as he saw me encouraging Those of Another Tribe against the believers. He screamed out to the believers to stop, as they marched into battle, but it was too late.

"What followed was only the most disastrous military defeat recorded in the history of all the believer's battles. The believers were not only defeated, but the Testimony of the Creator had been taken as they fled the field. The believers, who had been defeated just the day before, did not re-equip their forces nor change their strategy of attack or defense. They received their just punishment in the form of a thorough spanking, which cost them an approximate thirty thousand lives.

"They believed that the Testimony of the Creator would strike down Those of Another Tribe and leave them blinded and cowering while they easily finished them off. Yet, nothing could have been further from the truth. Those of Another Tribe were heavily armed and took not their previous victory as a guarantee. They re-equipped themselves and made their reinforcements ready to flank the believers and mounted their cavalry with spear, pike, sword, and shield. The believers were only saved from complete annihilation as they had no armor and those who ran were quicker than their attackers who stayed to finish fileting the fallen.

"I shouted to Those of Another Tribe to capture the Little Box as they looted and plundered the field, and they did just that. The Testimony of the Creator was now safely out of the possession of the believers, and I had half completed my task. Enormous loss and uncountable casualty was the name of the day and the buzzards were the proud recipients of a battlefield feast.

"The elder Ascent, who had many years about him, was then

notified by a messenger that his two wayward sons had been slain that day in battle. As he dropped to his knees, the messenger accompanied him and began sobbing in additional remorse. The messenger's words were dry and stuck to the roof of his mouth, while trying to speak. Ascent begged the young man to complete his words and tell him the entirety of the day's news. The messenger said, 'But my Lord…. The strength, the light, the hope of our people has left us! To our utter shame and defeat, The Testimony of the Creator has been taken by Those of Another Tribe.

"Upon hearing the horrible news, Ascent stood and his eyes dilated widely, he stumbled backwards and felt a sharpness in his heart. He reached his hands over his chest as the pounding there had silenced. He stumbled backwards falling over a chair, and then he too… was dead."

"How funny are the ways and working of things? The Testimony of the Creator had been taken not by any Hero or Prophetess, but by those who are unclean before the Creator and make offerings in the names of idols. My patience had not been in vain and now had come the time that I had long awaited. Be good my son I said, now is the time. I followed the Little Box back to the land of Ashod, which was settled by Those of Another Tribe.

"When it came into their threshold, they mightily proclaimed the Little Box as their plunder which incited them into triumphant celebration. The Little Box that housed the God of the believers was paraded through their city for the entirety of the day and night for all to see. They placed the Testimony of the Creator in the Temple of their Harvest God, as gods deserve to be in the company of other gods. They pleased themselves accordingly and made hedonistic celebration all throughout the night with heavy drink and open sex acts.

"Now the Testimony of the Creator was safely away from the believers, and it wouldn't be long before it would be in my possession. I could have easily lifted and carried it away myself, but why drive when one can be driven. So I would whisper to their priests and give subtle instruction that the Little Box be returned from whence it came. That night I added insult to injury, and entered their temple and shoved the statute of their Harvest God so that is was face down upon the ground.

"The following morning, their pagan priests awoke to find their god not upright, but fallen down in prostrate in front of the Testimony of the Creator. They did as ignorance does and repeated the same process and placed the pagan statue upright and continued their celebrations into the following day and night. The night drew near and torch fire warmed the night skies and once again, I crept in to the temple of their Harvest God and tipped the statue over upon itself, this time breaking the head and hands off from it. The following morning when their priests came in to make their daily observances, they became afraid and proclaimed that the believer's god had toppled the idol of their god to the ground in anger.

"They bowed and burnt offerings up to nothing and nowhere, and they meditated until coming into a trance like state. Their minds were already weak, but in such a state, I was allowed easier access to their subconscious minds, and I repeatedly whispered that the Little Box be sent back to whence it came." The serpent sighed heavily then paused from narration...

"What! What happened?" The Man of the Present asked.

"Its times like these that you really can't get upset at anyone else but yourself. I mean, if you want something done, you're really going to have to do it yourself!" the serpent sighed, shaking his head in disgust.

"I should've been more specific..." The serpent sighed a second time.

"I should've said 'take it back *to the mountain* from whence it came!' Because the following day, Those Idiots of Another Tribe hitched it up to a cart and took it right back to the believers from whence they got it! Then, I was right back where I started from! Shit! ... Man I tell ya!" the serpent quipped, while biting his lip and shaking his head at himself.

"The Testimony of the Creator, was now on the move so I followed its progress from the cliffs that overlooked the valley roads. The cart made its way without disruption as any who passed it saw the warnings and golden offerings that shrouded it as a cursed and evil thing. When it arrived in the fields of the 'House of the Sun,' an unlucky group of villagers happened upon it. In their ignorance, they placed their hands upon it and opened it and the temper of the Creator came upon the Land and consumed some fifty thousand lives.

"Initially, the villagers rejoiced upon seeing the Testimony of the Creator returned to them. Unfortunately, ignorance was prevalent amongst the believers and the Creator's true words had been lost to them. Their mothers and fathers had let the words of the Creator fade away and their children knew not the correct way to live. When the villagers opened the Testimony of the Creator, they beheld the awesome grace before them and their eyes became opened. They became physically ill and fell to the ground and died.

"I would not have believed it if I had not seen it with my own eyes. I would describe it as being similar to an addict who had become dependent on poison and then abruptly injected purity into their veins, causing an extreme reaction leading to death. The addict's body now convulsing from experiencing purity for the first time. It was overwhelmed to one so internally broken and burned. So, too, was it that the spirit of man who had wandered so far from the path of the Creator, that when they beheld a truth source so pure that it was shocking and painful to them. What once was a guide and blessing of life to them, had now become an elixir of death. Put quite simply… they couldn't handle their high!

"You see, you people throw around words like Ark and Covenant without fully understanding what those words actually mean. Put simply, an Ark is a symbol of wholeness. The structure of the chest that holds the Testimony of the Creator or the Ark, is similar to the structure of the human ego in the realm of the subconscious. Just as the ego provides the capacity for one to live in wholeness. So, too, did the Ark contain the laws for mankind to live in the same fashion. And what is wholeness you ask? A long, convoluted explanation, I'm sure, of long winded definitions relating to religion and ritual but nothing could be further from the truth.

"You see, wholeness is akin to integrity. It's a consistency related to an inner sense of qualities, while acting accordingly to the values, beliefs, and principles that one claims to believe. Wholeness and integrity are personal choices that you humans choose to live up to. A set of standards that you have said ... 'As God is my witness.' However wholeness, is an internal measure of one's own honesty up against their own hypocrisy. No one and nothing can tell you that you are, or are not, what's really inside of you. You might have everyone else fooled, but you can never fully fool yourself. Not to say, that you all do not try.

"Think of how painful it would be to see yourself as the lying, backstabbing, cum-gargling hooker that you really are. You clip-on tie, undercover, fag-mot, troubadour! You think no one knows about you? You addicted to the bottle, credit card spending, affluent, rape charging bitch. You think a surgeon's knife is going to make the misery go away? You think taking your failures out on a child makes you a big man? 'Remember, no matter where you go, there you are.' – Confucius.

"These cover-ups merely spin the wheel on a repeating cycle of pain, suffering, and perpetual hidden weakness called the in-human condition; that no one knows about except you and your shadow. I see you're pretty quiet over there, Man of the Present... everything alright?" The man remained silent looking down at the ground, clinching his fists, and gritting his teeth while listening to the serpent's words.

"You know the type, half-assed Hare Krishna-Christians always asking for money. One foot in, one foot out hokey pokey Muslims. In between praying five times a day, they go pick up a six pack of beer! And of course... the Zionist's! I wonder, if the rocks being thrown were diamonds, would you still fire rockets back at them.

"Let me ask you this, Man of the Present. If God is all knowing and all seeing; omnipotent, omniscient, and omnipresent, then don't you think God knows... that you're full

393

of shit?" A heavy silence came in like smoke and saturated the air in the cave, making it thick and hard to breathe for the Man of the Present. He became choked up and grabbed his chest as he gasped for air.

The serpent, seeing the man's discomfort, looked on for a few moments then broke the silence and said with a smile, "Of course... I didn't mean you!" The heavy air began to lighten and then became breathable again, and the man regained his composure. The serpent motioned towards the pool of crisp water with his tail, suggesting that he take a drink to refresh himself. The man leaned down and drank from the water and breathed deeply after patting his face and neck, bringing him back to a state of calm.

"Better?" the serpent remarked with sarcastic delight.

"Yeah... I'm fine." The man nodded slightly.

"Good... But know this, Man of the Present. Those who live in wholeness have nothing to fear; for sin and salvation are twin brother and sister, as both come from within. Let's continue shall we," the serpent said happily.

"There were so many dead bodies that day and if not for a small group of pious men who found the Testimony of the Creator and closed it, I wondered if the death would ever subside. Messengers were further sent to the inhabitants of the 'City of Woods,' notifying priests that the Testimony of the Creator had returned unto them and to come fetch it up. The Testimony of the Creator was brought to the house of a pious believer known as 'Father of the Vow,' where it was sanctified properly and further cared for by his son known as 'The Help.'

"The Testimony of the Creator ultimately rested there for many years before a beloved king appropriated it. The turn of events was upsetting, and I found further disappointment when the believers were reinvigorated by the young priest known as 'He to Whom the Creator Hearkens" or commonly as 'The Hearkened.' With the death of Ascent, The Hearkened took over spiritual leadership as he was correct and true in the eyes of the Creator. He was harsh soap on the backs of the believers as is the burning of Grandma's lye soap to the unclean.

"The Hearkened commanded the believers to reassert themselves before the Creator, then again would they make battle against Those of Another Tribe. In short time, the believers had purified themselves and were successful on their day of battle. I observed Those of Another Tribe flee from the battle field against a united army of the Creator's people. The believers were again on the narrow path of righteousness and The Hearkened stood as a Watch Tower to guide them to shore.

The Stone...

"After the battle, I observed The Hearkened set a stone on the road between two locations known as 'The Watchtower' and Shen. He made a small prayer there in thanks unto the Creator and placed the stone there as 'God as his witness.'

"I decided to head into what is now the hills of Samaria, however, while making my way down the solitary road, I encountered a man standing in the dirt completely naked with an expressionless look on his face. I stopped and looked around in confusion at the peculiarity of his exposure and the sheer site of him. As I approached him, he made no sudden movements, nor did he say anything at first. However, what was more curious was that there were no footprints leading up to his present location, nor were there any signs that he was heading in any particular direction. Therefore, I was unable to determine what direction he had come from or where he was going.

"He then said, 'My name is Stone, everything about my life is hard. When I stand tall, someone hits me until I break. When I fall to the ground, someone kicks me. And when I lay still, someone picks me up and throws me away. I am a Stone.'

"I thought on his words momentarily until coming to the full understanding of the complexity of his words. I then decided upon bringing him with me up into the hills to elevate his disposition. The Samarian hills towards which we headed were not very high, but were abounded by elevation on all sides. To the north, the Jezreel Valley, to the east the Jordan Rift, in the west the Carmel Ridge and the Sharon plain; and to the south by the Jerusalem Mountains. We arrived at a hill top ridge now known as the Kafr Qasim, where we looked out at the horizon over the coastal plains.

"When we reached the top, I asked him how he liked the view. He smiled and simply said, Goodbye."

The Man of the Present squinted, then asked, "Why did he say that?"

The serpent shifted his eyes back over to the Man of the Present, smirking then replied, "Because that's how he rolls…"

"After departing company with the Stone, I found humble accommodations in the Qesem Cave. The cave has existed undisturbed by man since the Lower Paleolithic era and was proof of early or pre-human life of some millions of years ago, that of course depends on your definition of… human. The cave sat just above a grouping of villages and the valleys were home to selective large-game that acted as a nearby market for quick pickings for one such as I. While I conceptualized my new plan, I took interest in the new priest who now headed the believers from afar.

"He was not so much different than the others who were divinely selected, but famously, he would come to be known as the last true judge of them. However, after the victory over Those of Another Tribe, The Hearkened instituted a time of rebuilding, and he exercised more power and authority than almost any other leader before him. He, in a sense, had become warden over the believers, but a warden is only a place holder, as soon there would come a true sovereign and head of state.

"A time of peace followed for the remainder of The Hearkened's days over the believers. It was many years that I rested and watched, and The Hearkened was indeed a true servant of the Creator. But a wandering eye, caught the believer's attention, and they saw wealthy foreign lords to whom all traveled and joined in festivals. The believers asked and said, 'Anoint us a king, so we too can be led by a true Lord and Commander worthy of our praises! Chose out from us one to become lord and begin us a royal line to rule the land.' Upon hearing the request, The Hearkened was troubled for he knew the awful things that came along with such dynasties."

"What's wrong with having a king? The Man of the Present

asked.

"The issue, my dear Man of the Present, is power," the serpent answered.

"Oh you mean, power corrupts!" he remarked, while gesturing with a finger swipe.

"More precisely... 'Power tends to corrupt and absolute power corrupts absolutely. Great men are almost always bad men.' - John Dalberg-Acton.

"It's not so much that the title of a king is an evil one, nor is it a condemnation to all the kings and queens of history. It is, however, the idea of absolute authority with little regard to oversight, in thinking said monarchs will not abuse said given powers. The Serpent continued.

"The believers would not relent in their asking for a king. Openly now, the leaders of every noble house campaigned for the anointing of one from their great tribes. The Hearkened then held counsel with the elders of each noble house and strongly advised them against supplanting a king above them.

"He then said, 'I hear thee and I understand why thou art fearful, but do not see this emptiness as a woe. We, the believers, have come through much struggle and hardship and have again found favor in the sight of the Creator. Perhaps the reason we have continuously been given new prophet, judge, and hero was because we were too weak to make it without them. Perhaps the Creator sees that we are ready to be on our own and do not need a watcher over us. We have been gifted with the care of the Testimony of the Creator, which are laws unto the whole of humanity. We have everything we need and we have the ability within ourselves to live in wholeness, just as we always have. Let us see this as it is, a test that we are truly righteous people and are able to stand tall as was always meant for us.'

"However, the believers again cried out, saying 'Give us a king that we may be envied and regaled in the eyes of our neighbors! Make us a king out from one of us to rule for generations as is our divine right!'

"Woe, unto you my brothers for this thing you ask you truly do not understand. A king is as close to a false prophet as ever there was one. Kings, enchanters, and magicians are made by men and only claim divinity out of greed and lust for power. Woe unto you and what you will have done unto yourselves," The Hearkened said with a distraught tone.

"However, I have convened with the Creator and hath been told to listen to the word of the people in all that they have asked. For if such a thing they ask, then a king will they receive. This is the manner to which it shall be done. This king among you, this king above you... He will take your sons to equip his armies and appoint them horsemen and charioteers. He will make them men of violence and of campaign, and they shall march and trample over the land.

"Your sons will not be of a loving sight, but will be the fear and scourge of humanity as they play instruments of war in the orchestra of your king. Those who set their ear and hands thoroughly upon the ground shall reap, sow, and harvest, to feed his dogs of war, and fashion instruments of death. And the best of them, yes your daughters, shall work within the king's ranks as cooks, bathers, seamstress, and wet nurse. Your fields too shall belong to the king, and all and everything of their bounty shall be placed at the tables of the king's servants. And this king shall implement taxes and take a percentage of all that ye shall own, build, and craft.

"And on that day, ye shall cry out unto the Creator because of the king which ye asked for, and the Creator will say, leave them until they satisfy their taxation, for ye have no representation. So as you wish, have it your way!"

"Then, from seemingly out of nowhere, did I see the Creator's voice come down and accompany The Hearkened. What was said was not for me so I was unable to hear, but I fathom it was regarding the identity of the coming king. I neared the home of The Hearkened and could see the presence of the Creator had just left him as he was visibly overtaken by the revelation. The Hearkened said out loud as he looked out a window and over the Land of his people, I cry for my people for this thing that they have done to themselves."

"So the people would have their king and the Creator would

have his prophet. Now the believers had separated themselves by church and state, and never again would the two meet as one. With my interest peeked, I stayed near The Hearkened to observe who this king would be and where he would come from. The Hearkened traveled to the Land of the 'Sons of the South' to make customary offering and perform ritual amongst the people. I waited and witnessed nothing miraculous that day, only The Hearkened who invited a simple herder to eat with him, who searched for his father's missing asses.

"The Hearkened returned from his midday meal with the herder and his servant, but took a peculiar interest with one so lowly. He walked with him to the edge of the village, and then it happened. A humble coronation and only by the unction of oil poured over the head of the herder as he kneeled. He kissed the herder on the head then bid him the Creator's blessing as captain and king over the believers. It was he… the king!

"I then focused my sights upon this man, I knew not his name but watched as The Hearkened pointed towards the Plain of Tabor to where he was to go. He and his servant journeyed towards the grave of the mother of He Who Would Increase, and they encountered two men who bid them well as they continued on to the Mount of Transfiguration, which was the same location of battle by the heroine judge, 'The Bee.'

"When they arrived, they encountered three men going towards the 'House of Sacred Stone.' Each of the men carried selected gifts and they made offerings of their supply unto the herder and his servant. They then journeyed to the Hill of the Creator, but were then called unto the presence of three hermits. The herder and his servant joined their presence as they played music for them, then they sat and gave instruction unto the herder regarding the specific teachings of the Creator. I listened and was astounded at their accuracy, but was intrigued as to why The Hearkened sent the newly anointed king away to a group of hermits instead of giving the instruction himself?

"From my understanding, there is a difference between one who is learned and knowledgeable compared to one who can teach and instruct. Let's say an athlete may be capable in a sport, however this athlete may not be the best to coach others to greatness. Whereas a coach may not be the best athlete, but has a fundamental understanding of the sport and an eye for talent to train a champion.

"These three hermits were not so much better or wiser, however I would say, they were guru. And a guru is one who has attained self-mastery and has fully realized his identity in connection with an omnipresent Spirit. And such a guru is uniquely qualified to guide a truth seeker through an inward journey towards perfection. Between the new king and the hermits, they initiated the guru-disciple relationship, to raise him to a level of deep understanding and wisdom for the omnipresent spirit.

"The Hearkened was truly a righteous man and one who was humble enough to set aside his own ego. He sent the herder away to the hermits as they were best suited to instruct the man who was to be king. If this king was to succeed, then he would need to embrace the Creator as his friend and true master and not The Hearkened who may be seen as king maker and the true authority behind the throne.

"They sat and prophesized and after they had completed, the herder stood and was changed. The herder and his servant then journeyed to the place of offerings of standing circular stones, where The Hearkened had been waiting for them. The Hearkened had summoned a congregation to the city of the 'Watchtower' then announced him as the king they desired, and from then on, he was crowned 'The Asked for King.'

"Now, The Asked for King was then accompanied by a troop of devoted and well trained military men, who would later become his official Royal Guard. Even though The Asked for King was anointed out from the believers as they had requested, descent stirred amongst the people and jealousy showed itself and he was despised. The Asked for King heard of the contempt, but took no physical action against those who despised him as he remained steadfast in the ways of the Creator. But, it would not be long before he would be tested and would soon meet his first enemy.

"Only a month had passed and the king of the land of 'Son of my People' had begun a campaign where he and his armies swept across the region enslaving all those he defeated. The king, known as 'The Snake,' had become infamous for a torturous practice where he gouged out the right eye of every conquered male and female in order to instill fear into all that would oppose him. He soon began enslaving the believers on the outer realms of the land. He then turned his sight upon the land of Dry Hills, were he began taking slaves by means of a siege laid upon the towns. Having no army to defend them, the towns sought out terms for surrender.

"The gracious Snake King offered them a choice, death by the sword or to live with one eye. The towns insisted that they be given time to make supplication unto the conquering army, and they bargained for seven days to prepare a feast unto their new lord and master. They secretly sent messengers unto the Asked for King for aid. The Asked for King boldly accepted and with the acknowledgement from The Hearkened, he assembled his forces and went out to meet Snake King in battle for the sake of his people.

"The Asked for King rode out with heavy horse and mounted Calvary and thousands of foot soldiers. The battle was immense and the Snake King led a massive army of heathens that had previously been known for hit-and-run raids, but were brought together for the purpose of conquering the land. The much larger believers army numbered three hundred thousand swords surrounded the heathen army and assailed them from all sides.

"The believers quickly regained the city and fired arrows from atop mobile battlements onto the heathen army. Enormous boulders were sent catapulting into the heathen ranks, crushing dozens at a time. The heathen army, then in disarray, were unhorsed and axed to death by skillfully wielding halberdiers. Finally, Snake King and The Asked for King met face to face on the battle field, but Snake King attempted to flee the fight. However, The Asked for King pursued him, then cleaved his enemy's skull with his sword.

"At the end of the battle, victory was declared in the name of The Asked for King and the land was returned unto the believers. Snake King's body was found and unfortunately, he remained alive, but slowly dying from his head wound. His body was then fittingly thrown into a snake pit where he was bitten until dead. The victory was celebrated and The Asked for King was fully accepted as the leader and captain of the believers. And so, a king stood above the believers and sits beneath the Creator and to his right, is overlooked by a prophet. I thought to myself, *a King had been anointed, but was he 'elect of the Creator?'*

"The Asked for King wasted no time and instituted an autocracy with absolute power over state and government. Now, The Asked for King ruled by decree and needed no approval from any council of elders or legislative assembly, and could impose punishments upon anyone. But after some decades of peace the believers again found themselves engaged in perpetual war against, their repeated enemy; Those of Another Tribe. Under the Mandate of Heaven, The Asked for King did battle and took with him every able-bodied male of his choosing. The battles ensued with such quick succession that any victory appeared meaningless as the other side quickly regrouped and retook any lands that were held by the opposing force. After two years of constant battle, the believers had grown into a military state as they were constantly on the offense.

"The Asked for King issued a stern decree: 'No time could be spent in leisure while the enemy was at the gate, all those who could fight must fight, all those unable must re-work, fortify, and supply.' None were spared and nothing was wasted... the days of The Asked for King were bloody and sore with war. Some three thousand fighting men accompanied The Asked for King while a thousand were set up in the south with reinforcements back in the main lands.

"Now, The Asked for King's eldest son, 'The Axiom' was known as the beginning of all reasoning. He was a model of loyalty and honesty, and his reputation was such that his word was unchallenged and accepted as true without controversy. In battle, The Axiom was a brave and skilled fighter and he notably scored a decisive victory against Those of Another Tribe. The believers were mobilized in war on all sides, but the Creator was with them and every direction they pointed their spear, they were victorious.

"The Asked for King was confident as their enemies were in retreat, their borders refortified, and had been successful over the last group of counter offensives. As was customary, he met with The Hearkened to hear the word of the Creator and to, again, sanctify himself."

The Hearkened said, "The Creator hath sent me to anoint thee captain above the believers and as such, thou have done well. Now, there is a task that the Creator asks of thee, but listen and do fully as I instruct thee. If thou shalt falter, trouble and worry shall be with thee until the end of thy days." The Asked for King lowered himself before The Hearkened and made supplication before the Creator and opened his ear to the seer's words.

The Hearkened continued, "If you recall The People of Prey and how they laid in wait against the believers while in exit, led by Law Giver. Thy kin have been slain and devoured, and The People of Prey, made feast of that which is ritually unclean. They are foul and hunt and feed on other men. They are thine enemy and are to be utterly destroyed. All they have, all that they are, young and old, male and female, spare none of them!"

"The Asked for King accepted the commands and assembled his armies together. With Those of Another Tribe beaten back, he withdrew forces from the front lines to assure the extermination of The People of Prey. And just as they had done, The Asked for King laid in wait for them in a valley. Then The Asked for King and his forces ascended upon The People of Prey and killed until the piles of bodies were as hills. And like a twisting of the food chain, where the predator becomes the prey, The People of Prey were hunted and slain.

"They took their time killing them, just as The People of Prey were known to slowly devour their captured alive, slowly licking their victims blood. Their sad victims watched The People of Prey conversing and cooking in communion for several hours, as the rest of them would be slowly consumed alive.

"The believers hunted The People of Prey from the 'Circular City' all the way to the wilderness of the north-eastern border of the 'Land of the Black Ground, Home of the River Bank.' Their king was located, while trying to flee, but they slew him not. He was held down screaming, as each finger was chopped off at the knuckle, thus he was declawed rendering him harmless. He could never hunt or capture another living thing. He would be forced to graze and chew on leftover carcasses and plants as an example.

"By that time the believers had been on the war path for such a long time, many had not seen any payment and were away from their families for extended periods of time. The Asked for King allowed scavenging to defeat low morale. However, The Asked for King was strictly advised against doing so, and thus broke the commandment of the Creator. But, then I heard a familiar rumbling from afar and could see the voice of the Creator descending upon The Hearkened. The following morning, The Hearkened came out to meet The Asked for King with news of his actions."

"I have done as the Creator hath commanded me, The People of Prey are utterly destroyed and are no more," The Asked for King reported to The Hearkened.

"The sounds I hear are not of nothing, but are the sounds of sheep and ox, of camel and fowl. Has thine army befallen sorcery and been changed into wild beasts?" The Hearkened questioned in observation.

"The believers remain true, the beasts of thine ear were those taken as spoils. Only the best of them were spared to be sacrificed unto the Creator. In these times of war, moral is key, the men must have something, surely my Lord sees that," The Asked for King said, in defense of his actions.

"Were my words unclear? The Creator charged you captain and said now go destroy The People of Prey and take nothing. This thing you have done is evil in the sight of the Creator and I am vexed for you now," The Hearkened said, then dropped his head in grief.

"I have done everything thou hast charged me with. We even have their king captured and declawed as evidence!" The Asked for King recanted.

"Know this, oh Asked for King, it is better to obey than to sacrifice. Your chosen decision is akin to idolatry as you have listened to the voice of the people over the Creator. In my heart of hearts, I feel that I have failed because of this thing you have done. You have rejected the Creator, so now the Creator has rejected you." The Hearkened said, now grief stricken.

"I am sorry, Asked for King, but this deed cannot be undone." The Asked for King dropped to his knees crying and begging for forgiveness. He pleaded that The Hearkened pray unto the Creator for forgiveness and to be given another chance, but The Hearkened shook his head, no.

"I am to tell you what the Creator hath said. The Kingdom that was gifted you shall not remain in thy possession and it shall be given to another whom is worthy. The strength of the believers will not remain with you nor those of your line, there is no repentance that will suffice. It was you who was anointed, it was you who was to embody the best of the people. It was you who was to lead the people to prosperity." The Asked for King now in tears, repeatedly begged for mercy and offered all his possessions and swore many offerings for the Creator's mercy and compassion to again favor him.

"Oh Asked for King, it was I who anointed thee, so I too share in this blame. If the Creator strikes me ill for remaining at thy side, then so too shall I be condemned. As we are men and are of a follied nature and is no man free from mistake. I shall remain with you till the remainder of my days, even as the Creator hath turned away from thee. I must fulfill what was left undone, so now bring before me their wretched king." The defeated king was brought in before The Hearkened bound by hand and foot and was placed before him on his knees. He looked up at the face of The Hearkened and could not hold gaze with him as The Hearkened was holy and his face shinned with the rays of illumination. The defeated king begged to be pardoned, then lifted up his swollen and bloodied, fingerless hands.

The hearkened looked upon him the said, "Thou art unclean and hath made feast upon men, so too shall the fires digest thee." The Hearkened raised an axe and with repeated blows did he divide the king into many bloody pieces.

"The Asked for King returned to his homeland in the hills, unsure of what was yet to come. However, the voice of the Creator followed The Hearkened and again paid him visit. It would happen sooner than I had predicted, and there would come a challenger to the throne. But The Asked for King would not go quietly, and the newly anointed would be faced with usurpation. I watched from a distance as The Hearkened rose early in the morn and took with him a heifer good for sacrifice. And without trumpet or priestly parade, but quietly did the seer go on his way.

"I watched him just as before when he had come into a humble place and looked there to which he selected one who was goodly above the rest, as did he do the same there. He came to the house of a man known as 'Onto,' who was upright before the Creator. Onto was known as a pious and learned man, who was skilled at debate. He specialized in arguing for the existence of the Creator against others who believed otherwise or in many gods. Yet, he did not see himself as a scholar, but as a truth seeker and was always studying the concepts of being, existence, and reality.

"Now, I have to be honest, Onto was a pious man, however I did not see anything special about him at first. But after further inspection, I looked and saw him seated with The Hearkened and saw his wife bring them hot drink poured from the same black, clay coffee pot which was heirloom from the lovely Widow. I knew then that the man Onto was the grandson of the Widow, and indeed the Creator had chosen well. The Hearkened called all the sons of Onto forth for inspection, and he sanctified all seven of them.

"The Hearkened looked upon each of the boys, but each time he shook his head, saying 'The Creator has not chosen of this.' The Hearkened then asked Onto if all of his children were present, to which he was informed that his youngest son was out in the fields tending to the sheep. The Hearkened then sent for the boy so that he may inspect him as well. Within no time, the youngest of Onto, a ruddy looking boy, came forward to which The Hearkened looked upon him and smiled."

"Do you know who I am?" The Hearkened said then, touched the boy on his shoulder. The boy remained silent then looked to his father before answering.

"You are the seer, come to sacrifice unto the Creator and bless the people of our village."

"Do you know why I am come unto your father's house?" The boy again looked at his father before addressing The Hearkened, then he shook his head, no.

"The Creator hath commanded me to come here, and here I would meet the one who was to be anointed captain above the believers one day. And I come here, and now I have found you." The Hearkened reached into his satchel and removed the horn of oil and stood above the boy and anointed him with the oil before his father and his brothers. Upon beholding the event, each of his brothers dropped down to one knee in agreeance with the decision of The Hearkened.

"And now the chess board was set, but there was a new piece set in play. The Asked for King, The Hearkened as Bishop, and now the boy who was just a pawn. But still, The Asked for King remained in rule, and a dark heaviness was continuously his shadow.

"Then, again, the believers came under attack by Those of Another Tribe. The uneasiness and repeated attacks were, no doubt, brought on by the misdeeds of The Asked for King that showed the spiritual weakness of the believers. Those of Another Tribe had invaded the 'Praised Capital City' and were sorely defending it. Those of Another Tribe had set themselves near the town of Azekah in order to take control of the Valley of Elah. The border town was advantageous as it was centered between the Praised Capital City and the lower foothills.

"The Asked for King met Those of Another Tribe with his forces to defend the Valley of Elah from the invaders. I stayed

407

out of it as this was a matched meeting of men and the Testimony of the Creator was out of harm's way. Those of Another Tribe stood out on an embankment, while The Asked for King stood out on an adjacent hilltop calling out and cursing each other. And then as the pride of the believers was bolstered, there came out from Those of Another Tribe a vilified warrior champion, as none alike had ever before been seen. He was not Gigantes, but a mighty big and strong man.

"He was battle tested and was armor fitted with a brass helmet, coat of mail, leg guards, and breastplate. He carried a fearsome spear and sword, and his shield bearer stood out to his left. He taunted the believers and called out to have any man meet him in single combat. He continued taunting them claiming that their God would surely deliver one as small as he into the hands of their mightiest warrior. He ended by saying, 'Let the day be decided by champion warfare and if ye be victorious, we shall serve you, but when I prevail, then it shall be you who will be slave to us!'

"The entirety of their army began chanting his name and shouting again and again, and they shouted in defiance of the feeble Asked for King. When The Asked for King saw the size of the Gath warrior and his fearless attitude, he grew quiet and was shaken, but he could not withdraw his troops. The believers stood silent, still holding their ground, but they had not the strength to return remark or to meet the Mighty Gath in single combat. To the utter shame of The Asked for King, the scene continued for some days. Every morning and every evening did the Mighty Gath return while the believers cowered beneath his giant stature.

"I took leave of the battle with the believer's barely retaining their numbers, but daily losing ground as they retreated from Those of Another Tribe. Each day in battle, they would rally and sanctify themselves, but when the Mighty Gath would show his presence on the battle field, they fled before him. I went down into the lower valley seeking a quick meal, as the lying dead bodies of men had begun to rot and the wounded stunk of cheese. And just as the grumblings of my belly had begun to beckon me, a grouping of lambs came into view. I took hold of one and hoisted it up and I could just about taste the mutton, but then... owe! Right, in my eye! Again! Then again, was I pelted with stones.

"I held on to the animal trying to locate the assailant before devouring the meal, yet they were still out of sight, but then I heard from around me, 'Release him fowl creature, and be gone! The flock of my father belongs not to thee!' I quickly surmised that the voice was that of my assailant who continued pelting me with stones. I then recognized him as the youngest son of Onto earlier anointed by The Hearkened.

"I stopped to let him see me, seeing him, seeing me, and then he gave pause and I said, And exactly what... do you think you are doing?" He looked in astonishment as I stood speaking eloquently before him, but he retorted in similar fashion.

"Demon tongue! Or do my eyes and ears deceive me? I stand in righteous defense of these lands against you, creature! For you attempt to pillage the lands of my father and take that which doth not belong to you! I shall not relinquish, nor shall I retreat from any darkness!" Seeing that the young man was steadfast in his stance, and I being trespass, I needed to end the aggression.

"I admit defeat young hero, surely I submit!" I released the lamb and it rejoined the rest of them, unharmed. The young man was about to leave, but I stopped him before he could leave, asking.

"But, may I have the name of my lord? For it would trouble me that I might not know the name of the one who hath stood up so faithfully in the name of the Creator of all life."

"I am 'Beloved,' son of Onto, Youngest of my brethren! And who are you that speaketh, creature?" the young man said strongly with his chest out.

"Ahh... Beloved are the youth! I see my status has been elevated from mindless monster to conversing creature," I said with an intriguingly sly tone.

"I am the Serpent of Old, and I mean you no harm Beloved youth. I merely descended upon thy sheep as means of midday sustenance. I am begging your forgiveness and am gracious for your compassion and mercy upon me in ending your assault and allowing me to live."

"You are welcome talking serpent, but I cannot stay and trade compliments with one of your sort. I must return to my brothers who are engaged in battle against Those of Another Tribe. I must bring them bread and meat for they must remain strong of body and spirit in order to do battle."

"And may I ask, why one so noble as thee are not engaged in battle as well? You are indeed brave as you stood against me without sword or shield, without armor or helmet. You gave no hesitancy in defending that which surly was lost, neither did you give worry or fear to thyself for thy father's honor and possessions."

"They have said I am too young to make war, but I am without fear and I stand ready to defend against those who are unclean before the Creator and mock my people!"

"Do not rush into battle, make time for thought and planning and be conscious of fear and worry; for they are valuable insights, as only the foolish are without fear as they are usually... the dead. But know this, 'So in war, the way is to avoid what is strong, and strike at what is weak.' – Sun Tzu.

"... but beware the enemy!"

"The enemy!' the young man's eyes moved back and forth as he thought to himself.

"You speak of the Mighty Gath who threatens and harasses my people! He makes the mightiest of men seem as feeble children before him, and how they tremble at the sight of him. But he is the one who should tremble, for the Creator is not at his side and his armor is only tough as sheep's wool to the butcher's knife. I will slay this enemy of my people. Indeed, thou art wise talking serpent. I am happy for staying your execution and not slaying you! I thank you for your insight. Be well, and may fortune allow us pleasant greeting again!" Beloved turned and ran down the hill without another word. I thought to call out after the young man but he was fast of foot and was already gone.

"I watched from a distance as Beloved joined his brethren

410

down in the trenches as he brought them food. When he saw the Mighty Gath up on the hilltop, he inquired of what would happen to the one who slayed the Gath warrior. The other men on the battlefield answered his inquiry saying, 'He who slays the Mighty Gath would be rewarded by riches and offered to marry the king's daughter.'

"Beloved stated proudly, 'I have come to fight, and I shall dispose of that which is unclean before the Creator.' The Asked for King commanded his assistants bring in the man who could slay the Mighty Gath. When they brought Beloved forth it was observed that he was only a youth, but completely without fear but strong in faith.

"Of one so young, how could you defeat such a great warrior who crushes all who oppose him?" The Asked For King proposed.

"Oh Asked for King, I am Beloved son of Onto, youngest of my brethren. It was I who from a young age was given unto the protection of my father's flock in the wilderness and on this day did I encounter a monstrous creature never before seen. Its size and countenance was abhorred and it spoke with eloquence and intelligence, but thy servant did not flee. The monster gave attack upon my father's sheep, but I defeated the demon with only thy beating heart stones and the Creator as my shield." Upon hearing Beloved's words, the congregation of soldiers let out into bellowing laughter as they knew the boy's words were folly and the aspect of his imagination. His elder brother, who stood over him, grabbed him by the arm commanding him, "Stop it! Enough of your games Beloved brother, the truth now!"

Beloved looked around seeing the disbelief in the men's eyes, then recanted and changed his story, "There was no monster, no talking creature. It was a lion that had pounced upon a lamb. I confronted him with only what I had, no weapons, but my shepherds staff, sling, and stones. I let out loud noises and waved my arms and then the lion let loose of his hold on the lamb. I thought it was my strength that frightened the lion away, but then I turned and saw that a bear was above me on a cliff.

The bear came down to claim the wounded lamb for itself. I admit I was afraid, but I held steadfast and remembered the words of the Creator and pelted the bear until it grew tired and fled. This is the truth of the matter, as I am but a youth, but this youth has no fear and is ready to stand against any man or beast in the name of the Creator." The men surrounding him cheered and raised their arms in strength after hearing his words.

"As none other has come forward, so let it be this Beloved youth. May the Creator be with you!" The Asked for King armed him with his helmet, armor, and sword. Beloved secured the sword in its sheath and headed out of The Asked for King's tent. Before leaving the area, he stopped and looked back and removed the armor against the advice of those around him. He grabbed his shepherd's staff and bag of stones and ran towards the hilltop to meet the Mighty Gath.

"The believers moved backwards and opened a path as Beloved ran strongly towards the hilltop to meet the Mighty Gath. The cheers emboldened the young man and Those of Another Tribe gave pause as the voices created a stirring on the battle field. All fighting halted as the stage was set for champion warfare as the believers had no doubt selected a brave warrior to face the Mighty Gath. But when Beloved climbed upon the hilltop mound, Those of Another Tribe fell out in frantic laughter at the sight of the boy. The Mighty Gath raised his arms to silence Those of Another Tribe and acknowledged the young warrior.

"Greetings of the highest sort! For the mightiest of the believers has come forth to do battle against me!" The entirety of the army of Those of Another Tribe continued laughing and jeered at the sight of the tiny boy who stood out, bold chested, in front of the towering warrior.

"But what's this? Thou cometh to me without armor or sword, without spear or even a shield. Dost thou see a whimpering dog before thee that thou come to punish me with only a shepherd's staff? Away with you boy, or I will filet thy flesh and feed your remains to the scavenger dogs and wretched buzzards of the air!" Beloved remained strong and never took his eyes off the Mighty Gath, and then took a step forward.

"Mighty are the sinful at play of war, but weakly of heart are they before the eyes of the Creator! No sword, nor shield can protect nor give thee parry against the might of the Creator. Submit and yield now before the armies of the Creator, as I will give thee no additional opportunity. Thou art unclean and I shall remove thy head leaving thee 'Uncovered!' Here, all will see the Creator's will done and how no weapon is stronger than faith. And when thou question thy defeat, thou shall question it in many pieces as the beasts of the earth partake of thy rotting flesh. He that stands in confrontation to the Creator is dumb and already dead, and is no contest for even a Beloved youth!"

"The eyes of the Mighty Gath filled with rage upon hearing the taunting words of Beloved. He threw his spear strongly, but missed as Beloved kneeled and rolled away. Beloved then remembered my words saying, 'Avoid what is strong, and strike at what is weak.' He then reached into his satchel and removed his sling and a grouping of stones and prepared to kick back at his enemy. The Mighty Gath drew his sword and made ready his advance. Beloved regrouped and raised himself and swung the sling around his head, while the Mighty Gath's eyes widened as he pivoted his weight forward and stepped to charge.

"Beloved slung a single stone upwards, perfectly aimed as he had done many times in play. He could knock a targeted fruit from a tree or paralyze a bird in flight. His aim was impeccable and unexpected by any soldier. The stone flew swiftly and struck the Mighty Gath where he was exposed in the forehead rendering him unconscious, causing him to fall forward down on to the ground. Upon seeing the sight of their fallen champion, the eyes of Those of Another tribe were agape as none could believe the incomprehensible sight.

"Beloved spared no time in allowing the Mighty Gath to recuperate from his temporary, fallen state. He quickly raced to his position and took hold of his now loose sword and raised it, bringing it down upon his neck and severing his head. Without a final word, the Mighty Gath was dead and Beloved, stood atop

413

his lifeless body, raised his head in triumph and let out a dominant rooster's crow!

"Those of Another Tribe were paralyzed by fear after beholding the sight of their champion fallen and beheaded by a trifling boy. Confusion and panic overcame them but before they could react, the believers were on top of them stabbing and slicing away at them. Those out front lost limbs and fell upon their exposed guts as they fell dying while the remaining fled screaming in defeat. Beloved remained atop the dead Gath's body claiming his carcass as his property. He stabbed the sword into the ground and wrapped the head of his fallen enemy in his tunic, while The Asked for King rallied to his position.

"Yeah, but how is it even possible that he could defeat a guy in full body armor and helmet with only a stone? I've heard this story before, but it almost seems a little too good to be true," The Man of the Present interrupted with a question.

"The mightiest of warriors, too, can meet their ends by the cost of their own arrogance. Even a boy can be taught to find the kinks in the strongest of armor. The story of Beloved defeating the Mighty Gath has become a legend all its own. But what some seem to take as divine intervention, seem to set aside simple physics. A hunting sling, which was used by the boy, is actually quite accurate a weapon.

"Whereas an arrow, or spear aimed and fired probably would not penetrate the breastplate, but it is the unexpected weapon that is most effective. A hunting sling is capable of launching a projectile at speeds exceeding 250mph. And as such, it is easy to master, is highly accurate, and generates a lot of power without the use of extreme force. Now being struck in the head by a fast-moving projectile such as a stone could cause a concussion. As described, the Mighty Gath fell down unconscious or dead. It matters very little if he remained alive, as his temporary paralysis gave the boy ample time to approach and sever his head without further argument."

"But wasn't he wearing a helmet?"

"Why yes, yes he was. Helmets are among the oldest types of protective gear worn during battle and warfare. What people do not seem to realize is that helmets were designed to protect the wearer from cutting blows by swords, or arrows, and later from low velocity musketry. However, in the time-period we are discussing, very few helmets were designed with a nose-guard to provide facial protection. Such styling of helmet did not take hold until the later middle ages. This encounter was no doubt a precursor to the later invention of the nasal helmet. Was it skill, divine intervention, or mere chance that allowed a boy to triumph over a giant of a man. What we learn is that very little is impossible and even the smallest are able to stand against the mightiest. Nothing is set, all one need do is believe and not be afraid to fight for what they believe in." The Serpent continued.

"The Asked for King then anointed Beloved, proclaiming him a mighty hero before the Creator. The Axiom, embraced him as his brother in faith and the two made an agreement to always be as one. The Asked for King then held a ceremony where Beloved was knighted before the entirety of the believers.

Interesting as it was, he believed that the promotion of a pawn to a Knight, was by his own doing. But the Creator is master of technique and pushed this pawn forward, through priyome and selective structuring of the game board. The Asked for King thought Beloved to be 'King's Knight' and of his file, which placed the board in a bind. Unfortunately, The Asked for King did not realize that he was 'bare' and was the only man of his color on the chess board.

"From that day on, wherever The Asked for King sent him, Beloved went out and did battle on his behalf. Beloved Knight, as he was now known, was graciously accepted and was a blessed sight to the servants of the Creator. Over time, his battles and victories could not easily be counted as he had journeyed far and battled long in the name of The Asked for King. But when Beloved returned to the capital and the entirety of the city came out to greet them, the ladies sang praises of their Asked for King, but sang louder for the Beloved Knight. And this angered and filled The Asked for King with jealousy and hatred.

"The praises of Beloved continued and The Asked for King then saw him as a threat. The Asked for King thought that, if left unattended, it would result in the depreciation of his position. And if The Asked for King did not make a move, he would be subject and placed in check." Indeed, it is true as they say, 'Jealousy is the fear of comparison.' – Max Frisch.

The Asked for King then said Beloved would be made general over his forces, which was the highest honor. Upon hearing the news, Beloved dropped to one knee in supplication of his king. Furthermore, The Asked for King waved his hand and in walked his eldest daughter who was known as 'Abundantly Beautiful,' then his second daughter known as 'Brook,' whom was in love with Beloved. She was petite and smaller than her elder sister, but she did easily captivate Beloved and he agreed she would be his wife.

"Highest and most proud of my fighting men, be thou now my son and further fight in the name of the Creator, for all I have shall be given unto thee," The Asked for King said, as he gave Beloved his blessing.

"Now Beloved was indeed entrapped and I pondered what quiet move had The Asked for King made against him. The betrothment to the king's daughter was definitely an intentional move, but it did not readily capture or attack him."

"I require no dowry for the price of my daughter, but I swear by the Creator of all life that thou doth owe me a bloody debt. For the enemies of our people still roam these borders unchecked. The maidens have sung that thou hast slain thousands, so I put to you, oh Beloved Knight, that for my daughter's hand thou shalt bring me a hundred hides of the enemy, to prove thyself before me." Yet The Asked for King surmised that he could not take the entirety of the army, but only a cohort with which to do battle.

"Beloved knew the region which he was heading and it was overrun by Those of Another Tribe, and many spies and scouts laid there. He knew he was being setup and sent to his death, but refusal would mean his imprisonment, so he accepted the debt. At the end of the battles, Beloved sat upon his horse in deep thought, "Why is it here in this place of blood and death, am I to do my best work? Shame for me, for I am not King's

Knight, but King's fool, and make war for one who would see me dead."

Then, to The Asked for King's astonishment, Beloved returned with the blood payment in full. I looked on in delight but as for now, the gameplay had halted, as The Asked for King and his Beloved Knight both took the time to strategize and make clever evaluation of their positions.

"The following day, The Asked for King paced the floor with contemptuous thoughts as he plotted deceit and death of Beloved. He summoned Beloved to his presence then sent the remainder of his subjects away. He sat and toyingly took hold of a javelin, twirling it between his fingers so as not to alarm Beloved. And then without warning, The Asked for King threw the weapon with lethal intent, as if to staple Beloved to the wall.

"Beloved was ever alert and moved to avoid being killed, and then fled out of the king's presence. The Asked for King made a second attempt while he fled but his aim was thwarted by an approaching maiden who was pierced straight through the abdomen leaving her dying on the floor. No one knew of the king's attempt upon his life, nor would any believe it, as all saw nothing but adornment and admiration like a father to a son. Beloved, now aware of the evil intentions set against him, sought out active maneuvering as he was now in a defensive position.

"

"The following day, The Asked for King summoned Beloved to his council, but knowing that Beloved would be hesitant to return, he made the meeting informal and had his son Axiom invite him. Beloved was now faced with a fearful choice, flee the realm in exile or return as he was still King's Knight and sworn by oath. But then, a bit of fortuitous information came unto Beloved who lived in a state of constant defense. Axiom approached him and embraced and removed a small blade from underneath his tunic and showed it to him. Beloved looked upon it and saw that the weapon was discreet and perfect for an assassination."

"My father called me to his chamber a few nights ago. He

enquired whether you and I were still close as brothers, to which I happily replied yes. He then asked me if I was brother to you by faith or by blood. I replied, that no bond could be greater than that which is between you and I. My father then asked me if I were loyal to you above the Creator, to which I replied nothing is above the Creator. What he said next saddened me and it is what has brought me here before you today, my brother. He said you plot evil and engage in idolatry with Those of Another Tribe, which is why the foreign princes sing of your praises. I spoke him false, but he swore upon King's duty, his words were true. I am ashamed to say it, but my father is a liar. This knife, he gave it to me... to kill you."

"And now?" Beloved looked back at Axiom with his heart racing, gripping his dagger.

"I am more devoted to you than I ever have been. My father has become obsessed with killing you, for what reason I do not know. I cannot disobey my father as it is against the laws of the Creator; but my brother, you are of me and there is none better." Beloved's eyes began to tear as he had no one to trust and in the midst of sinful plot, he was made safe and whole by Axiom.

"I must leave this place brother, for I am become enemy in thy father's eyes."

"I am sorry brother, but you will never be safe here. My father hunts you now and in this kingdom, there is no place that you can hide, as none will oppose him. Go out now and hide in a secret place." Beloved departed with swiftness and made good his escape.

The Asked for King did not stand idly by and called out alarms and raised the guards and pursued after Beloved. The entirety of the guards were out searching, every road and alley and there seemed little place for Beloved to hide.

"He crept along the rooftops with the poised digitigrade skill of a cat allowing him stealth. He made it home to his wife, where she kissed him and sent him out the back window to flee the night. Later, the guards were met by The Asked for King and reported that no one had come into or out of his home since the alarms rang. The Asked for King called them fools then rushed inside, bursting through the front door. He grabbed hold of his daughter, demanding she turn over her husband, as he knew he was there. She nodded that he was upstairs, so The Asked for King and his guards charged up to the bed chamber and saw a figure lying in the bed, cowering.

"They stabbed and slashed the body under the blankets but found only bed stuffing, cloth, and feathers bundled in deception. The Asked for King looked out the window seeing a hanging rope, then spit upon his daughter for her deceit. He then yelled at his guards, commanding them to pursue every shadow of the night until he be found.

"Beloved fled alone into the darkness, not knowing where to go, not knowing where to hide himself. There was seemingly no refuge available, but the Creator granted him mercy as he hid in the tall grass near the traveler's road. A cart drawn by two horses was pulled by The Hearkened and stopped near the place Beloved was hiding. The Hearkened summoned him, 'Come my son, we must flee with haste lest The Asked for King complete his assassination of thee.' Beloved hid in the cart and the two made good their escape to a small village on the borders of the lands.

"The village of Nob was a not much of a town, but more so a sanctuary for pilgrims making offerings unto the Creator. There were very few inhabitants save for the caretakers and a few villagers who farmed and turned over the proceeds for charitable gifts to the old, sick, orphaned, and the exiled. Beloved covered his face with a cloak so none could identify him and raise alarm as all of the land were hunting him. He approached the house of the priest known as 'King's Brother' as he was seen as almost family as he was The Asked for King's earliest advisor.

"Beloved entered the small temple for worship and shut the door behind him. He then kneeled and began a small prayer, after which the priest approached him from behind placing his left hand on his shoulder. Beloved removed the hood, showing his face to the priest. The priest gasped at the sight of Beloved as he knew he was a fugitive on the run."

"Now priest, you can raise alarm and have me imprisoned and brought before The Asked for King, but I was told by Axiom that you are friend. So as I put trust in my brother, I put my life in thy hands," Beloved spoke out truthfully.

"My son, keep quiet for The Asked for King has many spies, and he means nothing pleasant for you. How may I be of aid?" He said then, hugged Beloved tightly.

"I have nothing, and I am now cut off from returning unto The Hearkened who arranged transportation for me. I have no food, no water, no armor, or weapons. I'll take anything, whatever you have, it doesn't matter."

"I have no common foods, but only that which is hallowed here. If thou art clean, then take it to sustain you."

"I am clean and of an honest nature, these days past have given me no time for indulgence. But I need a weapon, something to defend myself with."

"This is a house of worship my son, we have no weapons of war here," the priest replied, opening his arms in emptiness.

"Damn! Then I go out naked! Without tooth or claw."

"Hold a moment, there is the sword of the Mighty Gath that ye had slain years ago." The priest walked behind an alter and underneath a robe was the Sword of the Mighty Gath.

"Take it. It is fitting that it should come back to you for this sword belonged to a mighty warrior and now it shall belong to you." Beloved received the sword that which he severed the head of the Mighty Gath when he was just a boy. The sword was single edged with a cross-hilted guard and curved like the lion's claw. Beloved reveled at the strength and sharpness of the blade.

"Legend has it that this sword has never met its equal on the battlefield as the Mighty Gath who wielded it was undefeated, save for you my son. That which you hath defeated, now becomes yours." Beloved gripped the sword firmly and said thanks unto the Creator for granting him his prayer. As he looked upon the mighty sword, he spoke out calling the blade ... 'Mameluke!' ... 'My Property!'

"Beloved covered his head as he crept out of the village now equipped with sword, Mameluke. Unfortunately, there was one spy, 'The Uneasy One,' who saw Beloved enter the temple and saw how he exited armed with a sword. The Uneasy One did not confront Beloved face to face, as he was aware of his battle record. So he sent word via pigeon post to notify The Asked for King that Beloved had been spotted on the road leaving the village Nob.

"Beloved, now alone out in the wilderness, looked around him and saw no place of safety. With his home land now against him and the years of war with Those of Another Tribe, he would have to travel quietly or face enemies at every turn. Tears streamed down his face, as he was lost and turned out, but he gathered his courage and said to himself. 'There are no good decisions before me, but indecision would leave me stranded and surely dead.' He raised the hood over his head and headed into the mouth of the Lion and into the land of Gath. His name there was venerated as their greatest accuser and most horrible foe, as he had slain their mightiest champion at just a boy's age. Even if none knew his face, the sword of the Mighty Gath would surely be recognized."

"Quiet now, they don't know you. You're just a weary traveler. Don't make eye contact, but do not appear suspicious. We will come and go... calm, and cool, like the wind," Beloved said to himself, upon entering the city of Gath.

"The land of Gath, however, was a circus of markets and loud people, who did not take kindly to strangers. It was not surprising that everywhere he turned, everyone wanted a fight. Not because he was threatening or argumentative, it was just the nature of the Gath people. The people of the markets began picking fights with Beloved, and some grabbed at his cloak trying to reveal the guarded weapon he carried underneath.

"He paid them no attention and continued to walk, but some took his behavior as insulting as he did not acknowledge their taunts. Some of the harlot women exposed their breasts and lifted their skirts up past their thighs as an invitation of company, for the price of a few coins. However, they too took his quiet demeanor as rude and called to their watchers, to harass this traveler who scoffed at the delights of Gath. He looked behind him and saw a grouping of men were now following him, with others ahead completely stopping their chores and focusing on him. He knew that he would be ambushed and most likely beaten dead, so he feigned madness and began drooling and stumbling and cursing the names of doves and rodents that had stolen his soul."

"I am the god of east wind! I am reborn anew and my light captures all who gleams upon thee! I am the savior of thine mortal ghost, who hath fallen a hundred times and risen a thousand!" He grabbed a wreath of dried hot peppers and bit into them, then boasted loudly with a raised fist.

"How sweet, thy earthly candies!" He laughed loudly coughing out bits of half eaten peppers that burned his mouth.

"Those who pursued him stopped in their tracks, seeing that he was indeed a mad man, and they waved off their pursuit. Beloved continued stumbling throughout the streets until ducking into an alley, then ran fleeing from the city. The night was kind to him but he had exhausted his water rations and was now lost in the hills after escaping the city of Gath. He had hoped to resupply there, but he only escaped with his person intact. He had traveled alone and now the moon had come up full and gleamed light on a small path through the hills. He saw a heavy shadow that glistened of fool's gold that was an opening into a much larger cavern, of what today is the Cave of Adullam. He needed shelter and a place to fortify so he came into the cave and laid down silently, secured and slept. Meanwhile, The Asked for King and his forces arrived at the village of Nob and singled out the priest who aided Beloved.

"Oh priest, where about is thy Beloved enemy?" The Asked For King said with interrogation.

"Lies are not within me, even though I know that I shall surely die this day. He that tarried here was unclothed and unfed. He inquired of me, so I bid instruction of the Creator, to which the Creator hath made none so faithful and honorable as thy Beloved Knight. For me to cast him out as he hath come in, would be a sin. I stand before you, oh Asked for King, steadfast and without sin."

"Then thou shall surely die!" The Asked for King said stepping closer to the priest until they were face to face.

"But I will not send thee out alone! All of your house and all of this village will go bloody out with you. Kill them, kill them all… and let him watch. He dies last!"

"The Asked for King commanded his men to slay everyone and everything in the village. But the soldiers were fearful of the Creator's wrath and would not draw swords against the priest village. The Asked for King repeated his commands to his men with anger, while they retreated back two footsteps in fear of slaying a priest. The Uneasy One stepped forward looking to gain favor in the eyes of The Asked for King.

"I will slay them. Alone if need be! Let the king's will be done! I am thy servant and shall be thy favorite," The Uneasy One stated boldly.

"The king removed his sword and gave over the blade to The Uneasy One who went running, screaming, and chopping violently throughout the village sparing none. He was drunk with madness and sinful lust as he hacked the skulls of kneeling women and kicked and booted dead their infants. He was not a fighting man and never was he accepted on the battlefield as a soldier. So inferiority was his shadow and the underlying cause of his angst and feelings of weakness, inadequacy, and inability to perform against his peers.

"He lashed out on those weaker and unarmed and took out his aggression as a means of esteem compensation. And when he completed the order, eighty-seven lay dead. He was a sloppy butcher and his clothing was stained with the blood of the innocent as he kneeled before The Asked for King, as if to be knighted for valiance. The soldiers surrounding the king looked on him not in respect, but in curse as a feeble thing looking for cheap acceptance from masturbatory relief. The Asked for King did not touch him on the shoulder, but only commented."

'Now finish!' And he smote the priest, in similar fashion.

"The following morning, the sun rose and shined through a daylight hole in the cave allowing light to enter and illuminate the cavern. Beloved awoke well rested in his position; he wiped the sleep from his eyes and saw standing before him an assembly of armed and rugged men. As he stood slowly, the cloak dropped from his back, exposing sword Mameluke at his side."

"Good Morning! Did you sleep well?" The leader of the men nodded happily standing proudly with his hands on his hips.

"Beloved looked around seeing that he was greatly outnumbered by the gang of outlaws. The cave that was his refuge was, no doubt, their hideout that he had unknowingly stumbled into the previous night. What was once a convenient hostel, was now the stage of a lopsided standoff.

"Yup! I'm guessing right about now, you're trying to figure how you ended up in this frying pan of a situation! You see compadre! Your mistake was jumping out of whatever double broiler brothel you were in, in the first place," the leader of the bandits said animatedly, motioning with his hands.

"Let me guess! You got a little too sauced and indulged a bit too heavily in the goodies of the Gath women, which cost more coin than you actually had. You, no doubt, found the brothel keeper's wrath none too inviting, so you fled making good your escape out here. But, unfortunately, whatever lashings the red-light wardens would have doled out to you is nothing compared to what we do to those who trespass here.

"You see, there are two types that end up here; either wealthy and lost, or lost without hope. And by the way you're looking, it don't look like you got any amount of wealth to buy your way out this sour pickle," the large gang of armed men looked on in silence.

"You are trespassing here! Now, state your business or be commended back to an eternity of sleep," the leader of the bandits commanded, then folded his arms over his chest with strength.

"I am Beloved! Son of Onto! Former King's Knight, and now fugitive of the believer's lands. And who are you that questions me?" Beloved answered confidently.

"They call me Baibars, and I am Chief Panther here," he introduced himself, while remaining in his confident stance.

"And this rebel… these are your men?" Beloved rebutted,

locking eyes with Baibars.

"Rebel?" Baibars smirked, then thumbed once over his shoulder at his men laughing heavily.

"Why... I see no rebel here. Why we're just a bunch of fun loving, crazy guys looking for a good time," the gang of men let out in heavy pirate laughter.

"You're bandits?" Beloved acknowledged.

"Bandits, thieves, exiles, the unwanted... or just about anyone who doesn't accept The Asked for King's way of life!" Baibars side stepped up on a boulder then waved left in introduction of the gang of men behind him.

"Those you see here were arrested for undisclosed crimes. We were given a choice, prison... or death! And, seeing as how there isn't much of a penal system in this land, going to prison is a death sentence."

"And how do you survive out here? By stealing?" Beloved further questioned.

"Yeah! We steal... but only from the dead!" The surrounding gang of men laughed heavily at the description of their deedful work." Beloved nodded his head in understanding. "Make him pay! Taxes! Tax him! Tax him! Ha! Ha! Ha! Ha! Ha! Ha! Ha!" The onlooking congregation of bandits yelled out taunts.

"Ahhh, yes! The Asked for Kings does enjoy collecting taxes," Baibars remarked, with a greedy smile.

"And if you can't pay?" Beloved added.

"More like we refused to pay. I turn over no payments nor submit to any king I never asked for."

"I have fought, killed, and bleed for that king. And now, the king hunts me as if I am the enemy," Beloved said solemnly.

"So the enemy of my enemy, is my... hmm." Baibars looked towards the sword at the side of Beloved.

"Say, that's a pretty impressive pair of scissors you got there! I've heard rumors of a sword similar to that one. It was said to have been wielded by a giant of a man. He was a Gath! The Gath's claim to be the bastard descendants of the Emim. The story goes that the Mighty Gath was undefeated and the sword he carried never knew its equal. And then there came not a

425

warrior, but a boy. And do you know what that boy did?"
Baibars asked rhetorically, staring back at Beloved.

"He cheated! Slick little bastard, dropped him with a single
stone from a sling! He never saw that coming did he? And then
the little S.O.B. went and chopped his head off. Real close shave
like!" The large gang of men remained silent while Baibars
orated.

"You know what I think? I think that sword would look
much better over here... on me," Baibars suggested, pointing
once at sword Mameluke, then patting his left side.

"So, you've heard of me?" Beloved said confidently, while
the cavern filled with heavy chuckling as the men watched him
intently.

"Everyone knows who you are, Beloved Knight. We just
wanted to see what you were going to say," Baibars admitted,
gesturing towards Beloved in recognition.

"Then you must know of the songs they sing about me."

"Ahh yes! How The Asked for King had slain hundreds and
his Beloved Knight had slain thousands..." The cavern again
filled with laughter as the men looked on.

"I love fairy tales, they make such wonderful bedtime
stories!"

"Actually, you're right... the stories are misstated. It wasn't
a thousand. It was tens of thousands!" Baibars and the gang of
men went silent hearing the confidence in Beloved's voice.

"There were so many that we lost count. Not in one day, not
even in a week is such a number possible! But every day, every
night, for years did I kill. I hunted and harassed them, and still
we killed. I slaughtered and ordered the deaths of so many that
Those of Another Tribe, began to be called The Few of Another
Tribe. The numbers that I have slain are only second to the
reaper himself and when I step onto the battlefield he fears his
title will not remain secure," Beloved raised and pointed a finger
waving it over the gang of men shaking his head unimpressed.

"And with the handful of a hundred you got in here, I don't
think you'd qualify for a haiku." The mob in the cavern stood as
the silence filled the cave, after hearing the rebuke by Beloved,

accepting and then doubling down on Baibars' threat.

"You want Mameluke? Come and take it!" Beloved looked down at the mighty sword at his side, then locked eyes with Baibars while standing ready.

"Baibars shifted his eyes watching as Beloved confidently tapped the cross hilted grip of the sword at his side. He felt his men behind him shrinking into a Lilliputian color guard, as they began to doubt themselves against the reputation of Beloved and the mighty sword. Baibars then sneered and huffed a laugh. He laughed again, then again, then again until the entirety of the cavern was filled with drunken pirate laughter. Beloved too, joined in laughing, thus ending the standoff. Baibars threw him an animal skin of water and from then on, they were one."

"Rumors began to spread that there arose a leader over the marauders and they were unified under one banner and were known as the 'Beloved Army.' Beloved commissioned the nearby villages of Aderet, Roglit, and Aviezer to farm and grow crops and in return they would provide them protection from raiders. The caves that were their fortified location included many cisterns carved directly into the rock face making water readily available. Access to the fortified caves was a well-kept secret and only those who knew the way and passing calls could navigate the wilderness to the hideout.

"Not long after, Beloved sent word to his father, mother, and brothers to come to the area and remain there under his protection, away from The Asked for King. They were brought secretly to the location unto the safety and protection of Beloved and his men. Soon, anyone of the region who was in debt, discontented, or persecuted, traveled and swore oath unto Beloved and he was captain over them too. At this time, those that followed Beloved were many and his army of men now numbered hundreds with fighting spirit.

"Now Beloved was cut off from The Hearkened and had no one to prophesize for him, but fortune was with him. For out of his fighting men, was such a seer known as 'Luck.' He was versed in the teachings and the commandments of the Creator and was gifted the sight of a prophet.

"Hearing of this, Beloved gave him rank as military chaplain. Luck proclaimed his willingness to fight and to stand with Beloved as he was militarily trained. But Beloved granted him non-combatant status and proclaimed that he was not to take direct action in the fighting. Luck accepted his post and carried out the fullness of his commission.

"Beloved, became a respected general, and he made simple marauders into a cavalry of warrior stock. He instituted intensive and rigorous training schedules, and through him, they became an organized garrison and masters of mounted combat skills. Although he was outcast, Beloved never gave up his duties as protector of the region. When he was made aware that Those of Another Tribe had regrouped and invaded the citadel of Keilah in the lowlands of Judah, the Beloved Army attacked and drove them out. However, even though he was victorious, he was constantly betrayed and The Asked for King was notified of his whereabouts. So The Beloved Army swiftly exited the area and laid in the wilderness of Ziph, in the Judean Mountains.

"The days that followed saw Beloved and his men hunted in the wilderness of Ziph. The Asked for King raised the bounty on The Beloved Army, so that none would hide them. Those that heard rumors of The Beloved Army marching in the hills and mountains too began searching them out. But cunning was their way and they evaded detection every time.

"They routed themselves in different paths so that one trail would lead into another, which circled back to their previous position making it difficult for anyone to determine their true path. After days of hiding and maneuvering, The Beloved Army found respite in the dwelling of Maon in the southern Judean hills. The following morning, they headed for the Ein-Gedi oasis to refresh themselves and trade with the local herders there for dried meats and grains. The oasis sits just below the Qumran Caves, which is where I encountered Beloved once again."

While they rode up the hills, Baibars stopped Beloved, and said with caution, "My Lord, I have heard rumors of a demon that haunts these hills and caves. A frightening leviathan that consumes men whole and steals their souls. Theses hills are cursed!"

"A demon you say, a leviathan... hmm? By chance, does this demon... speak?" Beloved replied with an intriguing smirk.

"They say men have heard an eloquent tongue calling to them and reciting hymns of the Creator, only to find a creature of ages lurking there in the shadows," Baibars advised, while clinching his sword.

"And I thought you weren't afraid of anything, noble comrade?" Beloved remarked, quietly folding his arms in his lap.

"Begging your pardon my Lord, all know I fear no man. But what can an army of swords and spears do against a creature of damnation?"

"I'll tell you what. I'll go on ahead and clear the caves, then I'll call for the men once it's safe," Beloved replied, then smiled contently.

"Alone?" Baibars questioned with high alert.

"If there be such a monster in there, it will make its presence known," Beloved stated with ease, dismounting his horse.

"What are you going to do?" Baibars questioned.

"You said the creature speaks, then I suppose we'll have a chat and I'll reason with it." Beloved answered, looking up at his comrade.

"And if the creature not be of reason, but of anger and vengeance?" Baibars rebutted, with concern.

"Then, I guess you're in charge from here on out!" Beloved answered jokingly, then headed into the Qumran caves. He took only a lighted torch with him, and stepped slowly allowing his footsteps to echo deeply into the darkness. The caves were filled with the melody of silence until he paused and spoke aloud."

"I am he that entereth the place of the unknown, the dominion of the unseen, and with me there are none. I bear no shield, no spear, no helmet... not even a sword." Beloved stopped suddenly after hearing a shifting of earth and the sound of heavy bellowing directly ahead.

And then with a commanding voice, I spoke from out of the darkness, asking, "And what of a sling?"

Beloved slowly replied, "No... not even a sling," He raised

the torch slowly, and beheld my presence before him.

"Then I am in no danger," I remarked, smiling keenly upon seeing him.

"And they said these caves were haunted by a most horrible apparition! One that consumes the souls of men," Beloved stated, with a smirk of relief.

"One must keep up appearances!" I replied with a sarcastic tone.

"It's been a long time, Serpent," Beloved said graciously, lodging the torch upright in a crevice and taking a seat.

"Too long, and happily it appears the years have been kind to you. And my, how you have grown from such a youth into a Beloved Hero."

"Unfortunately, I come empty handed, with no stray sheep this time," Beloved admitted, removing his gloves.

"I see you haven't got that wrist rocket with you either! It appears I can rest easy this time," I said jokingly, regarding our past encounter.

"And what brings you lurking about these caves, Serpent?" Beloved inquired.

"Oh! Just catching up on some reading. I came across a grouping of scrolls that are really quite interesting. I am really impressed at the detail included in them. Such a diligent attempt at historical and religious documentation. My only critique is the meshing of Hebrew and Aramaic throughout the 980 some odd texts here. You do lose a bit of the translation, but still, I can't complain for once having the time to take up some reading. But enough about me, how have you been?"

"There's tired, there's exhausted, and then there's what I am..." Beloved answered, wiping the fatigue from his face.

"I've heard of the bounty placed on your head. At first, I couldn't believe it, but then again I've seen how humanity exploits its own too often at times," I responded, looking upon Beloved, who was now a battle tested warrior.

"I don't know what to do. Each day is a test of survival and each day we ride harder and fight in closer quarters, and even then we're just trying to keep our heads above water. My men and I are running out of places to hide. The entirety of the region is against us and even those we pay and bargain with betray us as soon as the opportunity presents itself. I fear the Creator has left me and has allowed The Asked for King to reassert himself as I am with few options," Beloved admitted, in frustration.

"Fear not Beloved hero, the Creator may be silent but never has the Creator left thee. The path ahead of you is treacherous, but thou art surefooted. Does the goat complain of the rocky terrain? No, for he was built for it. Know that the Creator has made thee exceptional and a lesser man would have surely perished by know."

"My men are outside and we are seeking shelter so that we may rest and replenish ourselves. Our horses are weary and their heads hang low. I have nothing to give in payment for solace here. May I beg of thee for the safety of my men and our animals?" Beloved requested, showing his empty hands with nothing to offer in payment.

"The Beloved Army has no need to fear me! Besides it would be my honor to shelter thee, as it was you who spared me those years ago! But a word of advice, 'My son, keep thy father's commandment, and forsake not the law of thy mother. Bind them continually upon thine heart, and tie them about thy neck'... but beware the enemy!" the serpent recited, but was interrupted by Beloved before he could finish.

"He that hunts me! You speak of The Asked for King! He has proclaimed me and any who give aid to be of a hostile nation. I am sorely wounded in my heart for my own people hate me."

"Yes, that too, but that's not..."

"Shhh! Did you hear that?" Beloved interrupted me again, before I could complete the statement.

"These caves echo the approach of any for miles away. Still, the Creator hath made me in such a way, that I hear everyone, everything... everywhere." I said, letting out a slow gasp of whistling air.

"Damn! I thought we had more time. The Asked for King and his army numbering thousands are headed this way,"

Beloved remarked, overlooking the valley below seeing the king's forces down in the valley.

"Have no fear, Beloved hero they are miles away and the sun has almost gone to sleep. You have more than a full night's rest before they are even half near you. Rest the night, and tomorrow make good your escape" I offered with reassurance.

"Thank you Serpent. You are a most unexpected ally."

"That night, Beloved and three of his men crept down into the camps of The Asked for King. He located the King's tent and entered without raising alarm. But just before he moved to strike, he paused and instead, cut a piece of the king's tunic, then uttered, 'Wickedness proceedeth from the wicked, but my hand shall not be upon thee.' He signaled to his men and the group exited as quietly without being detected.

"The following morning, The Asked for King awoke to find part of his tunic cut off and footprints leading away from the camp site. He called to his men who stood watch and asked what had occurred that night. His men replied that no intruder disturbed the camps. The Asked for King pointed to the tracks leading away from his tent and his cut tunic."

"My beloved enemy was here and he could have killed me as I lay! But he silenced me not for he hath much mercy within him. That shall be his undoing," the king said, tracing the tracks with his eyes.

"Then a messenger approached the camp of The Asked for King and reported that, The Hearkened had died and his body was being prepared for burial. The Asked for King instructed his forces that they would return to attend the burial as was customary. The king's forces left the valley of Ein-Gedi and headed back to the city of Ramah to bury The Hearkened."

"One of Beloved's spies, came back up and reported that The Hearkened had died. Upon hearing the news, Beloved dropped to his knees and lay prostrate as he wept in prayer."

"He that hath anointed me should now rest in the heavens, for he was the best of them, and the last of them. And by the will of the Creator, it was he that anointed me to be Captain of the believers someday."

"Is it true? That The Hearkened anointed thee captain above the believers?" Baibars asked upon hearing the revelation.

"Aye! As none hath known it, except my family and The Hearkened. I was just a boy when he paid my father a visit and he looked upon me and said, 'The Creator hath chosen this.' And he washed me with oil from atop my head to my feet." Upon hearing the words, Baibars dropped to one knee and all the men seeing this followed in succession. Baibars and the men joined in swearing an oath of allegiance to Beloved, as follows, 'Say, do I affirm allegiance to that which hath been chosen by the Creator as captain over all. For I am thy servant and I renounce and forsake any other master of false claim.'

"My men! My Knights! I am pledged to the laws of the Creator and to thee as thou art pledged to me." Beloved raised his head and looked over the hundreds of men who kneeled before him in allegiance. He touched Baibars on the shoulder and the men let out a series of cheering in admiration of their beloved general and king. Baibars interjected a call and response of cheers then the group let out ululations to express their strong emotions and to commemorate the occasion!

"The Beloved Army successfully navigated the labyrinth terrain of the Judean Mountains for some days but still the region seemed endless. But then unexpected aid came in the form of a goat herder's wife, known as 'She that Giveth Joy.' She aided The Beloved Army and saw them through the mountainous paths and wilderness as the land was her home and she had traveled it many times. But by this time, The Asked for King had enlisted the help of the 'Pinnacle People' and had located the trail of The Beloved Army. And once again, The Asked for King made camp and Beloved and his men spied and came down into their camps. And just as before, Beloved stopped and could not kill The Asked for King, saying, "Let us not! As much as I wish it, I cannot slay him. I cannot inflict any worse punishment, than the pain and suffering that shall return upon his head." Beloved took The Asked for King's spear and returned up into the hills.

In the morning, Beloved called out to The Asked for King's

commander known as 'The Light', saying. "Oh great
commander Light, for thou art weak and foolish, as thou hast
left thy master open and without refuge,' Beloved said, pointing
and yelling furiously."

"Commander Light answered the call and came out on the
adjacent cliff. The two men now staring back at each other, were
separated by a gorge known as the Wady Malaky, which lies
between Hachilah and Maon."

"My master, lives and in no short time shall you be on your
knees begging forgiveness before him. And when my king
stands over thee, thou shalt be denied pardon and the last thing
you shall see is my sword swinging down upon thee."
Commander Light responded with strength, pointing back at
Beloved.

"The Asked for King is alive, but not because of thy
protection, nor thy skill, but by my compassion. As last night, I
came down upon thee with malicious intent; but yea did I stay
the blade," Beloved raised up the king's spear in his possession.
Upon seeing his spear The Asked for King, knew Beloved's
words were true. He was overcome by guilt and shame, then
came out and addressed Beloved.

"My beloved son, as I have called you many times, how I
have sinned greatly against thee. For greed and jealousy has
overcome me and now is my utter shame and damnation. There
is none greater than thee, there is none more noble and worthy
of praise. Thou hast spared my life, while I cursed thee. Only by
the grace of angels were you bestowed upon me, and how I have
repaid thee with spite. I cannot continue in this way and no more
shall I hunt thee. Thou art greater than me, thou art more ready
than I have ever been. I am sorry my son, I am sorry."

Beloved planted the spear firmly into the ground then
solemnly gave one final testament, "If thou betray me ever again,
then you shall surely die by thy own spear. And with spite, thou
art in check! Go now and never return."

"The Asked for King and his forces exited the hills, while
The Beloved Army overlooked from the cliffs. That evening,
Baibars and the men lit many fires and rejoiced for the war had

ended and The Asked for King would hunt them no more. But Beloved was silent and shared not in their gaiety. He withdrew into the solitude of the caves, with hot drink and a quiet smoke. Unbeknown to him, was my presence still there in those caves."

"There is nothing left for me than to wander forever in the land of my enemies without a home. And now, I have condemned us, for my men and I will know no peace as we shall surely die," Beloved said aloud, thinking he was alone.

"You regret your decision?" I said, creeping out from the shadows.

"Compassion is no elixir of the soul, but a curse of the weak. This candidate move I have committed too perplexes me and now I question it. I should have killed him when I had the chance. His pride knows no guilt, nor does he tire of false pursuit. The Asked for King is not a man of righteousness, nor does he think of anything but himself. I care too much, and as such, I am the one living like an animal, while he that hunts me lives in a palace and eats tender meats.

"I cry for my men as they and their families were wronged and chose to live in exile rather than bow to a tyrant. Because I was unable to do what was necessary to save them, I have doomed us. Out under the stars, here in these mountains, there is no land to sow, nor any livable space. Their families will either starve or freeze this coming winter, all because of my weakness,"

"Hmm... How to defeat him, without physically harming him?" I paused switching my eyes back and forth while thinking, then said, "Well you could always challenge him to... '!!Immoral Kombat!!' I then simultaneously began beat boxing the hypotonic theme song to Mortal Kombat, then followed with the signature scream.

Beloved was struck in confusion, by the simultaneous sound of vocal percussions mimicking drums, and my pop-locking head nodding. "Challenge him to Mortal what?" Beloved asked in befuddled confusion, completely missing the humor of the serpent's words.

"Well, I mean you could just say something really horrible,

about one of his nephews! Like, the one that's got downs syndrome. I mean physically, it's... it's not going to harm him, but morally it... it'd just be wrong," I explained, with suggestive absurdity.

"I do not find humor with your words, Serpent! And I would appreciate it if you would discontinue your facetiousness. I have distress about me and if you have nothing advantageous to offer, then leave me," Beloved said with serious tone, then folded his arms over his chest.

"I apologize, but I could not help but see the humor in the 'smothered mate' of a situation you have here. This is a man that has sworn death upon you many times and while under threat, you have responded with compassion each time. Very few could, or even would, do the same. At a time when you could have ended him you let him live.

"Compassion supersedes the cerebral rationale of justice and by so it motivates one to alleviate another's suffering by sacrificing of themselves. It is the key component of altruism and embodies the gold standard of 'Doing onto others as you would have them do unto you.' Is the Creator not attributed to being the most merciful, most compassionate? Then how could one ever regret such behavior? Yes, thou has been anointed as a king, but tonight thy actions have risen you above any mortal kingdom and into the heavens. And if the Creator's ledger should error in recording such deeds, then it shall be I who attests to them on that day of eternal judgment." Beloved was comforted by my words, then shed a solemn tear.

"... but beware the enemy!" I said with a solemn warning."

"The enemy!" before I could finish, Beloved remarked jumping to his feet.

"She that Bringeth Joy reported the presence of Those of Another Tribe in the lower lands, just days ago."

"Yes that too, but that's not what I..." I answered in acknowledgment, but was cut off before I could complete the statement.

"I thank you for your wisdom, Serpent. It is indispensable, but there is a task at hand. While we celebrate, Those of Another

Tribe rally against those who are unprotected," Beloved grabbed up sword Mameluke and came out atop his men and said with a thundering command.

"My men, are we soldiers of celebration, or warriors of fate? For Those of Another Tribe encompass the weak, while we linger in looseness filling our bellies and engage in pleasurable company. To Arms! There is a battle to be won!"

"The men yelled and cheered for their beloved general. They made ready their weapons, saddled their horses, and marched towards the Negev desert on the outskirts of the believer's lands. The Beloved and his commander, Baibars, led the army over a complete and full victory wiping out the invading armies of Those of Another Tribe who had supplanted themselves in the Negev desert. As payment, Achish the King endowed Beloved, the lands claimed in battle.

"Now, The Asked for King had repeatedly made supplication unto the Creator but received no answer. He called and sent out for prophets and seers but they, too, could offer him no answers. Now blinded to the ways of the Creator, he sought out an old woman in the city of Endor. He disguised himself and asked that she raise the spirit of The Hearkened, so he may prophesize regarding the upcoming battle with Those of Another Tribe.

"The old woman was said to be able to receive messages from the dead. But she warned him that The Hearkened was no ordinary spirt but a true prophet and if contact was possible, the result may be disastrous for all involved.

"Get on with it old woman, and do your work!" The Asked for King demanded.

"The old woman recited unknown words, then began a ritual, before falling silent. She sat motionless on her knees staring deathly wide eyed into the fire pit in the middle of the tent. A blue flame ignited and almost engulfed her, as she was hypnotized by the fire. Then a figure appeared to the right of the old woman. It slowly came into view and was The Hearkened who glowed with purity and light.

"Oh Asked for King, why hast thou risen me?" The ghost of

The Hearkened said, looking down at his hands and seeing he was in ghostly form.

"I have no eyes and no ears for all thy seers are false and the ways of the Creator are unknown to me. Those of Another Tribe are encamped and make ready their attack on the morrow's day. What shall I do, how can I defeat them? Speak to me of the Creator's benevolence and merciful will, as I am thy servant," The Asked for King, begged on his knees to the apparition.

"Oh Asked for King, of thee that I did anoint. Thou hast not executed the Creator's will, nor hast thou protected the believers as didst thou swear it. From the day thou disobeyed, the Creator did set the chess board against thee. The Creator selected me 'Bishop' and anointed a boy who was only a 'pawn' into a 'Knight,' and even then did thou show bad form in remaining in play as king. In the game of chess, the Creator plays perfectly and is always in positional advantage above thee. Brilliance is the Creator's every move, with sacrificial attacks and unexpected counters.

"There are no more legal moves available to thee, there is no escape, and thou shalt surely die on the morrow's day. So, too, shall thy seed be cut off and thy sons shall die in horrible fashion. Thou shalt know that before death approaches you that the believers hath been delivered into the hands of thine enemy and thy name shall forever be rent in shame." The Hearkened's spirit paused then said one last word before disappearing forever, 'Checkmate!'

"That night, Beloved faced a hard decision. He had dwelt in Negev, but now, he had received notice that Those of Another Tribe were going to make war against The Asked for King and the believers. Cowardice was not his way, nor was he keen to sit idle and do nothing. Beloved visited with Achish the King of Gath and afterwards, he and his men returned to their home in the desert of Negev. But when they returned, they found no welcome for them. They found nothing and no one as all had been burned or captured in their absence by the People of Prey. Those that were once thought gone and dead from the earliest days of The Asked for King had returned as a plague, and destroyed their home.

"Beloved and his men cried sorely and some of his men mourned so heavily that they cursed their beloved general, as it was his decision to leave their home unguarded. But Baibars quickly denounced such talk and swiftly disciplined the men, allowing Beloved to formulate a plan of attack."

"All supplies and provisions that could be recovered are prepared. Give the word and we are at thy command as always," Baibars reported to Beloved.

"As none could ever know it, I have found family and hope with men of such faith, honor, and integrity. That those who have stolen from us have brought upon the wrath of the Creator and justice shall be dealt through our hands, our swords, and our lances. But this place that we have called home is now at an end and we shall go to what is rightfully ours. The Creator thus sayeth, everything we have lost shall be returned. And those that have stolen and pillaged from us, surely shall die. Spare none of the People of Prey, for they are utterly unclean and are of a reoccurring disease," Beloved spoke out, gripping the reigns, seated atop his horse. The men, hearing the command of their beloved general, rallied and rode towards the land of the People of Prey to free their captured families and retake their possessions.

"The following day, The Asked for King was drunk and showed no signs of battle readiness for he knew his end was at hand. He looked over to his sons and wept, for their nobility would be ended as penance for his shame and misdeeds. Axiom, ever vigilant, looked to his father to make the rally cry before battle, but the king was silent. Axiom, took it upon himself to embolden the fighting spirit of their forces. And all at once, the entirety of the believers let out a mighty and vigorous yell.

"Axiom grabbed hold of their banner riding back and forth for the army to see and shouted to charge. The captains of Those of Another Tribe accepted and the two sides engaged heavily in war. But to their utter shame, the words of The Hearkened were true with pin point accuracy and detail. The believers fell heavily and were slaughtered on a seemingly endless day.

"But Those of Another Tribe did not let the believers flee and hounded them continually even across their borders. Those that lay dying were left to suffer and those that dropped their weapons in surrender were neither spared. The Asked for King was alive and fought in a drunken state and without care for his safety, yet he remained undefeated. And when he saw his sons fall by arrow and spear, they were lifted to their knees and their bodies held up until being beheaded in defeat.

"Axiom was he that was the best of them and his armor was pierced with many arrows and was his shield scratched with many blows, but he fought on and rallied to his father's side. Even though his father spat on him for his aid of Beloved, he looked upon his father and called him king. The Asked for King shed many tears and gripped his son tightly as he made his last stand. Axiom pushed his father backwards and commanded, "Go!"

"The Asked for King retreated and saw his son taken and beaten down with clubs as his body shook with tremors until dead. They hoisted his body up and tied him to an ass and paraded him as a follied trophy. The Asked for King was now exposed and had no pawns to shield him from enemy attack. He was pierced from behind by arrows as he fled. Finally falling to the ground, his lungs filled with blood and he was now on his knees. His sword, still in his hand, was little more than the cane of an invalid. He lifted his weapon and with the last of his strength, he tilted the sword upwards and fell upon his own blade dead.

"The battle had ended and The Asked for King and his three sons, were dead. Those of Another Tribe seized the Kingdom and claimed it as their own. On their day of parade and victory, they retrieved the bodies of The Asked for King and his sons and made bloody idols of them for all to see. They cut off their heads, arms, and legs and then reattached them to their torsos with broom sticks and straw costumes as their armor and crowns. They kicked down the doors of the believers' temples and remade them in the honor of their pagan gods in contempt of the Creator. And as a final insult, they took the newly mounted royal scarecrows and decorated the temple of their highest god, Ashtaroth, with their bodies for all to see.

"With The Beloved Army heading towards the believers lands, they encountered a man besieged of war, lost and frantic of the heat. He told of the outcome of the battle between the believers and Those of Another Tribe, 'The battle is lost and The Asked for King and his sons are made as foul decorations hanging in the temple of Ashtaroth,' the man reported, panting trying to catch his breath.

"The mighty and noble have fallen and all that we knew hath perished. The Land of Conquest which was promised us has been overrun and its defense and retake now falls to us. We are all that remains of our people. So now we go home and retake what is rightfully ours," Beloved spoke out to his men, looking towards the road ahead.

"Meanwhile, Those of Another Tribe, were secure in their position and feared no reprisal from anyone as they had defeated the God of the believers. The road from Ziklag back to the Land of Conquest took some weeks, which allowed The Beloved Army time to refit themselves with provisions.

"Then came a final act which was unexpected. While camping at 'The City of their Colleagues' Beloved was informed of a scant man who had possession of the crown of the slain Asked for King. It was then known that Beloved was the true and rightful anointed king, and was then crowned. The word was sent out and all those who were in hiding and who had fled the land came and swore oath unto Beloved as king. Now with their numbers reassured, The Beloved Army marched on to defeat Those of Another Tribe once and for all.

"The battle was terrible and the slaughter of men seemed endless, but The Beloved Army did their work and cleansed the land of Those of Another Tribe until none were left alive. Beloved then conquered the stronghold of Zion, claiming it for his own and making it his capital city. And finally, the bodies of The Asked for King and Axiom were recovered by a valiant troop from Jabesh-Gilead, and returned to where they were properly buried with honors befitting a king and knight of the

441

believers.

The battles and wars of Beloved were many as he cleansed the lands of all who opposed the Creator, until he stood as undisputed ruler of all that could be seen. Now, the wars had ended and peace and prosperity returned to the believers. The Creator looked on with delight as Beloved had defeated the troubles of men and the temptations of war, and had completed the oath as he had sworn. I looked on from afar when the Testimony of the Creator was brought out from its place of hiding and given its own house for the people to acknowledge the laws of the Creator. Baibars and The Beloved Army were given special release and title so that none could ever impose upon them.

"Beloved invited them to stay as nobility with lands to call their own. Some stayed, while others left as they were knighted warriors of the horse and were no good at farming and living quietly. He blessed them and held a feast on their behalf and the entirety of the believers turned out and bestowed upon them the gratitude of heroes. Those that left took with them their courage and honor, horsemanship, archery, and skills of war. To honor Beloved, they named themselves 'Mamluk' (Property of the King) for the sword of their beloved general, their beloved king. They departed the lands seeking glory, with their respect and honor, and thus… a warrior caste was born.

"And it was in the days of peace that I did encounter Beloved one last time, if not for the temptations of a woman. Beloved ruled justly and had many wives and concubines as was customary of king. And he did eye from his rooftop a woman of such legendary beauty and sexual appeal, that none of history have ever compared to her. She bathed herself outdoors with linen curtains to conceal her erotic appeal but her shadow created more envy than any poetry could ever inspire. "When Beloved saw her, he enquired of her being and status. He was informed that she was known as 'Daughter of the Oath' and was the wife of a trusted soul known as 'Fires Light.' The following day, Beloved returned and enquired of his servant to bring Daughter of the Oath to him alone in the night. His servant, ever mindful, did as his king advised him. And that night did Beloved lay with the wife of another man, and committed himself in wrongdoing as men are accustomed to folly. The following days and evenings were of heat, and the two found themselves engaged in illicit affair.

"But after some month's passing, a letter was received, as Daughter of the Oath proclaimed to be with child of the king's seed. Immediately, Beloved devised that Fire's Light was to be placed in the hottest battles, where he no doubt would fall and never return. And so, the deed was done and Daughter of the Oath mourned for her dead husband. But her mourning was soon overturned by celebration as she gave birth to a son and wedded her Beloved King.

"And then, I saw it, that awful sight and frightful glow. That which be the Voice of the Creator in gloom and of a displeasing tone. Then, not soon after was the infant son of Beloved and Daughter of the Oath struck with an unknown sickness that would not let go for sake of his life. Beloved called to every healer of the land, every seer to pray and work medicines to sooth and heal the child. But the child would not nurse, for his fever burned hot, and there was no release from this illness.

"Soon after, Beloved's parishioners began preparations to mourn the child, as they knew he would surely die. But Beloved would not hear of it and threatened to kill any who spoke of his son's death before his time had come. Beloved went into seclusion and made burnt offerings, fasted, and prayed for his son's life. And the voice that did answer was not of the Creator, but the voice was of mine, 'A riddle for you, oh Beloved King,' I called out from the shadows of the cave.

"Of all the times have you visited me, now is not a pleasing one!" Beloved opened his eyes and ended his repetitions upon hearing my voice.

"I say to you, a riddle, if thou will hear of it," I repeated.

"I have no time for your games, Serpent. I pray now for the life of my son and the Creator is silent on the matter."

"Interesting how you do not connect the two. You pray the Creator for an answer and here it is that I appear," I rebutted.

"Speak your riddle..." Beloved stopped, then slowly looked behind him cautiously, at me.

"There were two men who dwelt in the country, one rich, and one poor. The rich man was of note and great stature. He had risen up from nothing but still he hungered ever more. The poor man, too, was of humble origins, but was he blessed but with one little lamb. Now the rich man lived as such and the poor man did so as well.

"But then come a day that the rich man decided upon a feast. He called to him goods of splendor and fine wines of taste. He rejoiced with his council and indeed did they partake. But he took not only of his own supply, but stole every morsel from the poor man's plate. Now, how doth the scales and weights of justice tarry between the two? Identify the vandal, the thief, and name him enemy as such."

"Any man, rich or poor, who plots theft is surely a vandal and an enemy before the Creator and my kingship court," Beloved answered sternly.

"False!" With a half striking movement I said wickedly, half lunging at Beloved.

"The truth to you! I have answered your riddle correctly and you mock me in the hour of my misery," Beloved pounded his fist on the ground, then rose to his feet in anger.

"Enemies! Enemies all around me! From the days of my youth have I fought and struggled, against all those who curse me ill. The Mighty Gath whom I slay with only sling and stone. The Asked for King, who kissed me as a son, but hunted and swore me dead. Those People of Prey, I defeated after they burned the lands of lease, until finally did I smite them eternal enemy of my people, Those of Another Tribe! Now you speak in riddles of theft and deceit of an enemy, to which I am blind! I see no other that has haunted me all these years save for thee! Speak truth of me, dark creature... speak!" Beloved yelled in anger, standing in a fighting stance but without weapon in hand.

"The enemy... is you!" I replied with calm.

"But... how!" Beloved blinked, then momentarily stumbled in his tracks.

"I am sorry, I am truly, truly sorry! I tried to warn you. But you wouldn't listen. None of you do!" I said apologetically.

"I listened! To everything you said to me!" Beloved argued back, swiping away at the accusation.

"But only partially! As every time I became critical of your person, neither would you hear of it! As does the rest of humanity fall by its own ignorance.

"The Mighty Gath who fell was defeated not by a boy, but by his own arrogance. The Asked for King was slain not by weakness, but by his own jealousy and treachery on his people. The believers that gave great exit out of the Panopticon, that have constantly fallen under attack of Those of Another Tribe. It was their own internal failure of faith that brought repeated attacks and defeat, by not living in wholeness. The Hearkened, how he smiled upon you, he had so much hope and faith in you that you would be true and hold fast to the laws of the Creator. All those times we met, I tried to tell you…

"But for all the battles and trials, there is one darkness that follows you no matter where you go. And he that villainous shadow… is thy own reflection. Man continuously looks to his enemy across the battlefield, but he fails to see the enemy within himself, and is therefore defeated. For all that man will do, for all that he will build, conquer, and proclaim; in the end, it shall be he that is his own undoing. For he, is his own… worst enemy.

"Shame… shame upon me! Shame! Oh, my shame!" Beloved stumbled down to his knees sobbing and crying, shaking his head, pounding his fist until bloody on the ground.

"You were selected by the Creator and anointed captain and king over mortal men. It was you who were given might of sword and shield. With every blow you struck, you acted not in the name of vanity but in the Creator's name and for that, you were continually blessed. But this thing that you have done, you have stolen out of greed and lust. You partook of another's wife, and laughingly, did you plot death against him. And now, the Creator's decision is against you, and the life of your son is due payment." Beloved curled further on his knees in defeat as my words cut into him, wounding him with revealing truth.

"There is no need for you to remain here any longer, Beloved King."

"Why?" Beloved looked up, with eyes red, flooded with grieving tears. "No! I will not leave until the Creator has forgiven me! I will sacrifice all that I have! I will give up everything unto the name of thy fallen victim, for repentance. Anything, anything that I must do, to repay this horrible thing!"

"The Creator hath made me in such a way that my senses are intensely keen. And as such, I can smell death from miles away," I raised my head taking in a whiff of the stale cavern air, then advised him. "Go home to your wife, Beloved King. Your son is dead," I said with grim remorse and serious expression.

"Beloved began shuddering, as if the regret stretched him from the inside as he wept for the death of his infant son. Just then, a great horn sounded once, then twice, then again which signified the death of royalty. Beloved ended his crying then rested on his knees with his face in his hands, still shaking his head, then said, 'What are kings to men, but nothing more than high-posted ordinary fools. How they sing songs, and no doubt someday there will be a statue made of me. When they build this image of a noble man for all to admire and see, I pray there be an inscription in place of my name to read... the world's greatest fool!"

"Fear not, Beloved King, for the Creator hath found much favor in you, and you shall continue. And if the Creator grants thee another son, pray he fares wiser than thee..."

"I began to reach to comfort Beloved by the shoulder, but stopped as his grief was blanket enough, and silently departed the cave."

"So the enemy, was him the whole time. Out of all the battles and wars that he fought, the true battle was within himself," The Man of the Present summarized.

"Quite the revelation isn't it!" the serpent replied, glancing back over at the man.

"I know this is probably going to come out the wrong way, but... I thought you were the enemy," the man admitted.

"Me? Why would I be the enemy of one so... Beloved? What

fuels this continued contempt of me, Man of the Present?" the serpent said, tilting his head in question.

"Well, I mean that's what you are! That's what this whole thing is about, right?" the man pressed.

"Such irrational fear and repeated hatred of me. What an ill-seemingly, and devilish notion…" the serpent answered with a sinister whisper, then continued.

CHAPTER 11: THE LIE

"East was the west of the era, but it had been so long since I had ventured out elsewhere. I had spent ages hula-hooping the believers and it seemed theirs was the entirety of the world. I said to myself, if not now, when? So, I made good my exit and left the armies of men and the Beloved King behind and set out, once again, in search of rectitude. I put my back to the Land of Conquest and headed north east, out past the Euphrates River. I traveled some nineteen hundred miles, coming to a land that was lush and green as if it were made of emeralds.

"It was known as 'The Land of Counsel, the Place of Disputed Words.' But unbeknown to me at the time, I was set to witness an epic oral advocacy and dispute over the fate... of a 'Genuine Man.'

"The Land of Counsel was an arid, dry landlocked country and was one of only two doubly landlocked locations of the world, the other being present day Liechtenstein. The vast deserts were clean and scenic as I hopscotched through the endorheic basins. The Mediterranean climate was sweet and easy with touches of heat that made daily life comforting even when dipping and peaking at seasonal highs and lows. I refreshed myself meandering to and fro through a series of irrigated lands, finally, taking shelter in the Kyzyl Kum Mountains. I quickly grew tired of the scarce rations and feeding on Russian tortoises, desert monitors, and saiga antelope. I did, however, take interest in a group of nomads that were responsible for building the extensive irrigation systems along the rivers that fed the local homesteads.

"By that time, some cities had begun to bud with human activity and even some pre-government and culture began to take hold. But the growing silk trade from the east drew merchants and developed a silk route eventually making the cities into some of the most wealthy and powerful provinces of antiquity. The same region came to famed reputation and was later conquered by the great Macedonian general and further by the emperor of the Mongol Empire, but that is another story.

"But I had no interest in such things and the doings of man had utterly exhausted me into contempt, but then… there it was again. The voice of the Creator, this time a beautiful emission of light that bent and distorted air density into a shimmering light of an expanding, yet controlled, wave of intent. Unlike typical sound that travels until encountering the ear drum, the voice of the Creator meets physically, visually, and emotionally with its recipient, unlike any other sensation.

"I approached the voice of the Creator and saw a congregation of unearthly beings, now known as the sons of God. And standing there among them, engaged in a feuding debate, was a figure I had never seen before. The unknown figure then pointed towards a village of the land and the voice of the Creator accepted with acknowledgement, and then departed. The other beings bowed in agreeance and likewise disappeared. The unknown figure turned and then began walking in my direction.

"The figure did not appear to be solid, but was more of a reflection of a refraction of light, that mimicked the appearance of things, similar to that of a mirage. It continued towards me and still the optical phenomenon remained displaced as if viewing an object through a heat haze, but, alas, the figure was not a dream. It continued to draw nearer towards me almost as if it intended to walk right through me. I made my presence known, by raising myself in a defensive 'S' position and instructed it to make itself known before advancing any closer. The unknown figure then solidified and fully materialized, then said happily, 'Oh I'm sorry, I didn't see you coiling there. Allow me to introduce myself. I am 'Evil' and it's a pleasure making your acquaintance, Serpent!"

"You know me?" I asked the newly materialized apparition, while still coiled in an 'S' position.

"Everyone knows you," Evil replied, tipping his head slightly in a greeting fashion.

"I've never seen any creation like you before. Where did you come from?" I asked Evil, slowly twitching my tail with continued warning.

"From to and fro, from up there and down over yonder... quite possibly I'm from everywhere! You know something, I think it wasn't until just now that I came into existence. I only remember walking towards the Creator and joining the congregation of them over there," Evil said gesturing.

"And before that?" I asked, pointing back at Evil.

"Nothing! I guess I came from here, just only moments ago."

"Interesting, I thought the Creator only did such works in the Garden," I implied, biting my lip once.

"Oh! You mean did I come from the Garden! I'm from here and it wasn't the Creator who made me. They did!" Evil answered, thumbing down in the direction of the village.

"The Creator is maker of us all and I will not abide blasphemy by any," I asserted, with serious tone, rattling my tail furiously.

"Well not directly! He made them, they made me... Dad, Granddad. Same recipe, different cookware!" Evil clarified, connecting a smirk to a sly smile.

"You're saying that people made you?" I turned, looking out of one eye at Evil.

"This is their doing, not too shabby I'd say! I mean I could've come out looking like some sort of half-assed, inside out platypus! All things considered, I don't think they did too bad,"

Evil remarked, brushing himself off.

"I wasn't aware that people had mastered the ability of creation as of yet," I questioned, halfway speaking rhetorically.

"Now that you mention it, I don't think they have mastered it. Actually, I don't think they know they did it, but here I am!" Evil admitted, circling around to the left of my shoulder.

"You see, I have all their thoughts, from the very first of them, to the very last born. It's strange, knowing their desires, their fears and weaknesses," Evil expressed with gloom.

"So is that what you are?" I asked, attempting to confirm the identity of Evil.

"That's correct, I am the culmination of their very worst. I think they wanted something to admire and wonder at," Evil hypothesized, nodding in identification of himself.

"To admire themselves, like looking in a mirror," I added, with a slow nod.

"And you know what else? Me, thinks they want me to fight for them," Evil said, postulating his purpose.

"Fight for them? How?"

Evil replied, "As a prosecutor, like in a court room arguing on behalf of the people."

"You mean you're standing in judgment of some argument, as an accuser of sorts," I added, in further clarification.

"That's right," Evil acknowledged, raising up on his toes once, then rocking back down on his heels.

"But, if you're the prosecuting attorney? Who's the accused?" I asked, making eye contact with Evil.

"The Creator, of course!" Evil answered, with a big smile nodding once. I was struck in astonishment that showed plainly on my face.

"You see, the Creator asks too much of them. To walk in the ways of justice and morality, and live by the example of those anointed heroes and judges. It's too difficult. They would never admit it, but they despise their maker! For the Creator is overseer and taskmaster and oppressor. They'll never live up to such standards, that's why they fall wayward time and time again."

"That's not true... I've observed these people since the

beginning as I was there in the Garden with the first formed man and woman. They have goodness in their hearts but they are flawed," I responded in defense.

"I didn't start this argument, nor do I even agree with it. They sought my services out and brought me into existence through their whining and forever sinning. And as such, they've paid my retainer in full... so here I am!" Evil rebutted, opening his arms in presentation of himself.

"Guilt, innocence? It's all nonsense! Honestly, I'm pushing for a mistrial!" Evil admitted with professional clarity.

"I don't understand?" I admitted, wincing then shaking my head in confusion.

"Maybe it would be better if I showed you. Why don't you come down to that village along with me? You might enjoy this."

"What's down there?" I asked.

"Down there is supposedly a Genuine man that is said to be unlike any other of his day. It is said that he has never sinned once, and his heart is pure even when compared against the likes of prophets."

"Who is he?" I inquired.

"I think he is called something like 'Most Patient' or some silliness. But do you know how he is known to the people of his village? Even to those who claim him friend? ... He is 'The Hated.'

"But why! What has he done? What crimes has he committed to be the receiver of such ill will?" I pulled backward in dismay of the charge against the Genuine Man.

"Nothing! Not a goddamn thing! Well, not exactly nothing. You see his crime is one of excellence, faith, and piety. He gives wholly from his heart without expectation of repayment. He works and builds not for fame or social admonishment, but to better himself and those around him. He believes and follows through on his promises, while others are false and plot against their fellow man.

"No, his crime is that by his every goodly deed, perfect action, he spits on his neighbors and shines light on their flaws and weaknesses. He is so perfect that any who stand next to him look like children next to a full-grown man. And they hate it, they can't stand it. And it is that perfection that has made him hated. And when I get down there, he will become... 'The Persecuted.' Come on, you're going to want to see this!" Evil waved, beckoning me to accompany him down to the village.

We headed down to the village and I observed something peculiar amongst the people, then I commented to Evil. "They cannot see you either?" I questioned, as the villagers did not appear to notice either of us as we stood out boldly amongst them.

"People only see what they want to. Even though I am here by their accord, they deny my existence until it suits them to place blame upon me. But I am no more hidden or invisible than one's own reflection. It's always there, it only depends when one wishes to acknowledge the shadow they cast and see their ugly reflections."

"See there! There they go, right there!" Evil tapped me once, while pointing out three men walking through the markets. "Those are the friends of the one I spoke of."

"And they are the ones that have wished evil upon this man," I inquired, watching as the three men walked by.

"Of everyone here, they despise him the most," Evil answered.

"And they call themselves his friends?" I said, cringing at the sight of the men.

"Well you know what they say about friends and enemies, right. It's a shame though. It's so difficult to see people as the counterfeit plastic things they really are."

Plastic ware...

"Werewolves and bad dreams are from where they spawn, for plastic people are just what they're called. Mythology and folklore will tell you of shape shifting things, with clever-like capabilities of seeming like everyday beings. But those foe-some friends you see, are quite plastic and malleable things. Either purposefully or by accidental weakness of heart, be they fake or fearful of the consummate and well-structured of thought.

"Living lies in their hopeless dreams, the sing song themes

453

in their heads are nothing more than plastic thoughts. If their dreams were ever to come true, frightened of reality would they be, sending them back into their plastic box. Plastic people and their going nowhere plastic walk; can't you tell by the way the talk? Checking schedules according to appointments they're never going to keep. Tick-tock on a mock-clock, counting letters and reading numbers, all according to their plastic watch. Those are the type coming right out… of a cereal box.

"Most people who are fake don't even know it, they think they're genuine brand new. When actually, they're just recycled old sheets and smell like somebody's yesterday old farts. They tell lies only when you're gone away. Put them under scrutiny and heat, their lies don't hold up and melt away. Still, the best methods are straight talk and honesty, which keeps them at bay! Under the full lit moon, howling sincere madness they go, but be careful or they'll bite you; cursing you, with their plastic ways!"

"Evil was quite the conversationalist and was taken by his own humor, as he begged the question.

"Say there, Serpent! I've got a question."

"What's on your mind?" I replied, while still people watching.

"What do you think the people of the land of Uz are called?"

"Hmm… I never thought to ask it? Then again, proper demonym's are usually the name of the regional location conjoined with an ending of either; '-an, -ian, -ite, -er or -ish' or some other possible variant. Hm! Uz-ian, Uz-ite. I don't know, I really hadn't thought on the matter very much," I said with a simple shrug.

"Nope! They're called… Uzi's!" A-ha! Ha! Ha! Ha! Ha! Ha! Ha! Ha! Ha!" With a plotting straight face, Evil answered then fell out laughing hysterically, at his own bad joke.

"Evil began acting out the behavior of firing a semi-automatic weapon, while making rapid fire gun noises with childlike amusement. I stopped, dropping my head with silly disappointment still standing next to Evil, who continued acting out with immature amusement. He then changed his voice to impersonating Arnold Schwarzenegger, quoting movie lines from the 1984 film 'The Terminator,' saying,

"The 12-gauge auto-loader. The .45 long slide with laser sighting. The Phased plasma rifle in 40-watt range." Evil then paused, looking around slowly, then continued. "The Uzi nine millimeter!" A-ha! Ha! Ha! Ha! Ha! Ha! Ha! Ha! Ha!" Evil continued laughing hardily at himself, slapping me on the back, in an encouraging childlike manner, as I stood shaking my head in disapproval, then continued down the road with Evil catching up from behind...

"Here it is! This is the home of the guy I was talking about," Evil and I observed the Genuine Man working in a small garden just outside his home.

"Now look! This man and his wife have seven sons and three daughters. His is blessed of wealth and has flocks and herds numbering in the thousands. He began with but a few coins to his name, but through diligence and good business, he's prospered making his holdings the greatest in the land.

"He eats dinner with his children and their families weekly, sharing all that he has even with his neighbors and their associates. All he asks of them joining his table are that they bring a warm smile and a humble spirit to give thanks unto the Creator. Even though his children are of a righteous type, he prays repentance for them, just in case they unknowingly hold malice in their hearts." Evil paused, widening his eyes with sinful delight.

"Now, watch as this Genuine Man, becomes 'The Persecuted.' Evil lifted, then motioned his hands over the home of the man until the sounds of screaming and animal braying was heard echoing out from a distance. The villagers then began to stir and the man lifted his head from his garden and looked towards the commotions.

"What happened?" I inquired of Evil.

"Shhh! Here it comes! Here it comes! Here it comes!" Evil said hurriedly with amusement, waving his arm to silence me.

"And then four messengers came running from down the road to the home of the Persecuted Man. The first cried and sobbed with grief then fell upon their knees, saying, 'My Lord, forgive me, but the Captors have come into the lands and have stolen your oxen and asses and have killed the servants in the fields. What a horrid sight to bear witness to, and yet I am survived if not only to inform my Lord. Then the second and third messengers came from down the road and thus reported,

'Oh my master, please forgive our terrible news. While at the stables and barns, out from the sky fell rocks of fire, all the livestock are burnt up dead and roasted as black ash! We are come here to bear witness that no accident of arson set fire to my master's possessions, yet such a thing was frightful and we are escaped only of the blaze. Then three bands of robbers came and ambushed your caravans as they made ready their journey. All the goods and clothes, including the entirety of the annual stock has been stolen away.'

Then a fourth messenger delivered the worst news of all, saying, 'The news is grave and I am ashamed to speak of such loss. For I was invited by your eldest son for supper, but when I arrived, the house had collapsed. Inside of the house were your seven sons and your three daughters that made feast and drink. They lay dead now and await burial. I am come to advise you of the tragedy that befell your family. If not for my absenteeism, I, too, would be dead,' the fourth messenger reported, unable to hold eye contact with The Persecuted.

"The Persecuted stood silent, then nodded his head, sniffing up a tear. He thanked each of the men and gave them a coin for making the journey and advising him firsthand. He said blessings unto them and motioned them away as he was to inform his wife of the tragedy. He turned towards the door of his home, took one step, and then collapsed, fainting from the shock. His wife rushed to his side and brought him inside to recover."

"Alright… let's see what he does now," Evil remarked, smirking and looking on with enjoyment.

"What he does? What do you think he's going to do! He's probably going to die from grief or become a vagrant, as now his family is gone and he is penniless. Was this your doing?" I pressed, looking left at Evil in disagreement.

"Of course it was! What did you think I was doing? Giving blessing and glad tidings over his place?" Evil proudly admitted, speaking in acknowledgment of his work.

"But why? What purpose does striking this man with such malevolence serve? Even if those who despise him want to see him suffer, don't you think this is a bit much?"

"Forgive me, but I may have left out a bit of information earlier. This whole thing is a bit of a wager. Remember when you first encountered me back in the hills, I was engaged in a bit of an argument with the Creator, and it was the Creator who suggested this man, not me," Evil explained, holding a hand up in pause to explain.

"And then what?"

"The Creator said that this man was unlike any other, that he was perfect. I then reasserted that the Creator had taken favor with him and granted him protection because of his faith and good works. However, I argued that if divine protection were removed and replaced by naught, then this man, too, would fall. To settle the argument, the Creator bestowed me with dark ability to use against this man but made one consolation, which was not to take direct action against him."

"The Creator does not wager, nor bargain, or trade with any. The Creator commands... and that is all," I stated, while frowning in disagreement of the idea.

"Until me! Typically, you'd be correct, but I told you, this is why I'm here. It's to argue against the Creator on behalf of the people. Normally, the Creator wouldn't hear of such things, but I'm no everyday entity." Evil did a pirouette, curtsied, then remarked Ta-daa!

"Evil... at your service!" Evil tapped me, in a gesturing way and we entered the home of The Persecuted. We watched as he knelt crying, clinching, and pounding his fist on the ground.

"Alright now, here we go! Here, we go! Here, we go! Come onnnn, come on, come on, come on, come on!" Evil repeated impatiently, waiting for The Persecuted to curse the Creator.

"The Persecuted cried heavily, then walked to the long table where he and his family would sit for dinner. He walked around

457

to each chair and table setting that was now forever empty. He touched each of the chair backs and kissed the spoons engraved with his children's names from when they were young. He tried to calm the tears, but his grief weakened his knees and he leaned on the table to keep him upright as he bid his children goodbye. He then went and shaved his head and fell upon the ground in prayer."

"What am I, but a man of fatherless children, for it is I that have died this day. It is I that walk, but so too, did I come out naked of a mother's womb. To think that I was more is to forget that I am nothing. What was given was not forever, but grieves me to have it taken away. I cannot hate that which gives nor denies, for the Creator is everything and to the Creator does everything belong. 'The righteous cry and the Creator heareth, and delivereth them out of all their troubles. The Creator is nigh unto them that are of a broken heart and saveth such as be of a contrite spirit."

"Goddammit! You have got to be fucking kidding me... Shhhhhit!" Evil cursed aloud in frustration, while standing over The Persecuted while he prayed.

"You were expecting something else?" I said, looking over at Evil.

"Who in the hell takes four hits like that and still remains upright... jeeeeesh!" Evil cursed aloud, while we remained in the room observing The Persecuted, while he continued to pray.

"This fucking guy!" Evil remarked, shaking his head is contempt.

"You said it yourself! That this man is perfect and goodly even when compared against prophets. Even after everything you did to him, he still has not changed his ways, nor did he curse the Creator. It looks like you have lost your bet. Restore him and be done with it," I said plainly, shrugging at Evil's defeat.

"Not even! Time to double down! Come on, let's get outta here!" Evil swiftly grabbed me and we headed for the door. We left The Persecuted alone in the night and headed back up to the Kyzyl Kum Mountains. We returned back to the location where

Evil and the Voice of the Creator were engaged in debate the previous day. Evil stopped, then said,

"Just hang out here for a moment, I'll be right back."

"Evil then walked up and again joined the congregation of the Creator and the sons of God. This time, the voice of the Creator became quite animated and Evil backed off, but reasserted himself in the argument. The circle of unearthly beings then dissipated in similar fashion as before and Evil returned, where I was waiting."

"Alright, let's go!"

"You mean back down again?"

"Yup, it ain't over yet! You're gonna like this next part!" Evil said leading me back down to the village.

"We headed back down to the village and stood above The Persecuted's home. And just as before, Evil raised his arms and then a moaning of pain was heard coming from inside The Persecuted's house."

"We entered the home and saw The Persecuted in bed, moaning and aching while his body became sick and covered with sores from his head to his feet. His wife came in, and upon seeing him, gasped in disgust and terror. She administered medicine and washed him, then rubbed ointment upon him, then wrapped him with gauze. We kept watch over The Persecuted while he suffered, but he remained faithful and never did he curse the Creator."

"How long is this going to persist? This man isn't going to break, and all you're doing is torturing him," I argued, with reason against Evil.

"Perfect is a bold statement. It means that under the most extreme conditions one remains unchanged," Evil replied, stone faced and undeterred by the man's steadfastness.

"This is no personal vendetta I have against this man. But you have to understand, that making a man like this goes against what Creator wants for these people. The Creator must see the folly of his humanly work, as these people will never live up to the given commandment laws, it's impossible!"

"How is perfection or even seeking perfection wrong?" I

questioned.

"The idea of human perfection in itself is a crime. Humans aren't perfect. Why they're the most imperfect creatures that ever have been. There is a paradox that was or, excuse me... will be presented during the Renaissance: 'That the greatest perfection is imperfection.'- Lucilio Vanini

"And as such, Mr. Vanini will argue with Joseph Juste Scaliger over the philosopher Empedocles as follows: 'If the world were perfect, it could not improve and so would lack true perfection, which depends on progress.'

"And according to Aristotle, perfection means 'complete' or 'nothing to add.' And I argue against the Creator that such perfect men are an abomination to what the Creator asks of humanity. The Creator does not want perfect, the Creator wants growth and repentance, but how can one repent or grow if one is perfect. It is the paradox of perfection and my argument is that imperfection is perfect. And this Genuine Man, goes against the growth and development of humanity.

"Meaning the people who sin and fall wayward from faith are not wrong or corrupt. As a matter of fact, they're doing exactly what the Creator wants them to do. This is how they were made and what they were meant to do. They were made to sin, they were made to hate, to fight, to curse, to steal, to rape, and to inflict! This so called Genuine Man is the true sinner, for he can never repent, he can never be washed of sin... because he has none! What a fucking joke!

"The Creator mocks his creation daily with the riddle of life and virtue, only to have them circle the board, wait their turn, and then 'do not pass go!' By the very introduction of sin itself, the Creator has determined that humanity is to fail. If the Creator did not wish any fault or misdeed why create temptation? Why create value and worth? Why create misery and punishment? This man's very presence is contradictory to all that is good for humanity.

"This man's very being says that there is no better than what he is and his inability to scorn the Creator says so! Any real man would spit on the altars and shrines of the Creator. Wrong you say! Not even! For this man is something they will never be. He is contempt laughing at all of humanity, and his steadfastness is not helping anyone. He should swear oath of the pagan gods and dance naked for all to see, only to have fiery rage brought upon this village as example, which is what the Creator enjoys doing so much anyways," Evil argued, motioning and pointing up at the sky then down at the ground.

"But why do you think that this man's suffering is going to produce anything besides pain and misery?" I countered with question.

"Know this, Serpent. People are only as good as the situation they're in! If you take away their wealth, their social status, they're comfort, and a few of their toys. They can't handle it. If things are good, then they're good. As they say, 'they are blessed' and God has blessed them as such. But if they fall on hard times, if they lose their job, their spouse leaves them, their children die, they become sickly and weak, then God has mocked them and they, in turn, hate God. Their faith isn't real. Their faith is based in materialism and held up by their peers that envy and inflate their egos!" Evil jumped back in response.

"People and their blessings are as fake as the masks of society they wear! I merely want to even things out. Humanity should be graded on a curve. People like him over there are over achievers and make it hard on everyone else. The Creator has got to see that this guy goes against everything humans are. If he can be turned, then surely the others can't be held to such extreme levels of expectation."

Just then, The Persecuted's wife came into his room, and she said, 'Your infliction is great and your prayers go unanswered. You have lost everything and still you persist crying to a Creator who has forsaken you. You should be of some sense and curse such a being and allow him to end you, as this suffering of yours is unbearable to my sight!'

'The Creator will protect him and preserve his life; he will bless him in the land and not surrender him to the desire of his foes. The Creator will sustain him on his sickbed and restore him from his bed of illness,'" the Persecuted recited.

461

"Motherfucker!" Evil yelled out in anger, hearing The Persecuted's prayer.

"Come on, we gotta go. It's almost bed time."

"I'm not tired, nor do I...." I turned to advise Evil, but before I could finish he pulled me towards the door to exit.

"No, not us... them!" Evil grabbed me and we headed towards the home of The Persecuted's three friends.

"Hold on a second!" The Man of the Present interrupted.

"What's wrong?"

"How are you talking to the devil? What do you have a split personality now?" the man questioned, looking at the serpent with suspicion.

"I assure you, Man of the Present, I suffer from no psychosis of the mind nor am I conflicted between multiple personalities. Besides, the way I described Evil, was that at first it appeared like a mirage. And a mirage is not a hallucination nor a figment of the imagination, but a real viewable optical thing. Which is why demons have often been captured on camera. I however, cast no shadow nor reflect any image, and I recite, 'The fear of the Creator is to hate evil: pride, and arrogance, and the evil way, and the froward mouth, do I hate. Counsel is mine, and sound wisdom: I am understanding and I have strength.'

"We then arrived at the homes of The Persecuted's three friends and visited upon each of them while they slept. The first was known as 'As the Dawn Glows,' the second 'He that Loved,' and the third 'The Dawn Chorus.' I watched as Evil whispered subconscious suggestions to them in their dreams, and Evil said, *The Cold Dream...*

'To sow seeds of doubt, is but a simple thing even amongst the pure and most genuine. Men and women alike fuck for greed, want, lust, and plot. So does the pious hold such thoughts in a most perfect heart. For he that dwells in a house of clay, fears a heavy rain that may wash it all away. Builders of wood sleep securely they say, but that too is nothing more than an ashtray. To those who claim holy and portray morally right, their cloak is deadly camouflage like a shark's fin at night. How they put on such a good show, preaching of wrath and punishment but their turpitudes are shared only by the secretly elite. For pleasure and success to the bold are often nothing more than swindling luck. He must repent of his sins as he is no greater than any other who has fallen astray. But only if he admits his true crimes and begs mercy of us, as we are the true, and the most fearing of God."

"And I suppose you think these men will have further sway over The Persecuted?" I questioned Evil, as we headed back to The Persecuted's home.

"Like I said, people are only as good as the situation they're in. It's one thing to suffer alone, but what happens when one is ridiculed by his peers. In a difficult situation, one's friends or family come to reassure them that 'things will get better.' Even though they cannot physically take away the suffering, it does offer some comfort to the victim. When this support group is removed, the victim will feel alone, with no safety net to catch them as they fall. The fall from grace is a long and disorienting dive, and most people cannot stand to feel out of control even for a short time. It's a frightening felling, but I think this might just push him over the edge."

"The following morning, it was just as Evil had predicted, The Persecuted's three friends came to visit him. The three men sat and drank tea, and enjoyed some baked bread for that was all he had to offer. The Persecuted was comforted by the company of his friends, but the look in the men's eyes was actually one of glee, as now they had more than he did."

"My grief flows throughout my veins, it exits my nostrils and fills the very air, then I breathe in sickness and it too envelops me. Not only is my pride gone from me, but my heart is cold, and tears of mourning do nothing to ease the pain. My skin is sore with ailment and none can stand to see me for my appearance," The Persecuted told the truth of his dilemma, showing his illness to his friends.

"May we offer you comfort my friend for we are, too, sickened by your suffering. This evil that has befallen you is surely some mistake by the Creator. One so pious and steadfast has surely come under the calamity of a wicked grace." As the

Dawn Glows spoke first, then reached towards, but pulled back from touching his festering friend.

"All the things that were young and new, ready and full of value. I have heard some say to me that my friend only speaks truthfully, but his heart is like other men. Speak truthfully my friend. The doings of everyone is at some point none pure. Behind closed doors perhaps, quietly underneath the skin, where none can see. A servant's wife or their tender young girl by chance. The servant himself or his son that you paid to come dancing? The Creator sets judgment against you. Speak to us my friend, we will hear, understand, and forgive you," As the Dawn Glows implied, while looking grimly at The Persecuted.

"These things that have taken me, what sense or reason could there be. I hear your words my friends, but I bid truthfully, that I am innocent. The Creator knows what is right and what is wrong. Is my affliction punishment? For surely, I am without any blessing. The Creator is justice, but what justice is to be made of this?" The Persecuted defended, begging pardon of his friend.

"He poses a good question regarding justice," I injected while watching the four men conversing.

"How so?" Evil responded, glancing over at me.

"How can man be just with the Creator? Is it even possible? Where the concept of justice comes down to perspective. Justice and moral correctness is not one thing, but many concepts that depend on current law, field of ethics, religion, and social versus individual fairness. If you mean to imply that The Persecuted's situation is justice, then these men could be looking at it from either angle. Did he do something wrong to be punished, is this nature's way of balancing out life, or some crime he committed that was never adjudicated lawfully."

"So what's your point?" Evil asked, still observing the four men, but listening intently.

"What I'm getting at, is how humanity views the good and bad events that happen to them as a matter of justice or divine command. Many philosophers have grappled with the concept of divine command…"

"Ohh! I know what you're talking about now. Yeah, I know, it was that guy!" Evil interrupted, then snapped his fingers trying to recall the name of the person he referenced.

"You know! The guy with the face! He was always talking about philosophy and stuff..."

"The guy... with the face?" I repeated, back at Evil dumfounded by his extremely, general description.

"You know... the guy, he was always talking, with the beard. Greco-Roman- something, he had a dilemma one time. Jeesh! Why can't I... He was that one guy, with the philosophy, and the beard... you know who I'm talking about!" Evil continued still motioning with his fingers and pointing, as if that was making it any clearer.

"I really hate it when people do that. Like there has only existed one guy with a beard who always said stuff! Let me throw some random names out, because you said Greco-Roman... Socrates... Plato..."

"There you go, Plato!" Evil jumped, snapping his fingers.

"That's what I said... So, Plato, he's going to argue in the 'Euthyphro Dilemma,' the nature of piety, which can be presented as the question: 'Is X good because God commands it, or does God command X because it is good? Is the pious loved by the gods because it is pious, or is it pious because it is loved by the gods?' - Plato, Euthyphro' The whole thing is nonsense when you look at it. One might argue that this scenario itself is nonsense."

"How so?"

"Well as we stand over The Persecuted and his friends, they ponder that what has occurred is bad. And the reason for it is due to some sinful act by The Persecuted, which is the Creator's justice. However, unbeknown to them, that it had nothing to do with his actions. It's just a wager, as it was I who cursed him and the Creator who allowed it. So therefore, justice really has no meaning to the Creator, as the Creator does as the Creator pleases." Evil explained, then motioned showing a tit for tat gesture with his hands.

"You're right, it kinda takes us back to my original question.

Not is the Creator just with decision making, but how can mankind be just with the Creator? No matter what happens to them, they can never stand in judgment of the Creator for any doings or actions. They just have to accept it and go on."

"Like I said... that's why I'm here. The way things are, they can never have justice... or even revenge!" Evil winked at me, then we turned our attention back to The Persecuted and his friends.

"My words are sound, even though my physical appearance speaks of divine judgment against me. Righteousness is in every word I speak, nor have I ever spoken anything other, even when alone. I agree with you that if our situations were reversed I, too, would question what has brought such misery upon another, but in my current state I have no wisdom of the matter.

"I sit amongst you as I was just yesterday, the same man, the same person. Without my wealth, without my family, and yes without my health, I cannot turn away from that which built me up. I was thankful everyday then, I am thankful everyday even now. I have done no better, nor been any more sincere in my works than any other. So, too, must it be that I have done no more wrong, but still receive my share or life's pain, and I recite, 'Trust in the Creator with all thine heart and lean not unto thine own understanding. In all thy ways acknowledge him, and he shall direct thy paths.'

"You are so full of it, you know that? Why don't you just cut the shit!" The Dawn Chorus became angry at The Persecuted's defense. The other two men reached trying to calm him down as he was angry and The Persecuted's humble attitude.

"You walk around here acting like you're better than everyone else, when everyone knows that deep down, you're just like us. You've got your money and you love to sprinkle coin and alms on the unfortunate, don't you! Makes you look like you're so generous and kind. Everybody knows you lied and stole to get that property. The only reason you got the extra lands in that deal was because you blackmailed the previous owner. The Creator's blessings you say? It's bullshit! You're just a swindler and a hustler!

"You can sit there and act like this is all a mistake, but nobody gets sick for no reason. You laid down in sin with beasts and came up with an unnatural filth. Your lies cling to you like the smell of cheese on a gangrenous wound. If you won't own up to what you've done, then your lies are going to take you. And don't think I'm going down with you. The only way to save the body is to hack of the infected limb.

"We've been your friends through everything and we've even protected you many times when gangs of men wanted to jump you, because of your aloof attitude. And did we get anything, for everything we've done for you? No, all you do is invite everyone over when you want to show off. If you ask me, whatever you did is coming back on you... and now we're on top and you're on the bottom," The Dawn Chorus continued shouting then shushed his hand away at The Persecuted.

"There we go... its warming up now!" Evil nodded in delight watching the heated exchange.

"My very own friends mock me as if I withhold secrets and covet lies. I pray and am faithful without expectation. My fate is no different than any other of the earth. The best of the field is plucked from the ground. The prized pig once awarded is then slaughtered and presented for breakfast. Why do bad things happen to the good? In turn, why then do good things happen to the bad. Only the Creator can reason it," The Persecuted seated Indian style, begged the question before his friends.

"You know, I really gotta give it to him. After everything he stills speaks with reason and considers balance. Very few could do such a thing. He is cut from very fine cloth," Evil admitted, in respect of The Persecuted.

"But...?" I quipped back.

"Be it linen, cotton, or silk... when they are muddied with filth, they are nothing but a dirty rag," Evil spat in the direction of The Persecuted.

"Your words are true. The good and bad that happens in life, to whom, when, and why are difficult questions many times with no answer," I said considering the difficulty in understanding the Creator's reasons of good and bad.

"I thought we had settled this. There is no justice for them and the Creator doesn't care. The best they can hope for is simple pleasures, good meats, fine wines, pleasurably company, wealth, and the respect of their peers and the envy of others," Evil concluded, looking away then rolling his eyes.

"That's not true. Their lives have meaning, and I've seen it. So many of them are lost in a sea of hopelessness, but that doesn't mean they have no purpose. It is for each of them to find the meaning and purpose of their lives. Many of them will not reach their full potential, nor will they become any more than a face in the crowd, for they are only sheep. We are the wolves, but low, there are among them the few... the sheepdogs," Evil and I then turned out attention back to The Persecuted and his friends who continued to accuse him

"For all that you have done, my persecuted friend, one would think that you would have more wealth with the Creator. Perhaps you have short changed yourself. Have you some sinful debts that go unpaid by chance?" As the Dawn Glows asked, The Persecuted.

"Oh, my friend, I pray that all my doings have been tabulated correctly and none will bear witness against me that I am wicked or false. This question you pose is a correct one for many who prosper do so by the backs of others. But by no means do I believe that my success came at the expense of others," The Persecuted replied solemnly.

"Upon hearing the concept posed, I thought then asked the question aloud, Profit is a mortal concept, but is it possible that man can be profitable or perhaps wealthy by means of the Creator?"

"What are you talking about now?" Evil remarked, looking over at me.

"Well, men are seeking success in their worldly doings. They seek fulfillment and abundance by their work and through admiration by their peers. And one can look on themselves as wealthy by the amount of goods that they have collected," I further explained to Evil.

"Pack rats playing poker with a bunch of trinkets and

nonsense! In the long run, it will all break down and end up in a graveyard as yesterday's garbage." Evil concluded, shrugging off the idea.

"See, that's what I mean. Mortal wealth or money is meaningless. Which is why I think they hold to their religions so stridently. They are seeking something of value that will last," I further elaborated, slightly motioning forward then upward to the heavens.

"Mmmm…" Evil vocalized.

"When considering profit or wealth by means of economics, the function of money is a universal instrument of quantitative measurement. One of the interesting things about money and value is that objects are constantly increasing and decreasing in value. But what of wealth by means of the Creator? Does the Creator have a universal standard of quantitative measurement? Do prayers and offerings go up and down in value according to a divine stock market? And then I believe there is another question often posed when considering economics."

"And what's that?" Evil interjected.

"Quality versus Quantity? Take for comparison two pairs of shoes. One very fashionable and trendy produced by a highly profitable company. Now, a second pair produced by a shoe maker by hand. The first pair, all be it trendy, are made at lowered quality. While the second are made from high grain leathers, and constructed to the specific gait of the wearer. Now, if one were to ask profit and wealth between the two companies, you would say the larger company who produces thousands of shoes and makes more profit over the smaller business that only sells only a few hundred a year.

"Now ask the customer to determine the wealth of their shoe. The first has the latest, fashion trend and is no doubt the envy of all others on the catwalk. While their counterpart is, too, satisfied as they have a quality product to carry them securely and comfortably as a good shoe should do. However, after the first year, the trendy shoe is now out of style and has begun to fall apart; while the second shoe maintains its wear-ability and may only need re-soling. Now I ask you, if the Creator has any sense of value, profit, or wealth, what does the Creator consider; the quantity of ritual prayer offered, or the quality of faith in the believer?"

"You really enjoy this philosophy bullshit don't you?" Evil remarked with cynicism.

"You have to admit in our current situation as we look on The Persecuted and his affliction, they are asking it themselves. What is the meaning of prayer? Does faith have any real value? Is there some tabulation to be cashed out on that Day of Judgment where one's faith is worth its weight in gold? Or perhaps, it's just a nice thought, like volunteering and at the end of it all, they'll be rewarded with an 'A' for effort! But one last thing crosses my mind, and I ask... If it is possible to be profitable with the Creator, is it possible to be debt free?"

"Outside of The Persecuted's home was a young man known as, 'He that Mind's the Creator' who had volunteered to aid the Persecuted in his garden as he was too sick to work. He listened to the men inside arguing the cause of The Persecuted's affliction and the tragic losses. After several rounds of the men arguing and pointing blame upon The Persecuted, the young man could no longer hold his tongue. He stepped inside of the home and joined the men in debate, saying.

"I am young compared to the years of my host, but I cannot hold my tongue on this matter before me any longer. Of all men and women combined, none can truly know of the Creator's motives and will as we are only human and know not even what we do. Only the Creator knows and the Creator communicates in mystery, such like the dreams and visions while we awake in our sleep.

"The Creator offers help to those who ask for aid, as does the Creator forgive those of sin. But no man can stand in judgment of the wise as they, too, are tested with grief. Only the Creator knows the outcome and reasoning of their affliction, but chastising the pious is the habit of ungodly men. My years are few, but I have seen the light of the Creator as it saves those from the pit and returns youth to the flesh of the old. If this man be clean, the Creator grant him blessing and make him whole

470

again. Justice, wealth and profit are for men, the Creator respects nothing, but the wise have nothing to fear," He that Mind's the Creator said boldly, standing in defense of The Persecuted.

"I cry, I cry, how I have cried to the almighty and still my suffering is increased. Every one of my house, my children, of my name are no more. All those I once employed, I am now indebted to for I have nothing to repay their wages lost. My wife holds spite of me as she walks past me and her shadow greets me with disgust. I hear the children play outside calling the names of my dead sons and daughters. Saying as how they have been called home to the pits of fire, for the evils of my secret doings.

"I have nothing to eat but coarse meal and dry cakes, but even then my body resists me and swiftly rejects any sustenance I offer it. My friends whom I have shared and grown strong with, it is in this hour that I lean upon you, but in this trust fall, my spotters have failed me. Weakened I am, physically, financially, socially, but never in faith am I beaten.

"As I look upon each of you... my friends, I thank you for sharing company with me. I know not how long I shall live after this. I thank you for your words, even though sour and poisoned they are with accusation. Still, I am thankful for them, for now I know what you really think of me. I am a straightforward and honest man. I assist, I uplift, I acknowledge, and I offer without pride or lust in my heart. I want for all that which I want for myself. For everything that I have given, I did give purely without humor in my tongue.

"I know not why the Creator hugs me with an iron gauntlet and salutes me with a backhand. Perhaps there is an evil at work here, none can know it for certain. I hope you have enjoyed these last bits of food and hot drink I have to offer. Even of the sideways hospitality from that stubborn mule I call a loving wife. But before I kick you out of this empty shack that is my home, before I spit on you the last life out of a dry mouth, I say to you, each of you... my friends, my would-be brothers, with fake friends like you... who needs real enemies? Now get the hell outta my house! And don't ever come back here again!"

Evil clapped his hands, laughing at the condemning remark, then simply said to me, "Kill him!"

"What! Why?" I questioned in shock.

"Because fuck him, that's why! Now, kill him," Evil repeated, fixing his eyes on me.

"If you want him dead, then why don't you do it yourself?" I responded.

"Yeah... I kinda forgot to mention that part? You see, when I went back and renegotiated with the Creator, I agreed that I wouldn't kill him. But nothing was ever said about you," Evil raising a hand in defense.

"This man has suffered enough and now you want me to end him?" I further argued in question.

"What do you care? You kill people all the time! This isn't any different!" Evil reasserted.

"This *is* different! You want me to kill by your command. I take no part in these matters. If you want him dead, you will have to break your word with the Creator," I rebutted.

"Look at it this way, you'd be putting him out of his misery. In the afterlife, he'll thank you. So go on! Kill him!" Evil said again, lightly tapping me to ease the distrust.

I remained silent, refusing to kill The Persecuted, causing Evil to become angry, "What do you think you're doing? You think you're helping them somehow? You think they like you. They fucking hate you! You think all those times you got involved that they weren't repulsed by you! They'll never like you! It's been written! They'll curse you throughout the entirety of existence. Besides, these people are nothing but food to you!" Evil argued, motioning with both hands down at The Persecuted in front of them.

"I expect nothing from them. You would never understand it." The serpent said strongly, "The way I treat people has nothing to do with the way people treat me."

"Why do you think I brought you down here in the first place? All you do is kill!" Evil became further enraged at my refusal to kill.

"Wait a minute..." Evil paused pointing at me. "You don't

know do you!"

"Know what?" I questioned, making eye contact with Evil.

"But that's it, isn't it. You don't know what this is all about, do you?" Evil spoke rhetorically, with a downward tone as if I were a small child.

"You dumb fuck! You're just as blind and stupid as they are? What a waste!" Evil raised his voiced, continuing his verbal assault.

"He looked right at you..." Evil continued.

"He... what?" I said in confusion, shaking my head.

"Law Giver... when he came down from the mountain. He looked right at you, he said it right to your face! What did you think he was talking about! It's your name! It's your purpose!"

"My name, my purpose? My name is, Serpent..." I said plainly, blinking in confusion.

"That's not your name, that's just what they call you. You know as well as I do, that human words have no meaning to the attributes of one's actions and purpose."

"You know my purpose, the meaning of my life?" I asked.

"Yeah, I know your purpose... but I'll tell you what, though. If you kill him for me... I'll tell you!" Evil said holding the information over my head, then Evil continued heckling me while still ordering the kill.

"I was conflicted with wanting to know the purpose of my life, but refused to kill by command of Evil. I don't know how to explain it, but it seemed... wrong. Overwhelmed, I snapped in judgment then coiled quickly and struck, grabbing hold of Evil, piercing and inflicting him with venom. I coiled around him, bending him backwards slowly with constricting ease snapping his vertebrae until he was folded in half, and lay dead. I lopped his body to the side of me then spat, saying in disgust."

"You don't command me! And now you're dead! Evil bastard!" I turned and exited the scene, all together sick of the matter.

"Then there came a giggling from behind me, that became a snickering, then full on laughing. I turned back around to see the body of Evil repairing itself and coming back to an upright form. I stood in shock of seeing Evil come back to life and showing no signs of pain or injury."

"Sorry, fuck face. I guess today's just not my day! Ha! Ha! Ha! Ha! Ha!" Evil said laughing directly at me.

"I kinda liked you too! I do have to say that was a mighty nice try though! You know, if I had more time I'd find a supersized condom and stick you up my ass! Literally, for shits and giggles! Ha! Ha! Ha! Ha! Ha! Ha! Ha! Ha! Ha!" Evil further said, stretching and flexing his arms and back muscles.

"Snakes and stones may break my bones, but only one can ever truly hurt me! I should really fuck your shit up for that, but I got a better idea! One much, much, more suiting! You know what I'm going to do? I'm going to make them think you're me!" Evil said, with a scowl of a smirk.

"Why?" I remarked

"Because I can! And because you can't stop me. That's what you get for pissing me off! Now everything I do will be attributed to you!" A familiar rumbling came over the hillside and the voice of the Creator presented itself.

"Damn! Well I guess that means times up… oh well! He can have em!"

"So, you lost!" I said, watching as Evil prepared to leave.

"How do you figure?"

"You tortured that man. You took away everything he had and he never lost faith. You lost," I summarized.

Evil motioned at the three friends walking down the road leaving the home of The Persecuted, "Man, you really are stupid, aren't you? I got three for the price of one! I never even touched his three friends and look what happened? They have turned away from the Creator and now they belong to me. This is a numbers game baby! The Persecuted was never going to fall, I knew that from the beginning… he's perfect. Of humans, there are the strong and there are the weak, but no matter what, the strong will continue. They will always find a way.

"But the weak… it doesn't take very much. I didn't even have to touch them. I touched one who was faithful and they, being weak, fell without even a push. Their weakness is that they never really believed. The whole time, they were just going through the motions, and now the score is three to one! Ha! Ha! Ha! I love this casino called humanity, you gotta play the odds baby! See you around limp dick!" Evil turned and left walking and whistling an unfamiliar tune.

"I went back and saw The Persecuted in his home alone, weeping and shuddering. He could feel the aches of sickness overtaking him as his body further turned against him and the vapor of life slowly exiting his lungs. With his last strength, he lifted himself and prayed reciting, 'All they that see me laugh me to scorn; they shoot out the lip, they shake the head saying, he trusted on the Creator that he would deliver him, let Him deliver him, seeing he delighted in Him. But thou art He that took me out of the womb; thou didst make me hope when I was upon my mother's breasts. I was cast upon thee from the womb; thou art my Creator from my mother's belly. Be not far from me for trouble is near, for there is none to help.' The Persecuted now on his death bed continued,

'Oh my Creator, rebuke me not in thine anger, neither chasten me in thy hot displeasure. Have mercy upon me, my Creator; for I am weak. My Creator, heal me; for my bones are vexed. My soul is also sore vexed, but thou my Creator, how long? Return, my Creator, deliver my soul, oh save me for thy mercy's sake. For in death, there is no remembrance of thee, in the grave who shall give thee thanks? I am weary with my groaning; all the night I make my bed to swim; I water my couch with my tears. Mine eye is consumed because of grief; it waxeth old because of all mine enemies. Depart from me, all ye workers of iniquity; for the Creator hath heard the voice of my weeping. The Creator hath heard my supplication; the Creator will receive my prayer. Let all mine enemies be ashamed and sore vexed, let them return and be ashamed suddenly.'

"The Voice of the Creator then descended down upon The Persecuted and comforted him and healed him of his aliments and afflictions. He was Persecuted no more, and was made whole, as through everything, he remained a Genuine Man. And I, the serpent, heard the voice of the Creator that did say, and I

475

recite:

'Many are the afflictions of the righteous, but the Creator delivereth him out of them all. He keepeth all his bones, not one of them is broken. Evil shall slay the wicked and they that hate the righteous shall be desolate. The Creator redeemeth the soul of his servants and none of them that trust in him shall be desolate.'

"He cried as he was healed then he heard the voices of people gathering outside of his door. His wife call to him and it was there that all the people of the village and others from far away came to visit him. They each came and kissed him and thanked him for all that he had bestowed upon them in their times of need. Each of them gave him a coin and gift of beast or bread, seed or cloth so that all that was lost was replenished until he was more than doubled in wealth than before.

"Even that his children were killed too returned and he and his wife were granted more children that gave them joy. It was some many years before I returned to the Land of Counsel and laid eyes upon the Genuine Man. He had lived many additional years and saw his sons and daughters become generations. I visited the spot where Evil made debate with the Creator, and that's when he called to me."

"Who?" The Man of the Present asked.

"The Genuine Man, he was calling to me." I turned and headed back over to him, where he stood there smiling."

"You over there, come up and share hot drink with me. I would shame myself if not to offer hospitality to all who travel lonely. Please come and join me," he called out to me with an inviting tone.

"I hesitated at first, that he would invite me to share hot drink, and offered company and kindness. I approached him and greeted him with pleasantries."

"You... are not afraid of me? Even of my appearance?" I asked The Genuine Man

"I fear only the Creator. I admit, I have never seen one of your sort before. But I know the Creator is master of all, of me and of you. Besides, I know who you are and I do not hate nor have fear of you. Therefore, I love life," the Genuine Man said easily.

"How did you know?" I asked the Genuine Man.

"Know what?"

"About Evil... and the wager over your life?"

"I am aware of no evil wager," The Genuine Man replied, shrugging away at the idea.

"But you... but how? I mean the whole time that you were cursed and afflicted with suffering. You never lost faith, nor did you curse the Creator foul? You had to have known that it was Evil who was testing you," I further questioned.

"I speak nothing false to you. I was aware of no such deviation. I am only a man and I know very few things, but what I do know, I know to be true. 'These six things doth the Creator hate; yea, seven are an abomination unto him. A proud look, a lying tongue, and hands that shed innocent blood, a heart that deviseth wicked imaginations, feet that be swift in running to mischief, a false witness that speaketh lies, and he that soweth discord among brethren.'

"Therefore, I know that the Creator does not hate me and loves me. Some view life as a glass, half empty or half full, but I choose to look past the illusion. I look on life not based on what is offered or what possessions I think I have, but I press to see further meaning and the simplicity of it all, for it is nothing but sand and water. Some see themselves as being half way rich or half way poor, but the wise understand that the quantity of water matters little, with regard to the quality of it. Look past the illusions and see sand and water, for in the desert water is the same to every man.' the Genuine Man said, with a smile.

"I thanked him for his hospitality, leaving me to go on my way...

"So, he beat him?" the Man of the Present asked.

"Beat who?"

"Beat the devil... Because the devil is a lie!" the Man of the Present, said confidently.

"Interesting! It's not that I dispute your claim at all. It's just, well you say it with such ease and confidence. As if you know for certain the lies the devil will tell. As if you're, oh so prepared for the devil in disguise."

"Then what do you say it is?" the man further questioned.

"Oh, it's not for me, the devil's lie that is. But let me explain something to you, Man of the Present. I have heard that expression many times before, but there's something you don't seem to realize."

"And what's that?"

"The devil's lie, he knows it too. You see, in the battle for good and evil, there stands an accuser of you all. But what you think you know of him, is so very little, but he knows all of you better than you know yourselves. You see, Man of the Present, the devil knows what you know, he thinks exactly as you sing... very badly! But he doesn't tell you you are off key, he applauds you and encourages. You've been... running a race against a lame horse, all the while thinking you're stronger and faster than you really are. Every failure, every heartache that has befallen you, is nothing. The devil, yes, has set those things against you, but they are things that you could easily overcome. The devil *is* lying to you, but his lies are designed to make you think your faith and fortitude is stronger than what it really is.

"And then one day, he'll come a walking and he won't approach you in an unfamiliar fashion. No, No, No. He presents himself and challenges you not in unfamiliarity, but with your favorite sin. And then you'll say, 'I know you! You're the devil and you're a liar! I can beat you just as I have always defeated you.' And then the devil will remove the mask, he will unhitch the chains, and you, being overconfident, will accept the ill-fated race. And then on that day, the devil won't lie to you, he'll tell you truth, right to your face."

"Which is?" The Man of the Present questioned.

"That you are weak, a coward, a sadist, and criminal. You never got over that addiction, did you? You didn't turn away from children, you just paid someone else to while you gained release in voyeur. And in the end, he'll beat you, and you'll cry wondering why and how. And the devil will say... 'I am the devil and I am your favorite lie!' So, go ahead, keep humming that familiar tune, the devil is a lie, and you're right... because it's the lie that comes from within you!"

"And what of the devil... where did he go?" the man inquired of his whereabouts after parting ways with The Genuine Man.

"Oh, he's out there! Glad handin', Chi-litin', doin' his work... 24 hours a day!"

CHAPTER 12: THE TRUTH

"What's this?" the man asked, looking curiously at an unidentified object.

"What's what?"

"The man reached down and picked up a rectangular object wrapped in animal skins covered in dust, set on an opening in the rock face. He unfolded the animal skins revealing the hand stitched bindings of a book written in a language he had never seen before."

"This!" the man asked, as he raised the book showing the serpent. "What book is this?"

"Put! That! Down! … And do it now!" the serpent replied with a serious and demanding tone, then coiled himself and began rattling his tail.

"Ok, but just tell me…"

"Now!" the Serpent repeated his demand increasing the rattle of his tail, violently.

"I'm sorry, I just noticed it. I didn't realize it was there the whole time. What is it?" The man slowly recovered the book and placed it back from where it came. He then stepped a few feet away from it, showing the serpent he would not threaten it again.

"It's not for you, is what it is."

"It's a book, so how could it not be for me? I mean, isn't that what books are here for? So people can read them?"

"Not that one. That book is unlike any other, and is meant for the eyes of one, and only one," the serpent said, shaking his head with stern expression.

"Then how did you get it?"

"It was gifted to me long ago, and it shall remain here until the owner reclaims it."

"Who wrote it?"

The serpent sighed heavily thinking to himself, then replied, "I suppose telling you couldn't do much harm. But do me a favor first, step out of the cavern and look down that tunnel on your far left and tell me what you see. Don't go down there! Just tell me what you see," the serpent added.

"The man did as the serpent instructed and stepped out of the cavern and peered down the furthest tunnel on the left. The torch light he held was not bright enough to pierce the cavernous darkness, but down deep into the tunnel began to glow a light. The light was unlike the sun piercing an opening in a cave, nor was it the illumination from cave minerals dancing in reflection against each other. The light was heavenly, warm and glowing. The voice of the serpent called out beckoning the man back into the cavern.

"What did you see?"

"A light!" he replied, after rejoining the serpent.

"I don't know how to explain it. It was a light unlike any I have ever seen before. Wait… I've heard of a light at the end of a tunnel…" the man began to hyperventilate and then asked in fright, "Am I dead?"

"Hardly, my dear Man of the Present. You are very much alive. And you are correct, that light is unlike any other known to man, but let me ask you. How did you feel when you saw it?" The serpent chuckled heavily in response.

"I felt…it was strange, but it felt like… like I was home. There was something very familiar about… but how's that even possible?"

"That light, Man of the Present, is the light from the Garden… of Eden. That's right… it's just down that tunnel.

That familiar feeling you experienced was real, because *it is* home. It's where we all come from and one day, man shall return there to it."

"You mean... it's there, and I can go!" he responded, in astonishment of the revelation.

"... Not so fast!" The serpent dropped his tail, blocking the exit between the cavern and the man.

"You see, Man of the Present, the expulsion of man and womankind out of the Garden, was not a complete exile, one day mankind is to return. But that's something that has troubled me since I first learned of that fact. It's how the Creator made you all. With infinite curiosity and growth capability. For eons and millennia, none have known of the entrance here, at least... none have lived to tell of it. But one day, the location to the entrance of the Garden will become known and man will set his efforts on retaking it for his own. And when he does, he will gain access to the trees of divine abilities," the serpent further orated.

"What will happen then?"

"I posed that very question before, and I repeat. I do not know why the Creator made you all in such a way, nor do I know why the Creator will allow you all back, where your greed and lust for power will overcome you. But on that day, man will gain the full abilities of the trees and then man's power will rival the Creator's. There will be a struggle, and at first, man will lose and fall repeatedly, but man does not give up so easily. For soon after and with time, man will find a way. Yes... man will find a way to defeat the Creator, but that is a day I am not looking forward too."

"But why would anyone want to kill God?" he asked, stepping forward towards the serpent.

"All poor men wish to be rich, and all rich men wish to be king, and every king... a God! But we all know, there can only be one God. Unfortunately, Man of the Present, it is inevitable. I wish I knew why the Creator has set in motion such an outcome and ending. Perhaps the Creator is lonely and seeks companionship, perhaps the Creator enjoys a good challenge, or maybe the Creator is sick of the matter entirely, and can only retire when replaced by one so worthy.

"But, until that day comes, this is where I remain… I lay here and keep watch for those who come lurking and accidentally find themselves blinded by the light, revved up by Jesus juice, another runner in the… oh, you know what I mean! For I am gatekeeper and watcher of those who try to re-enter the Garden before man's due time. You asked who wrote that book. Well, I shall tell you. It was a man who lived long ago."

"What happened to him?"

"He died! Most violently… He fought against corruption and taught humanity to look within themselves for peace, and that everyone was equal in the eyes of the Creator. He was denounced and branded a heretic and a traitor. He was tortured, brutally beaten, flogged, and finally crowned with thorny instrumentation. He was sentenced at public trial and hung up on a wooden spike as an example of ridicule. That book is his written work and was given to me just before that infamous day."

"No! … It couldn't! You don't mean…" He gasped in denial with a look of fright.

"Yes… that's right! You know the one of whom I speak," the serpent said slyly, slowly nodding his head.

"But that's not possible? He couldn't read or write!"

"It appears they have succeeded in full detail. Oh, how those theologians have long worked to discredit his works and abilities. Let me ask you this Man of the Present, this is a man whom many believe was born of a virgin, could speak and conjugate from birth without instruction. Conducted miracles of turning water into fine wine, healed the sick and the blind, walked on water, and even brought the dead back to life.

"But oh, such a divinely inspired man was beaten so easily by illiteracy, leaving him dumfounded and hung out to dry! Tisk, tisk, if only he could read the writing on the wall! Ha! My dear Man of the Present, you humans have such impudent minds with such terrible imaginations. Is it not that they say, he was a great teacher and a wise priest?"

"Well, yeah."

"And do they not say that most great teachers and wise priests write books... hmmmm? The serpent let out a sustained sigh, emphasizing the mm's.

"You see, Man of the Present, none know of this book because it was not meant for any of you. It is for he, and he alone."

"But why would he give it to you?" he further questioned.

"To hold, for safe keeping," the serpent told, then drew closer towards the man.

"But why?" he pressed.

"For when he gets back of course!" the serpent replied keenly, with a toothy smile.

"But wait, I don't understand all this. The story, the Garden, and now this book... who are you?" the man questioned, trying to connect the dots against his own previous beliefs.

"I thought you would have figured that out by now. I suppose I cannot fault you, it took me some time to know and understand that question myself. Evil son of a bitch bastard was right! All along... it was in the details. When Law Giver came down from the Mountain, he looked right at me and, yeah, he said it right to my face. Evil was right. It wasn't until my encounter with Evil when it finally became clear to me," the serpent shook his head snickering at himself.

"I remember, while the believers were imprisoned in the Panopticon, and then, that night when the skies went dark and the Creator's will had visited upon the kingdom... and a sleep fell over me. Have you ever had an out of body experience Man of the Present? A feeling where you are asleep, but you can see and hear everything going on around you?" The man nodded in acknowledgment.

"That's what happened, when a sense of calm came over me. I could see the entirety of the kingdom and all of the people, believers and Citizen Masters alike. I could see myself moving but I could not control myself. There was a lethal smoke that seemed to take form and it moved in a familiar serpentine method as I do. Pushing off of surrounding surfaces in a wavy, sleek-like motion of lateral undulation. I followed the smoke as it went down every street and alley and each time it visited the homes and tents of all who resided in the kingdom. But those dwellings that were painted with blood, did we pass by quietly and in peace. I watched as it took the lives of newborns and infants, calves and kids were none spared.

"Grown men who commanded the king's army fell to their knees and were consumed by its presence. I felt the need to stop it, but I could only watch from above as this dream like state overpowered me. I have never felt a dream so real, and in the morning the land was filled with sorrow, for not one house was without one dead. I didn't understand it at the time but Evil's words made it all come clear.

"When Drawn Forth Son came down from the mountain after receiving revelation and he carried in hand the physical words of the Creator, he was then Law Giver and he looked at me and in his adopted language he said… 'He Who Completes,' and he was right. I always wondered what I was doing, just wandering the face of the earth killing and consuming. What was the purpose of it all? Was there any meaning to any of it? Evil mother fucker was right, I gotta give him that.

"Everywhere I went, everywhere I go, one thing occurs. There is one thing that follows… death! It's my name, it's who I am, it's… what I am!" The man's eyes grew wide with terror as he stood before Death himself, in serpent form.

"Feel no shame, Man of the Present, even I missed it. Since the beginning… back even before the Garden. My earliest thoughts were of darkness and chaos and I couldn't understand it. How I had memories of nothing and infinity, but I was there, and then that voice called to me. I was not formed yet, but I existed as an idea in the mind of the Creator. I remember tearing through the darkness and bringing an end to the eternal night. As it was then that I killed the night and brought forward the light. So it remains now that I end every lie and bring forward the truth, and I recite,

'The Creator possessed me in the beginning of his way, before his works of old. I was set up from everlasting, from the beginning, or ever the earth was. When there were no depths, I was brought forth; when there were no fountains abounding with water. Before the mountains were settled, before the hills were, was I brought forth. While as yet he had not made the earth, nor the fields, nor the highest part of the dust of the world. When he prepared the heavens, I was there; when he set a compass upon the face of the depths. When he established the clouds above, when he strengthened the fountains of the deep. When he gave to the sea his decree that the waters should not pass his commandment, when he appointed the foundations of the earth. Then, I was by him as one brought up with him and I was daily his delight, rejoicing always before him.'

"But, but, but…" the man stepped backwards in shock, stuttering.

"But what, hmm? Strangely, I am reminded of the Epicurean epitaph inscribed on the gravestones of the ancients: Non fui, fui, non sum, non curo: 'I was not; I was; I am not; I do not care.' But I am serpent and if ever I was to pose such a melody, a serpent epitaph would there be: 'There was not, I was; There is, I am; There will not be, I really don't care,' the serpent smirked to himself then continued.

"Consider this, Man of the Present, in the Garden, was it I that made you sin? You can debate it. But it *was* I… that caused you to die! You see, it wasn't the fruit that would kill you… it was me!" The serpent said, locking eyes with the man.

"But, but, but…" the man stood frozen stammering in shock.

"But what? I'm evil? My dear Man of the Present, the image of a snake in a garden is no scenario of evil. For a snake is a sign of a healthy garden. And indeed, the Creator's Garden was healthy and prosperous! My presence there was proof of that, and surely, as you stand here before me you stand testament to that truth. What did you expect to see there, furry, feathery, crawly creatures…hmm? For they are the true terror upon any garden setting. Yet it is my kind who are cursed, but it is we who give protection in such a garden setting just as I did then, as was the Creator's command.

"For man is born of innocence, and evil is not inherent to him. Evil is later learned and comes second if not thirdly to him. But one thing is with you from the very beginning, just as I was with you. Death! Death is with you before you have consciousness, before you leave you mother's womb... death visits upon each of you.

Why do you think it was that I went to the woman first? Because she was weak? No! For she is Giver of Life, and I am He Who Completes, and you? Why you're just a silly little man!

"You see, truth and lies are intertwined eternally, and the truth is the end to all lies just as death is the end of life. Your lives are a contradiction unto themselves. None of you are gifted life the same, as life does not come standard, but all lives are assured to end. Some of you are born crippled and frail, while others are given great strength but not the wisdom, nor drive, to make use of it. What pitiful lives you lead. Even when rearranged, your life is no better than a flies', save one character.

"Humanity has longed feared and hated me, but knows not why. Is it not that man hates what he cannot conquer, and fears what he does not understand? And what is death, if not the greatest unknown. And for all your workings, and all your doings, is there not one thing that man cannot defeat? You hate and fear me, not because I am evil, but because you do not understand me, and because you cannot defeat me.

"The Persecuted Man, he knew exactly who I was. As he said it, he had no hatred nor fear of me, therefore he loved life, and he did. He lived everyday with the acknowledgment of death, and he lived everyday as if it were his last, and I recite, 'Blessed is the man that heareth me, watching daily at my gates, waiting at the posts of my doors. For whoso findeth me findeth life, and shall obtain favors of the Creator. But he that sinneth against me wrongeth his own soul, all they that hate me love death.'

"But if you're guarding the entrance to the Garden, then how can anyone get past you?" the man asked.

"You must... kill me of course! But I am no easy slay," the serpent replied with fiendish delight.

"Yes, even death can die, but only one who is pure can defeat me. Look around you and behold the weapons of defeated heroes alike and the shields that failed to guard them. I suppose if it were possible for one man to live several seventeen lifetimes I assume he could find a way. But thus far, none have achieved such a feat."

"The story you told...was it true or just a lie?" the man inquired stepping forward.

"What does it matter? Those that lived are long dead, and can do no more than what they have already done. The stories of yesterday survive as fables of antiquity and become the motivation for dreams and war. Oh well! Tell me something Man of the Present, do you pray?"

"Sure, I pray for good health, wealth, and ease of life," the man answered easily.

"I too pray for these things; however, unlike you, your prayers are empty and foolish. The Creator has notably cursed you against ease of life and peace of mind, as your life will only bring struggle and contempt.

"The Creator did not punish me with difficulty of life and want for more than I can obtain. And it appears that on this day, the Creator has answered my prayers. I was earlier debating on taking-out or dinning-in, but here you are! Thanks be unto the Creator, who is forever my sustenance!" the serpent said, then raised himself above the man covering him in shadow, then said smiling, "Any last words?"

The man stepped backwards until his back was almost up against the wall. The shimmering light of the cave minerals caught his eye leading his gaze up to a final etching of olden words carved into the ceiling of the cave, to which he read aloud. 'Thou hast sore broken us in the place of dragons and covered us with the shadow of death.'

The serpent then closed in on the man and coiled around him squeezing him within an inch of his last breath. Before killing and devouring him, the serpent said lastly, "I am the Serpent of Old, the Serpent of ruin and curse. I am as the Creator hath made me. As it was then, so shall it be now. I am the death of all mankind, and I... am the truth!

TRUTH AND THE SERPENT

- The End -

ABOUT THE AUTHOR

Is it just me, or am I the only one who wants more than what's typically presented? Writing stories has always been a passion of mine that I rarely shared with others. As a child, I was often frustrated with the stories and characters I was presented with. I then began creating my own stories, and rewriting others with new endings or plot twists that I felt were lacking.

As a learned man, I have always found myself asking more in depth questions, and seeking out different meanings than my peers. Over the years, I have come to embrace that obtuseness about myself, and now I let it drive me. It was that same sense of curiosity and need for a deeper meaning that led me to creating Truth and The Serpent, my first full length novel. My goal as a writer is to generate intriguing, positive, and challenging ideas, while leaving the reader with plenty to chew on in anticipation of the next story.

WORK CITED

A listing of some of the sources used to create the narrative of <u>Truth and The Serpent</u>

1.   King James Bible: http://www.davince.com/bible Original Publish Date: March, 2001, Revised: January 2004

2.   The debate between sheep and grain: http://etcsl.orinst.ox.ac.uk/section5/tr532.htm

3.   'Without continual growth and progress, such words as improvement, achievement, and success have no meaning.' - Benjamin Franklin

4.   "The children of Adam are limbs of one body. Having been created of one essence. When the calamity of time afflicts one limb, the other limbs cannot remain at rest. If you have no sympathy for the troubles of others you are not worthy to be called by the name of man." Sa'dī, and A. Clarke. *The Rose Garden: Gulistan*. London: Ta-Ha, 2000. Print.

5.   Some thoughts on the Veil: http://www.suppressedhistories.net/articles/veil.html - Max Dashu Dashu, Max. "The Veil." *The Veil*. N.p., n.d. Web. 21 Nov. 2016.

6.   'Before you embark on a journey of revenge, dig two graves.' – Confucius

7.   "The Panopticon is a new mode of obtaining power of mind over mind, in a quantity hitherto

without example." Bentham, Jeremy. *Panopticon or the Inspection House*. Dublin: n.p., 1791. Print.

8.   "Power is no man's birthright, and it shall not be neatly packaged and legislated to any populace by any government or Kingdom." King, Martin Luther. *Where Do We Go from Here: Chaos or Community?* New York: Harper & Row, 1967. Print.

9.   "radical flank effect" as referred to by Herbert H. Haines."

10.   "If there is no struggle, there is no progress. Those who profess to favor freedom, and yet depreciate agitation, are men who want crops without plowing up the ground. They want rain without thunder and lightning. They want the ocean without the awful roar of its many waters. This struggle may be a moral one; or it may be a physical one; or it may be both moral and physical; but it must be a struggle. Power concedes nothing without a demand. It never did and it never will." Douglass, Frederick, Philip Sheldon Foner, and Yuval Taylor. *Frederick Douglass: Selected Speeches and Writings*. Chicago: Lawrence Hill, 1999. Print.

11.   In the *Two Principles of Mental Functioning* of 1911: "The human mind seeks pleasure while trying to avoid pain. After which he termed the phrase the 'unpleasure principle.' Legorreta, Gabriela, Lawrence J. Brown, Sigmund Freud, and Sigmund Freud. *On Freud's*

"Formulations on the Two Principles of Mental Functioning" London: Karnac, 2016. Print.

12. 'reasonable.' "... it no longer lets itself be governed by the pleasure principle, but obeys the reality principle, which also, at bottom, seeks to obtain pleasure, but pleasure which is assured through taking account of reality, even though it is pleasure postponed and diminished". Freud, Sigmund, James Strachey, and Peter Gay. *New Introductory Lectures on Psycho-analysis.* New York: Norton, 1989. Print.

13. 'Is God willing to prevent evil, but not able? Then he is not omnipotent. Is he able, but not willing? Then he is malevolent. Is he both able and willing? Then whence cometh evil? Is he neither able nor willing? Then why call him God? - Epicurean paradox

14. "If an omnipotent, omniscient, and omnibenevolent god exists, then evil does not. There is evil in the world. Therefore, an omnipotent, omniscient, and omnibenevolent God does not exist." – Epicurus

15. Selected Works by Jaques Lacan

16. *Mirages: The Unexpurgated Diary of Anaïs Nin, 1939–1947 "Motherhood is a vocation like any other. It should be freely chosen, not imposed upon woman.' Anaïs Nin*

17. <u>Impressions Of America</u>: "A man's face is his autobiography. A woman's face is her work of fiction." Wilde, Oscar. *Impressions of America.* Place of Publication Not Identified: Nabu, 2010. Print.
18. 'As long as she thinks of a man, nobody objects to a woman thinking.' Woolf, Virginia. *Orlando; a Biography.* New York: Harcourt Brace Jovanovich, 1973. Print.

19. "The true man wants two things: danger and play. For that reason he wants woman, as the most dangerous plaything." Nietzsche, Friedrich Wilhelm, and R. J. Hollingdale. *Thus Spoke Zarathustra: A Book for Everyone and No One.* Harmondsworth, England: Penguin, 1969. Print.

20. "A weapon does not decide whether or not to kill. A weapon is a manifestation of a decision that has already been made." Galloway, Steven. *The Cellist of Sarajevo.* New York: Riverhead, 2008. Print.

21. "Remember, no matter where you go, there you are." – Confucius

22. 'Power tends to corrupt, and absolute power corrupts absolutely. Great men are almost always bad men.' John Dalberg-Acton <u>Letter to Bishop Mandell Creighton, April 5, 1887</u> published in *Historical Essays and Studies*, edited by J. N. Figgis and R. V. Laurence (London: Macmillan, 1907)

23. "Nearly all men can stand adversity, but if you want to test a man's character, give him power." Abraham Lincoln (Removed apparently he didn't actually say that.)

24. "So in war, the way is to avoid what is strong, and strike at what is weak." – Sun Tzu Sunzi, and Lionel Giles. *The Art of War*. Place of Publication Not Identified: Simon & Brown, 2012. Print.

25. 'Jealousy is the fear of comparison.' – Max Frisch

26. 'That the greatest perfection is imperfection.'- Lucilio Vanini ... 'If the world were perfect, it could not improve and so would lack 'true perfection,' which depends on progress.'

27. 'Euthyphro dilemma'... 'Is X good because God commands it, or does God command X because it is good? Is the pious loved by the gods because it is pious, or is it pious because it is loved by the gods?' - *Plato, Euthyphro'*

28. Non fui, fui, non sum, non curo: 'I was not; I was; I am not; I do not care.' - Epicurean epitaph

Made in the USA
Charleston, SC
25 February 2017